INSIDIOUS DRAGON

A DEREK ALMER NOVEL

I0637253

Revised Second Edition

MARC LIEBMAN

Publisher:

Rotorhead Media, LLC
Savannah, TX

First edition copyright © September 2023 Marc Liebman

ISBN Paperback —979-8-9883127-4-1

Cover images from Vecteezy.
Proofreader: Diane Blythe
Virology Technical Advisor – Robert Fader
Book interior design by – Deena Rae; E-BookBuilders, adaptation for ebook

BISAC Subject Headings:
    FIC – 014030 – Historical/Thrillers
    FIC – 031050 – Thrillers/Military
    FIC – 06000 – Thrillers/Espionage
    FIC – 031090 – Thrillers/Terrorism

File version: 202304025-03.016

OTHER BOOKS

DEREK ALMER SERIES
Flight of the Pawnee

Failure to Fire

JOSH HAMAN SERIES
Cherubs 2

Big Mother 40

Render Harmless

Forgotten

Inner Look

Moscow Airlift

The Simushir Island Incident

AGE OF SAIL SERIES
Raider of the Scottish Coast

Carronade

Death of A Lady

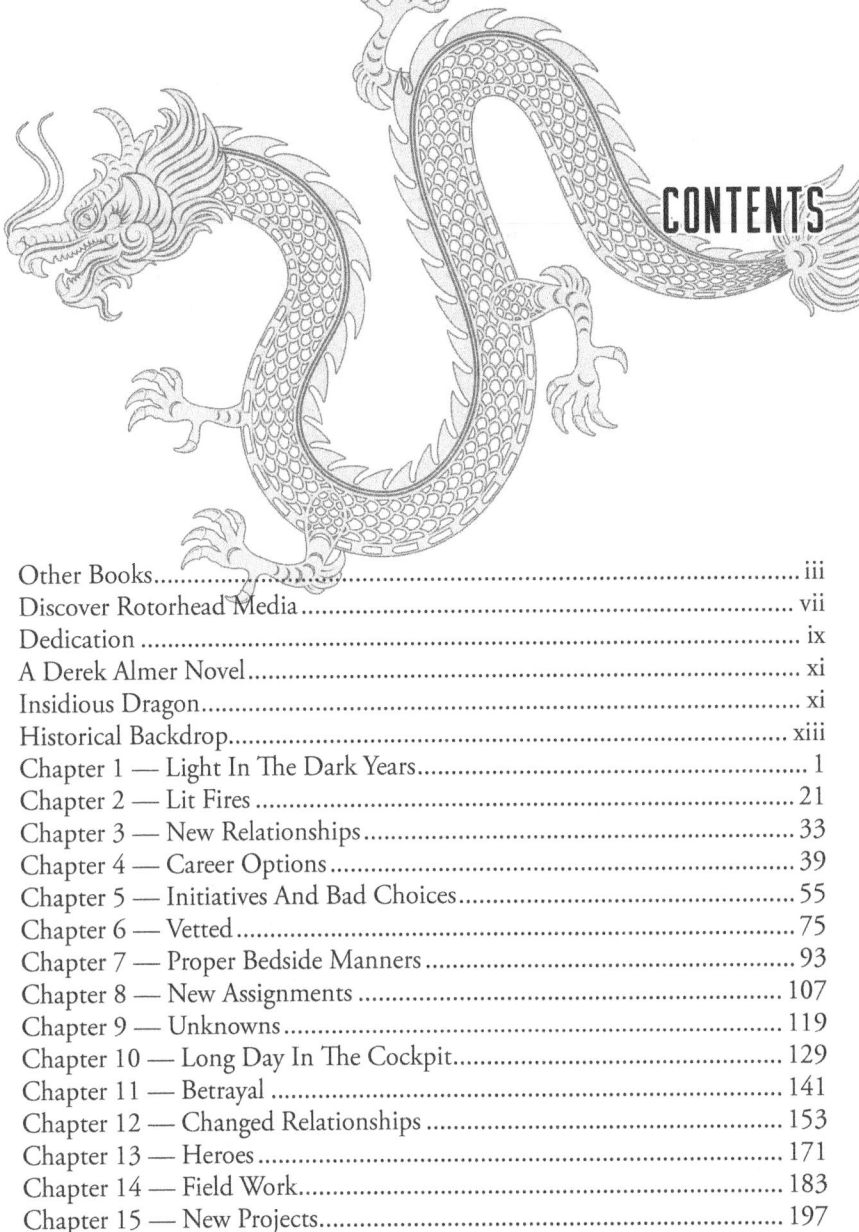

CONTENTS

DISCOVER ROTORHEAD MEDIA

Visit Marc Liebman's website – *https://marcliebman.com* – for information about Marc, his books, blog, and podcasts.

Check out Marc's blog on the period of approximately 1770 to 1816 which is the end of the War of 1812. Through his blog, you'll learn about events in American history that do not appear in American history textbooks.

You can also subscribe to Marc's newsletter by clicking on Contact Marc on the link *https://marcliebman.com/contact/*. His monthly newsletter contains information on what books he is working on, speaking events, podcasts, and other information.

You can also find Marc on Facebook at *https://www.facebook.com/marcliebmanauthor/* and you can watch his history and aviation podcasts on his YouTube channel at *https://www.youtube.com/channel/UC_sDoFQM5wupNaCeGIvKL1g*.

Marc hopes you enjoy this book. If you spot any problems, please contact him via the Contact Marc tab on his website and describe what you found.

If you have a moment, the author would appreciate you taking the time to leave a review for this book at the retailer's site where you purchased it.

Thank you for your support

War is a historic pastime for man. Despite the best efforts of well-intentioned men and women, it will never be stamped out. Over the centuries, we have managed to design and build and often employ weapons that kill people faster and/or more effectively.

Three types of weapons are, however, too horrible to contemplate employing in any kind of conflict. Only twice in human history have nuclear weapons been used and hopefully, the world has learned its lesson.

Number two are chemical weapons that were used widely during World War I, but not during World War II or Korea. One would have thought world leaders would have learned their lessons but we have seen them used in Syria and Iraq in the late 20th and early 21st Century.

Biological weapons are the third. During World War II, the Japanese employed them in their war against the Chinese. They learned the hard way that bioweapons are easy to employ, but the results can be unpredictable and sicken or kill more of your own soldiers than those of the enemy. Since World War II, Almost every major power has at least dabbled in bioweapon technology and some countries have developed deliverable bioweapons.

Unlike nuclear or chemical weapons, bioweapons can be delivered from a bottle dumped into a lake or water treatment plan or sprayed into a ventilation system of an apartment building. Delivery methods for bioweapons need not be complex or complicated.

This is a novel is dedicated to those who work tirelessly to find and expose those nations – Russia, the Democratic People's Republic of Korea, the People's Republic of China, and others – that continue to develop and maintain chemical and bio-weapon capabilities. The world needs to ensure that all bio and chemical weapons can never be used again.

A DEREK ALMER NOVEL

INSIDIOUS DRAGON

Senior Colonel Fang Sun of the People's Liberation submitted a concept of operations to the Central Military Commission, suggesting the People's Republic of China (PRC) develop a biological weapon to help achieve foreign policy goals without resorting to military force. His plan would have PRC agents covertly release the highly transmissive viruses or bacteriological agents in the targeted country.

To execute this plan, he wanted to build a laboratory placed under the auspices of the Chinese Academy of Sciences but run and funded by the PLA. What he needed was a virologist.

Enter Jun Lìn, a native of Guangzhou, whose doctoral thesis from the University of San Diego describes the risks of viruses such as poliomyelitis mutating. Senior Colonel Sun enlists her in the PLA's scheme to develop a biological weapon under the guise of wanting to prevent diseases from affecting the PLA's ability to defend the PRC.

Unknown to the Ministry of State Security and Senior Colonel Sun, Lìn has a cousin, Yan Huàng, who is a U.S. Navy intelligence officer. Horrified at what she is being asked to do, Lìn passes information on Sun's plan, code-named *Insidious Dragon,* to Huàng and suspects that Senior Colonel Sun is planning on launching an attack on the West. Afraid she will be arrested, tortured, and sent to a re-education camp, Jun Lìn asks to be extracted.

HISTORICAL BACKDROP

In World War II, the Japanese conducted at least 11 biological warfare attacks on Chinese cities using weapons developed by its infamous Unit 731. They ranged from polluting wells with typhoid germs to covertly introducing cholera, Bubonic Plague, smallpox, and botulism into the water supply of Chinese cities. The attacks killed at least 10,000 Chinese citizens and over 1,700 Japanese soldiers.

After the war, the Soviets imprisoned members of Unit 731 that it captured and built a new bio-warfare lab on the Japanese model in Sverdlovsk, a town in the center of the Soviet Union. The U.S. officially ignored Unit 731's horrific practices and gave the leadership immunity while its scientists studied the Japanese data.

During the Cold War, the People's Republic of China (PRC), the Democratic Republic of Korea, the Soviet Union, and the United States conducted research into both bio and chemical weapons. Thankfully, no country has launched a biological weapon attack on another country, at least so far.

One outcome of the horrors revealed by studying Unit 731's experiments is that 183 countries signed the Biological Weapons Convention of 1972 and agreed not to pursue or develop biological weapons. Several countries – most notably the PRC and the Democratic People's Republic of Korea – have only "accessed" the treaty. This allows them to continue researching biological agents that can be used as weapons.

Despite official denials, the People's Republic of China, the Democratic People's Republic of Korea, and Russia all have active biowarfare programs. In 2015, U.S. intelligence revealed that the PRC has 42 facilities dedicated to biowarfare.

Since the People's Army of North Korea has very limited medical capabilities, U.S. intelligence agencies also assess that the North Koreans prefer chemical or nuclear weapons to biological toxins. Why? Even their leadership believes biological weapons may be as lethal to their own forces and to those of their enemies.

In 1969 President Nixon ordered the U.S. to end its biological warfare programs. By 1973, all were all shut down. Exempted was research that would enable the U.S. to counter a bioweapon attack.

Marc Liebman
April 2022

INSIDIOUS DRAGON

CHAPTER 1

LIGHT IN THE DARK YEARS

The concrete floor beneath Liang Lín's bare feet was cold and the smooth surface and the chair's metal frame chilled her. Her hands were bound behind her; her ankles were chained to the floor.

The Ministry of Public Security interrogator bent at the waist so his face was even with Liang's. His sweat, which reeked of red chilis, told Liang he was from Hunan province. "What do you know about your father's defection?"

Liang glared at the man. Ever since her father Zimo and brother Tao left, she wished they'd taken her with him, but knew they couldn't. She was confident Zimo and his wife Shi would find a way to contact her once they were settled in America.

She shook her head to emphasize her words. "Nothing. He told me nothing! What I know comes from a letter I received four days later saying that he and my brother Tao had left."

Investigator Chen slapped Liang on both cheeks. "Liar. Your father and brothers are traitors."

Liang said nothing because there was nothing more to say. Zimo loved China and General Chiang Kai-Shek and hated the

1

Communists. The fact Zimo stayed in the People's Republic for as long as he did always surprised her.

"Chili Sweat," as she now thought of Investigator Chen, slammed his fist into Liang's solar plexus. Every cubic millimeter of air was forced from her lungs. For a few seconds, Liang saw stars in front of her eyes as she struggled to breathe.

"What did he keep in here?" Chili Sweat held up a photo of the floor of what she assumed was Zimo's apartment. A pried-up section of floor revealed a small compartment.

Liang again shook her head. The secret compartment could have been in anyone's apartment. "I don't know."

Zimo never showed her the secret compartment or what was in it. Liang said nothing believing the less said, the better. Liang was sure her interrogation was more about intimidation than finding out what she knew about the Huáng family's escape. With any luck, Zimo and his wife Shi, her brother Tao, and his wife Mei and their two children Ming and Yan, were safely out of the People's Republic of China.

The sound of her being slapped echoed in the small windowless concrete room. Liang felt her cheeks redden from the impact of Chili Sweat's palm. For a second, she debated if Garlic Breath would be a better name than Chili Sweat to take her mind off the pain Chili Sweat was causing.

Chili Sweat had arrested Liang just before she entered the headquarters of the Chinese Communist Party's (CCP) Guangzhou office. He grabbed her briefcase and purse before leading Liang to this room where she was patted down. Chili Sweat grinned as he grabbed Liang's groin and each breast before shoving her down onto the chair so his assistant could chain her ankles to the floor and pull her arms behind her. A belt was used to pull her elbows back and push her chest forward.

Liang had no idea what Chili Sweat's comrades were doing with her purse or briefcase. Nor did she care. Other than 50 yuan in cash there was nothing of value in either, other than her national identity card, her credentials to enter the CCP's office where she ran the accounting department. Elsewhere in the world, she would be known as the Controller for the CCP of the City of Guangzhou.

More slaps led to another blow to the stomach and one that landed squarely on Liang's left breast. Pain caused tears to stream down Liang's face as she glared at a smiling Chili Breath.

He put both hands on the armrests of the chair. "Now, tell me everything you know about your father and brother and why they became traitors."

"Read their files. Then you will know as much as I do."

Smack, smack. More slaps on the cheek. A knock on the door caused Chili Breath to turn around. "The judge is ready."

Another man entered carrying her purse and briefcase. Chili Breath threw Liang's shoes on the floor before he unlocked her shackles. A hood was pulled over Liang's head before she was led through several corridors. When it was pulled off, she found herself in front of a woman wearing the uniform of the Red Guards. Only the judge, a stenographer and an armed guard were in the room. Even Chili Breath had disappeared.

When Liang stood in front of the judge, the Cultural Revolution had been in full swing for six years. Each year there was a new phase and a new slogan. "Bombard the Headquarters" became the "Sixteen Points" which morphed into the "Destruction of the Four Olds" before "Down to the Countryside" became popular. "Cleanse the Party Ranks" was followed by the latest one, "Mango Fever."

Each phase purged more citizens from the party's ranks. With each wave of Maoism, another of Liang's friends would disappear, never to be heard from again. Standing in front of the judge, Liang thought it was her karma and turn to disappear.

"Citizen Liang Lín, you have been charged with knowing a traitor and not reporting him to the Ministry of State Security. While it is within my power to send you to a re-education camp, the fact that you are a senior administrator in the Communist Party of China and have served your country well mitigates your punishment. However, in the eyes of the party, you are now a security risk. Therefore, you will report to the head of the re-education department at Sun Yat-Sen University, where you will complete a course on our socialist system. If you pass, the university is authorized to hire you as an instructor or in another capacity. Fail, and you will be assigned to a re-education camp for five years. A note documenting these charges and punishment will be placed in your file."

The guard grabbed her bicep and led her out of the courtroom. There her husband, a senior inspector in the national police force, the Ministry of Public Security, waited.

Ai Lín gently reached out to hold his wife's arm, but she shrugged him off. Once they were outside the building and walking toward the car that Senior Investigator Ai Lin was entitled to use, Liang hissed, "Do you know why I was arrested?"

Ai nodded. "I found out after you were taken to the Ministry of Security's offices."

"Do you know they beat me?"

Again, Ai nodded. "I suspected they might. What did they ask?"

"Not much, but I would have died before I told them anything derogatory about my father or brother."

Ai pointed to the seat. "Get in the car. We have much to discuss."

Liang shook her head. "Not if it is about my father. Where is Jun?"

"In school."

"Good, take me home."

By the time Liang walked into their flat, her face was swollen. Ice packs on her cheeks that were already turning black and blue didn't help. Her breasts were painful to the touch and were turning black, blue, and yellow. Maybe, she thought, just maybe, I too should leave this country.

WEDNESDAY, JANUARY 7TH, 1976, 4:13 A.M. LOCAL TIME, GUANGZHOU

When eight-year-old Bao Gu heard the banging and shouting, he peeked out of the bathroom door. Red Guards had hauled his parents out of bed and handcuffed them. One of the six Red Guards slammed the barrel of his pistol down his brother's head as he pounded on the Red Guard's chest. Blood gushed from a gash as the boy crumpled to the floor.

Bao saw the front door to their small 55-square meter apartment cracked open and dashed for freedom. He heard several yells and then a gunshot. Concrete chips flew over his head as he slid down the stairwell railing with practiced ease and much faster than the policemen and members of the Red Guards could follow.

Once in the lobby, Bao saw the van and the police cars out front and slipped out a side window in the basement. Outside, he ran to a clump of bushes near another building until the hated Red Guards left.

He didn't want to return to the apartment that was, only a few minutes ago, a place he thought was safe and his home. With dawn breaking and the confidence of an adult, Bao walked to his father's parent's flat, a kilometer and a half from where he lived, or as he thought, used to live. He knew the route well from walking it with his parents at least twice a month since he was a little boy.

The clock in the lobby of his paternal grandparent's apartment building said it was 6:06 in the morning when he arrived. The kindly old man who was the concierge and logged the time and date of each person entering and leaving the building nodded as Bao, whom he'd seen many times, headed up the stairs.

GUANGZHOU, SUNDAY, JANUARY 11TH, 1976, 10:07 A.M. LOCAL TIME

Bao's grandfather advised that they wait a few days before going back to the boy's apartment. After studying the building for several minutes, they went inside. The area around where the door latched to the frame was destroyed. Cautiously, his grandfather pushed the door open and ducked under the tape that said, "Stinking Old Ninth," a reference to the intellectuals and academics hated by the Red Guards.

Bao found the dried puddle of blood where his older brother had fallen. Given that his body was not moving when he ran out, he assumed he died or was taken with his parents.

The Red Guards, supported by the CCP, listed Nine Black Categories of citizens - landlords, rich farmers, anti-revolutionaries, bad influencers, right-wingers, traitors, spies, capitalists, and intellectuals. All of whom, the Red Guards insisted, must be purged from society.

Bao's grandfather didn't know that by the time Bao's parents were arrested, the Red Guards had taken 142,000 professors and scientists into custody. If they were not killed immediately, most were sent to one of the May Seventh Cadre Schools where they would work with their hands in the fields and study the writings and teachings of Mao Zedong to learn to think as proper socialists. Most never returned to their homes.

Broken glass was everywhere in the ransacked apartment. The bookcases containing his father's collection of centuries' old books were toppled over and the books ripped apart. His father was, before he was arrested, a professor of Chinese history at Guangzhou University.

The room Bao shared with his brother was also a mess. Stuffing from their beds littered the floor. Bao picked out his school uniforms and other clothing he wanted and stuffed the garments into two drawstring bags.

Friday's newspapers listed those members of the Stinking Old Ninth that had been arrested. After his father's name, the chart listed professor and the damning words "bad influencer," "anti-revolutionary," and "intellectual." By his mother's name, the chart gave her profession as medical doctor. She was arrested because she was a "bad influencer," and an "intellectual." There was no mention of his brother or what happened to him.

Bao's mother was a pediatrician and someone he wanted to emulate by becoming a doctor. How and why a pediatrician could be a bad influencer was lost on the eight-year-old Bao.

When he returned to school a week after his parents' arrest, no one asked where he had been or why he had not been in school. Bao asked for his missed assignments and turned them in two days later. Life, as his grandfather and grandmother said, would go on.

SATURDAY, MAY 10ᵀᴴ, 1986, 2:16 P.M. LOCAL TIME, RANCHO SANTA FE, CALIFORNIA

Zimo Huáng pulled the small stack of letters out of his mailbox and as he walked back toward his house with a Spanish tile roof, he stopped suddenly. In the wad of envelopes and junk mail, one had the People's Republic of China logo in the upper left above the return address of its consulate in Los Angeles.

Random flashbacks of the years since his family escaped Communist China and settled in San Diego ran through his mind as he walked back to his house. Zimo started as a mechanical engineer at San Diego Gas and Electric. Now, 15 years later, he was the head of the department managing the utility's transmission lines.

His pace quickened. Once inside the kitchen, he put the letter from the consulate on the table, separate from the others. He looked at it for a few seconds, not wanting to touch it as if it was a hot potato.

Seeing his wife Shi, Zimo said softly as he pointed to the envelope, "In here, we will find out if our dream of seeing my daughter Liang and our granddaughter Jun will come true."

To escape, the Huàngs floated for three days down what the PRC calls the Shizi Yang River (a.k.a. the Pearl River when Guangzhou was part of the British enclave of Canton) before they landed on Lantau Island in the British colony of Hong Kong. When the British soldiers dropped them off at the U.S. Consulate in Hong Kong, they hadn't eaten for 36 hours.

Their immigration to the United States was quickly processed when Zimo showed his diploma from the U.S. Military Academy to the agent at the U.S. consulate in Hong Kong. He was one of a small contingent of officers sent to West Point by Chiang Kai-Shek.

Zimo also had copies of his letters from General Joseph Stillwell recommending Zimo to West Point and a second one from General John Sullivan saying that if he should ever want to join the U.S. military, he would act as a reference.

When the Huángs left Hong Kong for the United States, Zimo's granddaughter Yan was less than a year old and his grandson Qing was just three. The U.S. government offered three choices of places to live – San Diego, Los Angeles, or New York.

The family chose San Diego. Shi's first job was in a local elementary school's kitchen to help her learn English. The only native-born American cooking food was the manager; Shi's co-workers came from Mexico, Russia, and Iran. There was, she often said, much hand waving, pointing, and showing as they managed to serve 600 students a day. Each woman had the same three goals: earn money, learn English, and pass the citizenship test. Now, with a master's degree in nutrition from San Diego University, she was the San Diego Unified School District's Food and Nutrition Services dietician.

Shi touched her husband's cheek gently, "The pull of family is strong but we must be careful. We have made a good life here in America."

Her oft-made comment referred to Tao. He had become a wealthy realtor with rental homes, apartments, and small shopping centers all over San Diego. Through his firm, Freedom Real Estate, he was also an investor in several large commercial real estate projects. Tao's wife Mei learned both English and accounting at the University of San Diego and was now a CPA and the firm's accountant.

Tao's son Qing had just finished his freshman year at Stanford University as a pre-med student. Granddaughter Yan was about to become a junior in high school. She had her sights set on attending one of the U.S. military academies or earning an ROTC scholarship.

While Qing and Yan were growing up, Tao and his wife Mei educated the youngsters on traditional Chinese culture. Both grandchildren were fluent in Mandarin and Cantonese.

Shi's soft voice brought Zimo back to the present. "The People's Republic is not the China you remember. We do not know if this is a ruse. Remember Liang's husband Ai heads a department in the Guangzhou office of the Ministry of Public Security so she must tout the party line. Neither Liang nor I trust the Communists; neither should you. They may be luring you back to arrest you for being a major in the Chiang's army. Mao and his disciples have long memories."

In her letters, Liang used a code that Shi taught her so the words would look innocent enough but interspersed in the text were phrases that told the reader the actual content. Liang had written about food shortages, poor living conditions, and the idiocy of the "one-child policy."

Ai was a dedicated Communist who insisted Liang and he follow the Party's One Child policy. So while not having a son was disappointing, they would have no more children. To ensure Liang would not get pregnant, he used his position in the Ministry of Public Security to have a vasectomy.

Nodding to his wife's wisdom, Zimo took a small paring knife from the knife block and gently slit open the envelope. There were two pieces of paper.

Dear Mr. Huáng,

It is with pleasure that the People's Republic of China wishes to inform you that your temporary visa to allow your family to visit your homeland during the summer of 1986 has been approved. Please fill out the accompanying form so our office can complete the visa process and so you can make reservations at one of the hotels in Guangzhou on the attached list.

Each family member traveling to China is required to visit our consulate in Los Angeles so that we can issue the proper internal travel documents as well as stamp your U.S. passports with the visas. We recommend calling our office to make an appointment for this step which will take approximately an hour.

Below the text, three phone numbers were listed followed by the signature of the consular official. Zimo read the letter a second time and turned to Shi whose jet-black hair was now streaked with gray. The second sheet had a list of the hotels where his family would be allowed to stay.

"I understand and share your concerns. But remember, we are now U.S. citizens. If the Communists do not honor their commitments to respect the citizens of other countries, no one will visit the People's Republic and their Four Modernizations, just like the Great Leap Forward, will fall on its ass."

Zimo was referring to a program instituted in 1978 by Chairman Deng Xiaoping to encourage Chinese scholars, scientists, and students to study abroad. The goal was to enable the PRC to catch up to the West in four broad areas – agriculture, industry, defense and science and technology.

"My husband, you do remember what happened to that former member of the Red Guard, Wei Jingsheng who wrote the words *Fifth Modernization, Democracy* on the Democracy Wall. He was arrested, tortured, and sentenced to fifteen years in prison."

"I remember, but this will be a family reunion and maybe, Liang and Jun can emigrate if they wish now that the restrictions have been reduced."

Shi gently touched the arm of the man she had married in 1940. "My love, if you are right, the dark hours are now over. Let us tell Tao and Mei and make our plans."

MONDAY, JUNE 9ᵀᴴ, 1986, 2:26 A.M. LOCAL TIME, KUNMING

For someone who grew up in Shanghai, where it was humid and sticky most of the year, Major Fang Sun thought Kunming was a delightful place to be stationed. At 6,200 feet above sea level, the temperature rarely rose above 25^0 Celsius (77^0 Fahrenheit) in the summer. Yes, it was cold in the winter, but after a few days in the city, he understood why the Chinese Nationalists made the city their headquarters.

During the Cultural Revolution, Kunming was where the Red Guards would send those who fell out of favor even though the city was the People's Liberation Army's (PLA) headquarters of the Kunming Military Region. After he arrived, Sun learned the headquarters was being closed and consolidated into what would be called the Southern Theater Command and based in Guangzhou. This consolidation was part of a plan by the government to reduce the PLA by over a million men.

The young major's worries that he would be discharged from the army were set aside when his father, a major general, called to say that he was about to receive orders to the prestigious National Defense University in Beijing. There, his father told him, he would meet officers from each branch of the military and key government agencies. The relationships built in this school, Fang Sun was told, would be valuable as his career progressed. Do well and graduate, his father said, and soon you would be a lieutenant colonel.

The comforting news didn't help him sleep on some nights when he couldn't get the images of the battle for Lang Son out of his mind. On February 17ᵗʰ, 1979, the day the PRC invaded neighboring Vietnam, he was a platoon commander in the 460ᵗʰ Infantry Regiment, 164ᵗʰ Infantry Division, 55ᵗʰ Army Corps.

When the regiment crossed into Vietnam, there were 553 men in his battalion. They were part of the 300,000-man army the PRC had sent as a "punitive" expedition to convince the Vietnamese government to stop attacking the Khmer Rouge in Cambodia.

As a newly commissioned second lieutenant, Fang Sun believed his leaders knew what tactics to use. Quickly, he learned that they didn't.

Each time they came across a Vietnamese unit, the orders were the same, charge at the enemy. In three days, the four battalions of the 164th were cut to pieces. When his battalion was pulled out of the line, 51 men were left and Fang Sun was the only surviving officer.

Now, nine years later, he could still see the green tracers streaking through the air as vividly as they happened during the fighting. The screams of the wounded for whom there was no adequate medical care, the hydraulic sucking sound of a bullet hitting flesh were still as loud as when he first heard them. The memories wouldn't go away and there were many nights like this one, when he couldn't sleep.

There had to be a better way to defeat an enemy. What let Fang Sun drift off to sleep was that maybe, just maybe, he might learn what they might be at the National Defense University.

MONDAY, JULY 3ᴿᴰ, 1986, 5:38 P.M. LOCAL TIME, GUANGZHOU

Smoke from the cigarette curled up past the left side Ai Lín's face. In front of him, Liang stood at a position a drill instructor would call attention. She knew what was coming and it no longer bothered her.

Ai leaned forward, unblinking from the smoke. The only time an unfiltered cigarette wasn't in one of his yellow smoke-stained fingers was when he slept. Even when he was eating, a lit cigarette was in an ashtray on the table.

After 18 years of marriage, Liang still hadn't gotten used to the smoke. Everything in their apartment smelled like an ashtray, including her husband.

She didn't wince when the palm of Ai's hand smacked her cheek. It stung for a few seconds, but to her, it was the punishment of an amateur. Divorce was difficult in the PRC so her brain took Liang elsewhere. If she tried to divorce Ai, his position in the Ministry of Public Security would enable him to have her sent to a re-education camp from which she would never emerge.

She had resurrected her career and was a professor of finance and economics at Sun Yat-Sen University, one of the oldest and most respected schools in the country. Liang was sure that Ai believed that her position helped his career. That knowledge let her endure the abuse.

Ai held the letter from her mother Shi in front of her face as if it was contaminated, "What is really in this letter?"

"Just what it says. My brother Zimo and his family are coming to Guangzhou in July."

Deliberately, Ai put the paper down on the coffee table. "Your brother is a traitor and should be arrested as soon as he sets foot in the People's Republic."

"My brother and his family are now American citizens. Our government, which means the Ministry of State Security, has approved their visa. My father and mother have committed no crimes therefore the Ministry of People's Security has no say on whether or not they can come."

"And you intend to see him?"

"And mother, my brother Tao and his wife Mei and their daughter Yan who is a year younger than our Jun."

"What about their oldest son Qing?"

"He is at Stanford University and does not want to miss classes so I do not think he is coming."

"What if I forbid you to see them?"

"I will see them anyway."

Smack. Liang's check stung. Her determination to see her relatives was behind her words. "They will be our guests, but I will not invite them to this stinking smoke-filled apartment."

Smack, smack. Ai's palm hit both of Liang's cheeks.

Liang's defiance showed as she spoke, "It is your choice whether or not to join us. If you do, you can write a report saying you met with a capitalist millionaire and it may earn you another promotion!"

The lit cigarette flew out of Ai's mouth as he hit Liang in the stomach with his fist as hard as he could. She doubled over, not from pain, but as a show to let Ai think he was hurting her. The hours she spent every day taking bajiquan classes had strengthened her body and taught her how to absorb blows. The punch hurt, but she was determined not to let him know. The Chinese martial art also taught Liang how to deliver blows with her fists, elbows, and knees to disable an opponent.

Each time Ai slapped her, Liang imagined how she would parry a blow and deliver a punishing strike. She held back because hitting, or worse, hurting or killing the head of the Economic Crimes Investigation Division of Ministry of Public Security's Guangzhou's office would get her a bullet in the head or worse, sent to a re-education camp.

Ai pushed down on Liang's head and shoulders. "Kneel and do your duty to your husband."

Slowly, she unzipped his fly while Ai unbuckled his belt. Once the top button was undone, Ai's pants dropped to his ankles and Liang went to work with her mouth. She smelt a woman's vagina that wasn't hers. Ai hadn't touched her in ever since Jun was born. Who his mistress was, she didn't care. Liang forced what she was doing out of her mind. Her duty was to raise their daughter and ensure she didn't marry a monster like Ai Lín.

When Ai was spent, Ai let Liang stand, thinking he completely controlled his wife. Her face was impassive as she stared at the husband she hated. The reasons why she married him – love, he was a good, caring man, respected by his peers – were no longer valid. He was now something, not someone, she endured and hoped his chain smoking would send him to an early grave.

MONDAY, AUGUST 4ᵀᴴ, 1986, 9:12 A.M. LOCAL TIME, GUANGZHOU

Ai Lín couldn't wait to get to his desk. Right after he returned from his department's Monday morning staff meeting, Ai sat at his typewriter with the standardized GB2312 character code for Chinese. Computer terminals had not yet found their way to his department.

Once he had the form through the rollers, and properly aligned, he started typing, occasionally referencing his notes that had, among other things, the passport and visa numbers for each member of the Huáng family. A flash of his Ministry of Public Security badge and ID folder encouraged the hotel front desk manager at the White Swan Hotel to provide him with a copy of his log of foreign guests.

Referencing the heavy caseload of his investigative teams, Ai begged off most of the dinners in the evening with the Huángs, leaving his daughter Jun and his wife Liang to spend time with their relatives whom he refused to refer to as Americans. Also, before they checked into the White Swan, he asked a Ministry of State Security contact to ensure the hidden microphones were turned on in all the Huángs' rooms. What they would find, he told his contact, he did not know.

His report provided what background he had learned from Liang and the dinners and details from the Sunday he spent with them. In the action requested block at the end of the form, he typed, "All communication between Liang and Jun Lín and the Huángs should be monitored for potential crimes against the state, particularly espionage."

Ai left out of the report the budding relationship between Yan Huáng and his daughter Jun. While it alarmed him the most, he was afraid that it could reflect badly on him if he did not control the information flow. Liang was delighted that the two acted as if they were long-lost sisters which Ai saw as another red flag.

Every day, they disappeared as Jun showed Yan around Guangzhou. What was worse, Yan spent hours with Jun's friends answering questions about life in the United States. Later, Ai would add the friends Jun introduced to Yan to the watch list he submitted in his report.

TUESDAY, MARCH 8ᵀᴴ, 1989, 10:33 P.M. LOCAL TIME, GUANGZHOU

The library at Sun Yat-Sen University officially closed at 10 p.m. but Bao Gu had observed that by the time the last student left, it was closer to 10:15. For some reason, Bao decided to walk along the Xiaogang Park side of Dongxiao Road. When it bent to the right, he planned to take Qianjin Road to where he lived with his grandfather. Three years ago, his grandmother died from pneumonia. Antibiotics were, his grandfather learned, being rationed to those under 50. His grandmother was 71 when she passed away.

At 181.6 centimeters (5' 11") tall, Bao Gu was a lean but muscular 72 kilograms (147 pounds). In a crowd, Bao's head was above most. He had long legs and enjoyed taking strides that shorter men and women would find hard to match.

Ever since his parents were taken, Bao made few friends and kept his distance for fear of being arrested. His grandparents explained his existence by saying his parents died during an outbreak of cholera.

Bao was laser focused on getting into Sun Yat-Sen University's medical school, considered to be one of the PRC's best. Admission was extremely competitive and accepted only 1,000 new students per year from all over the People's Republic.

Members of the opposite sex were simply not in Bao's plans. Any invitations by female students to do anything other than prepare for exams were politely turned down.

He was lost in thought about a biology exam that the professor had postponed until Saturday morning and did not hear the soft footsteps behind him. Two men grabbed Bao and pulled him into the bushes that separated the park from the road.

Despite his yell for help, no one came to Bao's aid. One pinned his body to the ground and the other struck him in the chest. It was then the years of Shaolin training – a traditional Chinese martial art frowned upon by the CCP – that his grandfather insisted he learn took over. Bao kicked upward as hard as he could.

His attacker went from about to pounce on him to falling on his side, moaning, and holding his groin. Bao twisted an arm free from the second attacker who was trying to pin his arms down and jabbed two fingers upwards. They glanced off the man's cheekbone before going into his eye. The man fell back on his haunches, holding a bleeding eye.

Bao stood, his chest heaving as he took in deep breaths and looked at the two men he recognized as students at Sun Yat-Sen

University who often harassed Bao and his friends when they ate together at the cafeteria.

The one he kicked in the groin often bragged that his father was a member of the Central Committee of the CCP managed to get to his knees still holding his groin, and screamed at Bao, "You fuckin asshole. I'll get you for this!"

"I don't think so." Bao took off one of his shoes and slammed the heel into the side of the young man's head. The impact drove the boy's temple bone into his brain and he was dead before the upper part of his body hit the ground.

The other student who was still sitting on the ground, started to push himself away from Bao, saying, "I won't tell anyone."

"I know you won't." It took two blows on the side of his head to kill him the same way as he did the other student.

Bao looked around and seeing no one, he put his shoe back on and sat on a nearby bench to survey the scene. Convinced no one witnessed the fight, he hurried home wondering what he should tell his grandfather. In the end, Bao decided to say nothing because if his grandfather went to the police, bad things might happen.

FRIDAY, MARCH 10TH, 1989, 11:57 A.M. LOCAL TIME, GUANGZHOU

Bao Gu's "friends" were seven pre-med students – five women and two men – with whom he ate lunch with every day. They studied together in the library and before exams, crowded into one of their dorm rooms to quiz each other. Of the eight, Bao was one of two who didn't live in the dorm.

They were all laughing as they repeated a joke made by a professor during their calculus class when two investigators from the Ministry of Public Security were escorted to their table. Smiles turned to frowns as one man spoke and held up his badge and identity card for all of them to see.

"I am Investigator Lieu. Which one of you walks through Xiaogang Park on the way home?"

Bao held up his hand. The man showed a picture of the son of the Central Committee member. "Do you know this student?"

Afraid he would be arrested, Bao said nothing and tried to be impassive. Several of the girls nodded. "Yes, he tried to eat with us. When we asked him and his friend to go away, they overturned our trays. At least twice, they had to be escorted out of the cafeteria for rowdy behavior."

"Is this his friend?" Bao recognized the photo of the man whose eye he poked out. He forced himself not to react before shaking his head.

Another girl said, "Yes."

One girl asked innocently, "Why are you asking?"

Lieu said, "They were found dead in Xiaogang Park early Thursday morning."

The other pre-med student, a young woman from Guangzhou piped up. "Good, they got what they deserved."

Not wanting to miss a chance for information, Lieu asked, "Why do you say that?"

"Because they raped me last October and you, the Ministry of Public Security, did nothing. There should be a report on file. If not, my parents have a copy."

A pre-med student from Kunming added as she pointed to one of the photos, "That one came into our dorm in December and tried to rape me. My friends and I gave him a good beating."

"Will you come to our office and give us your statements?"

The two students said almost simultaneously, "No need. You should already have them."

The two investigators took the names of the two pre-med students who had filed reports. Then Investigator Lieu pointed at Bao and said, "You come with us."

"Am I under arrest?"

"Not yet, but we have questions for you."

Bao's backpack with his books was taken when he left the cafeteria. He was brought to a room in the Ministry of Public Security offices on the campus with a steel table bolted to the floor. A raised metal bar ran the entire length. Bao realized his chair wasn't bolted to the floor when he tried to slide it back, although from what he could see, it could be. Also bolted to the floor were rings that he assumed leg shackles would be attached.

He forced himself to be calm even though his stomach was churning. On the walk to the Ministry of Public Safety office, Bao wondered how they knew he walked either through or along Xiaogang Park. Bao steeled himself for what was about to come.

Lieu sat down in front of him holding Bao's national ID card. His partner moved to a corner where Bao couldn't see him. "Why were you in the park last night?"

"I walked through it on the way home from school."

"What time?"

"About nine-thirty p.m."

"Why so late?"

"Because I was studying in the library with my friends. The library closes at nine."

Lieu took the photos of the two boys and placed them in front of Bao.

"How do you know them?"

Bao forced himself to be annoyed. "I don't know them. As the others told you, they annoy us and we try to ignore them."

The man standing behind Bao slapped the back of his head. He didn't see the blow coming and turned to glare at his assailant who bitch-slapped him on both cheeks hard enough so his skin felt as if it was burning.

"We think you and your girlfriends killed these two boys. You ganged up on them in the park where no one would see you and killed them. Now, since you know the park and admitted walking through it on the way home, you are going to confess to these murders."

Bao said nothing.

BAM!!! A blow to the side of his head caused Bao's vision to blur. The investigator standing behind Bao yanked the chair out from underneath him, dropping him on the concrete floor. As Bao tried to stand, he was kicked in the side. Then, Investigator Lieu banged the chair down in its original position and commanded, "Sit!"

Once Bao was seated, Lieu slid a pad and a pen across the table. "Write your confession."

For a few seconds, Bao said nothing. Then he wrote, "Let me go."

Lieu read it, angrily ripped the sheet from the pad, crumpled it into a ball and threw it across the room. At the same time, the man in the corner slammed his hands against both sides of Bao's head. Before his head cleared, Bao thought the room was spinning.

He closed his eyes and then focused on the man's face before deciding to call the man's bluff. "My friends know I am here and have powerful friends. If I don't return to school, they will start asking questions of their parents and their parents will start asking questions."

The man standing behind Bao pulled him to his feet before jamming the tips of his fingers into his side. The air went out of Bao's lungs and the man kept Bao from collapsing as he staggered toward the open door. Before he was handed his backpack, Lieu stood on his toes so he could get his face as close to the 5' 11" tall Bao's as he could. "Remember, we will be watching you. What happened here is just a sample for you to remember. No one can hold out. Everyone confesses."

Bao slung his backpack over his shoulder and left. The time on the big wall clock in the Ministry of Public Security's lobby was 3:38 p.m. He was sure Lieu had no evidence from the fight. His pants, shoes and shirt were dumped in the trash well away from his grandparents' apartment.

CHAPTER 2

LIT FIRES

THURSDAY, JULY 27ᵀᴴ, 1989, 4:36 P.M. LOCAL TIME, GUANGZHOU

Walking back along Qianjin Road, Bao saw the column of black smoke ahead but didn't believe the fire was in his grandfather's apartment complex. He was about to start his last year as a pre-med student and wondered if he could keep his number one ranking. Bao was confident he would be accepted by either his first choice – Sun Yat-Sen medical school or his second – Guangzhou University. There was a third, the Southern Medical College, which he didn't want to attend because the medical school graduates must serve as doctors in the PLA.

When Bao entered the Sushe residential complex, he could see the fire he smelled two blocks away was in the building where he lived with his grandfather. Seeing the ambulances and fire trucks with ladders going to the fourth and fifth floors, he was afraid of what might have happened. Bao lived on the fifth floor where the concrete was blackened by smoke.

He tried to go through the barricades to the building but was stopped by a policeman. Bao showed his national identification card with his address to the policeman who pointed to where the evacuated residents stood behind a barricade.

Bao walked through the crowd back and forth three times, looking for his grandfather. Not seeing him, he asked a nearby fireman, "Have you gotten everyone out?"

The man shook his head. "No, we are still clearing the fourth and fifth floor hoping to find more alive." The fireman then asked, "What apartment do you live in?"

"Apartment nine on the fifth floor." His grandfather often told him that he picked apartment nine because the way the number is written in Mandarin was close to how the word "perfect" was written. Like most Chinese, Bao's grandfather preferred some numbers to others.

The fireman said, "The fire started in apartment seven on the fourth floor and then spread. Many of the residents on the fifth floor were taken down by ladders. We're just now getting to the apartments on the fifth floor. Wait here."

Bao stood resting his hands on the painted wooden barricade that fed the cold fear running through his heart and mind. He closed his eyes, willing his grandfather to be safe.

He saw the fireman speaking with another man and there was a lot of head nodding and shaking before the fireman started back to where Bao stood. His body language showed through the heavy coat firemen wore that foretold the news he was bringing.

"Mr. Gu, I am sorry, but your grandfather was found on the couch under a window he tried to open but couldn't. I am so sorry."

"When can I see him?"

"I do not know. All the bodies will be brought down after we finish searching the building. At that time, assuming it is safe, residents will be escorted to their apartments to collect whatever belongings they can carry. The state will find you temporary housing while the building is repaired. Please be patient. It will be a few hours."

Tears streamed down Bao's cheeks. He loved the man who raised him and now he was alone. Temporary in the PRC could mean years. Bao found an empty spot on the street and sat on the curb. He pulled his knees to his chest and sobbed.

TUESDAY, AUGUST 1ˢᵀ, 1989, 2:16 P.M. LOCAL TIME, GUANGZHOU

When he was allowed back into his grandparents' apartment, it reeked of smoke. There was almost no fire damage.

Someone had smashed the windows to let the smoke out. The couch where his grandfather had supposedly died, was untouched other that it was soaked with water. As he walked in, his feet splashed through puddles of water that dotted the floor.

The fireman who brought him to his apartment asked him to wait until he returned; then he would escort him out of the building. Bao could take what he wanted as long as it fit into cardboard boxes or suitcases the firemen could provide.

Bao nodded and went into the apartment. His grandparents had several old suitcases that could easily carry all his clothes. He wanted to save some pictures and several old books, but then realized how heavy the books were and put them back into the bookcase.

When he was sure the fireman had left, Bao went into his grandfather's bedroom and pushed his bed to the side. Under a carpet, he found the board and popped it open. His grandfather said that once he was dead, what was in there was his. The "what" was unknown other than he hinted that it was valuable.

In the hiding place, he found two bundles and two small velvet boxes. All were wet with water. As he unwrapped the layers of cloth and plastic around the bundle, he found himself holding two brown envelopes. The thinner envelope had a smaller envelope taped to the front. The thick one had five stacks of 100-yuan notes, each with 100 bills. He fanned through the money and was delighted that they recent printing that were valid in the PRC. Bao placed them off to one side and decided he would open the other envelope later.

Gently, he opened one of the velvet boxes and found himself staring at a diamond ring. How big, he did not know, but it was large. The other jewelry box contained a large broach in the shape of a butterfly. The body was a long green stone, the eyes were diamonds and the fillagree that made the wings were full of tiny diamonds. For its size, it was heavy. Both velvet boxes went into his pack along with the two envelopes.

When he was finished, Bao had his backpack, which was large enough to carry all his books and notebooks along with other items. He also filled a large expandable soft-sided suitcase that had rollers with clothes. Bao took the photos he wanted to keep of their frames placed them on top of his clothes before zipping up the bag. Then, he made sure the board and the bed were back in place.

50,000 yuan was a small fortune and once he was in the hotel room he was assigned and paid for by the state, he got down on his knees to search for a hiding place. It took a few minutes before he found a loose molding behind which he could hide the money and two jewelry boxes. As he put the board back in place, he wondered if he was not the first person to use this hiding place.

Exhausted, Bao lay down on the bed and fell asleep. He woke suddenly about three in the morning thinking about the envelope he had not opened. It was full of pictures of his parents and great-grandparents. On the back of each picture, someone wrote who was in the photo along with the date and location it was taken. Some were dated in the 1890s. Along with the photos, there was a handwritten letter to Bao from his grandfather.

My Bao,

Since you are reading this letter, it means I am gone, and you, my grandson are the last of our family. We still do not know after lo these many years where your brother is, or if he is alive. The authorities are very tight-lipped about what happened to your parents although I suspect they perished in a re-education camp.

The money, the ring and the broach is all we had left from much happier times. Your grandmother and I along with your mother and father fled Shanghai, to get away from the Japanese and then the Communists. We settled in Guangzhou because I could find work as an engineer and your grandmother as a nurse.

What follows is a family history, documented with pictures. For generations, our family worked for the Kadoories in their trading business. My father earned commissions and by Asian standards, my parents were well off.

The broach was made in 1893 in New York by Charles Tiffany and Company and was a present given to my mother by Emily Kadoorie. The structure is 22 carat gold, the stone is an emerald and both it and the diamonds are very high quality. The diamond ring was also your paternal great-grandmother's and she gave it to me to give my wife and your grandmother.

In the People's Republic, having such nice jewelry is not fashionable or even allowed. We have kept it hidden to keep it from being seized. I suspect that the ring and brooch are still quite valuable. And I suggest you keep them hidden until such time as you can leave the people's Republic which is not the China your grandmother, parents and I loved.

I am confident you will become a wonderful doctor. My only request is that you treasure and keep the pictures and this note and remember us and our love for you.

In the envelope, Bao found 50 pages of tersely written Chinese that covered the family's history from when his ancestors first worked for the Kadoorie family, beginning in 1873, first in Hong Kong, then Shanghai and how they managed to make it to Guangzhou. His grandfather also described how he bribed local Communists to provide him with papers showing he was a supporter of the Communist Party.

FRIDAY, NOVEMBER 25TH, 1989, 3:32 P.M. LOCAL TIME, GUANGZHOU

The papers given to Bao said that the state would pay for a room in a hotel until the end of December. By then, if an apartment had not been found for him, other arrangements to provide a place to stay would be made by the state.

What the "other" arrangements were, was not made clear and when he asked, the officious clerk glared at Bao as if how dare he question the state. Yet, time was running out.

Bao waited patiently in line until his name was called. The clerk behind the window asked for his papers and said, "We have no money to continue to pay for a hotel room for you. Are you still enrolled at Sun Yat-Sen University?"

"Yes."

"Then I suggest you move into a dorm or, on January 1ˢᵗ, you will have to pay for your room. The state has a favorable rate of 10 yuan per day, or 300 yuan per month."

While he had the money to pay for the hotel or a dorm room Bao had been very judicious in how he was spending it. He protested, "I am an orphan and a student and do not have the money to pay for a dorm room. That is why I was living with my grandfather."

"That, Mister Gu, is not the state's problem. Hotel or dorm room, those are your choices."

Bao had already gone to the Bank of China branch at 15 Changdi Road and rented the largest safe deposit box he could. To rent one, the bank required that he open a savings or checking account. He filled out the paperwork listing his father's old apartment as an address and counted out 1,000 yuan, the minimum amount required, for a savings account.

The clerk said the bank required that he list what would be placed in the safe deposit box. Bao responded, "Photos of my parents and grandparents as well as some mementos from my parents and grandparents. I'm an orphan and living in a dorm so I have no safe place to keep them."

The woman nodded and smiled. "That is very smart." Bao was led to a small cubicle where the empty box was placed on the table. He hung his backpack on the hook and waited for the woman who instructed him how to lock the box to leave. In went 47,000 yuan, the broach, ring, and the envelope with his family history.

Bao closed the box, slid it into the space and locked the door. He suspected that someone from the government would inspect the safe deposit box even though the laws stated no one could open it without his permission. If they did, Bao was sure he would be paid a visit by a government agent.

Back at the hotel, the manager was not very friendly or helpful. He said that the 10-yuan rate was only if the government was paying. The non-government rate was, the manager said, "15 yuan a night, paid a month in advance."

Bao forced himself to control his anger. He left sure the manager would pocket the five yuan a night difference. Arguing with the manager or asking for government to help was a waste of time. He'd be broke or dead long before the government did anything.

The dorms were full and Bao hoped that some students would drop out. When Bao explained his situation to the woman in charge of assigning dorm rooms, she was sympathetic but not helpful. The best she could do after seeing Bao's file and number two ranking meant he would probably be invited to attend medical school at Sun Yat-Sen. The best she could do was put Bao at the top of the list for a room. She recommended he work in the kitchen to earn money. Food for students working in the kitchen was free.

Bao nodded and asked her to schedule an interview for the job in the kitchen. Assured that he would be able to eat didn't change the fact that after December 31st, Bao was homeless.

THURSDAY, MARCH 22ND, 1990, 9:43 P.M. LOCAL TIME, GUANGZHOU

By the end of the first week of living and hiding out in the library, Bao had it down to a system. He'd eat at the school cafeteria after he finished his shift. Before going back to the library, he'd take a shower in the facilities for the staff whose apartments didn't have full bathrooms. In his backpack he had everything he needed to live.

He'd kept the bare minimum of clothes: two pairs of slacks, three shirts, three sets of underwear and toiletries, and all fit, along with a blanket, easily in his backpack. The rest of his clothes were crammed into his safe deposit box. What made the pack heavy were the books because he had to carry them all. Once a week, he went to a laundromat at one of the dorms and washed his clothes.

Each night around 9:30 p.m., he'd walk to the bathrooms on the second floor of the library that were the first to be cleaned. Once the cleaning crew left, Bao would lay out the blanket in a stall and sleep.

It wasn't perfect, but he was told that if he was admitted to the medical school, he could move into a small, studio apartment on campus that was paid for by the state. Food and clothing would be his only expense. In his mind, living in a bathroom for a few months was a small price to pay for a future luxury.

With the water running while he was brushing his teeth, Bao didn't hear someone enter the bathroom. The intruder Bao recognized as the librarian responsible for the medical library.

The woman surveyed Bao's set-up before asking, "Are you living in here?"

Bao nodded slowly and bowed his head. "Ms. Zhu, please don't get me expelled?"

"Do you not have a place to live?"

"I'm an orphan. There were no vacancies in the dorms and I have only the money I earn working in the cafeteria. It is not enough to pay for a dorm room much less an apartment.

Ms. Zhu, who was 151 centimeters tall (5'1") and 49.4 kilograms (~100 lbs.) commanded, "Pick up your things and come with me."

Bao knew an order from the woman who was probably in her late thirties, maybe early forties. "Where are we going?"

Daiyu Zhu looked at the tall young man who had a lithe, muscular body. "My flat. You can stay in my extra bedroom." Zhu waved her hand in the direction of Bao's "stuff." "This is nonsense. If the dean of the school learns that one of its top students was living in a bathroom, there would be much loss of face to say nothing of handwringing. So let us save them all of that and make sure you get into medical school."

Bao figured that she would learn more about Zhu's plans for him later.

GUANGZHOU, SUNDAY, APRIL 8TH, 1990, 1:22 P.M. LOCAL TIME

Bao studied the titles of the books on the shelves of the bookcase that filled one wall of Daiyu's apartment. In fact, against almost every wall, there was a bookcase, usually stacked two deep with books, most of which were in English.

Bao was sliding a book back he just finished reading called *Once Is Not Enough* by Jacqueline Susann. It slid in next to three books by James Clavell – *Tai-pan*, *Shogun* and *Gai-Jin*. Bao was debating on which one he would read next when he heard Daiyu's soft voice.

"Bao, did you like *Once Is Not Enough*?" Bao's head went up and down slowly. There was nothing like this printed in the PRC. Daiyu's hand caressed the small of his back, just above his belt and sent a rush through his body. It was the closest the attractive woman had been to him since he moved into her spare bedroom.

"Is this the first book of that type you have read?"

Bao closed his eyes, exhaled, and then said, very softly, "Yes, it was very enlightening."

"I have more books by Jacqueline Susann if you wish to read them. They are some of my favorites; too bad our government has banned them."

Bao turned around to face Daiyu. Quizzically, Bao looked at the librarian. "How did you get them?"

"I have my ways. One of my responsibilities is overseeing the purchase of books for the library." Daiyu who was wearing a robe over her bra and panties caressed Bao's cheek. "Come, let's have some tea. I think we have much to discuss."

The two sat on the couch and the conversation became one about their past lives which were very similar. Both Daiyu's parents were arrested and sent to a re-education camp early in the Cultural Revolution. Her father was a professor of Western literature and her mother taught history. As such, the Red Guards labeled both of Daiyu's parents as intellectuals, members of the Stinking Ninth, and bad influencers. Daiyu never saw them again.

She too was alone. One day, Daiyu received a telegram saying her brother had died gloriously in the service of the motherland and was buried at sea. Several months later, Daiyu received a letter from a shipmate saying that her brother, who was an officer on a nuclear submarine, and eight other crew members had died of radiation poisoning.

Daiyu was telling the story of her brother when Bao shifted to turn to face the librarian. The change in position moved Bao much closer to Daiyu who began caressing Bao's thigh and then between his thighs. Both stopped talking until Daiyu asked softly, "Have you been with a woman before?"

Bao shook his head.

"A man?"

A more vigorous shake of the head.

Daiyu put her fingertips on Bao's cheek and then kissed him gently. "Then, we know where to start."

That was the last night Bao slept alone until he moved into his small apartment that housed the medical students.

Once Bao had moved into his own apartment, both understood their relationship as sexual partners was over. By then, Bao had been educated by Daiyu on how to please a woman. He was an eager and excellent student with stamina and creativity, so much so, Daiyu introduced him to other women to participate in threesomes.

FRIDAY, AUGUST 10TH, 1990, 1:16 P.M, GUANGZHOU

The box sitting on the corner of Daiyu Zhu's desk was sealed with heavy packing tape. There was no name or address on the box, nor was any needed. Sitting in front of her was Senior Investigator Lieu who had slowly moved his way up the ranks of investigators in the Guangzhou's office of the Ministry of People's Security. Now Lieu ran the group that coerced their fellow citizens to spy on carefully selected targets considered either potential criminals or security risks.

Daiyu looked glanced at the box. "Those are what you wanted."

Lieu smiled and knew better than to use their titles. Who knew who was listening? He couldn't wait to start reading and add *Myra Breckinridge, Two Sisters, Julian, Myron,* and *Burr* to his collection of Vidal's work.

Daiyu slid a sealed envelope across the table. "In here is a recommendation that you acquaint yourself with a first-year medical student who will be, one day, a brilliant doctor. In there is my report and the comments of others who have experience with him. He is charming, discrete, and afraid of long-term relationships. He also has considerable stamina and is, therefore, perfect for your department."

"What's his name?"

"Bao Gu. Pay him well. When he finishes medical school, he will be an asset to our country. I feel obligated to say that if you interfere with his studies and prevent him from completing medical school, I will ensure you are exposed."

Lieu knew exactly what Daiyu meant. If his superiors learned of his sexual preferences, he would be sent to a re-education camp from which he would not emerge alive.

CHAPTER 3

NEW RELATIONSHIPS

THURSDAY, AUGUST 13ᵀᴴ, 1992, 4:53 P.M. LOCAL TIME, LOS ANGELES INTERNATIONAL AIRPORT

The press of the crowd outside the immigration hall at Thomas Bradley International Terminal at Los Angeles International airport surged forward toward the fencing as people began to exit. Small in stature, Zimo Huáng held Shi's hand firmly as they angled through the throng to a place on the fence separating passengers from those waiting for them.

Once there, he held up a sign with Jun's name in Chinese characters. He needn't have bothered. Shi jabbed him in the ribs and pointed to a young woman emerging from the terminal. Her wave was acknowledged by Jun who was pulling a large roller bag on top of which she had a smaller one.

Zimo pulled Shi along through the people jostling to either get to the fence or move to greet a loved one. Not knowing quite what to say, Zimo let Shi hug her granddaughter before he did the same.

Even for a Chinese woman, Jun was small. She was only 5' 4" tall and at 45 kilograms (~100 pounds), thin. Zimo thought that Jun if she wanted, could be a model, just as his granddaughter Yan could be. To his eye, they could have been fraternal twins.

Jun was in LA because San Diego State University had accepted her in their microbiology doctoral program. Besides her top grades at Sun Yat-Sen University in Guangzhou, Tao's offer to pay her living expenses, paved the way for her exit visa under the new policy of Four Modernizations (agriculture, industry, defense, and science and technology). Her U.S. F-1 visa application stated Jun planned to stay in the U.S. for six years to enable her to finish her doctorate. If Jun decided to stay after graduating, she would have to apply for a resident's permit.

With his hands on Jun's shoulders, Zimo spoke in Cantonese, "Granddaughter Jun. It is a delight to see you. You look wonderful. How was your flight?"

Jun answered in halting English. For much of the flight, she rehearsed the questions and the answers. When she checked in for the flight, she spoke English and the Cathay Pacific agent at Hong Kong's Kai Tek International Airport responded in Cantonese. At each step of the way, Jun spoke English knowing there was a difference from lessons in school to using the strange language in every situation. "Very long. I must thank Cousin Tao for paying for a business class seat. It was most comfortable."

Zimo took the hint and responded in English. "You can tell him tonight at a family dinner to celebrate your arrival. How is your mother?"

"She is well."

"And your father?"

"He too is well but immersed in investigations as usual." Jun chose not to share the constant fights, Ai's beating of Liang, or discuss the unhealthy tension between her mother and father.

Translation – my father put his dedication to Guangzhou's Public Security Police's 5th Bureau's investigations of murders, rapes, robberies, etc. above his family.

"Well, you are here. I know you must be tired, but are you hungry? It is rush hour, so it may take us a few hours to reach San Diego."

To come to LA, Jun rode the train from Guangzhou to Hong Kong where she boarded the Cathay Pacific flight to Los Angeles. This was the first time she'd been outside Guangzhou, much less the PRC or ridden in an airplane.

"Grandfather, I am hungry and would like to try a cheeseburger."

Zimo smiled. "Can you wait an hour or so and we will take you to a place in San Diego?"

Jun nodded her head and Zimo accelerated his BMW 533i out of the parking lot. With her eyes fixed on the sights outside the car, Jun said nothing. Once they were south of I-5, jet lag won and the 22-year-old fell asleep.

FRIDAY, AUGUST 14ᵀᴴ, 1992, 6:43 P.M. LOCAL TIME, RANCHO SANTA FE

The sound of a car door closing loudly stopped the conversation in the living room between Tao, his unmarried son Qing, and his father. Zimo stood up since the door closing signaled Yan's arrival from Los Angeles where she was about to start her senior year.

Tao stuck his head in the kitchen and addressed the women preparing chicken, beef, shrimp, and vegetables for fajitas. Jun said, after she had her first hamburger, she didn't want Chinese food; she wanted what Americans eat and Mei Huáng was happy to oblige.

The Huángs stood in the background so that Jun would be the first to greet her cousin. When Jun arrived at LAX, Yan was in a class she didn't want to cut and risk her almost 4.0 GPA. The two young women hugged each other. Yan being almost a head taller at 5' 10", broader and more muscular, thanks to years of practicing Kung Fu and Tai Chi.

While physically mature, Jun would tell you that her small stature resulted from many years of only having at most two meals a day, thanks to food shortages.

"Welcome to America, Cousin Jun." She sniffed the air and smelled the cumin from the marinade. "I see you are about to be introduced to the Mexican version of moo shu!!!"

Jun looked at her cousin quizzically, which Yan took as a hint to explain. "Fajitas. Vegetables and meat in a flour tortilla. It is very similar to moo shu chicken or pork… "With a smile, she added, "but spicier!!! It is so good to see you."

Back in 1986, Yan was in what she said was her rebellious teenager period. When told about the trip to the PRC, initially Yan didn't want to leave her friends. She went only after Zimo and Shi insisted. Now, Yan would admit that not wanting to go was a stupid position to take.

Ever since, Jan and Yun wrote to each other every month. In her letters, Jun was careful not to reveal details of her life Ministry of State Security censors would find objectionable. Yan never mentioned she was attending UCLA on a Navy ROTC scholarship.

SATURDAY, JUNE 12ᵀᴴ, 1993, 11:07 A.M. LOCAL TIME, LOS ANGELES

The auditorium for the commissioning ceremony had enough seats for the 53 midshipmen about to be commissioned and their families. The front rows were reserved for the midshipmen, officers, and NCOs in UCLA's NROTC unit.

When each midshipman was called to the stage, the commanding officer read their name, degree, and in the case of Yan's, a bachelors' degree in international affairs, summa cum laude. He noted that Ensign Yan Huáng would report for training as a Naval Intelligence Officer at the Naval and Marine Corps Training Center in Dam Neck, VA.

Once exams were over, Yan had no reason to stay in LA and moved out of her apartment and came back only for graduation. She already had her orders. She said good-bye to her friends in the unit, knowing she may see many on active duty. When Yan introduced her cousin Jun to her friends, Jun said she was working on a doctorate in microbiology. That kept the conversation away from the fact that she was a citizen of the People's Republic of China.

They were cruising on I-5 well south of LA and headed to San Diego when Jun said to her cousin. "I am proud of you that you chose to serve your country, America. From what I can see, it is worth serving. In the People's Republic, the party tries to control everything one does and how we think at the same time, and the government officials are corrupt. I have not, nor shall I say anything to my mother or father that you are about to be an American Naval Intelligence officer."

Surprised at the candid admission, Yan replied, "Thank you. They might ask you to try to turn me into a spy or force you to return before you earn your doctorate. I don't know which would be worse."

Jun stared out the car window. "My country's visa requires that I return after six years. The only reason I will return to China earlier is to take care of my mother and father if they are ill. Before I left, my mother urged me to stay in America. Please do not tell your parents that my mother and father hate each other. Being here in America spares me of witnessing their fighting. Nevertheless, I owe much to them just as I owe much to Uncle Tao and Grandfather Zimo. Without their help, I would not be here."

Jun's words hung in the air. Both women knew if they were overheard in the PRC, Jun would soon be having a very uncomfortable session with officers from the Ministry of State Security that could lead to a sentence of several years in prison for uttering counter-revolutionary ideas.

Yan turned to another subject. "What about men? Are you interested?"

Jun shook her head. "I am here to earn a doctorate and learn as much as I can. And, if I fall in love with an American, what then? I doubt he would want to go back with me."

"If he is an American citizen, you could become one."

"That would make things worse for my mother and something I will not do." What Jun did not say was that before she left, her mother said, "If you can stay in America, do not worry about me. It is my karma to live with Ai and die in China."

Jun felt guilty about leaving her mother to live with the monster her father had become. She had seen the black and blue marks on her mother's body. Ai knew exactly where to hit her so the bruises were hidden by the cheongsams Liang wore.

CHAPTER 4

CAREER OPTIONS

Ensign Yan Huáng was about to leave the N2 – Intelligence – spaces for the admiral's office when Vice Admiral Broderick's aide called to say the admiral was running late. He didn't think it would be long before the Commander, Seventh Fleet, was ready. Disappointed because she'd spent the past hour prepping for the meeting, Yan Huáng pushed her pile of briefing slides to the side of her desk.

The sudden delay gave Yan time to reflect on the whirlwind she'd been living since arriving in Japan. Right after she was commissioned, Yan attended the Naval Officer Intelligence School in Dam Neck, VA, and was surprised to receive orders to the Seventh Fleet Staff. Normally, intelligence officer billets on numbered fleet staffs were filled by second-tour lieutenants and lieutenant commanders. The N2 – the Chief of Staff for Intelligence – was a commander which is the equivalent of a lieutenant colonel in the Air Force, Army, or Marines.

When the aide called, Yan put her slides and notes under her arm and headed aft, down the passageway to the Admiral's office.

Vice Admiral Broderick first words to Yan after she was introduced were, "How is your Chinese?"

"Sir, I am fluent in both Mandarin and Cantonese and can speak and read Hakka but don't consider myself fluent."

"Outstanding, Ensign!" The three-star admiral's comment led to a conversation about three ships from People's Liberation Army's Navy (PLAN) impending port visit to Tanjung Priok, the port for Jakarta, the capital of Indonesia. The naval attaché to Indonesia was tasked with arranging a visit of the new PLAN Type 053H2G frigate and the admiral wanted Yan to go.

That was less than three weeks ago. When Yan arrived in Jakarta four days before the port visit, Commander Williamson expected an experienced officer who had recently served on frigates or destroyers. He viewed Yan as a wet behind the ears ensign who didn't know anything about ships.

Yan came armed with whatever intel CIA and DIA could provide on *Huainan* on which the number 540 was painted on her bow. *Huainan* had been commissioned in December 1992 and was considered by DIA's analysts one of the most modern ships in the PLAN's fleet. The frigate would be accompanied by a 430-ton Type 037 sub-chaser and the *Dongting Lake*, an 11,000-ton Type 904 supply ship.

Admiral Broderick wanted Yan to use her knowledge of Chinese culture to learn about the capabilities of the ship and its crew. Eager to show off its new ship, the PRC's embassy in Jakarta scheduled a reception for the *Huainan's* officers the night before the tours were to be given.

Williamson's first excuse for Ensign Yan not being on the invitation list was that he didn't know she was coming until two weeks ago. Her look told Williamson that his excuse was bullshit. She had a copy of the Personal For message from VADM Broderick to the State Department's representative on the Commander Pacific's staff advising him that Ensign Huáng was being sent as his representative. Williamson was copied on the message.

The commander then said that Mess Dress which was required for the reception. Yan smiled and said, "Mine was cleaned and pressed just before I left Yokosuka."

Yan had decided not to say she didn't want to report to a three-star that the officer he'd sent as his representative with the blessing of

CINCPAC was not on the guest list unless he kept making excuses. Williamson, who had been the Naval Attaché for less than a year knew that in the world of naval operations, Indonesia was in the Seventh Fleet area of operations and a port visit by three PRC ships was a big deal.

Ten minutes later, Williamson dropped her official invitation on the desk she was using, followed by the briefing book on who would be at the reception. Curtly, he told Yan an embassy car would pick her up at five, cocktails and hors d'oeuvres were at six.

To Yan, the reception was a non-event. She was the only woman in uniform at the event and wasn't surprised that more officers weren't interested in who she was. As an ensign, none of the People's Liberation Army, Air Force, or Navy officers – all the equivalent of commanders and captains – spoke to her. As the most junior officer in the room and a woman, they probably assumed she didn't know anything of value and was, therefore, not worth their time.

Williamson left her alone which gave her time to surreptitiously look for cameras. She assumed everyone was being photographed and microphones were recording whatever was said. Standing at what was for her, a chest high table, Yan dropped a napkin. On the bottom of the table, there was a black box in which the AA batteries were visible.

Back in her hotel room, Yan made notes of the entire event, even listing the food served and what was available at the bar. Each conversation, brief as they were, were noted.

The next morning, Commander Williamson arrived at her hotel in a black Suburban that took them where *Huainan* was tied to a pier. Before walking up the gangway, the frigate's executive officer introduced himself and asked them to leave their cameras in the car, noting that at the end of the tour, they would have their picture taken with the *Huainan*'s captain.

In each compartment where they stopped, a PLAN officer explained its purpose in Chinese. Then the captain, whose name tag said his last name was Hé, translated the description in English. To Yan, the Chinese seemed to be carefully rehearsed and what was said in Chinese wasn't accurately translated.

In the last compartment of the tour that in a U.S. Navy ship would be called the combat information center, *Huainan*'s operation officer, Lieutenant Gáo, explained all the positions and their roles. As he spoke, he kept looking at Yan. With all the displays blank, Gáo's explanation was that all the systems were turned off since they were in port.

As the most junior officer, Yan was the last to leave and walk onto the main deck. As she was passing through the hatch, she felt a hand on her shoulder. It was Lieutenant Gáo who spoke in Chinese, "Ensign Huáng, you speak Chinese don't you?"

Yan looked at Gáo blankly as if she didn't understand. She was sure that Gáo and Hé were not their real names.

He repeated the question in English.

Yan responded, "Why are you asking?"

"Because I could see you paying attention to me when I was speaking and not when Captain Hé spoke. So do you speak Mandarin?"

Yan responded in Mandarin, "And two other dialects."

By now, the others on the tour were in a group having their photo taken with *Huainan's* captain leaving Gáo and Huáng alone on the main deck just outside the hatch to the ship's combat information center. The Chinese officer was a good head taller than Yan and his aggressive stance made her take a step back so her back was against the steel of the superstructure.

"Where did you learn Chinese?"

"From my parents."

"Where were you born?"

"My secret." Yan was not about to give this man any information. *Already Gáo knows that I know that his captain was deliberately misleading his visitors. This could cause Captain Hé to lose face if he learns the truth. That was Gáo's and Hé's problem, not mine.*

Gáo pointed to her single ribbon above the left pocket on her summer whites. "What is your warfare specialty?"

Sure that the Chinese Navy officer was fishing for information, Yan said, "I am too junior to have one." *If Gáo and Hé can lie, so can I.*

"You read all the placards on the sensor stations in our combat information center, didn't you?"

Yan smiled and saw Commander Williamson standing a discrete distance away. "Lieutenant Gáo, Commander Williamson is waiting for me now that our tour is over, so I must not keep a senior officer waiting."

Once in the car Yan began sketching the bridge and the frigate's CIC on a pad she had left in her purse. When she finished, she labeled each item. Williamson watched and said nothing until she finished.

"What are you planning to do with those drawings?"

"They are going to be part of my report. Why."

"May I have copies?"

"I'll give you a copy once they are finished. They lied to us and they didn't use their real names. I read all the placards I could. For example, Captain Hé said their air search radar had a range of 100 kilometers, yet there was placards for 150 kilometers. The ones I can remember will be in my report."

"May I ask what Lieutenant Gáo and you were discussing?"

"He figured out I spoke Mandarin and he wanted to know what my warfare specialty was." She then recounted what happened and ended by saying, "Gáo knows I know that neither Captain Hé nor he used their real names and that they lied about the ship's capabilities. If he doesn't tell Hé, then he loses face for hiding the truth. If he tells Hé, then the captain loses face. If Gáo doesn't tell his captain and Hé finds out, it could be career over."

Williamson nodded his understanding. "Interesting. How did you determine they were not using their real names?"

"Simple! Their name tags didn't match the names they used."

The black Chevrolet Suburban stopped while the Marine Guard opened the gate to the U.S. Embassy. After he got out, Williamson leaned back into the vehicle. "Ensign, I'm impressed. I can't wait to read your report."

Yan's phone on her desk jangled, ending her recollection of the visit to the *Huainan*. It was Vice Admiral Broderick' aide. She picked up the bundle of slides for the briefing she intended to give before she left for Indonesia and headed down the passageway with the staff's senior intelligence officer, Commander Lester Lansing. The aide, a newly promoted lieutenant commander, was also affectionately referred to as "the Rope." He was waiting for Yan when she arrived outside the admiral's office and pointed to the office with large table covered in green felt that could seat 12. One chair at the end had a covering with three stars. At the far side of the office, there was a large steel desk along with a well-used, brown couch with over-stuffed chairs with the same leather.

As she entered, Yan could see the door to the admiral's living quarters was closed. VADM Broderick waved to the couch and sat in one of the armchairs. Lansing sat opposite the vice admiral leaving Yan alone on the couch.

"O.K. Ms. Huáng, give me the elevator speech of your analysis. Then, I'll ask you questions. If we need to, we can look at your slides. Deal?"

Yan nodded. "Sir, the punch line is quite simple. Right now, the PRC's navy is in a transition from a coastal defense force to being a true, blue-water navy. From a timeline perspective, we won't see much change until just after the turn of the century, but if they continue at the pace they are currently proceeding at, by 2005, we'll see surface action groups supported by supply ships operating four or five hundred miles from their coast. By 2010, they'll be experimenting with carrier task forces. I don't think they'll have an operational carrier task force that can deploy for months at a time until 2015 at the earliest. Will they be able to challenge us at sea? Not in the foreseeable future, but my guess, in twenty years, we'll have a formidable adversary."

Neither Admiral Broderick nor Commander Lansing said anything for at least 30 seconds. "Ms. Huáng, you have all the facts and figures to support these conclusions?"

"Yes, sir."

The admiral looked at the N2 as if to say, have you seen her data and analyses. Lansing answered the unasked question. "The entire staff tried to rip it apart and couldn't. Then she presented it, unofficially of course, to the PRC Navy experts on the CINCPAC staff and they gave her kudos. When we socialized it with DIA, they said it fills in some of the blanks in their analyses."

"When do I get to see the formal report?"

Yan pulled the report she had at the bottom of the stack of slides. "Sir, here it is. I am still tweaking it, but I'll wait for your input before the N2 and I ask for your endorsement and forward it to CINCPAC and DIA."

The admiral nodded. "I'll give this back to you after I've had a time to digest it." After he put the report in his lap, the admiral asked, "Have your new orders arrived?"

"The JO Naval Intelligence officer detailer called this morning to let me know that orders to report to COMCARGRU Seven in San Diego by March 1st were in the works. The message orders should arrive any day."

Everyone in the admiral's office understood JO meant junior officer. Yan pronounced COMCARGRU just as the acronym was spelled and meant Commander, Carrier Group. By asking to go to Carrier Group Seven, Yan was asking for back-to-back sea duty tours. Normally, officers rotate between sea and shore assignments.

Volunteering for two sea duty tours in a row was viewed favorably by promotion boards assuming Yan received excellent annual fitness reports during the second tour. The added experience would give her a leg up when requesting plum billets within the Navy's intelligence community.

SATURDAY, FEBRUARY 7TH, 1998, 9:36 A.M. LOCAL TIME, WAITSFIELD, VT

For February in Vermont, the temperature was a balmy 20°F. No wind meant no wind chill. Better, yet, a storm dumped 18" of fresh snow the night before.

Derek Almer arrived at the base lodge at 8:16 a.m. wanting to get on one of the first chairs going up the mounting. By the time the lifts began taking skiers up the mountain at nine, most of the trails will have been groomed. As someone who skied Sugarbush North a lot, he knew where the places were to enjoy skiing knee-deep powder well into the morning.

The staff members gathered at the base of the Green Mountain Express chair lift, waiting to ride up the mountain and welcomed Derek when he slid into line at the base of the Green Mountain Express lift . He'd been skiing Sugarbush North since he was four and was well-known to the staff as both an instructor and one of the top local racers. It was also where his mother worked half days on weekends in the lift ticket booth in exchange for season passes for the family at both Sugarbush North and South. Everyone waiting at the lift wanted to get to the top of the mountain before the paying customers and be the first to ski in the fresh untracked snow.

From the top of Mount Ellen, Derek skied down Elbow to the base of the North Ridge Express. Already, the snow cats towing rollers had packed the snow in the center of the trail leaving plenty of deep snow along the tree line. From Elbow, Derek dropped onto Hammerhead, a narrow trail full of moguls that led down to the base area. The snow had filled in the troughs and the tops of the bumps were barely visible. As he turned back and forth, the sensation was like a mini roller coaster. In some places the snow was shin deep, in others, thigh deep.

Derek pulled up at the base of the Green Mountain Express at the end of his run and leaned on his poles as he watched four young women walk toward the lift and plop their skis on the snow.

One wearing a light gray parka and black ski pants peeled off to talk to an older woman. She yelled to her friends to go up saying she'd catch up. Derek recognized Lois van Doorn, Sugarbush North's ski school director, the college age woman was headed to. Van Doorn spotted Derek standing alone and walked over with the young woman.

Van Doorn spoke, "Derek, are you still planning to come to the instructor clinic in late March?"

"I am."

"Great." Realizing that she had not introduced the two college students, Lois spoke to the young woman. "Sorry, Adrian. Let me introduce you to Derek Almer, ski racer extraordinaire! Derek, this is Adrian Gutenberg, another of my potential ski instructor recruits."

Derek smiled, picked up Adrian's poles that had fallen over and used them to point to the lift. "Shall we?"

They were the only two on the four-seat chair that started up the mountain. Just after the first lift tower, they stopped abruptly. Derek was automatically interested in Adrian since the young woman could ski. He turned around to look down the mountain. "They're loading one of the ski patrol sleds onto the lift. Adrian, are you from around here?"

Here, in Derek's mind meant Waitsfield, Warren, Waterbury or even Burlington.

"Nope, born and raised in Newton, Massachusetts. It's outside Boston. You?"

"Born and raised in Burlington. Are you up here with your parents?"

Adrian laughed, thinking that is nice way of getting at how old she was and why she was at Sugarbush North. "No, I'm a sophomore at Middlebury. You?"

From an athletic standpoint, Middlebury College was one of Norwich University's rivals in hockey, ski racing, soccer, and other sports. Culturally, the two schools were worlds apart. Norwich is the oldest private military college in the U.S. and primarily an engineering school. Founded in 1819, the school was credited for inventing what is now called ROTC.

Middlebury College was a private liberal arts college founded in 1800. In addition to traditional curricula, it was known for its foreign language school. About half again larger than Norwich, Middlebury was a member of the Little Ivies (Amherst College, Bates College, Bowdoin College, Colby College, Williams College, and Wesleyan College) – i.e. small, elite liberal arts colleges in New England known for their educational excellence and highly selective admissions practices.

"I'm from the arch enemy, Norwich."

"I gathered as much.

The chairlift started to move. Derek shifted so he could face the young woman. Adrian pulled her goggles forward and then up on her head before putting on a pair of sunglasses. The move let Derek see her bright blue eyes as Adrian brushed strands of brown hair back under her hat.

"What's your major?" Derek was trying to make conversation.

"Poly Sci."

Adrian didn't ask what Derek's major was and he wondered if the admission he was at Norwich turned her off. So, Derek changed the subject.

"So, how well do you know this mountain?"

"Pretty well. I ski Sugarbush South more than North, but on a weekend like this, my friends thought that North would be less crowded."

"Well, if you are interested, I can take you to areas where the powder won't be skied off for most of the day." Derek held up his hand. "Not trying to be pushy, just helpful. I've been skiing Glen Ellen, Mad River Glen, and Stowe all my life."

"Tell you what, if my friends are waiting for me, then no, but if they're not, then you're on and I'll find them later."

"You're on."

"So, Derek, are you one of those military guys?"

He laughed at the words. "If you are asking if I am in Norwich Corps of Cadets, then yes. I have a Navy ROTC scholarship and am hoping to become a Naval Aviator after I graduate."

"So you want to fly jets like in the movie Top Gun?"

"Yup. Did you see the movie?"

"I watched it with my boyfriend when I was in high school. At the time, he was really into airplanes. The flying scenes were very exciting and Tom Cruise and Val Kilmer are easy on the eyes, but I didn't dig the macho aura of the characters."

"I don't think Naval Aviators are macho, confident in their skills, maybe even a bit arrogant, but macho…."

Adrian grinned. "I rest my case."

Derek flipped up the bar and they slid off the lift to the side. Adrian didn't see her friends. "I guess I'm yours for a few runs. Pressure is on to show me runs with fresh powder. Just don't leave me stranded in the woods."

"I'll do my best and will stop to make sure I don't lose you."

MONDAY, APRIL 20TH, 1998, 9:49 A.M. LOCAL TIME, GUANGZHOU

The doctor's office in the clinic for senior members of the Ministry of Public's Security was both clean and sparse. Ai Lín fidgeted as he looked out the window suspecting he was about to hear bad news. For weeks, his cough had gotten worse. Now, the phlegm was speckled with blood. As a life-long chain-smoker, it was hard to quit, but when the coughing started, he'd stopped smoking, much to the delight of his wife Liang.

Ai was thinking about his life and how he managed to survive Mao's purges in the 50s and the Cultural Revolution. Now, he ruefully thought, some disease, not a bullet may end my life.

Behind him, the door opened and the doctor who had ordered the X-rays and tests entered carrying a folder and a sheet of film. The physician waved in the general direction of the other chair in the office. His choice was the examining table or the chair. Ai nodded and chose the chair which let the doctor sit in the swivel chair at the small desk.

"Commissioner Lín, allow me to be blunt, the news is not good. You have Stage IV small cell lung cancer. In the medical profession, you have what is known as an "oat-cell" carcinoma. My oncologist colleagues and I believe that surgery is not feasible since you have tumors throughout both lungs and in, we suspect, all your lymph nodes. Here in the People's Republic, we do not have the drugs that can slow the growth of the tumors down or even kill them."

Ai waved his hand to cut the doctor off. He was just told what he suspected; he would die soon. "How much time do I have left?"

"One or two more months before you cannot function normally. At which point we will bring you into a hospital and make you comfortable until the end."

Ai nodded. "Thank you, doctor." He stood up and before he reached the door, he turned, "I presume that my diagnosis will be reported to the ministry?"

The doctor nodded.

"Please give me a few days to tell my superiors."

Again the doctor nodded. "The bureaucracy works slowly."

Ai left, knowing precisely what to do and who to tell. The most important person was Liang who, despite their strained and very tense relationship, had been nagging him to see a physician.

THURSDAY, AUGUST 27TH, 1998, 6:46 P.M. LOCAL TIME, SAN DIEGO

Jun was worried that she had not heard from her mother since May. As a dutiful daughter, she wrote every month to keep her informed of her progress. In her last letter, sent in the middle of June, Jun enclosed several pictures of her from her graduation with a doctorate in virology. She assumed the letters were intercepted and opened before they were delivered to her mother which is why none of the photos included any of her relatives.

When Jun arrived in the United States, her mother gave her a well-worn copy of Mao's Little Red Book from the Cultural Revolution. The family had two copies acquired by Ai and both were signed by Chairman Mao. When she went through immigration on the way to the United States, the inspector was impressed and showed his comrades Mao's inscription to her father.

To a PRC government employee, the book was a sign of cultural purity. For Jun and Liang, the book had another purpose. It enabled Liang and Jun to communicate without a censor learning the true content of the letter.

The system Liang taught her daughter was simple. Early in the letter, use a number. That would tell her mother the chapter, the next number the page in the chapter. The third number indicated which word on each line was to be used.

It was cumbersome to use and took some back and forth to be able to send terse messages, but worth the effort. In the pile of mail from her inbox, along with the usual store flyers, there were two letters. She read the Chinese on the stamps that commemorated the 90th anniversary of the birth of Comrade Li Fuchun. The return address on one told her that it was from her mother.

Yan remembered from the political courses she was required to take that Fuchun was a close friend of Mao and became the Vice Premier of the People's Republic of China. Fuchun is considered one of the founders of the country's socialist economy.

Carefully, Jun used scissors to cut open the end of the envelope and then dumped the two thin pieces of paper onto the kitchen table in her two-bedroom apartment. Gently, she unfolded the paper and smoothed it out before putting the scissors on it to keep it flat. From the desk in the small bedroom she used as an office, Jun picked up Mao's Little Red Book along with a pad and pencil.

Looking at the letter, Jun recognized her mother's precise strokes with the fountain pen with a wide point she preferred to use that made the Chinese characters. The letter wasn't encrypted.

My Dear Jun,

I humbly apologize for not writing sooner, but this is my poor attempt at explaining why. Your father passed away after what is described as a brief illness. He had lung cancer caused by his constant smoking. Ai did not suffer long and I was at his side when he took his last breath on July 16th, 1999. I wish he had listened to me long ago and stopped smoking. He was buried with honors on the 21st. So now you know why I have not written.

Tears filled Jun's eyes. She had to smile at her mother's reference to trying to get her father to quit smoking. From her early teens, both she and her mother nagged Ai to stop smoking. It filled their apartment with a noxious smell and made their clothes stink. Yet, Ai wouldn't quit and now it killed him.

As a little girl, she adored her father. As a teenager and college student, she loathed him for how he treated her mother. She kept reading, surprised what her mother wrote was not encoded.

My position as a professor of finance is not in danger and before your father died, he informed me that you are being ordered home. He suggested you be careful because those who have studied abroad are often viewed with suspicion. He also said that the state has great plans for you after you return, but he could not find out what.

I am well and hope to see you soon.

All my love,
Your mother

Reading between the lines, Jun suspected that the letter from the People's Republic's Los Angeles consulate that arrived on the same day would request she return home. She ripped it open and it confirmed her suspicions. The immigration official who sent the letter included a form on which she would give them her travel plans to return to the People's Republic by the end of the year. The letter also asked her to make an appointment at the consulate so she could be issued her new identity documents.

Jun brushed away her tears and dialed a familiar number in Maryland she knew by heart.

A familiar voice answered. "Hello."

Jun didn't' waste any time. "Yan, they want me to go back by the end of the year."

"I thought you were going to stay and work in a virology lab in San Diego for two more years."

"So did I, but I just got my recall letter."

"Are you going to return?"

"Yes, my mother is now a widow, so I do not have a choice." Jun explained what was in Liang's letter and the consequences if she did not."

"Have you told Grandfather Zimo and your Uncle Tao?"

"No. You were the first I called. I will see them this weekend. It is very important that I see you before I leave."

"I will take some leave. I'll call you on Monday to tell you when I will be in San Diego."

"Good." They talked for another few minutes before hanging up.

Yan was in DC working on an expansion of the analysis she started on the Seventh Fleet Staff. The message orders to leave Seventh Fleet and report to Commander, Carrier Group Seven were not what she expected. She was ordered to detach immediately and report to the carrier group staff in San Diego, arriving no later than February 10th, 1998. When she called the staff, they said she could ride the airlift leaving on February 27th for Norfolk because the staff was sailing on the *U.S.S. John C. Stennis* (CVN-74) on February 28th. The seven-ship battle group was scheduled to return to San Diego on August 26th, 1998.

On the deployment, *Stennis* went straight to the Arabian Gulf (a.k.a. known as the Persian Gulf if one lives in Iran) via a transit of the Suez Canal. After four months on station, the ship headed for San Diego, stopping in Perth and Hobart, Australia and Pearl Harbor, Hawaii before docking at North Island Naval Air Station.

Back in the U.S., Yan received orders to the Defense Intelligence Agency (DIA), headquartered in Anacostia, Maryland, which is where she was when Jun called. Along the way, she was promoted to lieutenant and received her second Navy Commendation Medal. The first was awarded by the Commander, Seventh Fleet, the second by Commander, Carrier Group Seven. At DIA, based on a recommendation from Admiral Broderick who was now the Chief of Naval Personnel, Yan was the action officer for the expanded study.

At DIA, Yan's office was near Glenn Young's, whom she dated until Young graduated a year before Yan. He was on leave in CA when she arrived at DIA and within hours of seeing her, asked her out.

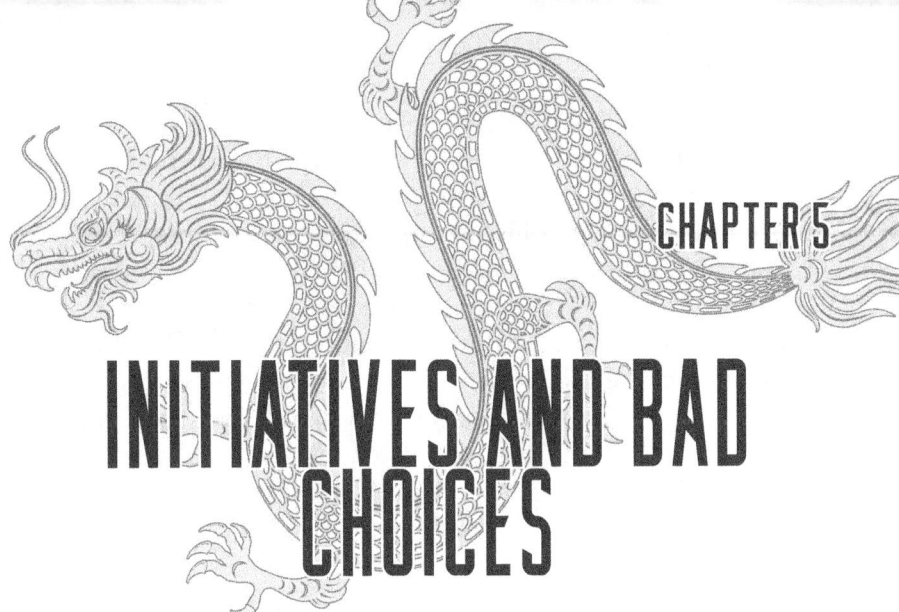

CHAPTER 5

INITIATIVES AND BAD CHOICES

After graduating from the National Defense University, Fang Sun's career took great leaps forward. First, upon graduation, he was promoted to lieutenant colonel; his new assignment was with the 71st Group Army staff headquartered in Xuzhou. When he checked in, three of its divisions were deployed into Beijing in an exercise to impose martial law if there was a replay of what happened in Tiananmen Square in 1989.

Sun was assigned as the group army's chemical and biological warfare officer. Before reporting, he had attended a four-month-long school on chemical and biological warfare. Sun's takeaway from the school and this assignment convinced him there were ways to use bioweapons off the battlefield to change a population's trust in its government.

Three years later, he was promoted to colonel and given the command of the 535th Infantry Regiment in the 179th Motorized Infantry Division based in Nanjing. Fang Sun's next billet was on the

PLA's General Staff as its Director, Unconventional Warfare, Strategic Plans Department. A year later, he was promoted to Senior Colonel.

The stocky, but not overweight senior colonel closed the door to his office after telling his administrative assistant that he did not want to be disturbed. He had just received a call from a People's Republic Liberation Army general who was the chief of staff to a chairman of the Central Military Commission (CMC). The caller told him to create a discussion document as soon as possible that expands on what they discussed a week ago. If the CMC thought the concept had merit, then Sun would be asked to develop a plan that the PLA would execute. His memo was sparked by an idea he developed after a visit to one of the PLA's biological warfare sites.

The PRC signed the United Nations Biological Convention in 1984 but kept the biowarfare site he visited along with three other fully operational facilities. From his training, Sun knew were in direct violation of the 1984 treaty. Since the PRC was not part of the actual negotiations, by "accessing" the treaty, it means that they will legally be bound by its provisions even though the PRC was not one of the original signatories. Accession, he learned at the Chemical and Bio Warfare school, had the same legal force as signing and ratifying a treaty. As far as Sun was concerned, treaty violations were the purview of the Ministry of Foreign Affairs. He was just doing what he was told.

Sun stacked all the routine paperwork on one side of his desk so only his original notes that led to the conversation, a copy of the U.N. Biological Convention in both English and Chinese, and a pad were in the center of his desk.

The note that came with the copy of the treaty said that the People's Republic had accessed the treaty on November 15th, 1984 and was one of 183 nations that agreed to abide by the treaty. Article I of the U.N. Biological Weapons Convention read:

> No state shall ever in any circumstances develop, produce, stockpile, or otherwise acquire or retain:
>
> 1.　　Microbial or other biological agents, or toxins whatever their origin or method of production, of types and in quantities that have no justification for prophylactic, protective or other peaceful purposes.

2. Weapons, equipment, or means of delivery designed to use such agents or toxins for hostile purposes or in armed conflict.

Sun didn't care what the words said. He thought the treaty was just another attempt by the world, and the United States in particular, to restrain the People's Republic's freedom of action and keep his country from developing weapons that would enable it to become the dominant power of the world.

From his personal files from the bio-warfare course, Senior Colonel Sun took out two charts he asked one of the medical doctors at the school to help him create. One was for known bacteriological diseases and the second was for viruses.

Across the top of each, he had the names of diseases in alphabetical order using their English names. To be on either chart, the disease had to be highly communicable and patients needed drug treatment(s) and/or hospitalization.

Vertically, the chart had boxes that answered eight questions. One, where was the disease found geographically? Two, how was the disease transmitted?

Question three identified the geographic regions where the disease was more prevalent than others. How the disease was treated was the subject of question four. In the answer, the primary medicines used to target the infection and their efficacy were listed.

Question five on Senior Colonel Sun's list: was there a vaccine? If so, how was it administered, was the vaccine readily available, and how effective was it? Number six identified where the disease was still infecting the population.

In Senior Colonel Sun's mind, questions seven and eight were the most important. Number seven identified the mortality rates in four ranges – under 13, 13 – 25, 26 – 60 and over 61. Question eight asked, what were the long-term effects, if any, on an individual, assuming they didn't die from the disease?

Senior Colonel Sun had several pages of notes to support the charts' entries on ledger-size (279mm X 432mm or 11" X 17") paper. The data reminded him that while many of the diseases were eradicated elsewhere in the world, some were still found in the southern parts of the People's Republic.

Other than medical care and a lack of medicines, he had two questions: Why? And how could he use them to his country's advantage?

His suggested course of action came from reading analyses and documents from biological research labs outside the PRC. Some were public, others he suspected by their markings had been stolen. Also in his possession were the People's Republic's internal analysis of the SARS pandemic and those from other countries.

Pencil in hand, Sun began writing. The words came easily since they had been formulating in his mind for months.

Project goal: create biological weapons that can overwhelm a target country's medical system and enable the People's Republic to achieve its foreign policy goals without using military force.

Project scope: the People's Republic should:

* Create highly transmissive viruses or bacteriological agents with high infection rates while at the same time, developing vaccine(s) and/or drugs to treat the disease(s); and

* Once developed, recommend testing the agents on a prison population within the PRC to learn their effects.

Project execution: once new viruses/bacterial agents have been either identified or developed, the PRC can:

* Release the agents covertly.

* Once the target country's population is infected, offer to "develop and produce" a vaccine. The swift deployment will demonstrate the superiority of the PRC's medical research capabilities.

* PRC offers the vaccine to the country with a political/foreign policy price tag.

Recommendations: build one or more laboratories designed for this purpose and:

* Place them under the auspices of the Chinese Academy of Scientists.

* Fund the labs through monies appropriated for the PLA.

* *Position the laboratories as medical research facilities so they will not be covered by the U.N. treaty.*

* *Acquire designs and equipment from the West since the PRC does not have the knowledge.*

Timeline:

* *First lab can be built by the end of 2000 if work begins within three months.*

* *Estimate that the first "testable" weapon can be ready within 10 years.*

Sun made several revisions, then retyped the memo and stamped the single sheet of paper Top Secret at the top and bottom. Once in an envelope marked Top Secret, he had the document couriered to the general who requested it.

WEDNESDAY, OCTOBER 13ᵀᴴ, 1999, 10:02 P.M. LOCAL TIME, LOS ANGELES AIRPORT

There were tears in Jun's eyes as she walked into the Tom Bradley Terminal. With each step, she felt the freedom she enjoyed over the past six years was being peeled away. To delay the inevitable longer, Jun decided she would spend what she thought as her last night of freedom in Hong Kong before taking the train to Guangzhou.

Besides her new identity documents, Jun had papers telling her to report to the Guangzhou Institute of Biomedicine and Health's Institute of Chemical Biology on Monday, November 1ˢᵗ for assignment as a biological researcher. Other documents informed her of her title, pay and authorized a one-bedroom flat near the facility. The institute was a member of the Chinese Academy of Scientists and a short walk from where her mother lived.

Also in Jun's possession were two Little Red Books, one she brought with her plus one of two printed in the U.S. - Yan had the other copy.

THURSDAY, NOVEMBER 25TH, 1999, 12:22 P.M. LOCAL TIME, BROOKLINE, MA

What started as a run through the trees in knee deep snow last winter had blossomed into a serious relationship. Before and after his midshipmen summer "cruise," Derek drove his 1992 VW GTI 16 Valve to Boston on weekends. Whenever he wasn't in Brookline, Derek worked at Sugarbush North clearing brush and helping with whatever tasks Lois van Doorn assigned him. In Brookline, Adrian was interning with, as he learned, her father's real estate development firm.

An invitation to the Gutenberg family Thanksgiving feast was, Adrian explained, a "really big deal." Thanksgiving was Derek's introduction to her extended family and would be taken as the indication that he was "the chosen one" and that Adrian and he were "serious." Not even her former high school beau had been so honored.

While Derek's family was well-off, at least by Burlington standards, the Gutenbergs were wealthy by any measure. They lived in a 5,000 square-foot, four-story house built in the late 1880s on a one-acre, heavily treed lot in Brookline, one of Boston's more exclusive neighborhoods.

On his first two visits during the summer, Derek stayed a few miles away at a Fairfield Hotel near the junction of Interstate 93 and Route 128. When Adrian's mother Miriam heard he was paying for hotel room, she said nonsense, you stay at our house but no funny business. As in, you will not sleep with my daughter in my house until you are married.

Derek was given a room on the top floor in what that were once servants' quarters. He had his own bathroom and the ceilings in each room slanted in. The room he was given had a small octagonal window that overlooked the front yard and beyond the 130-year-old oak tree, he could see the street – Buckminster Road.

With no classes during the week, Derek originally planned to leave Burlington on Wednesday so he could spend the weekend before Thanksgiving with his parents. Instead, they insisted their middle son go to Brookline. Derek laughed when they asked when they were going to meet their potential in-laws.

A maid opened the door and led Derek to the kitchen so he could say hello to Mrs. Gutenberg. He planned to ask what he could do to help but stopped when he found not only Mrs. Gutenberg, but Reena, the wife of Adrian's older brother Samuel, and Adrian's older sister, Sharon in the kitchen. After perfunctory hellos and glad you are here, Derek sensed his presence, just as it was in his house when his mother was cooking for a major event, was not wanted.

Adrian rescued him by leading him out of the huge kitchen that had been remodeled and modernized. Pulling his face toward hers so they could kiss. "Glad you are here so you, my knight in shining armor, can save me from this madness. Let's go someplace."

Derek was dumb enough to ask, "Why aren't you helping in the kitchen?"

"Reena and I don't get along and my mother knows it. I think Reena is a social climber who married my brother David for money, not love. I see right through her as if she is a window and she doesn't like it."

Derek's older brother was married and his sister-in-law Dannielle and his mother got along quite well. His baby sister Elaine was a freshman the at University of Vermont and was glad she didn't have a serious boyfriend that he'd be asked to "evaluate."

On Tuesday afternoon before the big Thursday feast, Adrian led Derek by the hand into a second-story room she referred to as the library. Its book lined walls made it look like one. She pointed to a table as if to say, "sit there." Adrian took a photo album off one of the shelves, sat in the chair next to Derek and opened the book. "These photos were taken last Thanksgiving by my brother David."

For the next half hour, she went through the 22 adults and children as if she was briefing the president of the U.S. who was about to enter a reception hall full of diplomats he didn't know.

"What if I don't put names to faces?"

"The first time, they'll laugh, the second time, when they see you hesitating, they'll reintroduce themselves. After that, who knows? You are my first boyfriend invited for Thanksgiving and I want you to be prepared."

"You mean I am going to be grilled?"

"Yup."

"Maybe I shouldn't have come?"

"Oh no. My mother insisted I invite you since you tick all the necessary boxes. You're good looking, smart, white, Jewish, come from a good family and are not gay. You were going to have to run this gauntlet someday, so we might as well do it now."

Derek took her attempt at humor the wrong way. He was annoyed. "What did your mother do, conduct a background check?"

"My mother is an excellent judge of people. If she didn't like you, you wouldn't be here. My father is very protective of the family's wealth which is another reason you are under the microscope. And yes, he probably had a background check done on you. While we are not the richest in Boston, we're easily in the top one hundred, probably top fifty."

"I don't want any of your family's money."

"I know that and my mother senses that but please understand, my father is always suspicious. At least once a year, someone attempts to scam him or get him to underwrite some fake cause. It just goes with the territory."

Adrian put her hands on his cheeks and pulled his mouth to hers. "Look, I love you, but I want you to come into my family with open eyes. We have our warts just like everyone else!"

Derek came downstairs late Thursday morning after a long workout in the gym on the third floor and a shower. He found Adrian reading a book to one of her nieces. The downstairs had been transformed into a small banquet hall.

In the dining room, there were two tables. One, with silverware in settings for eight, was for the children. The other longer table had 16 place settings. The Rosenthal China was the same as his parents "good dishes." He bet that, unlike his parents who bought them when his father was stationed in Germany, the Gutenbergs bought the high-quality China in the U.S. Derek suspected the silverware was Sterling and the glasses Waterford crystal.

In the living room, a man in a tuxedo was setting up a bar that would have made a restaurant proud. Two women, dressed as maids, were putting place cards on the table telling Derek that seating was assigned.

"Derek, I am glad you are here."

The native Vermonter turned around to see Miriam Gutenberg who held out her hands. To someone who grew up in a middle-class family, this set-up was overwhelming.

He took Miriam's hands who gently squeezed his. "I am sorry we have not had time to sit and talk this week, but as you can see, Thanksgiving is one part meal, one part family gathering of a full nest, and one-part social event. Come into the kitchen where we can have some privacy."

Derek assumed Miriam was in her fifties as she led him into her "inner sanctum" - the kitchen. She asked the maid arranging cheeses on a plate to, "Please give us a few minutes."

Miriam poured Derek a glass of red wine, then one for herself before holding it up to signal a toast. "Health and happiness to Adrian and you." They both took a sip before Miriam continued. "My Adrian is quite taken with you and I see the feeling is mutual. Just so you know, I believe serving in our country's military is an honorable profession and I applaud you for your choice of careers. My husband Michael didn't and preferred to go to Canada. Please don't hold that against him. Many members of my extended family think those who protect us are Neanderthals who can't do anything else. So, be warned. How you respond to their jabs and snide comments is up to you. I, for one, will cheer if you push back politely, but firmly. Please don't let them goad you into a shouting match."

Derek nodded. "I understand. Many of Adrian's friends at Middlebury are the same way. We've come to a mutual understanding in that I'll defend their right to make millions if they pay their taxes so people like me have the wherewithal to protect their freedoms and fortunes."

The older woman held up her glass. "Well said. Now, to my second topic. If you should decide to propose, we have several large stones in settings that are over a hundred years old. If you want one of these heirlooms, please ask me and we'll meet at our vault so you can choose one. Adrian knows they exist but has not seen them."

Derek put his glass down on the counter to give himself time to think. "Mrs. Gutenberg, thank you. Your offer is generous beyond belief. However, if you don't object, I would prefer to buy Adrian a ring with my money."

"I gathered that is what you would say, but please don't go heavily into debt just to buy her a ring with a big stone. If you do, both Adrian and I will be mad at you. So, the offer still stands. Do not be afraid to ask."

"Understood."

They – Miriam and Derek – were walking out of the kitchen when Adrian spotted the pair. Miriam went off to talk to one of the maids leaving Derek to answer Adrian's questions.

"What was that about?"

"Well, it appears that I am not about to be excommunicated from the Gutenberg family and am encouraged to keep seeing you. I was also warned about the opinions some of your relatives hold of the military."

Adrian made a face, "I forgot about that." She took his hand, "Come, and let us meet my relatives who are just starting to arrive. This way, we can sample all the appetizers before they are gone."

On prior visits, Derek had met some of Adrian's siblings. She had a sister Sharon who was 28, three brothers – David, 34; Saul, 32; and Samuel. Sharon and Samuel were fraternal twins. Then there was 30-year-old Ian who came out as a transvestite in high school. At age 18, he had his name legally changed to Ilana. As Adrian explained, if one didn't know, one would think he was a woman.

In the "World of Gutenberg" – Adrian's term for her family – her father presided over Pilgrim Real Estate, Inc. as its president. He was also the president of Pilgrim's Real Estate Investment Trust (REIT) which owned 121 hotels around the world and apartment buildings in Boston, Chicago, Philadelphia, and New York catering to wealthy residents.

Fifty percent of the hotels owned by the REIT were in the U.S. and were top-tier Marriott (JW Marriott, Marriott, Ritz Carlton, and Courtyards) and Hyatt (Hyatt Regency and Grand Hyatt) brands. The rest of the hotels were located around the world with ~10% in Canada, ~20% in Europe, the remaining 20% split between in Argentina, Australia, Israel, New Zealand, and Mexico.

Pilgrim began in the late 1880s when Israel Gutenberg, Michael's great, great, great grandfather began buying land around

Boston and contracting to build homes for wealthy Bostonians. He also branched out to build townhomes on Beacon Street and the profits enabled him to build the house on Buckminster Road. After WWI, Israel Gutenberg branched out into owning hotels.

Pilgrim had three operating units. The REIT that owned the hotels; a hotel and apartment management group led by David that managed the properties, and the real estate development unit led by Samuel that acquired land and built either hotels or apartments. Adrian had made sure Derek knew that her brother preferred Samuel, not Sammy.

Adrian's sister Sharon, a graduate of Cornell's School of Hotel Administration, worked for her brother David. Trained as a chef who spent a year in France and another in Italy, Sharon focused on food and beverage service at their hotels.

Ilana was a partner in a small law firm specializing in LGBT rights that was pushing the Massachusetts' legislature to pass a law allowing gays and lesbians to marry. His life partner Randy Bergen was a partner at the law firm that handled Pilgrim's real estate contract matters. In Adrian's briefing on her family she made a point of saying that Ilana got crossways with his father when he tried to convince him to hire Randy as Pilgrim's general counsel. The conversation, Adrian said, didn't end well. Neither talked to each other for months until Miriam forced the two to have a private dinner where she played referee.

Adrian was surprised when Ilana and Randy were the first to arrive. After being introduced, Ilana's first words were, "Derek, how do you like the idea of gays in the U.S. military?"

Derek wasn't taken aback because given Adrian's brief, he had an answer prepared. "Doesn't bother me at all as long as they are willing to share the risks."

"So you don't mind flying with a gay co-pilot?"

"Nope. If he or she is qualified and good, then it doesn't matter what their sex, religion, race, or skin color is. All that matters is how well they do their job."

Ilana made a face. "That's a simple answer to a very complex social issue."

"No, Ilana it is not. The bottom line is how good are you at doing your job. Nothing else matters."

"So you don't think that the military discriminates against women or gays and lesbians?"

Derek was now on a roll and he could feel Adrian squeeze his hand as a warning. Ilana had come prepared to test her boyfriend as if he was on the witness stand. "Ilana, by definition, the U.S. military is a discriminatory organization and must be. We discriminate against those who can't pass the physical and mental tests. We will not allow into our ranks diabetics who need insulin daily or anyone who needs daily medications, or those who have heart problems, and the list goes on and on. To be a pilot, one needs 20 – 20 eyesight and fit a specific physical and mental profile. So, no, I don't think we discriminate. History has taught us what mental and physical profiles are needed to be successful in combat and that's who we let in our ranks. If you qualify, welcome aboard. If not, sorry, go find another line of work."

Derek looked Ilana right in the eyeballs. The transvestite was almost as tall as Derek who was 5' 11" and slender. She – the pronoun Ilana preferred – had dark brown, shoulder-length hair. Randy said nothing other than an introductory "Hello, it is nice to meet you." Ilana's mouth opened slightly but no words came out.

Sensing it was time to end this conversation, Derek smiled as he said, "As I think they say in court, the witness may step down. Ilana, I think I answered your question. Adrian and I are heading off to sample some of the delicious appetizers Sharon created."

With that, Derek followed Adrian into the living room where plates adorned almost every flat surface. As they walked hand in hand, Adrian pulled Derek's hand down so she could whisper in his ear. "That was a very nice job of putting Ilana in her place."

During the dinner, Derek answered questions about his major and what he wanted to fly in the Navy. Adrian and Derek, even though they were the two youngest, were seated next to each other on the left side of her father with Adrian closest to her father. Sitting next to Derek was Saul and his wife Leah.

The only question that was not about cars, family, if he liked Red Sox or the hated Yankees, Patriots or Celtics, came from Saul about halfway through dinner. "So, Derek, after you complete your obligation to the Navy, what do you plan to do?"

This was another question Derek had prepped for. "Short answer is I don't know. Assuming I earn my wings in 2001, my contract end of service date will be, unless the Navy and the government decides otherwise, 2012. A lot can happen in those years. However, I can assure you I will evaluate my options carefully and pick a career I find interesting and one in which I am confident I will be successful."

Saul followed up quickly. "Just out of curiosity, if you had a crystal ball, what do you think those careers may be."

Derek noticed that conversation at their end of the table stopped. All were waiting for his answer which had an unasked question – are you planning to come into the family business? "Saul, that is an interesting and difficult question that has a binary answer – stay in the Navy until I retire or leave the Navy. Leaving opens a host of options. I could become an airline pilot, go to work as an engineer or program manager for a defense contractor, open a business, or become a ski bum. Who knows? Right now, I am focused on becoming the best Naval Aviator I can be. I've wanted to fly since I was a little boy, and now I have my chance. So that is my focus. I'm sorry if that doesn't answer your question."

He felt a hand caress his inner thigh. Derek wasn't sure if Adrian approved what he said, or was asking "what about me?" That was a subject they both knew was coming and he wasn't ready to pop the question. In his mind, that day was coming and coming soon.

SUNDAY, NOVEMBER 28TH, 1999, 1:42 P.M. LOCAL TIME, GUANGZHOU

When she reported to the institute, Jun was told that she needed to attend classes to "reacquaint" her with the People's Republic of China. There was no apartment ready nor was the institute prepared to pay her. When it finally did, the clerk handed her an envelope with the wrong amount. This mistake took weeks to correct since the admission there was an error caused several to lose face. And, after all, the state cannot be wrong. Jun concluded that she would not be assigned an apartment until she completed what she called the re-indoctrination course.

The classes were incredibly boring and an attempt to "prove" the superiority of the CCP's system. Each day Jun sat through lectures on the PRC's constitution, its government and the CCP's brand of communism. After living in the United States, the propaganda was so far from the truth, at times she had to lower her head to keep the instructor from seeing her laughing.

When Jun reported to the Guangzhou Institution of Biomedicine and Health, she was ushered into the office of Senior Administrator Doyi Siew. She could tell he was studying her file because she could see her picture. In his first few words, Siew noted her late father was a senior commissar in the Ministry of People's Security and served his country for over 40 years.

This past Friday, Siew said she was still being vetted. When the Ministry of State Security and commissars conducting the course were confident that Jun could be trusted after living in the U.S. for six years, she would be allowed to begin working at the lab. Meanwhile, she had to remain patient.

When Jun was having breakfast with Liang, her mother suggested they walk off the meal in the Houlushan Forest Park, not far from her mother's apartment complex. After strolling for about half a kilometer and listening to her daughter vent, Liang touched her daughter's shoulder.

"I have a letter from your father I promised to give you once you returned." She didn't use the word United States because she and her daughter were convinced that the Ministry of State Security had microphones hidden throughout the park, particularly near benches. This was another reason they walked and Jun kept her voice down.

The letter was in her father's style and unopened. "Mother, do you know what father wants to tell me."

Liang suspected what was in the letter, but was not sure, so she said, "No, other than your father wanted me to give this to you."

Gently, Jun opened the envelope and unfolded the letter. She could see the letter was dated June 16th, 1999, a month before Ai died.

My lovely Jun,

It is most unfortunate that I will not live long enough to have this conversation with you so this letter must suffice. Even though your mother and I have had our differences, she has agreed to give this to you upon your return to the People's Republic and encourage you to carry out my wishes.

I have heard good things about your studies through my contacts within the Ministry of State Security. By earning your doctorate in microbiology you have justified the faith the Party had in you and honored your parents.

It is, however, time for you to consider marriage. Both your mother and I know you pushed everything else aside to earn your doctorate in a foreign land. But now, you must do your other duty and marry, reproduce, hopefully, a son for your country.

To that end, I have selected a young man — Bojing Zhao - who comes from a wonderful family. Currently he is assigned to the 75th Regiment of the Ninth Fighter Division's maintenance staff. They fly J-7s from Guangzhou East air base.

I know his father well and have met his son several times. Bojing is handsome, hardworking, smart, and loyal to his country. The two of you would produce beautiful grandchildren on which your mother will dote.

Please honor my memory and wishes by marrying Bojing.

May you be as lucky as you desire and all your wishes come true. And in this marriage, may you have mutual love and respect and give birth to one or more sons.

Your father

Jun turned to her mother. "Mother, did you know about this arrangement?"

"No. I suspected your father was making this arrangement, but he did not, as you know, confide in me very often."

Jun struggled to contain her anger. She didn't want an arranged marriage but now that one was set up, she may not have a choice.

"Mother, have you met Bojing Zhao?"

Liang's voice was solemn. "No. Last night, I read the letter your father gave me a letter instructing me on what I should do and what arrangements he made. In accordance with his wishes, I will contact the Zhao's. I suspect Bojing is eager to meet you."

Jun's urge to run was married to the feeling of being trapped. Maybe she should have filed for immigration to the United States. She returned only out of her loyalty to her mother and a sense of duty to care for Liang as she aged.

Looking into her mother's eyes, Jun said, "Does Bojing know I think that communism is crap and doomed to fail. Given a choice, I would prefer to live in America."

Liang took her daughter's hands in hers. "Jun, I know you came back to Guangzhou only for me. I would never say this when your father was alive. I suffered through the last fifteen years or so of our marriage being beaten and humiliated. Ai's death took away the physical pain but left me with the emotional pain. Even if I do not agree with this, I am duty-bound to ask you to carry out his wish. So here I am … Widowed, alone, and unhappy. Only you, my lovely daughter, bring me joy and happiness."

The two women hugged. Jun did not want her mother to see her tears. She felt sorry for her mother and now, to honor her father, she was being encouraged, the English word she would choose was "forced" to marry someone she did not choose, know, or even love.

If there was a bright spot, maybe the marriage will convince Ministry of State Security investigators that she is to be trusted. In those few seconds, Jun vowed she will bury herself in her work and that will be her love and salvation.

SUNDAY, DECEMBER 4TH, 1999, 6:08 P.M. LOCAL TIME, SAN DIEGO

Lieutenant Commander Glenn Young stood proudly at the end of the aisle watching the woman he'd been chasing since he first laid eyes on her when he was a junior and Yan was a freshman. The time for Yan to walk down the aisle allowed a few moments for him to reflect on how he wound up here.

Orphaned at eight, unwanted by his relatives, Young was moved from one foster home to another every two or three years. In high school, he lived with a Chinese family who took him only because the state paid them to do so. From them, Glenn Young learned the value of education and after applying, was awarded a Navy ROTC scholarship through which the Navy paid for his tuition, room and board, books, and fees. He worked in a MacDonald's four nights a week and on Sundays to earn spending money over and above the monthly stipend of $150/month paid to him by the Navy.

Young wanted to be a Naval Aviator, but when he failed the flight physical, the NROTC unit commanding officer suggested he become an intelligence officer since he could speak Spanish – learned at one foster home – and Chinese learned in another.

Growing up, Young viewed almost every situation as a transaction, i.e. what am I going to receive versus what I must do. While he received some affection from his foster parents, love was something new to Young. All the foster parents did was put food on the table, a roof over his head and as few clothes on his back as they could get away with. Everything else he paid for with his own money earned in part time jobs.

While the Huáng family would have preferred that Yan marry someone of Chinese descent, they liked Glenn. He was serving their adopted country and while his Mandarin was horribly accented, they took great delight in helping him expand his vocabulary.

Just before their marriage and honeymoon, Jun's evaluation of the PRC's military capabilities was sent back to her by the Director of the DIA with a short note.

Fantastic analysis. Well done.

Am having the head of the CIA's and NSA's China desks contact you to see what you can glean from their data. When you're done, this will go to the NSA and POTUS.

The NSA was the National Security Advisor and POTUS was the President of the United States. Cool beans, Yan thought. Not bad for an immigrant Chinese Girl.

The director's note led to another month's worth of work before it was classified Top Secret, Specially Compartmented Information, Code Word *Dragon Breath*. With that, what Glenn laughingly called, another "turd" found its way to Yan's desk in the Directorate of Analyses.

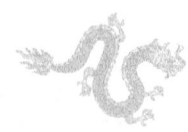

Right after Glenn and Yan returned from their honeymoon on Maui in the first week of January 2000, Glenn returned to his job in the DIA's personnel department. He often remarked that there wasn't much intelligence work, just hundreds of personnel and administrative headaches that he liked to solve.

Waiting on Jun's desk was another tasking note from the Director.

> Lieutenant, find out where Saddam Hussein's chemical and bioweapons went after Desert Storm. Authorization to dig through all agency databases follows. Project is TS/SCI code word *Salt Serene*. Need to give POTUS the answer in 90 days.

In early February, she was getting ready to go to the dojo, something Yan did four days a week to keep fit, reduce stress. Kicking or punching a heavy bag was, she believed, very therapeutic.

Yan had been practicing martial arts since she was 10. Her first black belt was in Kung Fu to which she added a black sash for Tai Chi. Now she was adding Tai Kwon Do to her skills.

What kept her out of the dojo this morning was the urge to puke right after she woke. Glenn didn't hear her gagging in their bathroom because he was making breakfast. At first, Yan thought she had some sort of flu and then remembered that she hadn't had a period since they returned from their honeymoon on Maui.

A visit to the clinic on Anacostia two weeks later confirmed Yan's suspicions. She was pregnant.

Glenn's first reaction was surprise and shock. And then, he was happy. Soon, there would be the pitter-patter of little feet around the three-bedroom, two-bath house they bought just before they were married. Glenn was considering a civil servant position inside DIA once his commitment to the Navy was up. Yan was confident that she could bounce between NSA, CIA, and DIA for the rest of her career and not have to move or deploy.

The only rub in the impending new arrival ointment were her grandparents. Both insisted that once the baby was born, they would move to Anacostia and provide daycare for the child. When Yan pushed back, they insisted, saying that it will be their pleasure. In the end, she relented.

After spending two weeks in Israel evaluating the intelligence held by the Mossad and its equivalent of DIA, Aman, Yan was convinced that what Hussein had was the infrastructure – labs and plants, and the people – but no weapons. What few the Iraqis had were not found by the allies after the war and didn't work. She was also convinced that the vehicles used to transport the components to make the nerve gases sarin and VX were moved across the desert and into Syria.

Her report was submitted in April and it wasn't popular reading at DIA and even less so at CIA. Few challenged the underlying facts or conclusions. What went to POTUS and his advisors was beyond her control.

CHAPTER 6

VETTED

Liang looked at her daughter who took a deep breath and nodded as if to say, let's do this. Both wore form-fitting cheongsams, Jun's a bright red with gold dragons; her mother's, a much more subdued one in dark green with white flowers. Rather than push the doorbell, Liang rapped on the door. Senior Commissar Huan Zhao saw Liang, then he turned to the diminutive Jun. His eyes opened and jaw dropped.

Bowing slightly, Huan spoke softly, "Miss Jun, the pictures your father showed us do not do you justice. Thank you for honoring us by coming to our humble apartment."

Both Liang and her daughter reciprocated by bowing, making sure that neither their heads nor their bodies angled down more than Huan's. He made a sweeping gesture toward the inside of their apartment where his wife Nuo stood. Her gray-white hair was tied in a neat bun on the back of her head complimented her cream-colored cheongsam. Standing well back in the living room, Bojing bowed formally. He, like his father, was wearing a Mao jacket. His was PLA Air Force blue and his father's a light gray.

As Jun entered, Bojing spoke softly, "Miss Lín, I am most honored that you agreed to meet me."

Jun sensed that this was as difficult for the young man with the wire-rim spectacles as it was for her. She tried to put Bojing at ease by extending her hand, "The honor and pleasure is mine."

Jun was impressed by both the quality of the cooking and the amount of food Nuo had prepared. There were more than enough slices of the barbequed pork dish main course called char su. Add in the steamed rice, scallion pancakes and spring rolls and the Zhao's had put more on the table than Jun and her mother ate in two meals. Jun wondered if the Zhao's had hoarded food to prepare for this event or had just splurged.

During dinner, the parents kept quiet as Bojing asked about Jun's time in the United States. She was sure he was comparing her answers to the propaganda he was fed. Jun learned Bojing had joined the PLA AF through a program modeled after American ROTC and was three years older than she. After graduating with a mechanical engineering degree, he went to school for a year to learn aircraft maintenance before being sent to an aircraft maintenance unit. After being promoted to captain, he was assigned as the deputy commander for the aircraft maintenance battalion of the 25th Fighter Regiment. The unit flew J-7s from Huiyang Air Base. The J-7 was an upgraded version of the Russian MiG-21 designed and manufactured in the PRC.

Dinner was followed by a leisurely stroll through a nearby park. Jun and Bojing were followed by their parents who gave them space for privacy but still appear as chaperones. As they were about to re-enter the Zhao's apartment building, the young officer asked Jun if he could take her to lunch the following Sunday.

Jun touched his cheek in a very Western gesture and said yes. Her act committed Jun to being courted and eventually marrying the young man.

TUESDAY, JANUARY 25TH, 2000, 8:06 A.M. LOCAL TIME, GUANGZHOU

At the staff entrance for the Guangzhou Institute for Biomedicine and Health, there was a guard station where one had to show one's badge and be logged in. After the guard wrote down Jun's name and the time, he handed her a note ordering her to report to the institute's administrator's office as soon as she arrived rather than go to one of the large meeting rooms used as classrooms.

Walking down the green tiled hallway with the beige walls, if Jun didn't know better, she thought the building could be in the United States. Everything, down to the placards denoting the office, Jun believed was copied from U.S. architectural guidelines. The only difference was that the individual and department names were in Chinese.

When she walked into Doyi Siew's office, his administrative assistant, a man in his late forties named Fan Mah, said, "Go in, he will see you now." The officious man went back to whatever he was doing. Other students in Jun's "re-education" class referred to Fan Mah as "The Hammer" because whenever Siew wanted to deliver bad news, Mah was sent.

Siew, whose first name loosely translated into English as "the One," stood and then waved to the chair in front of his desk. Siew's voice was pleasant which was unlike her first meeting when his manner and tone was cold. "Comrade Doctor Lín, please sit. May I pour you some tea."

Jun was guarded. This was the first time she'd been addressed as doctor by any of the staff. Her doctorate was in microbiology not in medicine. Up until this time, Jun was always addressed as Comrade or Citizen Lín. She didn't know how to interpret Siew's sudden pleasant mood. The man had a reputation of being dour bordering on unpleasant.

Siew was completely bald and each time he addressed their class, he wore a black suit, white shirt, and a red tie, usually with gold stripes as he did today. Jun wondered what else was in the man's wardrobe.

Before she sat down, Jun slid off the Targus backpack she bought in San Diego and leaned it against the chair. It doubled as a briefcase and purse. "No thank you, Comrade Senior Administrator Siew."

Jun hated addressing people as Comrade. The re-education course had a protocol session on how to address one's fellow workers. The instructor said that one should use the word Comrade followed by their title as sign of respect. For one's untitled peers, one could or should use either "comrade" or "citizen" and the individual's last name. Only family members, the class was taught, were to be addressed by their first name.

Siew slid a folder across his desk with several sheets clipped to the top. "The Party has decided to assign a one-bedroom apartment in the Lianhe Residential District to you. The apartments, I am told, are new, quite nice and are fitting for someone of your education and position. Take this paper to the apartment complex office and they will show you your flat. They will also provide whatever help you need to move in. The complex is about a four kilometer walk from here or you can take the bus. There is a map of the best route from the Guangzhou Science City to Lianhe attached to the authorization."

Jun read the sheet before bending over, unzipping the top of the backpack, and sliding the papers into section where she kept her notebook. She'd look at the map later. "Thank you, Comrade Senior Administrator Siew."

Nodding at her use of the proper language, Siew slid the second sheet off the top of the folder that Jun assumed was her personnel file and placed it in the center of the desk. "I have spoken with many of the senior researchers on our staff who have spent some time reviewing your course work, your master's, and doctoral theses now that they have been translated into Mandarin. They agree that you should be assigned to the virology lab. You will be assigned to study viruses and their effect on humans which is your area of expertise. More, I am afraid, I do not know."

Siew held out the second sheet. "Take this paper to the security office where you will be issued your new credentials. Once you have them, they will call Comrade Doctor Ng who is your supervisor and he will show you to your lab."

By bowing her head, Jun showed her gratitude. "Thank you, Comrade Senior Administrator Siew for your assistance in this assignment. I am sure I will do my country proud."

Jun hoped her answer sounded sincere but was really canned. In her mind, the phraseology was a mockery because she didn't care if her work benefited the Communist Party, it only had to benefit the human race.

Siew stood. "I presume I will receive many good reports on your work."

His statement said the meeting was over. Jun stood, bowed slightly before saying, "I am sure you will. Again, thank you for your assistance."

Getting her new badge took only a few minutes. Dr. Jiang Ng was a tall thin man. He took both her hands in his and bowed his head, "Dr. Lín, it is a pleasure to meet you. Your resume is most impressive. You are our only trained virologist. The rest of us were trained as doctors to fight infectious diseases." He pointed to the door and in an open area between building, Dr. Ng stopped abruptly. "On behalf of the institute, I apologize for you having to go through all that political nonsense. Arguing with party functionaries is a dangerous business if you know what I mean. Inside the labs, you can speak freely and do not need to call anyone comrade. That is nonsense! We do not allow commissars or any party functionaries in the lab unless they are escorted. What I would like to suggest is that we – that is the four other medical doctors and you – have lunch together at the cafeteria to discuss the research you will undertake. I must warn you, your new colleagues are very interested in the San Diego State University's facilities, so you will be asked many questions. Please do not make comparisons that someone could misconstrue as being unpatriotic. I am sure that the party or the Ministry of State Security has planted a spy in our midst."

"I understand."

Dr. Ng smiled. "Please do not be offended by those who are jealous of where you received your doctorate."

How does one answer that? Yes, I had the grades, but I am sure my father pulled strings. My doctorate makes me more valuable to the state and the CCP. Jun gave a politically correct answer. "I was very lucky and I will do my best to share what I learned."

Smiling, Dr. Ng pointed the way to the door where she would enter her world, the virology laboratory.

TUESDAY, FEBRUARY 8ᵀᴴ, 2000, 11:13 A.M. LOCAL TIME, BEIJING

Senior Colonel Fang Sun had a two-headed problem on his hands. First, he was surprised at how fast the approval came to develop a plan of action to carry out the concept he outlined in his memo. He was instructed to include specifics on how the lab would develop a bioweapon, test it, and then deploy it in a foreign country. While the PLA's planning guide gave him the steps and what had to be covered in each section, he had no idea how to build much less equip a facility that would have the capabilities he wanted.

No one on the general staff had the necessary expertise, so Sun had to find experts with the knowledge. Some were at the school he attended, others were in the PRC's scientific and medical community. This meant a whole new set of approvals and clearances for his Top-Secret program code named *Insidious Dragon*.

Colonel Sun was ordered to maintain a list of those who knew about the project and what they were told. By inference, the general who approved the project wanted the number who knew the true purpose of the program to be kept to less than six. This precluded going back to the chemical and biological warfare school's staff.

Second, was the timeline. The general on the Central Military Commission who gave him the go-ahead wanted a fleshed-out plan to review by the end of June, less than five months away. He suspected he would have to threaten and cajole bureaucrats who stood in the way to meet the deadline. It wasn't ideal, but Sun would do what was necessary.

His administrative assistant brought him a classified description of the Chinese Academies of Science and learned there were six divisions in the academy:

1. Chemistry
2. Information Technological Sciences
3. Earth Sciences
4. Life Sciences and Medical Sciences
5. Mathematics and Physics
6. Technological Sciences

There were 13 regional branches in each division and he began paging down the lists to find the ones that he thought might have the needed expertise. Sun's list had seven names:

1. Institute of Genetics and Developmental Biology
2. Chengdu Institute of Biology
3. Guangzhou Institute of Biomedicine and Health
4. Shanghai Institutes for Biological Sciences
5. Institute of Neurological Science
6. Suzhou Institute of Biomedical Engineering and Technology
7. Wuhan Institute of Virology

He read the descriptions of the research focus of the seven and decided the Wuhan Institute of Virology and the Guangzhou Institute for Biomedicine and Health were the ones he should contact. He ordered his administrative assistant to schedule calls with the heads of both facilities.

SUNDAY, FEBRUARY 13ᵀᴴ, 2000, 3:22 P.M. LOCAL TIME, GUANGZHOU

Bojing was convinced that his father made a wise choice for a wife the moment he began talking with Jun. He, just like Jun, was opposed to this arranged marriage, but his resistance melted away the more he met with Jun. Now Bojing couldn't conceive a future without Jun.

What Bojing did not know was how the arrangement came about. When Ai – Jun's father – and Liang began discussing sending their daughter abroad to earn her masters and doctorate, they knew that without a "sponsor" in the Ministry of State Security, Jun had no chance of securing the necessary exit visa.

Ai and Huan became friends while attending a Ministry of State Security school for future officers. While their lives separated, each man had a network the other could leverage for intelligence on how policies were interpreted. While there was no quid pro quo, both knew the information flow had to go both ways to maintain the value of their networks.

A doctorate from a major U.S. university was considered extremely valuable and was considered Jun's dowry. However, her six years abroad would cause some in the Ministry of State Security to worry Jun was corrupted by U.S. culture and not loyal to the party and the state. Others would think her training brought value to the People's Republic.

On the advice of his father, Bojing would not notify his commanding officer of his intent to marry Jun until the wedding date was selected. Bojing's position in the military required a vetting process, something Huan would ensure Jun would pass.

FRIDAY, MARCH 3ᴿᴰ, 2000, 12:07 P.M., LOCAL TIME, MIDDLEBURY, VT

Derek waited outside the front door of the building where Adrian shared a two-bedroom apartment with another student. He'd already loaded her skis on the roof ski rack of his '92 VW GTI 16 Valve and her boots and poles were in the back. She came out laughing with another woman Derek hadn't seen before. Adrian handed him her bag and suddenly becoming very serious. "So, again, tell me where we are going?"

"To a foreign country."

"Montreal so we can ski at Tremblant or Gray Rocks?"

"*Mais non, ma Cherie.*" No my dear. Derek held the door open and Adrian slid into the Recaro seat which held her hips and upper body snugly and comfortably in place by the side and upper body bolsters. The Recaro's looked uncomfortable, but once one's butt was settled in place, they were very comfortable, especially on long trips.

Derek turned the key, and the two-liter engine with the European model's dual overhead cams snarled into life. When Derek tested it on a dyno, the engine was producing 150 hp at the front wheels, 15 above the rated horsepower of "normal" GTI 16Vs that were imported. Adjustable Koni shock absorbers and stiffer front and rear roll bars made the car handle much better than the stock versions which were no slouches on a windy, twisty road.

The free-flowing Abarth exhaust system did an excellent job of muffling the sound, but when the engine was revved, everyone around knew that it was attached to a high-performance engine. Amazingly, the car was relatively quiet when cruising in fifth gear and had a comfortable ride, even on bumpy roads.

"So, please tell me where we are going?"

"Someplace I'm pretty sure you've never been. We're going to splurge a bit and stay in a five-star boutique hotel called Auberge St. Pierre that has only twenty-six rooms, one of which is ours until we leave."

"You know my parents want to see me over spring break."

Derek had a mischievous grin on his face. "And that my love, will happen. During the day, we will ski on a mountain that will test your skills. In the evening, we'll drink wine and make mad passionate love until the wee hours of the morning."

Adrian shook her head thinking, sometimes, this man she loves was nuts, absolutely nuts. The good news was that he wasn't like anyone she'd met in Boston which is another reason why she loved him.

"What town is this Auberge St. Pierre in?" Adrian asked in French. Before they met, she had spent her sophomore year at the Université Grenoble-Alpes studying political science in between runs down the nearby ski slopes. She came away fluent in French, but also had a deeper appreciation of why the United States was so different than Europe.

"Quebec City."

"*Bon.*" Good. "*Combien de temps nous faudra-t-il pour y arriver?*" How long will it take us to drive there?"

"*Quatre heures et demi, maximum et nos arrive juste à temps pour le dîner.*" Four and half hours, maximum, and we arrive just in time for dinner.

"*Donc le domaine skiable c'est le Mont St. Anne?*" So the ski area is Mont St. Anne.

"*Oui, et les conditions sont excellent!*" Yes, and the conditions are excellent.

Grinning, Adrian settled back into the Recaro seat to enjoy the ride as Derek rowed up and down through the gears when needed.

The Canadian border guard appreciated Derek's attempt to speak French and waved them through. Interstate I-85 was now Canadian 133 which he followed to where it joined Route 235 and then Canadian A-20.

In Drummondville, while Derek filled the tank with gas, Adrian hopped out and bought two bottles of water and two Cokes along with baguette, a piece of Appenzell cheese, and 250 grams of sliced Piller's Old Forest Salami. On A-20, the posted speed limit was 100 kmph, but those who were driving the speed limit were getting "run over" by faster traffic. Derek kept the GTI 16V in a line of traffic cruising at 130 kmph (79 mph).

Adrian fished out the Leatherman that Derek kept in the glove box, wiped it off with a napkin and handed him slices of the baguette with cheese and salami. With no cup holders, Adrian had the food in her lap and both held their Cokes between their thighs.

"So, have you ever been to the Auberge St. Pierre?"

Derek, who had his mouth full of bread and cheese, shook his head.

"Do you have an address?"

Swallowing, he said, "I do. It is marked on the map of Quebec City. So when we cross the Pierre LaPorte Bridge, you get to navigate."

Adrian rolled her eyes. Map reading was not one of her better skills.

The clerk at the Auberge St. Pierre didn't ask either for their passports, only Derek's credit card. He showed him his passport because on the back of the card, he'd written "See ID" in the signature block.

Holding hands, they followed the bellman down the hall on the third floor to their room which overlooked the Rue St. Pierre in the heart of the old city. The bellman stacked the ski bags in the closet, put the bags with their clothes on the two foldout stands. Derek handed the man a Canadian $20 bill and he left.

Adrian had already inspected the room and rested her forearms on his shoulders. "Very nice. Shall we work up an appetite before dinner?"

SATURDAY, MARCH 4ᵀᴴ, 2000, 11:13 A.M. LOCAL TIME, QUEBEC CITY

Saturday it was cold and snowy, and both Derek and Adrian wanted to walk around the historic city rather than ski. They were on a parapet overlooking the Plains of Abraham where the British defeated the French during the Seven Years War. Their victory gave the English control of Canada.

Flakes from the heavy snow had almost covered Adrian's ski hat and shoulders, but Derek didn't care. This was the moment of truth. She was looking out over the park when Derek tugged on her hand as he got down on one knee.

Holding out a ring with a three-carat square diamond and half carat stones on either side, he said, "Adrian, my love, will you marry me?"

"Oh my God, now it all makes sense - the hotel, the mystery, coming to Quebec City. You want to me to introduce you to my family as my fiancée when we go to Brookline."

Derek was still on his knee. "Adrian, you didn't answer my question."

Feeling silly, she started laughing and then pulled him up so she could French kiss him. After they finished, she pulled off her mittens, and slipped on the ring and held it up in front of her face. "Of course, I will. I was wondering when you would ask."

WEDNESDAY, MARCH 8ᵀᴴ, 2000, 7:32 A.M. LOCAL TIME, GUANGZHOU

The bus stop was 300 meters from the entrance of Jun's apartment building. On most days it would not have been a problem, but today, the skies had opened and it was pouring rain. At this hour, the shelter would be packed with people, all trying to stay dry.

Jun took a deep breath, popped open her umbrella, hoping the wind wouldn't collapse its flimsy metal structure. The noise of the rain on the fabric almost drowned out the soft male voice behind her.

"Dr. Lín." The implied word stop was not needed. Jun turned around to see a man a head taller than she who looked familiar, but she couldn't put a name to the face.

"Good morning, I am Senior Doctor Bao Gu…. It is perfectly acceptable that you don't remember me. Please, do not apologize for not recognizing me. I run the immunology practice at the institute. I didn't know you lived here at Lianhe."

"I just moved in on February 14th."

The two started toward the bus stop where people were packed together. For those inside the shelter, the metal roof provided shade in the summer and protection from the rain. Sheets of water from the rain poured down the sides splattering those on the edge of the mass of people.

Senior Dr. Gu nudged Jun. "Come, let us take a cab. My treat."

While cabs were plentiful and inexpensive, they were not something Jun could afford every day. They slid into a cab that slowed so that it didn't splash them. As Dr. Gu told the driver where they wanted to go, he pulled the plastic hat that surgeons use to keep their hair from falling onto the operating table off and shook his head revealing his jet-black hair.

Neither talked much during the 15-minute cab ride to the Institute of Biomedicine and Health. As they emerged under the portico, Dr. Gu asked, "How about we have lunch in the cafeteria?"

There was something that Jun liked about the senior doctor and she accepted. So far, Jun hadn't made any friends amongst her co-workers which, she thought, was probably a good thing. Other than Bojing, his parents and her mother, Jun realized she knew no one in the sprawling city of Guangzhou and needed a friend. Maybe Dr. Gu was that person.

At a break in the afternoon, Dr. Gu walked into his office and closed the door. Sighing in resignation, he dialed a familiar number. The voice of a man he detested answered. "Lieu."

"This is Doctor Gu. I just had lunch with Dr. Lín."

"Excellent, keep me informed."

Bao hung up the phone feeling disgusted with himself. He felt he had no choice ever since Siew promised that he would hang the murders of the two boys on his head. As the senior investigator said when they met when he was in medical school, "He didn't need evidence to charge him and during interrogation, he could beat the truth out of him."

No one, Lieu told Bao, could hold out forever which he thought, was probably a good thing. It was something that Bao never forgot.

FRIDAY, MARCH 10TH, 2000, 4:46 P.M. LOCAL TIME, BROOKLINE

Derek led Adrian to the kitchen where Miriam was preparing dinner for her husband, Adrian, and Derek. "Excuse me, Mrs. Gutenberg but I must introduce you to someone."

Miriam looked puzzled because the only people in the kitchen were the three of them. Her husband Michael wouldn't be home until about 6:30. With a flourish of his arms, Derek said, "Mrs. Gutenberg, may I introduce you to the future Mrs. Adrian Almer."

Miriam broke out into a broad smile and hugged her future son-in-law. "When did you propose?"

Before Derek could answer, Adrian wanted to tell her version of the proposal as she held out her left hand. "He proposed when it was snowing heavily and cold as hell on the parapet of the old fort in Quebec City."

Derek nudged her, "Do tell her the most important part."

"You're never going to let me forget, are you?"

"Nope, tell your mother."

"I got so excited and started babbling, he had to remind me to answer the question."

"Congratulations. So, now I am in wedding planning mode. What have you sorted out?"

Adrian nodded to her fiancé, as if to say, you tell her. "I graduate in May and start flight training in June. Adrian will finish her senior year next spring so if all things work out as planned, we're thinking late August 2001. To earn my wings, depending on the pipeline, its twelve to fifteen months, and I should know sometime early in the fall what month."

SUNDAY, MARCH 12ᵀᴴ, 2000, 5:19 P.M. LOCAL TIME, BROOKLINE

Sunday dinners were a big event in the extended Gutenberg family and unlike other dinners which started at seven, this one began at five because Adrian and Derek had to drive back to Vermont that evening. Although not all the children and grandchildren attended every week, missing two Sunday afternoon dinners led to uncomfortable questions.

After the blessing of the food they were about to eat and before the appetizers were served, Michael Gutenberg tapped his fork against his glass to get everyone at the table's attention. "Everyone, Adrian and Derek have an announcement."

Excited, Adrian shoved her hand out over the table. "We're engaged. The wedding will probably be in August of next year!"

After the flurry of congratulations followed by a toast, things settled down. Ilana was heard to say, "Great, now we will have a fucking fascist militarist in the family."

Miriam's face contorted in anger, "Ilana, what did you say?"

Before the transvestite could speak, Derek held up his hand, "Ilana, I have taken an oath to uphold and defend the Constitution of the United States. I take that commitment very, very seriously. This oath means that someday, I as well as many other servicemen and women may die in defense of the freedom that allows you to make such a statement. So, before you repeat your comment, I suggest you count your blessings. Until you do something to protect the freedoms that enable you to live the lifestyle you have chosen, besides paying taxes, I suggest you keep quiet. Or better yet, thank those willing to defend your freedom of speech."

Ilana started to ball up her napkin but before he could do anything, his mother said, "Don't you dare move away from this table."

Michael Gutenberg stared at his son. "Your mother is right. Derek's answer was right on point, if I must say and, it would be good for Randy and you to remember that my largesse only goes so far. I think you need to make a formal apology to Derek and my daughter. NOW would be a good time!!!"

The silence that followed was poignant. Ilana made an apology that was acceptable. Then, the chatter over the wedding and the young couple's plans as well as other family and business topics brought the conversation and the noise level back to normal.

THURSDAY, MARCH 16TH, 2000, 7:06 P.M. LOCAL TIME, GUANGZHOU

When Jun started working in the virology lab at the Guangzhou Institute for Biomedicine and Health, she had high hopes that she would be researching viruses affecting the health of the Chinese people. Her research as both an undergraduate as well as at San Diego State University suggested that Guangdong and Guangxi were breeding grounds for pathogens. In those two provinces, millions live in a humid, warm climate and near wildlife – bats, ducks, chickens, fish, rats, etc. – known to be carriers of disease. Guangzhou, where the institute was located, is the capital of Guangdong province.

Add in people bathing, drinking, and using water where infected animals live, one has a petri dish for disease development. Several pandemic diseases – SARS, bird flu, Hong Kong flu – all originated in the region.

Compared to the University San Diego's labs, Jun thought the Guangzhou Institute of Biomedicine and Health's virology facility was woefully underequipped. She suspected that walking around and taking notes during the workday might make her co-workers suspicious, Jun waited until all her co-workers left before taking an inventory of the equipment in the lab that she thought should be replaced.

Back in her flat, Jun powered up the Apple PowerBook G3 she brought from the U.S. It contained her research notes and the documents that supported her masters and doctoral theses and had a list of the equipment she used in her research. Also, she had a copy of the World Health Organization's (WHO) "Guidelines on Establishment of a Virology Laboratory in Developing Countries." The document was by the organization's Southeast Asia office and she thought it would provide a starting point.

Her mother pointed out that her PowerBook G3 did not have the PRC's government approved applications needed to use any of the search engines available in the country. To do so, she would have to buy a computer and an operating system licensed in the PRC that enables the government to monitor where she went on the Internet.

Using her mother's laptop, she found that many sites available to those outside the PRC were simply not available. Liang warned that emails were tracked, often read by members of the Ministry of State Security.

Unless she wanted her Apple PowerBook G3 compromised, Liang suggested she buy a computer sold inside the PRC. Powerful laptops like the one Jun liked were expensive and licensed so the government knew who owned computers and when connected to a network, government agents would know where the machine was anytime it was online.

Jun was making notes about the lab's only autoclave on a pad when she heard the lab door open. The WHO document – one for sterilization and one for decontamination. It was Dr. Ng. Behind him were two-armed security guards who stayed, as per the protocols, outside the laboratory. The doctor's voice was firm and commanding, "Dr. Lín, what are you doing?"

Jun, who didn't think she was doing anything wrong, said, "Doctor, I am taking an inventory of our equipment. Much of it is old. We, according to the World Health Organization's recommendations, don't have what we need. I would like to suggest how we can upgrade the capabilities of the lab by acquiring new equipment."

Dr. Ng nodded slowly. "Dr. Lín, if you wanted an inventory of the lab's equipment, I am sure Senior Administrator Siew could have provided one. As far as new equipment, the People's Republic is a poor country. We cannot afford what America can."

Jun didn't say what was on her mind which was rather than spending trillions of yuan on modernizing the PLA to keep up with the Americans, the PRC could spend a few million on developing cures to diseases that plague its citizens.

Instead, she said, "Dr. Ng, we do not know the answer if we do not ask. I have a list I brought from San Diego State University that I can compare to our inventory and the WHO recommendations. We then can ask the Party to buy these items we will use for the good of our fellow citizens."

Dr. Ng turned and waved at the guards. Dr. Lín wasn't a threat to the facility, she was a threat to the CCP's dogma and decisions. He went down this route when he first arrived at the lab. It resulted in some new equipment, much of which was what Dr. Lín is calling old. So, he will let her carry the torch forward and fight the bureaucrats. He did it once before, and his body and mind still had the scars.

CHAPTER 7

PROPER BEDSIDE MANNERS

TUESDAY, MARCH 21ST, 2000, 9:58 A.M. LOCAL TIME, GUANGZHOU

When Senior Colonel Fang Sun arrived at the Guangzhou Institute for Biomedicine and Health, the day had just started. Data he'd requested for *Insidious Dragon* was slow in arriving. The delays increased his frustration caused by his underestimating the difficulty and time needed to create his plan.

He learned during his visit to the Wuhan Institute of Virology that it had just begun the certification process to become a certified Level Four Biosafety Laboratory (BSL-4). Its senior administrator had been given permission to speak with Canada's National Microbiology Laboratory and the CDC in Atlanta to learn more about the certification process.

Sun's takeaway was that the Wuhan lab was years away from certification. He didn't need or want certification, just the capabilities. He did, however, make a note to request the Central Military Commission follow the lab's progress and keep him informed.

Adding to Sun's frustration was that another of his other projects was way behind. If he did not deliver on time, he would lose credibility with his superiors and worse, face. His fears led to an early morning call to an official who was the roadblock. During the call, he counseled him on what would happen if he didn't produce the requested data within 24 hours. Sun believed every so often, a "public hanging" of a bureaucrat was needed to improve efficiency and maybe, just maybe, this man should be one.

Punctuality was another one of Senior Colonel Fang Sun's habits. He believed if one walked into a meeting less than five minutes before its scheduled start time, one was late. At 20 minutes past eight, 10 minutes before the meeting was scheduled to begin, Sun walked into Senior Administrator Siew's office.

Siew was reading one of the documents he wanted to show the Senior Colonel. If the Army officer wanted copies, then he would log them as such. Ministry of State Security policy required that his office track who made a copy and what was copied. His office had the only copier in the institute.

After standing to greet Sun, Siew offered green tea which Sun accepted. After he took his first a sip of the aromatic liquid, Siew slid a copy of his proposed agenda across the desk. Sun's initial questions were about the facility, not about biomedicine, so he felt confident he could answer the senior colonel's questions.

On the institute's organization chart, an infectious disease doctor was shown as the president. However, as the senior administrator, Siew had the power of the purse, controlled assignments, and had to approve all promotions. His responsibilities made him the de-facto head of the institute.

Sun glanced at the four items on the agenda – introductions, tour, discussion of the institute's capabilities with members of the staff selected by Sun, and lunch.

Sensing an opportunity to show his value, Siew said, "Senior Colonel, before we have our discussion with the virology staff, I may have a document that meets your needs. It was prepared by one of our young doctors. On our tour, I'll point her out and you can decide if you want to interview her."

Sun nodded and stood up. "Excellent, let us get started."

Throughout the tour, Sun asked what he thought were intelligent questions. When Siew could not or didn't think he was the best person to answer, he tapped on a window or knocked on a door. Quickly, the expert was summoned and eagerly answered Sun's query.

On the fifth floor, Siew pointed to a small woman wearing a white lab coat and a mask speaking with a man similarly attired. Seeing Siew, Dr. Ng started to walk to the window. The administrator shook his head and held up his hand as if to say, no, don't come.

Siew said, "That is Dr. Ng, the head of the virology lab. He was talking to one of our new doctors, Dr. Jun Lín whom I believe you should interview, and whose file I suggest you review. She may have the knowledge you are seeking."

Sun grunted an acknowledgement and the tour continued. Re-entering Siew's office, Sun asked, "Where is the doctor's file and where may I meet with her privately."

Senior Administrator Siew was prepared for the question with a surprise of his own. "I think this document which is Dr. Lin's suggested list for equipment will be of interest to you."

Senior Colonel Sun looked at the table of contents thinking this is exactly what I need. "Senior Administrator Siew, what have you done with this document?"

"Nothing yet. I was planning to send it to the Academy of Sciences along with a request for funding for both the equipment and the modifications to this facility. The Institute's virology lab could use modernization."

Siew's statement was a bald-faced lie. He was planning to bury it until his phone conversation with Sun and the tour. Now, he would promote it since a member of the PLA general staff was interested in its contents.

The senior colonel's face was an expressionless mask as he tried not to betray his excitement. This woman could help me finish my plan, assuming she is politically reliable. If not, afterwards she could be made to disappear.

The institute's administrator anticipated Sun's next question. "Next to my office, there is a conference room I reserved for you for the rest of the day. My assistant Fan Mah will ensure you are not disturbed and if you need anything, please ask Mah."

Sun nodded and left taking the list of items needed to modernize the lab along with Dr. Lín's file. Paging through her file and the list, he prepared his questions. The room had a black phone without a dial. When Sun picked it up, the man known as "the Hammer" answered, listened, and then dialed a number for the security guard on the third floor. Fan Mah instructed him to bring Dr. Lín to Senior Administrator Siew's private conference room.

A sharp, "enter" from within the room followed the guard's rap on the door. Once the door was open, Jun saw the stocky Army officer she'd seen touring the facility with Siew.

Senior Colonel Sun stood and waved to a chair. "Dr. Lín, it is a pleasure to meet you. Please, sit down. I have many questions about this…." He held up the equipment list Jun prepared. Her heart sank because she immediately thought she was now being investigated, just as Dr. Ng thought might happen. She decided to say nothing.

"May I ask why you compiled this list?"

"Am I under investigation?"

Senior Army Colonel Sun sat back and laughed. "Oh no, this is exactly what I needed for one of my projects. I have some questions about the equipment and where it can be purchased." *But if needed, I could have you arrested and tortured to see if there is a threat to the party behind the compilation of this list.*

Jun still didn't relax. She didn't trust the man in uniform. There was way too much of a coincidence between when she gave the list to Dr. Ng and Senior Administrator Siew's questions about its contents. Now, she is sitting in a room with a senior army colonel. Not good karma!!!

"Dr. Lín, where did you get the list of equipment you recommended?"

"San Diego State University has a virology lab with this equipment. That is where I earned my doctorate in microbiology. What's on the list is from memory and the equipment I referenced in my theses since I cannot access the university's website from Guangzhou." *But you know that, Senior Colonel Sun. I am not going to tell you that I have a PowerBook G3 in my flat that is illegal to possess.*

"If you were able to access the internet, could you go to the university's web site and make a copy?"

"I no longer have credentials at the university. What I would do is contact my academic advisor and she would send me the list."

"Dr. Lín, what was the topic of your doctoral thesis?"

"Dangers of the Poliomyelitis Virus Morphing and Preventing Its Propagation Throughout the World."

"Would you give me a summary that an army colonel could understand."

Jun nodded. "Before I do, again, if you want a copy of the thesis, it is a matter of public record and can be acquired from the university. I translated it into Chinese for the institute."

Colonel Sun nodded, "I want a copy." He turned to pick up the phone, asked Mah to make him a copy and then nodded to encourage Jun explain her thesis.

Jun started with why she picked poliomyelitis as the virus. It was, she said, thought to be eradicated in Europe, North America, and most civilized countries. However, Jun noted, significant outbreaks still occur in underdeveloped countries. As a virus, there is a chance that it could, if it has not already done so, mutate, thereby negating the worldwide attempt to eradicate the disease. A mutated strain could be milder or more devastating to those who contracted it which would require new vaccines and treatments to be developed.

The PLA officer held up his hand. "Where do you think this would occur?"

Dr. Lín smiled. "My thesis ranked the most likely locations where it could take place."

Jun then rattled them off in order of which area was the most likely to have a morphed version of the virus. She started with Southeast Asia – Burma, Cambodia, Laos, Thailand, and Vietnam. Then she listed the two provinces in the People's Republic where she knew from her research polio still existed. Next on Jun's list were central and southern India followed by Equatorial Africa, Indonesia, and Equatorial South America.

A few seconds went by as Senior Colonel Sun forced himself not to stand up and cheer. "Dr. Lín could you come to Beijing to help me with my project. I am sure that Dr. Ng could do without you for a few weeks."

"Before I say yes, assuming I have that choice, may I ask why the People's Army is interested in my work?"

"Fair question, doctor. The Army is considering a dedicated facility to research possible cures for diseases our soldiers may catch in the defense of our country. We want to be prepared."

Both of us know it is a short step from researching diseases to creating biological weapons. If I suspect this is the goal, I will do my best to derail the program even if it costs me my life. Jun bobbed her head in agreement. "I will tell Dr. Ng that I may be called to Beijing for a few weeks."

"Excellent." *If you didn't agree, I could compel you to come and that would not be pleasant.* "I will make the necessary arrangements for accommodations befitting someone of your rank. Do you need a chaperone? I see by your file that your mother lives in Guangzhou. Would you like her to accompany you?"

"That would be preferable, but not necessary." *Does he know that by summer, I may be the wife of a PLAAF major?*

That night, Jun sat down and composed a letter to Yan saying she is working in the virology lab at the Guangzhou Institute for Biomedicine and Health and she is seeing a young man by the name of Bojing Zhao. Embedded in the message, Jun wrote:

> PLA Sr. Army Col. Fang Sun very interested in my doctoral thesis. He asked questions about how to equip a virology lab to create vaccines for mutated viruses. Am being brought to Beijing to help develop requirements.

The next day, Jun posted the letter and spent the extra money to send it airmail, hoping she would live long enough to receive a reply. Jun did not consider herself a spy. War was bad. Biological warfare of any flavor was unconscionable.

WEDNESDAY, APRIL 5ᵀᴴ, 2000, 11:46 A.M. LOCAL TIME, FORT MEADE, MD

Jun's letter on the flimsy Aerogram stationary arrived via a Federal Express package. She had addressed the letter to Yan at her grandparent's address in San Diego. Her mother forwarded it via Federal Express to her granddaughter.

A phone call from Mei alerted her to the incoming package that would be delivered late in the morning. The timing was perfect because Yan could stop by their house after her monthly visit with her OBGYN doctor. Now almost four months pregnant, she had a noticeable baby bump.

The couple bought the house in Glenn Dale, Maryland, thinking that both would be assigned to DIA for several years. The house was a 25 to 30-minute drive to either DIA headquarters on Joint Base Anacostia-Bolling on the Maryland side of the Potomac and to NSA's headquarters on Fort Meade.

The trip in her metallic red Honda Accord coupe that came with a handling package gave Yan time to think about what she wanted to say to Captain Ellis. She enjoyed shifting the manual transmission of the car that was a wedding present from Glenn and to make the Accord sportier looking, she replaced the stock wheels with a set of aftermarket alloy wheels.

Jun's plan to stay at DIA went askew when NSA asked for Yan to be assigned to its Chinese desk as a linguist and analyst. The head of the China desk, Lester Ellis who was a retired Navy captain had read her analysis of the PRC's military growth when he was at DIA and thought she would be a good fit for his group.

Each time her background investigation used to grant her access to code word and specially compartmented material was updated, Yan was careful to provide a statement about Jun and Liang. Up until she decoded Jun's letter, the fact that Yan had a cousin with a doctorate in microbiology and was working in the Guangzhou Institute of Biomedicine and Health fell into the "nice to know" category. Jun's note changed all that.

Captain Ellis was not in his office when Yan arrived, so she went to her desk, logged in, and started looking at the intercepts flagged for her review. Yan was engrossed in reading a decoded message from the captain of a Type 093 nuclear-powered attack submarine beginning sea trials. His complaint was that when they called on the reactor to deliver more power to accelerate, the boat filled with unacceptable levels of radiation. Satellite imagery accompanying the transcript showed the submarine surrounded by tugs in Huludao Harbor, less than a mile from the Bohai Shipyard where the sub was built.

The jangling of the phone on her desk startled her. It was Captain Ellis. "Lieutenant, I understand you wanted to see me?"

"Yes sir, when it is convenient."

"How about now because I wanted to see you?"

"I'll be right there."

Captain Ellis stood when Lieutenant Huáng walked in. She was wearing what was known in the Navy as working khaki and she had not yet started wearing the maternity version, even though the "regular" uniform was now becoming tight around her mid-section. Ellis spoke sternly, "Lieutenant, I see you are out of uniform."

Quizzically, Yan looked at her boss, "Sir, if you prefer, I will start wearing maternity clothes."

Trying to keep a stern face, Ellis shook his head. "No, Lieutenant, it's the insignia on your collar. It shows you are a lieutenant when you are entitled to wear these."

Ellis picked up the red Vanguard box he'd bought at the exchange containing the gold oak leaves worn by lieutenant commanders. "The O-4 board results are out and you've been selected for lieutenant commander. Congratulations!" The captain tossed the box to Yan. "If you wish, I'll pin them on, or we can have a formal ceremony."

"Now is fine!"

As he exchanged the two silver bars that looked like railroad tracks with the gold oakleaves indicating she was a lieutenant commander, Ells added, "You don't have a date of rank yet, but by the powers invested in me, I am frocking you."

In the Navy, it was the commanding officer's choice to allow officers who were selected for the next highest rank to wear the insignia of their new rank. They would not receive the increase in pay until officially promoted.

While he finished changing Yan's collar insignia, Ellis said, "After you leave here, my admin will have the letter officially frocking you so you can get a new ID card."

He held out his hand. "Congratulations again. Now, what's on your mind?"

"Sir, I think it best if you sit down because this will take a few minutes." Seeing Ellis' look of concern, Yan said, "Sir, it is not bad news, it just takes some context so we can make a decision."

Ellis made a gesture with his hand that said come on tell me. Yan explained who Jun was and then slid the Aerogram and the decoded message across the table. The captain sat back in his chair as if he was punched in the chest.

"So, if I understand you correctly, your cousin sent you a letter telling you that the PLA is about to create a biowarfare program using medical facilities ostensibly built for public health."

"Yes sir. I think that is a step too far. She is being asked to help design and equip one and she doesn't buy the cover story."

"Do you?"

"No sir."

"That makes three of us." Ellis took a deep breath. "How do you communicate?"

"By letter." Yan explained that Jun sends them to her grandparents who forward them to her. She then said, the PRC knows Jun has family in San Diego but does not know she has a cousin in U.S. Naval Intelligence.

"What kind of code do you use?"

"Sir, it's a one-time pad using Mao's Little Red Book from the Cultural Revolution. It's a pain in the ass but is simple and secure."

Ellis laughed at the reference to Chairman Mao's book that was the bible to the proponents of the Cultural Revolution. "Who else knows about Jun?"

"I provide updates on my background check so the agency knows. This is a new development."

Ellis' tone was serious. "I'll say."

"Captain, what do you want me to do?"

"Respond asking her to keep you informed and not to take any risks. Then, we'll see where this goes. Start a file so we have an audit trail. If Dr. Lín winds up deeper in this program, people inside DIA, CIA as well as NSA will want to know. They may want to take control."

"Sir, I don't think she'll work for them. Jun trusts me, she doesn't trust government intelligence agencies, if you know what I mean."

"Understood. However, I must tell someone to keep our asses out of hot water. At most, there will be only four people who know this secret, Dr. Lín, you, me, and my boss. The message that I will deliver is that Dr. Lín may become a treasure trove of intelligence but must be controlled by you or the source goes away."

Yan nodded her head and left the office wondering what Jun had learned since she wrote the letter.

FRIDAY, APRIL 14ᵀᴴ, 2000, 6:10 P.M. LOCAL TIME, GUANGZHOU

In Beijing, Dr. Jun Lín was treated by Senior Colonel Sun's staff as if she was a fountain of knowledge about Western virology labs. On the excuse she would share the information on the equipment to be ordered with Senior Administrator Siew, Jun was allowed to keep both paper and electronic files on CDs.

Before she left Beijing, Senior Colonel Sun handed her the authorization that let her keep the Lenovo computer she had been using to download information from Western websites. The document acknowledged that access to this growing phenomenon called the Internet from her home would not be possible without it. The document would be given to Senior Administrator Siew who would allow her to use the machine inside her lab at Guangzhou Institute of Biomedicine and Health. She wasn't sure if the lab had a data line that would work but she would try.

On the 3.5" floppy discs in her purse, she had copied everything that Senior Colonel asked her to download onto four sets of diskettes. One would be kept in the lab and the others she would keep.

Walking through the Beijing Capital International Airport, she spotted a kiosk operated by DHL. Stopping abruptly, she asked if she could send a package from the kiosk to the United States. The clerk said yes and then bragged that once it is sealed in a DHL bag, it cannot be opened without the sender's permission.

Quickly, she filled out the waybill using a fake return address, used the table with packing materials to wrap the diskettes in bubble wrap and place them in a DHL envelope. She then wrote a short note saying to the clerk that "My cousin may find a business opportunity here in the People's Republic."

Jun paid for the shipping which was almost a quarter of a month's pay and watched as the clerk dropped the package into the locked box. It would be, the clerk said, delivered in three days.

In Guangzhou, Jun fully expected to be arrested for espionage, but the only person there to greet her was Bojing. He was driving his father's car and on the way to her apartment, he stopped in Houlushan Forest Park. Smiling, he handed her a bottle of water and suggested they take a walk. Jun suspected what was coming and had steeled herself to say yes.

While she liked Bojing, Jun was not in love with him even though it was clear, he was in love with her. Marrying him was a way to honor her father's wishes and repay him for facilitating her U.S. education. Marriage to Bojing was her karma.

The young man didn't wait long. In a quiet place, he turned and got down on both knees as he held both Jun's hands. "Jun, I adore and love you. Would you marry me?"

Jun tugged on Bojing's hands as a signal for him to stand up. "I will only say yes if you are standing up and agree that in the marriage, we are equals in all decisions."

Bobbing his head vigorously, Bojing agreed. "Yes, yes, that is the way of the future. Men and women must be equal even though it goes against the traditions of our people."

On the way back to her flat, they agreed on a small wedding on the first Sunday in June with only a few friends. Bojing said he must tell his commanding officer who will arrange for an Air Force security officer to interview her.

"I just spent two weeks with Senior Colonel Fang Sun on the People's Army's general staff helping him with a top-secret project. I think I will pass."

"I will so inform our security officer."

They rode in silence for the rest of the way back. Jun allowed Bojing to hold her hand between shifts.

FRIDAY, APRIL 21ST, 2000, 5:33 P.M. LOCAL TIME, GLENN DALE, MD

The Federal Express office called Yan to let her know of an attempted delivery. When asked, they said the driver could return between five and five-thirty. An ID and a signature would be required to accept delivery.

On her way out of NSA, Yan wrote Captain Ellis a note saying that she was going back home to accept delivery of a package of diskettes from the PRC that her mother sent. She would bring them to NSA that evening and needed clearance to get them in the building.

Before she left the house, Yan scribbled a note to Glenn saying she was at NSA and he was on his own for dinner. Backing out of the driveway, her mobile phone rang. She stopped to answer and it was Captain Ellis asking her to call when she nears the agency. Since she had diskettes, there is a protocol to follow before their contents can be examined.

Two NSA computer experts were waiting at the entrance and took the diskettes before they all went to the secure conference room used by Captain Ellis' team. On the table were two briefcase sized steel boxes that looked like computers. Each one had a small diskette receptacle connected by a cable to the metal box.

One technician introduced himself as Bill and the other as Mike. Knowing NSA as she did, she wasn't sure if those were their real names. The man whose name was Bill nodded and Yan ripped open the Federal Express box. Inside was a DHL envelop Yan cut open with scissors and found eight 3.5" diskettes, each with Chinese characters and numbers, one through eight.

Before she touched any of the diskettes, Mike held up his hand and shined a blacklight on the paper. Seeing nothing out of the ordinary, he put his briefcase on the table, popped open the lid revealing rows of bottles, swabs, and other chemical testing paraphernalia. He pulled on a pair of rubber gloves and went to work. Yan wasn't clocking him, but she thought it took him about 15 minutes before he nodded and said, "They're clean. You can touch them."

Mike picked up the disk with the number 1. Yan looked at the Chinese characters, "It says meeting notes. What are you going to do now?"

"Check the files to see if they are infected. Then, if they are not, we can take them to a computer downstairs that can read them and if needed, copy them."

Captain Ellis spoke. "No copies will be made unless either Lieutenant Commander Huáng or I am present and approve."

Bill nodded. "Understood." He slipped the diskette into the reader and tapped on a small keypad. There was a whirring sound and a stream of numbers and letters flew across the small green and white screen. When the test was competed, the diskette popped out.

"This one has a bunch of files in Word 98. They are all clean."

It took less than 10 minutes to check all the diskettes and all were clean. Bill handed Yan a diskette reader. "This will let you download the diskettes onto your workstation. The rules say that I must watch you download the diskettes and then take the reader back. Captain Ellis must secure the diskettes in a safe and they cannot be inserted into any NSA computer."

The four moved to Yan's computer. One by one, the diskettes were downloaded and put into a folder. Yan sampled the files and saw the Chinese characters. With the files now on her computer, she handed the reader back to Bill and he and Mike disappeared down the hall after being thanked profusely by both Captain Ellis and Yan.

"What do you think you have?"

"Frankly, I don't know. I scanned one of her meeting notes and it listed a PLA Senior Colonel Fang Sun on the General Staff and mentioned a code name. Beyond that, I don't know."

Ellis looked at his watch. "It is almost eight. I suggest you go home, get you and your child some sleep. Tomorrow, come back refreshed and go through the diskettes so you can give me a sense of what we received before we do anything rash. We need to make a record of their receipt as well as an inventory so we don't wind up making big rocks into small rocks at Leavenworth."

Yan laughed and left. When she got home, Glenn gave her a big hug. "So what's the hush hush late work about?"

She just looked at him. Her husband, who was still in DIA's personnel department, shook his head. "I know, if you tell me, you'll have to kill me. How about we snuggle until you two want to go sleep."

MONDAY, NOVEMBER 13TH, 2000, 2:16 P.M. LOCAL TIME, LANHAM, MD

Beginning the week before Yan was due, Glenn took leave and both were hoping that Yan would deliver on time. But then again, Mother Nature gets a vote. At just after ten-thirty in the morning, strong labor pains started and unlike the ones earlier in the week, these, Yan thought, were real. Less than an hour later, Yan was in the delivery room and at 2:16 p.m., Min Young, seven pounds, eight ounces and 20 inches long came into this world.

Grandmother Mei (Tao's wife) and Great-Grandmother Shi (Zimo's wife) were staying with the Youngs and immediately went into action. First item on the agenda was to let the extended family know. Liang was sent an airmail letter.

Glenn, who was an orphan, was learning how the extended Chinese family took care of their own. He'd accepted without argument that the now retired Zimo and Mei were moving into an apartment a few miles from the Young's house. This way, when Yan went back to work, rather than drop Min off at a daycare center, she would be cared for by her great-grandparents who also provided baby-sitting services if the Young's wanted to go out for dinner.

At first, Glenn saw the elder Huáng's presence as an intrusion in their privacy but quickly understood the benefits of three generations living together. Plus, they did not have to pay for daycare - that was expensive - plus Mei was an outstanding cook!

CHAPTER 8

NEW ASSIGNMENTS

MONDAY, FEBRUARY 26TH, 2001, 10:07 A.M. LOCAL TIME, GUANGZHOU

An excited Senior Administrator Siew rapped on the door to the lab where Dr. Jun Lín worked. She was supervising a lab technician in a back room while he diluted a sample using a rack of six pipettes and wasn't paying attention to the noise at the door.

Dr. Ng waved at Siew to say he saw him there and then waited until the procedure was finished and properly logged. When one sample was placed in a centrifuge, he interrupted and didn't attempt to hide the sarcasm in his voice. "Dr. Lín, one of your admirers wants to speak with you."

"I wonder what he wants now?"

"Dr. Lín, when dealing with Senior Administrator Siew, remember the Chinese proverb – a man who cannot tolerate small misfortunes can never accomplish great things."

Nodding as she peeled off her latex gloves, Jun said, "So, true, so true. Let us see what today's crisis is about."

From the airlock, Jun went into the locker room where she took off the booties on her shoes, her mask, and the cap covering her hair. She left her white lab coat on as she walked into the hallway that led to the observation room. "What brings you to the virology lab, Senior Administrator?"

Excited, Siew pointed to the elevator, "Come, come. I must show you something that will make you smile. I think the Party has finally seen the value the Guangzhou Institute of Biomedicine Institute of Health delivers. We have, as you will see, been rewarded for our initiative."

Puzzled, Jun followed Siew through the back of the main building to a loading dock. There, she could see men unloading a container with large boxes. She recognized the brands and names of the equipment. They were on the list she created for Senior Colonel Sun when he asked what the Guangzhou facility needed to modernize.

Turning to Senior Administrator Siew, she said, "This is wonderful, but as the Americans say, this is getting the cart before the horse. We must modernize the building before we can put this equipment to work."

"What do you mean, Dr. Lín?"

"The institute is at best at biosafety level 2. If we upgrade the building to Biosafety Level 3, we can do even better work."

"But that costs money. We don't have it."

"I think I can convince Senior Colonel Sun to find the money for the modification. In the meantime, I suggest you put all this valuable equipment under lock and key."

Senior Administrator Siew pointed down the corridor. "Please, come to my office and let us call the good colonel."

Senior Colonel Sun came on the line shortly after his assistant took Dr. Lín's call. "What can I do for you, Dr. Lín?"

"First, I want to thank you, the PLA, and the Party for its generous purchase of equipment for the Guangzhou Institute of Biomedicine and Health. Without your support, this purchase and prompt delivery would not have been possible. We are most grateful."

Senior Colonel acknowledged her thank you and then said, "I hear a but in there somewhere."

Dr. Lín smiled then leaned over to get her mouth closer to the speaker phone. "To make full use of this new equipment and accomplish the things we discussed last spring, we need to upgrade the institute's facilities. We are only at Biosafety Level 2 and to get the most from this new equipment, we need to be at least a Level 3. To get to a four, we would have to demolish one building and start anew. That would take too much time, but I think we can modify our building and upgrade it to a Level 3 facility without too much trouble. What we need is an architect who understands biology labs who will help us purchase a set of Level 3 facility designs. From there, the architect can adapt them to our building. Then we need a reliable contractor who can follow the designs to the letter and who can acquire quality materials." Jun paused and then decided to play to Sun's ego. "I am sure, Colonel Sun, you can with your contacts, find these people."

"To say nothing of much needed money."

"That too. However, we can be up and functioning as a Level 3 lab long before any new built lab can come online."

Senior Colonel Sun said nothing for a few seconds. What Jun just said to him was that *Insidious Dragon* could have its first facility to begin testing concepts very quickly while its new, Level 4 building was being constructed.

"I like the way you think, Dr. Lín. Thank you for bringing this to my attention. I will be in touch."

Dial tone. Senior Administrator Siew looked at Dr. Lín. His appreciation of her skills just went up several more notches. "Do you think he will find the money?"

"Yes. And faster than you or I think."

As she walked back to the lab, Jun realized that she owed her cousin a letter. Her niece Min was about three months old and would provide the topic.

SUNDAY, JULY 8TH, 2001, 10:31 A.M. LOCAL TIME, PENSACOLA, FL

By being in Pensacola, Derek kept out of the wedding planning fray. His mother Rhea was routinely consulted by Miriam Gutenberg as the planning progressed. When needed, she drove to Brookline and was a guest at the Gutenberg's house.

Both Adrian and Derek wanted a small wedding with only immediate family and close friends. Derek was thinking 100 people max, Adrian, 150. Miriam on the other hand, was thinking of 250 or more.

Every Sunday morning, Derek was part of a weekly call with Adrian, Miriam and when appropriate, his mother. Sharon's spectacular wedding had a guest list topping 400 and was concerned that Adrian would be slighted by a smaller event. Eventually, Miriam agreed to her daughter's wishes and the invite list was whittled down to 126 and the date was set for Sunday, August 26th, 2001.

While the planning was going apace, Derek whizzed through the primary phase of flight training at VT-1. There, he flew the T-34C Turbo Mentor which was a new production T-34B that had its 225 hp, six-cylinder engine replaced with a 550 horsepower PT-6 turbine engine. All the students that finished primary at the same time with Derek were sent to VT-2 at Whiting Field, just north of Pensacola.

He was very disappointed but put his head down hoping his top of the class grades would earn him a coveted jet slot. It was not to be. He was offered a choice of entering multi-engine pipeline to fly E-2s or P-3s, neither of which Derek wanted or helicopters. Derek chose helicopters.

He passed his last check ride on June 26th and called Adrian and then his father to let them know the winging ceremony was on Friday, July 6th. She was already planning to fly down on the 30th for the week of July 4th. His parents, brother and sister arrived on Tuesday, the 3rd. Derek's father, Cy Almer and Adrian both were on the platform to proudly pin his gold wings on his chest. Derek wasn't sure who was prouder, he or his father, Colonel Almer, USAF (retired).

For the days his family was in Pensacola, Derek rented a two-bedroom condo on Pensacola Beach while he and Adrian stayed in a one-bedroom unit in the same complex. While he was sure that his mother didn't approve, Rhea didn't say anything.

Adrian and Derek's family left the day after his wings were pinned on. He checked out on the 9th and headed west to San Diego with orders to report no later than midnight, July 22nd to Helicopter Anti-Submarine Squadron Ten (HS-10). The unit was the Navy's West Coast Fleet Replacement Training Squadron a.k.a. the H-60 RAG (Replacement Air Group) for the SH-60F and the HH-60H that Derek would fly in the fleet. RAG was a term left over from World War II that was still used in the Navy.

Once he finished the four-month transition course, Derek had orders to Helicopter Sea Combat Squadron Eight (HSC-8), known as the Eightballers at Naval Air Station, North Island. HSC-8 was part of Carrier Air Wing 11 scheduled to deploy in early 2002 on the *U.S.S. Nimitz* (CVN-68).

So the timing was perfect – drive to San Diego, check into HS-10, go through two weeks of ground school then take two weeks leave beginning on August 17th, get married on the 26th and return after Labor Day. Adrian and he planned to spend their honeymoon while driving from Brookline to San Diego.

She'd been accepted at the University of San Diego's law school and classes started on September 10th. When Derek called HS-10's admin officer to make sure that his plan was feasible, the lieutenant commander laughed, said, "Yes. Thanks for the heads up."

Most students arrive, Derek was told, and tell him that they are going off to get married.

While he was in San Diego, Derek found a two-bedroom apartment to rent for a year to give the couple time to find a house. Derek expected to be in San Diego for the next six years, first as a member of HSC-8 and then later as an instructor at HS-10.

TUESDAY, SEPTEMBER 11TH, 8:59 A.M. LOCAL TIME, FORT MEADE

Where Yan worked at NSA was deep inside its sprawling complex. To enter the building, she needed to insert her badge which contained a computer image of her photo and fingerprints was encoded. At those entrances where fingerprints were required, she inserted her badge into the slot and pressed whichever finger was required onto the small screen. To enter where she worked, she entered a six-digit code that was changed every six months.

Captain Ellis' team worked in a windowless, open area divided by 8' X 8' cubes, each with a workstation. Printers and fax machines were on tables along the walls outside the cubes. Only Captain Ellis had a private office. For meetings, two conference rooms qualified as

SCIFs (Sensitive Compartmented Information Facilities) to support his 42-person staff of intelligence officers from each of the services and NSA employees. Unless one ventured out of the space, they were, as a practical matter, cut off from the outside world.

When Captain Ellis stepped outside his office and yelled, "Everyone, listen up! Drop what you are doing and come to the large conference room in two minutes."

Rarely did Captain Ellis resort to this tactic to call a meeting. Their large conference room had chairs for 18 at the table, and with all 42 in the room, it was standing room only and packed. Ellis was grim-faced as he flipped on the large flat-panel TV set used primarily for video conferences. He held the remote in his hand. "The United States has been attacked. Two airliners flew into the World Trade Center in New York and a third crashed into the Pentagon. More I don't know. So, when you return to your desks, finish what you are doing so you can take on new projects at a moment's notice." He pushed the button to turn on the TV. When it did, the announcer was talking about a fourth airplane, American Flight 93 that crashed in a field in Pennsylvania.

"Like I said, we're under attack and the info I received is out of date."

THE SAME DAY, 9:46 A.M. LOCAL TIME, NAS NORTH ISLAND

Derek was sitting in the cockpit of an HH-60H parked on the ramp, going through what he called the switchology of the checklists and emergency procedures when the word was passed that the squadron was to muster immediately in the hangar ASAP.

Like many who were busy doing their jobs, most did not know what had happened in New York City, the Pentagon, or the field in Pennsylvania. The first launch went off as planned at 0830, and Derek was scheduled to fly at one in the afternoon.

Three of the helicopters were pulled out of the hangar to make room for the 300-plus officers and enlisted men and women to gather. The squadron CO was standing on the maintenance platform so he was well above everyone.

"If you have not heard, terrorists took control of American Airlines planes and crashed one into each of the World Trade Center Towers in New York, a third into the Pentagon, and a fourth has supposedly crashed in a field in Pennsylvania. We are under attack... While I have no official orders to do so, I am putting HS-10 on a war footing, which means we will compress the flight syllabus to get all the students to the fleet as soon as possible. The first launch will be tomorrow at 0700, which means the brief is at 0600. Last launch will be at 2200. I have ordered the TVs in the squadron tuned to a local news channel. In the meantime, do your jobs and when you go home tonight, kiss your wives and children, and tell them how much you love them because we are all will be working long hours. My gut says we are going to war!"

His announcement was a step change to Derek who, when he checked in to HS-10 after earning his wings, he was told that the transition course for "nuggets" – Naval Aviators right out of the training command – was four to five months. Now, it would be much shorter.

TUESDAY, NOVEMBER 27 TH, 2001, 9:18 P.M. LOCAL TIME, GUANGZHOU

In the months after Senior Administrator Siew and Jun discussed upgrading the Guangzhou Institute of Biomedicine and Health's virology laboratory to Level 3 had been a whirlwind. Out of nowhere came architects to re-design the interior of the building. That took a month. Once it was blessed, the construction manager arrived with electricians and plumbers and workers who demolished existing walls and built new ones. Magically, in a country which couldn't feed itself and in city with many unfinished buildings, the skilled labor appeared along with whatever was required to build a Biosafety Level 3 lab.

It seemed to Jun that neither money nor materials was a problem as the renovation of the fourth, fifth and sixth floors were completed. Approvals that Senior Administrator Siew said would normally take months, if not years, happened in days.

The fast pace of the construction attracted attention and suddenly, the National Academy of Sciences became interested in what was being built. Demands, not requests for visits and information from Academy bureaucrats arrived daily. Senior Administrator Siew passed all the requests and the answers on to Senior Colonel Sun who approved some, but not all of them. Siew told anyone inquiring about the lab that it would be a showcase of what medicine and science can do in the People's Republic.

The most obnoxious bureaucrat from the Academy of Sciences was Dr. Toghon Tang. He appeared for last Friday's official tour and sat directly across from Dr. Lín, staring at her while she gave a short presentation on the modifications being made. Tang had walked into Senior Administrator Siew's office last Friday demanding a personal tour and Jun was tasked by Siew to show him around. She disliked Dr. Tang from the instant they were introduced and thought he took pleasure in giving those around him headaches.

Tang's business card said he was a senior director in the Beijing office that oversaw life and medical sciences facilities such as the Level 3 Bio Lab being built at the Guangzhou Institute of Biomedicine and Health. Jun suspected that Senior Colonel Sun either went around Tang to get approval for the lab or more likely, started the project without Tang's knowledge.

Even the well-connected Senior Administrator Siew didn't know who Tang was. When Siew called Senior Colonel to ask for approval to show Tang the facility, surprisingly, the PLA Army officer agreed to let Jun show him around. His only instruction was to be polite and give him the one-yuan tour.

Once the certification process began, no one except members of Dr. Ng's team and two officials from the World Health Organization assigned to oversee the certification process would be allowed in the lab. Given the support from the Western Region of the World Health Organization in the design and construction of the lab, Dr. Ng, Jun, as well as the WHO team leader were confident that the certification process would be completed by the end of January 2002.

The lab's new organization chart showed that Dr. Ng was responsible for administration and overall operations and Dr. Lín was its research director. The chart showed that Jun would have another virologist or immunologist and six lab technicians working for her on special research projects. Two more virologists and 10 more technicians would work under Dr. Ng.

Neither Dr. Ng nor Jun was sure where the new staff would be found. When discussing the qualifications for the new workers, Dr. Ng had an old Chinese proverb at the tip of his tongue – Ripe fruit falls by itself, but it doesn't fall into your mouth. In other words, they would have to go find them, something that Senior Colonel Sun could facilitate by giving them access to personnel files and data they did not have.

Jun thought they were rid of Tang, but today he was back like a recurring migraine. Senior Administrator Siew brought Dr. Tang to the conference room and promptly excused himself leaving Dr. Ng and Jun at the table. Tang put a battered brown, soft-sided leather briefcase on the table and unbuckled the straps.

"So, Dr. Lín, you are quite young to be a research director. The good Senior Colonel Sun obviously thinks quite highly of you."

Jun said nothing. Age, in Chinese Culture, was considered a valued qualification, sometimes more so than actual skill or knowledge. She despised Tang's holier than thou manner. His first name was the same as one of the last Mongol Emperors, Toghon Temür. Given his imperious manner, she thought it was appropriate.

Taking a deep breath, Tang reached into his briefcase and placed a packet of cigarettes and matches on the table. Dr. Ng was quick to say, "Dr. Tang, we do not allow smoking anywhere in this facility. If you feel the need to smoke, we have designated smoking facilities outside the side doors."

Defiantly, Senior Doctor Tang started to pull a cigarette out of the pack. Dr. Ng spoke again, this time much more firmly. It was the first time Jun had ever heard him raise his voice. "Again, Dr. Tang, we do not allow smoking in the building. If you insist, I will call security and they will forcibly remove you from this building. We do not want any smoke – tobacco or other – entering in the ventilation system because it may compromise our labs and affect our patients."

Dr. Tang pursed his lips and pushed the cigarette back into the pack with his index and middle fingers stained pale yellow, just like

Jun's late father's. The pack and matches went back into his briefcase. Coughing, he pulled out two folders. "As you know, the People's Republic has spent a considerable sum of money on this new lab. Funding for many other projects approved by the Academy were pushed aside. Therefore, the Academy will be closely following the research of the lab. Apparently, both of you will be given freedom to …." Tang paused for the right word. He wanted to use raid but settled on another "… recruit from other medical labs throughout the country. I am told that Dr. Lín is to be given priority on the top ranked doctors coming out of our medical schools. However, all appointments to the lab must be approved by the Academy of Sciences which means, more specifically, me. Any request for additional staff will be sent by Senior Administrator Siew to me for review. If I approve, then you may interview the candidate and, if so desired and with my explicit approval, bring him or her here."

Again, neither said anything to let Dr. Tang continue. "I feel it necessary to remind both of you that whatever research is conducted in the new lab is to be considered a state secret. Some research, I am told, will be Top Secret and I presume you know what that means. The Ministry of State Security will vet anyone before they are employed. I will leave it to both of you to ensure that your staff understands the requirements of keeping top-secret research away from the prying eyes of our enemies. Need I say more on this?"

Both Dr. Ng and Dr. Lín shook their heads.

"Excellent. Then, once the lab is certified for operation, I believe Senior Colonel Sun wants the theories in this doctoral thesis explored as the lab's first project."

Tang slid a copy of Jun's doctoral thesis across the table to Dr. Ng. Smiling, he said, "The state, meaning my office, has some current data we can share on the polio virus in the People's Republic."

Jun's body language gave her thoughts away. Tang said, "Dr. Lín, the Army, the party, and the people have gone to great expense and effort to provide you with a first-class virology laboratory. To sound like a capitalist, it is time you began to repay their investment."

Jun could not wait for Tang to leave. Both Jun and Dr. Ng, who had read her doctoral theses understood the implications of what they were about to begin. And both were powerless to resist.

That evening, Bojing sensed his bride's unhappiness. Jun couldn't give him many details other than to say that the Academy of Sciences was asking Jun to conduct research in the new lab that she doesn't think is appropriate. He suggested that the Ministry of State Security will twist her time in the United States as a justification for any perceived resistance or disloyal act.

Jun understood. She was already disloyal to her country but, she rationalized, for a good reason.

Seeing his wife nod acceptance, Bojing led her to the bedroom, hoping to make her feel better. Each time they made love, Jun enjoyed the pleasant sensations. Despite Bojing's efforts, she was not in love with him, and she never reached the same heights of passion that he did.

CHAPTER 9

UNKNOWNS

Since their first taxi ride together, Bao Gu and Jun Lín had become friends, often having lunch at the institute, and sometimes walking together to work. However, now that she was married to Bojing, Bao realized he must be careful.

Bao wanted to walk away from their relationship after Jun told him of her intent to marry Bojing. When he relayed the information to Senior Investigator Lieu, he was told to find a way to continue and expand it. Bao objected strenuously. Lieu reiterated his threat to have Bao arrested on trumped up charges claiming that he knew the truth about the fight.

He believed his actions were fully justified but it would be futile to try to prove his innocence in the PRC. What Bao resolved to do was essentially nothing. He would report every month that nothing was new, i.e., Jun was happily married to Bojing.

This morning, they were talking after a staff meeting and Bao asked about Bojing. Jun said Bojing was spending the night at the Guangzhou East Air Base. He had just been promoted to major, an event they celebrated on Saturday, January 25ᵗʰ. Tomorrow, his unit, the 25ᵗʰ Fighter Regiment, was participating in a live fire exercise and he wanted to make sure that the airplanes were ready.

Hearing that, Bao suggested that they go out to dinner. Jun surprised him by accepting.

After they ordered, Bao leaned across the table and whispered, sure that they would not be overheard in the noisy restaurant. "Jun, I don't know if you realize how much the staff looks up to you for what you have done for the institute. Even Senior Administrator Siew thinks you walk on water."

The American-trained virologist laughed and said, "All I was trying to do was to upgrade the lab's capabilities. Never did I dream we would have a Level 3 lab so fast. It makes my head spin and I wonder what steps we missed."

Bao didn't change his position and he said softly. "Rumors are flying about the project your research team is about to attempt. It is as if everything in the new lab is top-secret."

She wanted to tell Bao that it was, but he wasn't cleared or even granted access to the lab. Instead Jun said, "What we are doing is so important that if I fail, I will wind up forgotten in a prison someplace in Mongolia. If we succeed, I will be a hero of the Party."

Bao laughed. "I have confidence in you. Everything will turn out well."

They finished dinner and Bao escorted Jun back to her apartment. Finally, he had a tidbit for Senior Inspector Lieu.

THURSDAY, JANUARY 10TH, 2002, 2:43 P.M. LOCAL TIME, GUANGZHOU EAST AIR BASE

Bojing heard the thump that sounded like a muffled explosion. He could see smoke pouring from the alert hangar two down from where he was supervising the refueling and re-arming of another J-7. Each alert J-7 was armed with two PL-8 Thunderbolt missiles and carried three drop tanks, one under each wing and one under the fuselage to extend their range.

The thump was much louder than when the fuel was ignited when the fighter's engine started. Bojing yelled at two of his subordinates to tow the airplane being refueled out of the hangar along with the other one they just finished arming.

Bojing ran toward the fire ordering men he passed to follow him. When he arrived at the hangar, the tail of the J-7 was engulfed in flames. Fuel was pouring onto the concrete floor of the shelter from the plane's ruptured fuselage fuel tank. The pilot had the canopy open and was trying to unstrap and climb out of the airplane.

Two men emptied the CO_2 extinguishers on the fire. Their efforts, Bojing thought, were brave but were like pissing in the wind. He grabbed the nozzle of the fire hose from the wall and pulled it toward the starboard side of the plane.

He felt the heat from the fire on his skin. When he was close enough to use the foam that the firefighting system was supposed to contain, he signaled for the man to charge the hose. Feeling the hose inflate, he pointed the nozzle at the burning fuel on the hangar floor just as the blast fragmentation warhead on the PL-8 missile hung on the starboard wing exploded. The small, square tungsten steel fragments shredded Bojing, the pilot, and the six men carrying the hose and the hose itself.

The tungsten fragments punctured the wing and centerline tanks, adding their fuel to the fire. The explosion set off the rocket motor on the missile on the port wing and whomever came after Bojing faced two rocket motors burning in the middle of a jet fuel fire. There was no back-up fire suppression system or another hose in the hangar.

The arriving fire truck crews now had to put out a raging inferno inside a hardened aircraft shelter. Streams of firefighting foam from their trucks eventually brought the blaze under control. By then, the bodies of Bojing and the seven others who died were burned beyond recognition.

SUNDAY, JANUARY 13TH, 2002, 1:03 P.M. LOCAL TIME, GUANGZHOU

Huan Zhao heard a sharp knock on the door to their apartment. When he opened it, Huan saw two PLA Air Force officers in dress uniforms. One he recognized as Colonel Zhen Wang, the commander of the 25th Fighter Regiment. Solemnly, the colonel asked if he could come in.

Bojing's father bowed his head and stepped back, fearing the worst. His wife, Nuo put her hand to her mouth, managed to find her way to the couch and collapsed on its cushions. Huan sat next to her and wrapped his right arm around her shoulder and held both her hands with his left.

Colonel Wang came to attention in front of the couple and saluted. "I am sorry to inform you that your son, Major Bojing Zhao was killed during an air defense exercise. The details of which are classified, but I can assure you that he died bravely and gloriously for his country."

Huan immediately thought what he heard was a carefully rehearsed statement that was bullshit. "What happened?"

"Sir, I cannot tell you because the details are classified."

Nuo asked between sobs, "Did he suffer?"

"Again, Mrs. Zhao, I cannot tell you. What I am permitted to say is that his remains have been cremated and his ashes will be delivered to you or his wife in a few days. We are required to ask his wife if she wants them first."

"Have you told his wife yet?"

"No, we are going there next."

"How many others died with our son?"

"Senior commissioner, I am sorry, but I cannot divulge that information. It, too, is classified."

Colonel Wang again said he was sorry for their loss and Major Zhao was well-liked by his men and will be missed. And then the Air Force colonel was gone.

Once the door closed, Nuo hammered her husband's chest with her fists, screaming that her son, her only son, thanks to her country's stupid one-child policy was gone. Then, she collapsed in a heap, sobbing.

Jun Lín was reading a book wondering when Bojing would be home. She was wearing a tightfitting white cheongsam with red dragons that Bojing liked that looked sexy and attractive.

On the table, she had the places set. In the kitchen, what a chef would call the "mise en place" work was done for his favorite dish, chicken with snow peas, bean sprouts, water chestnuts and scallions all diced and put in little bowls. The rice was already made and being kept warm in their rice cooker. Once Bojing was home, all Jun had to do was turn on the gas burner under the wok and start cooking.

When Jun heard the knock, she thought it was Bojing. She opened the door with a big smile, only to see the solemn Colonel Wang and a captain. The colonel bowed slightly at the waist and asked if he could come in. Jun had no idea why an Air Force colonel she had seen only at her wedding was suddenly at the front door to their apartment.

Slowly, Jun backed away from the door, thinking that a colonel at her front door meant something bad had happened to Bojing. Colonel Wang pointed to their small couch in front of the large, at least for People's Republic of China, TV Bojing loved to watch.

Jun sat on the edge of the couch looking up at Colonel Wang who saluted and intoned, "I am sorry to inform you that your husband, Major Bojing Zhao, was killed during an air defense exercise. The details of which are classified, but I can assure you that he died bravely and gloriously for his country."

Jun let out a painfilled wail. Tears streamed down her cheeks. She looked up at the colonel and asked the same question, what happened? She heard the same answer as the Zhaos.

She tried a different question, "Cannot tell me or will not?"

"Cannot. The incident is classified top-secret."

"Well, so is my work. Why am I not cleared?"

The colonel ignored her question and asked, "Is there someone who can stay with you during this trying time?"

"My mother lives nearby. I will call her."

"Would you like me to have one of my officers wait until she arrives?"

"No, colonel, that is not necessary. Thank you for the offer."

Colonel Wang's formal demeanor softened. "Dr. Lín, Major Bojing often spoke proudly about the work you do for our people at the Institute of Biomedicine and Health. He was a very popular officer and well respected. He had, as I am sure you know, many friends." The colonel's tone hardened. "Please do not contact his friends to ask about what happened. If you do, it will go badly for you and those who answer your questions."

Jun nodded numbly and said, "I understand."

When the colonel left, Jun called her mother who said she would come over and spend several nights with her. Jun then sat down on the couch and tears streamed down her face. She was not sure if they were from grief for a young man who died way too young or relief because now, she was out of a marriage she did not want. While she respected and cared for Bojing, she did not love him.

MONDAY, JANUARY 14ᵀᴴ, 2002, 7:10 A.M. LOCAL TIME, GUANGZHOU

When Bao Gu didn't see Jun at the institute's Monday staff meeting, he wondered why. Normally she arrived early and often she and Dr. Ng sat next to each other. All Senior Administrator Siew would say was that Dr. Lín would not be in for a few days.

To Bao, this was news that could be reported to Senior Investigator Lieu, but before he did, he wanted to know more. After work, Bao knocked on the door to Jun's tenth floor apartment.

Seeing Jun and her bloodshot eyes confirmed his suspicions that something unfortunate happened to the American-trained scientist. Bao said as he entered, "What's happened?"

"Who are you?" The strong feminine voice from the kitchen caused both doctors to turn their heads. "Mother, this is my friend Dr. Bao Gu from the institute who is head of the immunology department. Bao, this is my mother, Senior Professor Liang Lín."

Bao turned to face Jun's mother and bowed slightly. "From what I have heard, you and your daughter have a wonderful relationship. She talks about you all the time."

"Thank you, you are most kind. My daughter is not going to work for at least a week."

Bao turned to Jun. "Are you ill?"

"No…" Jun sniffled because the news of Bojing's death was still raw and the refusal of Colonel Wang to provide any details made her angry. "Bojing was killed yesterday. The People's Air Force won't tell me what happened."

The immunologist made a face. "That sounds typical. They don't want anyone to know the cause that may reveal that some of their officers are incompetent." Bao changed the subject, "Mother Lín, I can stay with Jun if you need to go to work."

Jun shook her head vigorously. "No, that is not necessary. I promise I won't jump off the balcony or slit my wrists."

Liang left to go back to her apartment after Bao left. She promised to be back before dinner leaving Jun alone with her thoughts.

She picked up a wedding photo and looked up at the sky. "Bojing, you were a very good man who loved me. You didn't deserve what happened to you. I will miss your good humor and smile. Rest in peace."

The next morning after Liang went to work at Sun Yat-Sen University, Jun composed a short note to Yan telling her Bojing was killed in an accident but provided no details. That was the uncoded portion. In the coded text, she said the lab was being tasked to study poliomyelitis and other viruses to see if they might mutate. Satisfied the note was innocuous enough, she mailed the prepaid airmail letter at a China Post facility and returned to her apartment before her mother arrived from the university.

Jun packed Bojing's uniforms into one of the bags he was issued when he was a cadet. Into another, she carefully placed his civilian clothes. Looking at the two cases and a cardboard box with his shoes, all Jun could think about Bojing's life was reduced to a few framed pictures, two suitcases and a box. What a pity! But the act helped her grieve.

THE SAME DAY, 10:13 A.M. LOCAL TIME, GUANGZHOU

While Jun was packing Bojing's clothes, Bao dialed a familiar number.

"Lieu."

"Senior Investigator, this is Dr. Gu. I have some interesting news."

"Define interesting?" For weeks, all Bao Gu would tell Lieu there was nothing to report. Now he has some interesting news. His impatience got the best of him in his tone of voice.

"Dr. Lín is now a widow."

Silence. Then Lieu spoke trying to hide the surprise in his voice. "Her husband was killed in an accident out at Guangzhou Air Base. The Air Force is classifying the accident that killed Major Bojing Zhao as Top Secret."

"That is interesting." Lieu waited for a few seconds then said. "Well, you have your assignment, get to it."

"I am going to continue being her colleague for a few months and see what happens."

"Good idea, but don't wait more than a month before seducing her."

"What happens if she refuses?"

"You need to ensure that doesn't happen."

Bao sat their listening to a dial tone before he hung up the phone thinking three months was more appropriate. Seducing Dr. Jun Lín will be his pleasure since she was the most attractive woman Lieu ever assigned him.

TUESDAY, JANUARY 15ᵀᴴ, 2002, 10:07 A.M. LOCAL TIME, GUANGZHOU EAST AIR BASE

Jun was pouring tea for her mother when there was a sharp knock on the door. The two women were planning to take a walk in the morning and then eat lunch at a nearby restaurant.

Again, there was an Air Force major standing at attention when she opened it. He bowed deeply from the waist and held out an envelope horizontally with both hands.

The officer came back to attention after Jun took the proffered envelope. "Dr. Lín, the 25th Fighter Regiment is having a memorial service on Saturday, January 18th for your husband and the others who died. Colonel Wang requests that you honor your husband's regiment by attending. The envelope has the formal invitation, the agenda and other information. We will provide a car to take you to and from the ceremony. There is a number for you to call to confirm your attendance."

"You may inform Colonel Wang that I will come."

The officer bowed again. "We are most honored. I will so inform Colonel Wang."

Moments after the officer left, the phone rang. "Allo…"

"Jun, this is Nuo. Did you receive the invitation?"

"I did and I said I would attend."

"We have no choice. What are you going to wear?"

"All black."

"Then, I will wear all white." Both women knew that black and white were traditional Chinese mourning colors. They talked for a few more minutes to ascertain how each was dealing with their grief and hung up.

Liang offered the black dress she wore at her husband's funeral which fit her diminutive daughter.

SATURDAY, JANUARY 18TH, 2002, 10:17 A.M. LOCAL TIME, GUANGZHOU EAST AIR BASE

Eight J-7s were parked in a neat row and the 800 plus men of the 25th Fighter Regiment were in ranks of 100 when Jun arrived. The car stopped where there were chairs for the families of the nine men who died. Behind the chairs, the men of the 25th were arrayed in eight ranks of 100. Between the families and the airplanes, there were nine tables covered with red cloth on which there was an official photograph of the man draped with a medal and an urn with his ashes.

The Commander of the Seventh Air Division made a short speech praising each man's bravery. Starting with the most junior man, the medals and urns were presented to the families in turn.

Bojing's medal, Model Hero First Class, came with a gold and red ribbon. Jun handed the picture to Nuo who propped it up on her lap. At the end of the ceremony, the families were led to staff cars that took them home.

In her apartment, Jun gently placed the urn on her table. She lifted the lid and took a small sample of the powder and put it in a plastic bag.

MONDAY, JANUARY 21ST, 2002, 9:11 A.M. LOCAL TIME, GUANGZHOU

On her first day back at work, Jun went to Dr. Ng and said she wanted to run a DNA test that she didn't want recorded. Dr. Ng asked the technicians to give the two doctors a moment. Jun dropped samples of the ashes into tubes for the polymerase chain reaction process. Within seconds, Jun had her answer and didn't need to finish all the tests. There was not a shred of human DNA in the ashes which came from burned wood, mostly bamboo.

CHAPTER 18

LONG DAY IN THE COCKPIT

9/11 changed everything. Within days after the World Trade Center collapsed into a smoking pile of rubble, all the students were told they were about to start flying seven days a week so they could report to their squadrons as soon as possible.

The terrorist attack was a shock to everyone, but the impact on the Navy's tempo of operations was palpable. HS-10's first flight of the day now briefed at 6:00 a.m., launched at 7:00 a.m. and the last launched around 10:00 p.m. If Derek wasn't in the cockpit flying, he was in a simulator handling emergencies or learning ASW tactics or studying for an upcoming flight or a simulator ride.

Adrian was immersed in her courses. Non-class time was spent in the school's law library or studying in the spare bedroom of their apartment. Many nights dinner was take-out and both were too tired for sex.

Two weeks after 9/11, HS-10's executive officer (XO) stopped Derek in the passageway after he'd just finished debriefing a flight in which the helicopter lowered a sonar dome into the water and the sensor operator in the back practiced pinging while the instructor grilled him on tactics.

The XO, with whom Derek had flown once, was an academy graduate and addressed his subordinates as either Mr., Ms., or Mrs. "Mr. Almer, got a minute?"

"Yes, sir" was Derek's cheery reply even though he was dog tired. He followed the XO into his office. The commander held up a piece of paper. "You are about to get what some may call a 'Navy good deal.' *Stennis* departure has been moved up to November 12th, so I've promised the Eightballer's skipper that I will deliver you as a full up round by November 1st. From what the training officer tells me, you're doing well, so plan on flying twice, maybe three times a day. Sometime between now and November 1st, you'll go to SERE school."

A "full-up round" meant a fully qualified co-pilot in both the HH-60H and SH-60F helicopters flown by HSC-8. SERE stood for the Survival, Escape, Resistance and Evasion course. It was a 10-day school in which the students are taught how to survive in the wilderness and spend four full days in a POW camp that is one-quarter step away from the real thing. In the camp, students are beaten, waterboarded and taught the skills needed to survive and resist if captured.

"Aye, aye sir. I'm game."

"Good, now get out of here and don't embarrass me when you get to HSC-8."

Derek kissed Adrian good by on November 10th, 2001, at North Island Naval Air Station and boarded one of the two C-9s that would take him to Seattle. There a bus carried those not ferrying the squadron's 12 helicopters – eight SH-60Fs and four HH-60Hs – to the *U.S.S. Stennis* (CVN-74) tied up at a pier in Everett, Washington. Those flying in the helicopters as well as the aircraft in the air wing would fly aboard the carrier on the 12th as it passed 50 miles west of Los Angeles.

In his interview with the CO of HSC-8 on the day he checked in, Derek was asked which "HAC Track" he preferred, ASW or combat search and rescue (CSAR)/logistics. HAC stood for helicopter aircraft commander. Without hesitating, Derek said CSAR. The CO looked at him and said ASW is where it is at in the helicopter community and having a CSAR background may adversely affect him later in his career. By his advice, the CO was subtly trying to point out that CSAR/special ops flying was a bastard stepchild in the Navy helicopter community.

"Sir, I understand, but I like the special operations and CSAR missions. If it means I fly a lot of plane guard and parts runs, so be it."

Derek's arrival brought the number of Naval Aviators in HS-8 to 27. If it were at full strength, the roster would have had 36 names. Pilots and aircrew were unofficially divided into two unofficial detachments - 18 who flew the SH-60F and nine who flew the HH-60H.

With two months taken out of HS-8's work-up schedule, new personnel were still arriving. Derek was the seventh Naval Aviator in the HH-60H detachment so as soon as they were at sea, he was in demand as a co-pilot.

Stennis along with the cruisers and destroyers of Carrier Group Seven arrived on station North Arabian Sea in late-December and the F/A-18s of Air Wing 9 began flying strikes into Afghanistan. The carrier steamed back and forth roughly 50 miles south of the Pakistani coast between the ports of Gwadar and Ormara to minimize the flight time needed for the F/A-18s to reach their targets.

Pages in Derek's logbook became filled with entries indicating he was flying 60 hours a month. When he arrived at HSC-8, he had 326 total hours of Navy flight time and no call sign.

Now, he'd passed 500, the minimum number needed to qualify for a HAC check and had a call sign – Racer. It came about since he often used the term that he would "race" about to get something done. It had nothing to do with his ski racing background.

Back at North Island, the process was more structured, requiring a simulator ride, oral and written exams, along with a flight in the helicopter. At sea, the HAC flight check simulator ride was dispensed with.

When Derek walked out to the HH-60H, the rotors were shut down, but both engines were turning. The crew was doing what was known as a hot fuel. The aircraft commander Derek was flying with today pointed to the right seat and said, "You're playing HAC today."

Talking to the pilots getting out of the HH-60H, side number 607, everything was normal. Derek was still tightening his straps when the radio crackled. "Angel 607, eta liftoff."

The official HAC, Gavin Ritchie, looked at him as if to say, you're the aircraft commander, you answer the air boss. Derek glanced at the fuel totalizer which indicated the helicopter had 4,000 pounds (~588 gallons) on board. This was the only H model that didn't have an external tank fitted. Derek keyed the mike, "Gold Eagle Tower, Angel Six Zero Seven, request permission to engage."

The air boss, satisfied his question was answered, responded with one word, "Cleared."

Derek twirled his finger over his head and the enlisted man standing in front of the helicopter held up a balled fist while he looked under and on both sides of the helicopter. Satisfied that only the two members of the Eightballers line crew were near the helicopter and out of danger by standing next to the wheels, the enlisted man twirled his arm around his head.

Lieutenant Gavin Ritchie, HSC-8's HAC with the most experience in the HH-60H, read off the items on the checklist and Derek gave the proper response before Derek pushed the throttles for the two GE T700-401C engines to the stops to make sure each was generating its full 1,662 horsepower.

Ritchie's call sign was Richman. He earned the moniker when he checked into his first squadron. He often, when donations were being solicited, claimed poverty.

With the turbine engines at full speed, Derek looked at the engine gauges which were white vertical lines on the central display unit. Everything was normal and he heard from the aircrewmen in the back that they were ready. Derek said, "Engaging" and pulled the rotor brake back from the notch where it kept the rotor blades from turning like a parking brake and pushed it up into the off detent to allow the blades to start turning.

Within seconds, the rotors were at 102 percent RPM and Ritchie noted over the intercom that the gauges looked good so Derek keyed the mike, "Gold Eagle Tower, Angel 607 is ready for take-off."

Technically, the helicopter wasn't because they hadn't finished the take-off check list, the last item of which was remove the chocks and chains. He was not going to have them pulled until the Air Boss cleared him to take off.

"Angel 607, cleared for take-off and cleared to starboard delta. Wind on the nose at fifteen knots."

Ritchie said the take-off checklist was complete and signaled to pull the chocks and chains. Derek waited until the two linemen stood off to the right front of the helicopter, each with a chock and two tie-down chains. The senior aircrewman said over the intercom, chocks and chains were gone.

Derek pulled back the rocker switch to transmit on the UHF radio. "Angel 607 lifting. Cleared starboard delta."

To increase the power to take off, Derek raised the collective. This was a lever-like object on his left side that controlled the pitch of all the blades. At the front end of the collective there was a small box with switches that controlled the moveable searchlight, its brightness, and the chaff and flare dispenser.

Angel 607 weighed around 20,000 pounds which was 1,900 less than its designed maximum take-off weight when Derek raised the collective. He added enough power to lift the HH-60H into a hover four feet over the deck. As the helicopter rose, he added forward cyclic because, if he did not, the carrier would steam out from underneath him and the wind would push him back down the angle where jets were sitting on the catapult waiting to be launched.

Ritchie pointed to the central data unit display and keyed the mike. "Power looks good."

Derek clicked intercom twice as he added more power and pushed the nose down. The HH-60H accelerated. By the time it reached the end of the angled deck, the airspeed indicator showed they were passing 40 knots. At 60 knots and about 100 feet over the water, Derek turned left and passed behind the carrier climbing to 200 feet.

Overhead, the first pair of F/A-18s passed by with their hooks down and began their break approach to the left which would bring them around to aft end of the carrier for landing. The first four aircraft had trapped aboard when the radio cackled.

"Angel 607, Contact Combat on button 3. They have work for you."

Ritchie rogered the radio call, selected the third preset frequency on the UHF radio and keyed the mike. "Gold Eagle Combat, Angel 607 is up."

"Roger, Angel 607. We have a request to take a medical team out to a friendly vessel to triage a badly injured sailor. Pigeons are 220 at 90. Are you able?"

Derek looked at Ritchie who was on his second long cruise with HSC-8. He was also the aviator in the squadron with the most hours in the HH-60H. "Racer, don't look at me, you're the HAC today, your decision."

"Gold Eagle Combat, we'll go. Suggest medical team brings out a Stokes litter and, when we come aboard, we would like to top off."

"Roger. Will advise the tower. Details on the ship to follow. Stand-by this frequency."

Derek acknowledged the call. When he was done, Ritchie said, "Good call on asking for a stokes litter and more gas. Ship's pigeon's estimates are notoriously inaccurate."

"Mr. Ritchie, this is Petty Officer Grayson. When we touch down, I am going to dash down to our aircrew spaces and get the combat medic pack. Hambleton can supervise the refueling, get the passengers on board and stow the litter."

"Roger that."

They made six orbits, staying at 200 feet and about a quarter mile on from the carrier. Derek was thinking that it would be nice to have one or both external tanks but 607 had a leak in the hoses inside the starboard stub wing. Due to the tempo of operations, HSC-8's skipper, Commander Huerta didn't want to take the time to remove the stub wing and make the repairs. He also rationalized that most of the flying the H models did was within 50 miles of *Stennis* and 607 didn't need the extra fuel.

However, six times, by Derek's count, the H models were sent a hundred miles or more from the carrier. Each time, the additional fuel was needed.

"So, HAC wannabe, what's the plan?"

Derek looked at Ritchie, not surprised by the question. "Once we top off and take off, we'll have about three and a half hours of gas. So, we climb to three thousand feet and fly out toward the ship at one hundred and twenty knots. I'd turn on our ESM system to see if we can pick up their radar. After about an hour, we climb to five thousand, do an expanding circle search. If we don't see the ship, after about thirty minutes, we RTB to *Stennis* and should arrive with about 30 minutes of fuel. Now, if we find the ship, we take on fuel if we can."

RTB was return to base, a term everyone on board knew. Ritchie was about to say something when the radio interrupted. "Angel 607, Combat. Air Boss advises we're going to bring you aboard after the next pair of F/A-18s trap aboard and will give you fuel. Do not shut down the rotors. Intel is sending a package of info on the ship that will come out with the medics, copy?"

Derek looked at Gavin who nodded. "Angel 607 copies."

"Angel 607, Combat. Contact combat on button one once enroute."

"Roger." Button one meant that he would select channel one which had the frequency for combat pre-selected.

On their brief, Ritchie told Derek that while he will do things in the cockpit as requested, Derek is going to have to talk, fly and navigate as if he was flying solo. Ritchie said he will take the initiative only if it is a safety of flight issue.

True to his word, Grayson loaded the medical pack that rescue air crewmen use on MEDEVAC flights if they must provide medical care to a survivor before he or she can be airlifted. Seeing it, the surgeon and the corpsman who brought their own "stuff," gave Grayson a thumbs up. He also brought several stands that were used to hang IV bottles on a Stokes litter.

Once they were enroute and cruising at 120 knots at 3,000 feet, Ritchie opened the manila envelope given to him by the surgeon. In it, there were photos of the French *Floreal*-class frigate, *Capitaine Dreyfus.*

Built in 1981, the frigate was approximately 300 feet long, had a beam of 45 feet and displaced 2,600 tons. On the aft end of the ship, there was a helicopter deck designed to accommodate a French Panther helicopter - about two-thirds the size of their HH-60H. It did mean, however, that theoretically, they could take on fuel via a process called Helicopter-in-Flight Refueling (HIFR).

"Angel 607, call sign of your destination is Zola. We've got them on JTIDS and are talking to them on SATCOM. They have several casualties from a flash fire. All they have is a corpsman on board. Their air search radar is down. Revised pigeons are 220 at 130."

Derek rogered the call before turning around to look aft. "Grayson, how many stokes litters can you get in the back and still carry the four of you?"

"Four, sir. Two on the floor and two I can hang with straps from the overhead."

"What about room for you?"

"It'll be cozy, but we can move stuff around to get everyone onboard."

Ritchie looked at Derek with a quizzical look as if to say, what are you thinking?

"Richman, I think we may be making several trips."

The senior HH-60H HAC pointed to the multi-function display. "We're out of radio range so we have nothing. TACAN just crapped out, so we're dead reckoning."

Derek nodded. Fear was growing in his gut that if the winds were bad and they stooged around looking and cannot find *Capitaine Dreyfus*, they might end up swimming.

"Angel Six Zero Seven, Retro Seven Zero Three, how do you copy?"

Retro was the call sign of VAW-112, the airborne early warning squadron on *Stennis*. They flew E-2Cs.

Ritchie held up a pencil over the pad on his kneeboard saying he'll take notes and pointed to his mike saying he'll talk. "Retro Seven Zero Three, this is Angel Six Zero Seven, we copy you loud and clear."

"Roger that, squawk 4162 and ident."

Ritchie dialed in the digits on the APX-100 transponder and pushed the button that would cause the blip that represented the helicopter to flash on the controller's screen.

"Angel, Six Zero Seven, radar contact. Turn port ten degrees and Zola is twenty-one nautical on your nose."

Ritchie rogered the instruction and Derek changed heading.

"Angel Six Zero Seven, be advised that Retro Seven Zero Three has been tasked to provide command and control for this MEDEVAC. We have comms with Zola as well as Gold Eagle."

Derek scanned the horizon. "Ship, twelve o'clock, about five miles." He started a slow descent and the radio crackled again. This time the voice had a French accent. "Zola has a ready deck, wind is thirty degrees to port, wind approximately thirty kilometers per hour."

The side of the ship aft of the bridge was blackened by smoke. The frigate was leaving a wake, but not much of one. Derek guessed *Dreyfus* was making about five knots.

Smoothly, Derek eased the helicopter through the burble caused by the ship's superstructure and into a position about 20 feet over the helicopter deck. The hoist went down with the doctor first. Before he touched down, one of the *Dreyfus'* crewmen touched the cable with a grounding wand to dissipate the static electricity which, while not strong enough to electrocute a man, it could knock one on his ass.

The corpsman went down right after the doctor. Before he pulled away, Derek keyed the mike. "Zola, we would like to take on fuel. Is that possible?"

"*Attendez un.* I am sorry, wait one."

A different voice keyed the mike. "Angel 607, give us five minutes to rig the hose."

Derek keyed the mike to acknowledge and eased back on the cyclic and raised the collective slightly to let the frigate sail out from underneath the HH-60H. Derek accelerated to 60 knots and climbed to 100 feet and began a lazy circle behind the frigate.

"Angel Six Zero Seven, your doctor has asked if you could lower your crewman with his medical pack."

Another acknowledgement and another approach to the back of the *Capitaine Dreyfus*. Grayson went down the hoist and disappeared into a hatch on the side of the hangar. Their second air crewman, Ron Hambleton, raised the fuel hose with the hoist, looked at the fuel sample that was free of debris and plugged the hose into the receptacle in the cabin. Topped off with fuel, the hose was lowered and Angel 607 continued to orbit on the port side of the ship, about half a mile away at 200 feet.

"Angel Six Zero Seven, this is Dr. Zelen. I am going to send the ones that need more than I can do here back to Gold Eagle. You'll have the four worst ones on board with and me. Then, Zola is going to land its helicopter on which we will put two more patients and the ship's corpsman. You will lead the Panther back to Gold Eagle as fast as you can."

Derek answered and began to approach the French frigate. He kept the helicopter in as steady a hover as he could. Grayson and some supplies in a pack was the first on board, followed by one Stokes litter, then another. When all four were on board, Derek slid the helicopter off and slowly climbed to 3,000 at 60 knots. He could hear the controllers on the E-2 giving the Panther vectors to his helicopter. When Hambleton said the French helicopter was sliding in position on the starboard side, Derek started to accelerate. Glancing out the starboard side, he could see the Panther keeping station about 50 feet outside his rotor disk and slightly in right echelon. He kept beeping the nose down as he coaxed the HH-60H up to 140 knots.

"Racer, let me fly. You've done enough." Ritchie was keying the mike with his left hand and pointing to his chest. Derek took his hands and feet off the controls and tried to relax. His legs bounced up and down and his hands shook slightly.

Richman waited a few seconds before speaking again, "Racer, normally, we would have been switching back and forth to share the flying. But I'm impressed. Are you up for another round trip, or should we have someone else go?"

"No, I want to go back if needed. We started this - I want to finish it."

Ritchie nodded.

Grayson said that *Dreyfus* had a fire in the motor room for their main radar. When one of the sailors opened the hatch to put out the fire, there was an explosion that spread to their combat information center which was partly demolished. Four men were killed outright. The six brought to the carrier were the most severely injured. There were still about a dozen more that will be fine once their burns heal. The frigate, he said is headed toward Carrier Group Seven so that the less severely injured can be treated on board *Stennis*.

When they shut down Angel 607, Derek looked at his watch. It was almost dark and the time was 7:52 p.m. He'd been in the cockpit for almost 11 hours and was exhausted from the two trips to the *Dreyfus* and back. Ritchie filled out the maintenance paperwork and handed Derek the log of the mission he kept. "We'll flesh this out after we take a shower and have something to eat in the Dirty Shirt mess."

There were two officer wardrooms on *Stennis*. One below the hangar deck which required the uniform of the day and had two sittings for each meal. The officers were served by the stewards.

The "Dirty Shirt" mess was on the level below the flight deck and there was no "dress code" to eat there. It had a short order menu as well as a buffet and was open 24 hours a day. Most of the officers in the airwing preferred the Dirty Shirt for the simple reason they didn't have to change out of flight suits and they could eat when they chose.

Walking down the passageway with Derek after they fleshed out their notes, Ritchie stopped at the door to his stateroom. "After you type our notes into the computer as our mission report, I'll get the skipper to sign your HAC letter. Well done!!!"

Derek nodded. Days and missions like what he flew today confirmed why he chose the CSAR/Logistics HAC track.

CHAPTER 11

BETRAYAL

The weather outside may have been cold, windy with snow beginning in the evening, but inside the Young house, Yan was sitting at the kitchen table seething. For the third week in a row, while gathering clothes to take to the cleaner, she found lipstick, make-up, and blond hairs on Glenn's white uniform shirts that he wore with his service dress blues.

Next Monday was Yan's first official day back at work after her 12 weeks of maternity leave. However, she had not been absent from the office. Two weeks ago, Yan went back to work part time, arriving around 10 and leaving around two.

She came into the living room where Min was asleep in a bassinet next to her grandmother. By the look on Yan's face, Mei sensed a storm was brewing and asked, "What has you so upset?"

Yan tossed one of the shirts to her mother who needed only a few seconds to find the incriminating stains. "Is this the first time?"

"No, the third."

"Are you angry?"

"Yes. Glenn has betrayed Min and me."

"What are you going to do?"

"Get even, but before I do, I need my ducks in a row."

Zimo Huáng came into the room with a cup of hot, green tea for his wife. Having overheard the conversation, he asked, "Do you want me to follow him?"

Yan thought for a second. "He has been going to Dam Neck on Monday to the Naval Intelligence Officer School for the past three months. I think it would be a good idea, but don't tip him off. I'm going to take pictures of these shirts and put the hair in a plastic bag. I'll note the date, where it was found and you can witness it."

When she returned, her father handed Yan a sheet of paper saying call this number. The law firm was recommended by the family law firm in San Diego noting that they had a successful and well-respected divorce practice. He suggested Yan let the attorney advise what to do.

TUESDAY, FEBRUARY 19TH, 2002, 11:12 A.M. LOCAL TIME, FORT MEADE

On the way to her first official day back at work, she dropped Min off at her grandparent's apartment and found that leaving at 6:30 a.m., the traffic was lighter. She was in her office by 7:15 a.m. rather than closer to eight.

When Yan arrived, after all the "glad to have you back full time" comments, she grimaced at the stacks of transcripts she needed to pour through. Despite her efforts over the past two weeks, the pile hadn't gotten smaller. Many of the transcripts had notes and questions with references to other transcripts and topics of interest.

Around 11, Yan called the Defense Finance and Accounting Office representative at NSA she knew. Dari Ramos was a Filipino native who served in the Navy for 20 years as a DK – disbursing clerk – and earned her citizenship before coming to work at NSA.

Yan tapped on the door frame and Dari gave her a big smile as she came around her desk to hug Yan. "Welcome back, how's Min?"

Pictures followed. When they finished the mother talk, Yan asked, "I'm getting our taxes ready and seem to be missing a bunch of Glenn's orders and per diem filings for trips to the NIO school in Dam Neck on these dates. Glenn works for DIA. Can you look them up and print me copies?"

"Sure. What's his social security number?" Ramos, who had six grandchildren, tapped away at the computer. The hard drive whirred and the printer behind her desk began spitting out the orders, accounting data and completed travel vouchers for reimbursement known as Form 1351-2s.

She handed the stack of documents to Yan who thanked her. As she left Ramos office, the Filipino said, "Don't be a stranger!"

"I won't." She almost bumped into two people as she flipped through the 1351-2s and the accompanying receipts. None had a hotel receipt which begged the question, where was Glenn staying?

WEDNESDAY, FEBRUARY 20TH, 2002, 5:16 P.M. LOCAL TIME, DAM NECK, VA

Glenn backed his well-used, 1995 GMC Sierra Club Coupe pick-up with 126,000 plus miles on the odometer out of the driveway. The truck was the first vehicle Glenn bought and he lavished attention on it. With the light blue smoke that came from the tailpipes and the knowledge the engine was burning a quart of oil every 1,000 miles, he'd concluded that either he was facing an expensive engine rebuild or buying a new vehicle. Neither of which the penny-pinching Glenn Young wanted to do. Yan often kidded him that he was so cheap, he squeaked when he walked.

He headed for I-495 where he had two choices. Continue through the heavy DC traffic to I-95 south or get off I-495 at Maryland Route 301 South which was the fastest way to make the 230-mile drive to Dam Neck in the morning. Maryland Route 301 South intersected I-95 northeast of Richmond and then he took I-95 to I-295 to I-64 to Norfolk and Dam Neck. The drive took between four and four and a half hours.

Right on schedule, Zimo spotted the metallic green pick-up and pulled the Malibu he rented from Avis in behind. He thought that if Glenn was alert, he'd spot his silver M5 with California plates.

Four hours and 14 minutes later, Glenn pulled into the parking lot of the Naval Intelligence Officer school. Zimo who had to stop for a visitor's pass, arrived at the school just in time to photograph LCDR Young enter the building. Zimo had come prepared with a map of the base and moved around, parking in different parking lots before returning to watch Young exit the building at 11:33 with a young woman. He followed them to the exchange's food court for lunch before they returned to the school giving him a chance to photograph the pair again.

At 4:46 p.m., Zimo watched Glenn get into his truck he tailed to a small house in North Virginia Beach. Glenn parked his truck on the street and entered the front door after it was opened by the same blonde he saw at the school. Zimo managed to take pictures of the two kissing.

Zimo found a hotel nearby, checked in and called his granddaughter. They agreed that after he attempted or took pictures of them in the morning, he should return to Glenn Dale.

THURSDAY, FEBRUARY 21ST, 2002, 6:30 P.M. LOCAL TIME, GUANGZHOU

Jun unlocked the door to her apartment and found a letter on the floor. She left it there while she put her briefcase on the counter and took out a pair of latex gloves from a box she had in the apartment to wear when she sliced red Tien tsin peppers. With them on, she studied the sealed envelope wondering what was inside.

Curiosity got the better of Jun, so she slit it open with a kitchen knife. Inside, there was a picture of the hangar taken right after the fire was put out and showed the burned corpses where they fell. The unsigned note looked as if it was produced on a typewriter.

```
Major Bojing Zhao was killed trying to fight a fire
caused by an engine that exploded when the pilot
added power with his throttle and attempted to
taxi out of the hangar. Turbine blades punctured
the main fuselage fuel tank and the leaking fuel
```

```
caught fire. Heat from the fire caused the warhead
of one Thunderbolt missile to explode and then the
second one.

Seeing the fire, Major Zhao did not hesitate to
attempt to try to put the fire out. However, our
fire-fighting systems are not adequate. Fragments
from the missile killed Major Zhao and the men who
followed him. They paid the price of not having
an effective fire suppression system in any of
our hangars.
```

For a few seconds, Jun debated what to do with the note. She decided that the Zhaos should be told. And then, she decided to keep the note to herself thinking it will only rekindle their pain. Jun didn't know a similar note was delivered to each of the families of the men who died.

Nuo Zhao gasped when she saw the photo, knowing one of the bodies on the ground was her son. Guang Zhao's reaction was different than his wife Nuo's. His training and experience from years as an investigator for the Ministry of State Security took over when he said, "This is a violation of national security. Whomever delivered this letter is a traitor. Colonel Wang said the incident was classified top-secret. This could be the work of a counter revolutionary. I will have this letter fingerprinted and we will launch an investigation."

Nuo faced her husband. "No Guang, you will do no such thing. One of those bodies is our son. I will not have you dishonor his memory just because someone in his regiment wanted the families to know the truth."

"I have no choice."

"Yes, my husband, you do. For once in your life, you can be a father, not an instrument of a state that keeps the truth from its citizens. Assuming all the families have seen this photo and read this note, you can't force them to forget what they saw or read. All you will be doing is ruining a man's career who wanted the victims to know the truth. And, by doing so, you will call more attention to this accident than it deserves."

"I have taken an oath to protect this country."

"Damn your oath and damn the government who hides the truth."

"You know I could have you arrested for what you just said."

"Go right ahead. Arrest a grieving widow who just learned her son was shredded and burned in an accident. Be my guest!"

Nuo ripped up the note and photograph which she put in her mouth and swallowed. "Now you can add destroying evidence to the charges." With that, she stormed out of the living room and into the bedroom, slamming the door for emphasis.

FRIDAY, MARCH 1ST, 2002, 6:22 P.M. LOCAL TIME, GLENN DALE

Yan heard Glenn slam his truck's door closed and came down the stairs of their split-level home into the kitchen. As she did, her grandfather nodded and disappeared into the basement. Min was at her grandmother's apartment.

Not hearing or seeing his wife or child, Glenn Young put his bag and briefcase on the tile floor just inside the front door. "Yan?"

"In the kitchen."

Glenn followed the sound and saw his wife leaning against the counter with her arms crossed. "How was your trip?"

He made no attempt to kiss or hug his wife. "Productive. Long." He paused and then asked, "How'd you like being back at work?"

"No biggie. I'd been working back into it for a month. Still, Captain Ellis had a stack of work for me."

"I'd have guessed that. What's for dinner?"

"How about a beer?"

"Good idea, I could use one."

Glenn slid into one of the chairs at the kitchen table while Yan took a can of Tecate out of the refrigerator and tossed it to him. Glenn snatched it from the air and popped open the can. This gave Yan time to take the thick folder off the counter that had been behind her back.

She slid out a 5" X 7" photo of Glenn and the blond woman at the front door of the house in North Virginia Beach. The photo was placed on the table in front of Glenn who almost choked on his beer.

"Who is she?" Yan put three other photos on the table in a row. "I assume you were sleeping with her because on your 1351-2s, you don't claim expenses for a hotel room, breakfast, or dinner. Only lunch."

Form 1351-2 is the Department of Defense's standard voucher that members of the department use to file travel expenses. Receipts are required for all expenses listed.

Glenn's jaw clenched and she could see his cheek muscles working. "It's O.K. that you don't answer. That will come out if we go to trial. So here's the deal. You agree to an uncontested divorce. We each keep what assets we brought into the marriage, but you move out over the weekend. I live in the house until I am transferred to my next duty station. Visitation, none. You don't spend any time with Min, so why bother."

"And if I don't agree?"

Yan put the divorce filing on the table. "We go to court. It will be ugly and probably public. Your clearance may be suspended while they figure out if you've been compromised and it will ruin your career."

"Where will I stay? I need to pack my things."

"Packing? My grandfather and I did it for you. Everything is in boxes in the garage and neatly labeled. It should all fit in your truck. Grandfather Zimo and I will be happy to help you load."

"I want to walk through the house to see if you packed everything."

She knew Glenn well enough to know he had a temper. She forced herself to remain calm even though she suspected a cauldron was brewing. "Not a problem."

Glenn stood up with fire in his eyes and took a step toward Yan. "You sanctimonious Chinese bitch. You're a fucking disaster in bed." He charged Yan and tried to hit her in the face. Years of training in dojos took over and Yan easily parried the blow with her left hand and slammed the palm of her right hand into Glenn's chest. He staggered back and leaned against the counter for support.

"Glenn, don't. You know I have third-degree black belts in Tai Chi and Tae Kwon Do and can beat the shit out of you."

Glenn yanked a 10-inch chef's knife from the knife block by his right hand. He took another step toward Yan, jabbing the knife in her direction. Yan stepped back, giving her time and space to defend herself.

Yan's eyes went back and forth between the knife and Glenn's eyes, trying to anticipate his next move. Glenn tried slashing. Yan dodged the stroke and managed to land a blow on his side, just below his ribs.

Still he came on, Yan retreated, this time, around the table. Glenn lunged across the table and again missed.

"Glenn, stop or I will shoot." The voice was soft, menacing and commanding. Glenn turned to see Zimo Huáng holding a .45 caliber Model 1911 pistol in right hand and a video camera in his left.

Seeing the .45 pistol less than 10 feet away, Glenn dropped the knife on the floor. Yan kicked it away and stood just outside arms-length from the man who was soon to be her ex-husband. There was fire in her eyes and coldness in her voice. "Your walk-through has been canceled. Now get out of this house. If you contest the divorce in any way or threaten or attempt to harm either my grandparents, Min or me in any way, this video will go to the police. I will insist you be charged with assault with a deadly weapon and attempted murder. You and I know the charges, even if you are not convicted, will end your Navy career. Now, Grandfather Zimo and I will watch you load your truck. Do not ever, and I mean ever, come back here. From now on, the only contact you will have with me is through my lawyer."

After Glenn drove away, Yan sat on the couch in their living room emotionally drained. Her father handed her a glass of bourbon and she sat, hunched over, holding the glass thinking how she could have been so stupid to marry a man who turned out to be a monster.

"Drink, my child. It will calm your nerves."

Yan took a sip, then another and then a gulp. She didn't like whiskeys of any type, but this time, once her body began absorbing the alcohol and sugar, she felt calmer.

"Grandfather, would you have shot Glenn?"

"Yes. One more strike and he was dead."

"I did not know you had a gun."

"I have a concealed carry permit for California as does your father and Maryland accepts my permit. So, I have it legally. It would not have been the first time I killed a man and no jury would convict me for defending my granddaughter from a man trying to stab her with a knife."

Yan nodded. "Thank you. Let us watch the tape and tomorrow, I will take it to my lawyer to have him keep the original and make a copy that I will keep in my safe deposit box."

"Granddaughter, what do you think your husband will do?"

"I do not know. I hope he does not fight me."

Her grandparents insisted on spending the night. Yan suggested that they move in with her and they agreed, depending on what it cost to get out of their lease that had almost six months left.

The next day, as Yan headed to NSA, she was surprised that she felt freer than she'd felt in months … and cleaner. Others managed to raise a child as a single parent, she would do so as well and had an advantage – her grandparents – and if they were nearby, her parents.

SUNDAY, MARCH 24TH, 2002, 3:12 P.M. LOCAL TIME, SAN DIEGO

It was the San Diego Unified School District's spring break and Adrian had no one to spend it with. The other wives in HSC-8 were off busy with their children. Back in the beginning of the deployment, she went to many of the squadron's officer wives' functions, but as the workload from law school increased, she found it easier and easier not to go. That was until a month ago when Juanita Huerta, the CO's wife showed up at her front door insisting they go to lunch.

Juanita took her to a restaurant with the best Mexican food she had eaten since arriving in California. A week later, Juanita invited to her house for lunch to teach her how to make several Mexican dishes. At the time, Adrian didn't realize the difference between what was served in California from what was served in Texas.

Juanita's family came from Monterrey, Mexico, and she met her husband when he was at Texas A&M. They ate fajitas and made chili that Adrian took home. It was at this lunch that she learned that beans do not belong in chili.

The CO's wife was blunt and funny when she described the challenges of being a cruise wife. It was lonely and, holding up her index finger "It is this or a dildo."

Adrian started laughing. It was the first hearty laugh she had since Derek had left.

Juanita continued with a broad grin on her face. "Felipe and I have three kinds of sex. There's making love which is when we have the time and there are no kids around to interrupt us. Then, there is sex which is what we have when we are in a hurry or its just spur of the moment. Last, there is fucking. That's when Felipe has been away on cruise or temporary duty and we haven't seen each other in months."

Adrian blushed noticeably at the older woman's bluntness but then broke out into laughter that just wouldn't stop. Still, Adrian needed a break from the memorization and studying she was enduring as a first-year law student. Going back to Brookline for a few days was rejected. It would, Adrian suspected, just make her lonelier when she returned. And a visit to Brookline did not solve the other major problem – she was horny as hell.

In the summer between her sophomore and junior year in high school, Adrian lost her virginity in a summer romance. Vladimir, the son of a Polish immigrant, and she made love at his parent's house since they both worked. When Vladimir's parents moved to Chicago, the relationship ended before she would have broken it off.

After Vladimir, there was Jacob whom she met in her synagogue confirmation class. The opportunities for sex were few, and were, in her mind, way too short. At Middlebury, opportunities to have sex in the dorm were difficult. Dorm rules forbade members of the opposite sex in the rooms behind closed doors or after nine at night. Sex required planning and cooperative roommates. The motels in the town frowned on students renting rooms for the night.

As a straight A student, Adrian was allowed to live in an apartment off campus after her sophomore year abroad. At first, she wanted one by herself, but gave in to her parents' wish to have a roommate to split the cost.

Derek, she found, met all her requirements. He had stamina, loved to experiment with different positions, caressed her body's sensitive areas and used oral sex to get her orgasmic before entering her. His creativity in bed was one of the reasons she fell in love with him.

But now he was on a carrier, 10,000 miles from her bed, and she was incredibly horny. The selection of dildos and vibrators Derek gave her, part in jest and part serious to use in his stead, had become boring.

She dropped her wedding and engagement rings into a small dish where she put them when she wanted to take them off. On went a pair of jeans and a sweatshirt that said Red Sox on the front and drove to an adult bookstore named Mercury where Derek bought the toys on her nightstand. Before entering, Adrian pulled a Red Sox baseball hat down so the beak was on her forehead.

Adrian looked at the shelves of sex toys and BDSM paraphernalia before stopping at a wall with books. She was reading the back covers when a soft voice came from behind and startled Adrian, "May I help you select one?"

Adrian turned toward the voice coming from a light-brown skinned woman slightly taller than her whose long tresses of black hair hung down over her shoulders. The woman had soft black eyes that invited a response. "Do you want a story that is just sex or one that has a little plot to it?"

Adrian smiled. "A plot would be nice."

"How graphic do you want the sex?"

"I'm not squeamish, so I'd like it pretty descriptive."

The woman squatted down, selected three books and as she stood up, smoothed out her pleated skirt. Holding them out, she said, "These have a lot of variety."

Adrian read the back covers and then looked at the woman. "Cool. What else do you have?"

"Lots more. My name is Rosa de la Cruz, what's yours?" Rosa held out her hand.

"Adrian."

"Nice to meet you. Let's go over to another rack in the back."

On the walk over, Adrian noticed that Rosa was wearing a cotton turtleneck that showed off her body as well as two-inch heels that clicked on the linoleum floor. She had muscular legs inside flesh-colored panty hose.

Turning, Rosa smiled at Adrian. "So, these books have plots as well as lots of gratuitous sex. This one, *Lotus Bloom*, is about a consultant who starts dating a transvestite. Ultimately, he becomes trans and falls in love with a man."

Rosa pointed to another book titled, "*The Pair.*" It's about two lesbians who fall in love, one of whom made millions selling a software business and is now into vintage sports car racing, then she turns professional sports car racing and competes in races like the Daytona 24 Hour and the Sebring 12 Hour. Her lover is a successful nightclub owner. It's the first in a five-book series that are, in sequence, *The Racer, The Grinders, The Champion,* and *The Repeaters.*"

Before Derek, to Adrian, cars were just something that one drove. Now, she was more aware of the differences and had ordered a Porsche 911 Turbo for Derek as an anniversary present when he returned from the cruise. Her eyes widened when she realized that Rosa was handing her books that she wrote.

"Are you the author?"

"One in the same."

"Would you sign the ones you wrote?"

"Sure."

"So why are you in the store?"

"I'm half-owner." Rosa carried an armful of books to the register. She looked at the name on the credit card. "Are you a law student at U San Diego?"

"I am. How did you know?"

"I'm slowly working my way through law school and I thought I saw you in the class on torts." Rosa scribbled a short note on the inside cover of each book. As she rang-up the books, she said. "I don't socialize with anyone in my classes."

Adrian started laughing. "Me neither. But it is not every day one meets an author of pornography!"

"Thanks, but that and five bucks might get you a meal at McDonalds. Have a good day."

Adrian left thinking that if she likes the books, she'll stop by to see if Rosa had published any new ones.

CHAPTER 12

CHANGED RELATIONSHIPS

D r. Toghon Tang leaned back in his chair watching the smoke rings he'd just created rise toward the ceiling as he thought about the memo he just read. It originated in the State Council of China and was passed to him as the Director of the Immunology and Virology Department in the office of Life Sciences in the Academies of Life Sciences.

The memo authorized formal negotiations with the U.S. Center for Disease Control and the French Centre International de Recherche en Infectiologie (CIRI) for the design of a Level 4 Biosafety lab that would be the first of its kind built in the People's Republic. All the needed equipment and training in France for a cadre of scientists was included in the scope of the relationship. The finished lab would far surpass the Level 3 lab run by that pushy, American-trained virologist, Jun Lín.

The memo was classified Secret so Tang could not make a copy. However, he knew someone who would be very interested. Doing so would show the value of his network and that he is a trusted citizen of the state.

FRIDAY, MARCH 29TH, 2002, 6:02 A.M., LOCAL TIME, NORTH ARABIAN SEA

Derek kept his HH-60H at 120 knots, 40 feet off the water. A second HH-60H flew in right echelon, about 500 feet away. Their target was a freighter suspected of carrying small arms and ammunition intended to support insurgents in Iraq. U.N. sanctions forbid such imports and the freighter became a target of interest when it left the North Korean port of Wonsan.

The vessel, *M.V. Hibiscus*, took a circuitous route to avoid detection and interception. Their intelligence brief showed where the ship was loaded, but before the Navy could intercept and seize *Hibiscus*, it disappeared into the vastness of the Pacific and now the Indian Ocean.

M.V. Hibiscus was spotted the day before by a French Atlantique maritime patrol aircraft operating out of Réunion, a French Department approximately 420 miles east of Madagascar. Surveillance was turned over to American Navy P-3s flying from the island of Diego Garcia in the British Indian Ocean Territory which monitored *Hibiscus'* progress. The *Aegis*-class cruiser *U.S.S. San Jacinto* (CG-56) was dispatched from the battle group with two of HSC-8s HH-60Hs along with flight crews and 10 enlisted along with 16 SEALs. Their mission was to stop, search, and if necessary, seize *Hibiscus*.

San Jacinto was selected because its hangar could accommodate two SH-60s and one could be tied down on the flight deck with its blades spread, ready to launch. The SEALs had been flown out to *Stennis,* and when he heard about the mission, Derek volunteered to lead the helicopter detachment designated HSC-8 Det 100.

Before they deployed to *San Jacinto*, both crews practiced swooping down on the supply ship accompanying the task force and letting the eight SEALs fast rope onto the deck. The crew reduced the evolution – flare the helicopter, toss out the rope and the eight SEALs sliding down to the deck – to 15 seconds.

The battle group's intelligence officers believed *Hibiscus* would attempt to slip through the Straits of Hormuz early in the evening, emerge into the Persian Gulf during darkness, and then hide amongst the thousands of ships in the gulf as it ran for the Iraqi port of Um Qasr. Their job was to seize it long before it reached the Straits of Hormuz.

"Hammer Nine, Retro Seven Zero."

Vera Hotchkiss was Derek's co-pilot. She was behind Derek at HS-10 and met the *Stennis* when it arrived in Hawaii for its Operational Readiness Inspection. At first, she was overwhelmed and didn't do well in the ASW world, so she was pawned off on Ritchie. Between Derek and Ritchie's tutoring, Lieutenant Junior Grade Vera Hotchkiss became a stellar 2P and now was about to become an aircraft commander. Vera got the call sign "Tapper" because when she was impatiently waiting for an answer to a question, she'd tap the ground with her right foot.

"Retro, go." Vera was being salty. Hammer Nine was the call sign assigned to Derek's helicopter for this mission. Hammer Ten was his wingman. Both helicopters were monitoring the frequency but Hammer Ten would only transmit if required.

"Bozo is on your nose at twelve nautical. No emissions other than its surface search radar which is turned on for about two minutes to get a radar picture and then turned off."

Vera clicked her mike twice.

"Hammer Nine, Big Chief Actual says mission is a go. Good luck."

Two more clicks. Big Chief Actual was the call sign of the admiral commanding the task force.

Vera turned her head to look aft at Lieutenant Junior Grade Nicholas Connor who graduated from Norwich in the same class as Derek. Petty officer Grayson keyed his mike. "Ready in the back."

Twenty-six miles to the east, *San Jacinto* was ploughing through the aqua-blue waters of the Indian Ocean at 20 knots. In the chair on the right side of the captain in the ship's combat information center was a Coast Guard lieutenant. On the left was a Navy JAG officer who specialized in maritime law. Both were required to provide law at sea expertise to ensure that the Navy followed maritime law regarding seizing ships in international waters that were carrying contraband.

Derek and Connor's SEALs were about to execute what was known in the Navy as a Visual Board, Search, and Seizure (VBSS) operation. The seizure would only come if there was contraband on the ship.

In the growing light, Derek could see *Hibiscus* moving through the water at what looked like its reported speed, 12 knots. He adjusted the heading so the two helicopters would approach from the stern. While Hammer Nine was unloading its eight SEALS, call sign Pancake, Hammer Ten would provide cover with its M-60 machine guns and attempt to contact the ship on the VHF frequencies it should be monitoring. Once Derek pulled out, they would exchange roles and Hammer Ten would let the second group of SEALs fast rope onto the merchant ship.

Photos of *Hibiscus* showed an open area over the hatches in the middle of the ship where he could hover to let the SEALs fast rope down. They had been practicing hovering 60 feet above the deck with a rope 100 feet long. Once the last SEAL was on the deck, Grayson would let the rope fall onto *Hibiscus* rather than let it hang and risk catching it on the freighter's rigging as the helicopter departed the hover.

Coming from *Hibiscus'* stern, when the nose of Derek's HH-60H passed the stern of the freighter on the port side, he hauled back on the cyclic and pushed down on the collective. The helicopter groaned and vibrated as it decelerated from 120 knots to less than 10. A little bank and push of the left rudder and the HH-60 entered a hover between the cranes and masts amidships on *Hibiscus*.

In his headset, as he was flaring the helicopter, he heard, "*Hibiscus, Hibiscus,* this is the U.S. Navy. We suspect you are carrying cargo in violations of U.N. sanctions. Stop and heave to. Repeat, stop, and heave to so we can board your ship."

A stream of tracers zipped across the front of Derek's HH-60H. He sensed the weight of the helicopter reducing as the eight SEALS, each weighing about 200 pounds went down the rope. Behind him he heard the clattering of the M-60 fired by AW1 Grayson. "SEALs away!!! Rope's away!!! Let's go!!!!"

Derek dumped the nose and pulled up on the collective just has he heard a series of dull thwacks. The yellow master caution light came. "Tapper, talk to me."

"Stand by, boss, am trying to figure out what we have and don't have."

"Boss, keep us alongside so we can help the SEALS." Grayson's voice was made harder to understand by the rattling of his M-60."

Derek banked the helicopter so it was parallel to *Hibiscus* and so he could watch the firefight on the deck. A man came out on the wing of the bridge and started firing a PKM machine gun at his helicopter. Rounds thwacked into the helicopter and two hit the armored sides of Derek's seat before the shooter was cut down by a burst from Grayson's M-60.

A glance at the instrument panel showed the master caution lights on, but the helicopter was flying normally. "Vera, talk to me." When Derek didn't receive an answer, he looked and saw her slumped over, coughing up blood. The side of her flight suit was already dark with her blood. "Grayson, Tapper is hit. See what you can do for her."

Keeping the helicopter straight and level to let Grayson get his co-pilot out of her seat gave Derek time to look at the caution and advisory panel. Caution lights made up the top two thirds of the panel and the ones showing "pitot heat failure," "main rotor de-ice failure," "ice detection system failure" glowed bright red. In the lower third, the yellow advisory lights showing the cargo hook was armed and the engine inlet ice detection systems were on. None of them were critical to staying airborne so Derek pushed the reset button on the top center of the instrument panel and the lights went out.

Before he climbed between the seats, unstrapped the 110-pound woman, pulled her into the cabin and began triage, Grayson turned his M-60 over to Hambleton who kept firing short bursts from his M-60 to provide cover for the SEALs on *Hibiscus*.

During the training command, in an emergency, Derek was taught to aviate first, then navigate, and when you have it all sorted out, communicate. More thwacks and more warning lights came on telling him that the #2 hydraulic system was showing zero pressure and the #2 generator was offline. Engine and transmission oil temperatures and pressures were all normal; however, the #2 engine was, according to the torque gauge, only developing about 80% of the power of the #1.

"Hammer Nine, Bozo is secure. We have three casualties, beginning search, need MEDEVAC."

"Hambleton, how's Tapper?"

"Sir, she's in a bad way, but I have her stabilized. We need to get her to a doctor, ASAP."

"Hammer Ten, can you pick up the casualties. I've got one on board who needs a doctor, ASAP."

"Roger that!"

"Hammer Nine, this is Trout 5. We're about five minutes out and can provide gunfire support. Suggest you RTB Lone Star."

Trout 5 was the *San Jacinto*'s SH-60B. As his HH-60H crossed the stern of *Hibiscus*, Derek could see *San Jacinto*, less than two miles away. "Grayson, Hambleton, stick your heads out the side and tell me what we're leaking. I suspect, if we land, we're going to be hard down so I want to stay turning and burning for as long as we can."

"Hammer Nine, Retro Seven Zero Zero, this is Pancake One Actual. The holds of this puppy are full of weapons, ammo. There was a small platoon of about 25 Republican Guards on board. Eleven are dead, four are wounded, the rest, along with the crew are prisoners."

"Roger, this is Retro Seven Zero Zero, we'll pass the info on to Big Chief."

"Mr. Almer, we're bleeding hydraulic fluid down both sides along with some oil. Sir, I'd recommend shutting her down so we can see what all the damage is."

"Roger that."

"Hammer Nine, Lone Star, you have a ready deck, medical team standing by."

Derek landed gently on the cruiser's helicopter deck. Before he shut the engines and rotors down, four men lifted Vera onto a stretcher and with Grayson holding the IV bottles, headed into the hangar and the cruiser's small dispensary."

Quickly, Derek went through the shutdown check list and pulled the rotor break to stop the rotors. "Hambleton, get the guys to fold the blades so we can pull the helo into the hangar. We don't want to foul this deck any longer than we have too."

He was about to toss the checklist onto the co-pilot's seat when he noticed it was covered in Vera's blood. In a maintenance space just forward of the helicopter hanger, he found a role of paper towels that he used to wipe up as much blood as he could.

After dumping the blood-soaked paper towels into a nearby trashcan, Derek asked a petty officer wearing a *San Jacinto* ball cap where the dispensary was. The sailor said follow me. When Derek asked why all the men were lined up in the passageway, he was told they were standing by to donate blood.

Hammer Ten made two trips to bring wounded to the *San Jacinto* before it too shut down. Derek counted 32 bullet holes in Hammer Nine, most were in the overhead around the engines and transmission. The generator took two bullets, one that knocked off the wire connecting it to the airplane's electrical system. The #1 hydraulic fluid reservoir was emptied when three bullets destroyed its integrity. By contrast, Hammer 10 was hit by only nine bullets, none of which did any damage other than punch holes in the helicopter's skin.

Derek went back to the helicopter and stared at the boron epoxy slab that protected his hips, side, and shoulders that was hit by four 7.62mm from either a PKM or an AK-47. His examination found where a fifth bullet grazed the back of his seat and slammed into Vera's seat. Another glanced off the armor and from the blood spatter, he determined it went into her side.

"Sir, Miss Hotchkiss is out of surgery." Derek turned to see AW1 Grayson who was wearing a bloody surgical gown. His watch said it had been an hour and a half since he landed on *San Jacinto*.

He didn't have to ask the next question.

"Her left lung is fucked up, but eventually she should be fine. Doctor says she may need more surgery, but she'll live unless something unusual happens. We're going to keep her here in a stateroom until we can transfer her to the *Stennis*. Hambleton and I will watch her. You sir, need to go write an after-action report on a very successful op."

Derek nodded numbly and headed aft to get the input from the others on the raid. In his mind, with two SEALs and Vera wounded, it was a high price to pay for a ship full of small arms.

SATURDAY, MARCH 30TH, 2002, 7:43 P.M. LOCAL TIME. GUANGZHOU

It had been almost a month and a half since Bojing died and Senior Investigator Lieu had been turning up the pressure, insisting Bao ask

Jun out on a date. So far, he refused, more importantly, he believed Jun wasn't interested. He wasn't going to ask until he was sure she was ready to date him or someone else.

Bao suspected Lieu was very interested in the secret work that Jun and the new Level 3 biolab was performing. It was information Lieu could use. In a society where information was power, tidbits of juicy information could be used to remove a rival and possibly send the person to a re-education camp or prison. Lieu's suspicion that Jun was a traitor was just the excuse to pressure Dr. Gu.

To have something concrete to report other than Jun's polite refusal of his offers for meeting anywhere outside work, Bao decided to take a bolder step. He would knock on her door late in the afternoon thinking all Jun could do is say no.

When Jun and Bojing were married, Bojing was entitled to married quarters on the air base, but there was a waiting list and the base was an hour or more by bus from the institute. They elected to stay in Jun's apartment and Bojing rode his Jianshe 150cc motorcycle back and forth to work.

After they were married, Jun learned to ride the bike just as she learned to drive a car when she lived in the U.S. She hadn't ridden the bike since Bojing was killed and hadn't decided what to do with it. As she was changing into a pair of jeans, she saw the two helmets on top of the armoire they bought to hang his uniforms in. Now, it was mostly filled with her clothes.

Seeing the helmets, and with the nice weather outside, Jun thought it would be a good day to ride the bike around Houlushan Forest Park. It would something to do that was different.

Living in the U.S., Jun was familiar with U.S. motorcycle practices and insisted that Bojing buy the best helmets they could afford and wear boots. The protective clothing that was readily available in the U.S. was, if one could find it, very expensive in Guangzhou.

Jun was tying her shoulder-length hair into a ponytail so it would fit comfortably under the Shoei full face helmet she insisted they buy when she heard the doorbell ring. Not expecting anyone, Jun finished tying her hair.

"Who is it"

"Bao Gu."

Jun stopped, took a deep breath before cracking open the door. "This is a surprise. Is something happening at the institute?"

"No, I just wanted to see how you were doing."

Jun hesitated and then opened the door a bit more. Bao Gu was the only "friend" she had at the institute. Other than her mother, Bojing and his parents, and Bao, Jun knew no one in Guangzhou. How to begin a "social" life was one of the things on her mind. She was a widow after just a few months of marriage. How does her newly changed social status figure into what she does next? When should she start dating? How does she meet a man?

"It has been a rough few weeks but I am fine." *My mother has been a big help. She's the happiest I've seen her in memory.* Jun opened the door. "Bao, please come in. My flat is a mess and I was on my way out."

Bao nodded and stopped just a few feet inside Jun's apartment. Seeing the helmet, Bao asked, "Do you have a motorcycle?"

"My late husband did and he taught me how to ride it. I was just going out for a ride."

"What kind of motorcycle do you have?"

"Jianshe 150. Bojing said it was based on a Japanese Yamaha design and that Yamaha had invested in Jianshe."

"Oh, interesting." Bao Gu knew nothing about cars or motorcycles. Until he became a doctor, he could afford neither. Now he had enough money, but before he could drive a car, he'd have to learn how.

Trying to be sociable, Jun offered, "Would you like a beer or some tea?"

"A beer would be nice."

Jun went to the refrigerator, popped the lids off two dark brown bottles of Zhuijiang beer. "Do you like to drink from a bottle or from a glass?"

"Bottle."

Jun handed him the bottle and then expertly poured hers into a glass so that there was an inch of foam at the top. She held up her glass and said, "Friends!"

Bao did the same and said the same word.

Pointing to the couch, Bao sat at one end and Jun sat in a chair that was perpendicular to the couch. She pulled her legs up under her butt. "So what really brings you to my door in the middle of a Saturday afternoon?"

In other words, besides checking up on me, Bao what do you want?

"Invite you to a dinner. You've turned down having lunch with me."

"Bao, I like you, but I am not ready to date. I need more time."

"How about a lunch at work with just the two of us? Pick a day."

Jun thought that was harmless enough. She responded by saying, "Ask me after the Monday morning staff meeting." They talked for a few more minutes and when Bao finished his beer, he left. He would let Inspector Lieu know that his task of getting Jun to agree to a date had been accomplished.

SATURDAY, APRIL 20ᵀᴴ, 2002, 8:26 P.M. LOCAL TIME, GUANGZHOU

On average, April is the fifth rainiest month in Guangzhou, when on average, 231 mm (~9 inches) of rain falls. Senior Professor of Economics at Sun Yat-Sen University An Wu popped open a large umbrella as soon as she opened the cab's door while trying to keep dry. She was only partly successful as she reached into the car for Liang Lín's hand. The umbrella moved off-center and both women laughed as the rain wet their hair.

The two women walked into the apartment complex where many of the school's senior staff lived. They were headed to the eighth-floor apartment of the head of the university's International Business School.

An and Liang met when they were forced to attend re-education classes. Both had been "re-habilitated," both were 55, and both were widows – An at age 38, and Liang at 52. An's husband was an PLA Air Force pilot whose PRC copy of the Soviet MiG-17 known as the

Shenyang J-5, came apart in mid-air during a practice dogfight. A design defect in the fighter's fuselage known to the Soviet designers caused his fighter to come apart in certain, high g maneuvers.

As the pair waited at the elevator, Liang asked, "Tell me again who is going to be here?"

"Women with similar interests."

An was referring to the novels – *Price of Salt* by Patricia Highsmith, *Nightwood* by Djuna Barnes, and Jane Bowles' *Two Serious Ladies* – she saw on Liang's desk one day she stopped by to see if she wanted to meet for dinner.

"I'll bet you'll know a half a dozen people."

Liang nodded and said nothing. She had mixed feelings but agreed to go with An. If nothing else, to meet women with the same desires she had. Long before Ai died, she had started reading novels, forbidden to most Chinese, with lesbians as the major characters. She borrowed them from Daiyu Zhu who had an extensive collection in a locked room in the university's library. It was an open secret to everyone but the commissars that the illegal books were there.

There were, by Liang's estimation, about 30 women in what she guessed was a 100 square meter (1,076 square feet) apartment. An believed there were over 100 lesbians and just as many, if not more, gay men on the university staff of several thousand. Technically, homosexuality was a crime in the PRC, but the police didn't prosecute a man or woman for their sexual preference unless another crime had been committed. Then, homosexuality was another charge they could pile on.

An was right. Besides Daiyu whom she believed was bi, Liang knew, by her last count, eight women she thought might be gay.

Tables and chairs were pushed aside in the living room to make room for couples to dance. An slid her hand into Liang's and led her to the floor where they found some space.

As they danced, neither woman said anything. Liang felt her pulse racing and her heart beating with excitement. Both increased by an order of magnitude when An pulled her close and gently kissed Liang on the lips.

"An, are you trying to seduce me?"

"Do you want to be seduced by me?"

"I do, very much so."

An French kissed Liang and when they came up for air, she whispered, "That makes me very happy." She pulled Liang closer so their bodies were touching breast and thigh. An again kissed the woman she wanted to make love to ever since she learned Liang became a widow.

SATURDAY, MAY 25ᵀᴴ, 2002, 9:18 P.M. LOCAL TIME, GUANGZHOU

The rain had stopped, leaving behind cool 22⁰ Celsius (about 70⁰ Fahrenheit) with almost oppressive 90 percent humidity. To Jun, it didn't matter. She'd spent the afternoon primping and prepping for her dinner date with Bao.

She decided to dress as if she was going out in San Diego rather than Guangzhou for no other reason but to send a message that she wasn't a traditional Chinese woman.

Some CCP commissars would frown on her bright red mid-thigh skirt, not for its color, but for its length. The party encouraged Chinese women to dress conservatively, not provocatively. A mid-thigh miniskirt was borderline. She wore a white blouse opened so one could see her cleavage and from the right angle, the white bra. All her good clothes were bought in Bloomingdales or Nordstroms before she left San Diego.

When Bao opened the door, he smiled as he took in the woman who could have been a model. "You are truly beautiful."

"Thank you. You're quite good-looking for an older man." Bao was four years older and laughed.

After a leisurely dinner, they were sitting on Bao's couch facing each other sipping glasses of locally made baijiu, a liquor made from glutinous rice. Bao decided that this was the moment. He slid his hand into Jun's who responded by squeezing.

Gently, Bao pulled and Jun slid closer so their faces were only two feet apart. Something in Jun's eyes told Bao, Yes, and their faces slowly closed the gap until their lips touched and pulled apart. Then they were together in a passionate series of kisses. Bao pulled Jun close and after a few more kisses, Jun pulled away.

After a few minutes of breathing heavily and looking at Bao, Jun rested her head on the immunologist's shoulder letting Bao stroked the back of her head. Bao whispered, "Jun, I have been wanting to kiss you since we first met. I am sorry if I offended you, but I can't keep my hands off you."

Jun looked up and they French kissed deeply. "I am not offended." She didn't say what was on her mind and that was she felt stirrings in her loins that she never felt with Bojing.

Bao leaned forward so they could kiss. When they stopped, he stood and held out his hands. Jun took them and they looked at each other for a few moments before Bao saw what he thought was a slight nod.

Bao looked into Jun's eyes as he took both of Jun's hands into hers and said, "Jun, if you feel uncomfortable, tell me to stop."

Jun bowed her head obsequiously as if to say, "I am yours."

The next morning, the smell of spicy diced pork steamed buns and a bowl of rice porridge woke Jun. She sat up in bed as Bao put the tray with the two dishes and a cup of green tea on her lap. Jun made no attempt to pull up the sheets to cover her naked body.

During the night, at a pause in their lovemaking, Bao told Jun about Daiyu Zhu and how he made it through medical school. Deliberately, he left out the incident in the park in which he killed his two attackers and Senior Inspector Lieu's pressure. Some would call it coercion, others blackmail.

Then he told her that when first arrived at the Guangzhou Institute of Biomedicine and Health, he dated a radiologist. The relationship lasted until early 2001 when the woman was sure she was dying of radiation-caused ovarian cancer. The two slipped into the radiology lab and disassembled their Chinese made X-ray machines and found no lead shielding in the machines or in the walls.

When Bao went to Senior Administrator Siew, his answer was he will submit a report. Someone, Siew assured the dying woman, will be punished.

No one, to Bao's knowledge, was ever arrested and the machines, still without the necessary shielding, are still being used although Siew managed to procure lead lined aprons for the X-ray technicians who were only allowed to use the machine twice a week.

When he made eye contact with Jun the first time on Lieu's insistence, Bao was hopeful that the new virologist was a kindred soul. Senior Investigator Lieu told him that Jun was educated in America, which made the woman all that more interesting.

Later, when Bao heard that Jun was going to marry Bojing, he sensed that Jun was playing the role of a dutiful wife but was not happy. And now, Bao said, the woman of his dreams just spent the night with him.

Both the tale about the woman radiologist and his pursuit of Jun were close to the truth. Senior Investigator Lieu ordered Bao to seduce the radiologist who was suspected of anti-party activities. She was not. All the woman wanted was to ensure that the X-ray machines were safe.

As Jun ate, Bao slid a hand underneath the sheets to caress Jun's thigh, who put her hand on top of his, "Stop. I am famished so let me eat."

Bao sat on the edge of the bed smiling as Jun devoured the meal. He took the tray back to the kitchen. Back in the bedroom, Bao knelt on the bed in front of Jun and reached for her hands, not quite sure of what she should say.

Jun said what was on her mind. "Bao, I feel wonderful. Never have I enjoyed so much pleasure."

"So, you are not upset with me?"

Jun shook her head vigorously. She reached for Bao's penis. "Oh no, I want to make love to you again and again. But if we become steady lovers, it will be complicated."

"I think not. There are no institute rules about doctors dating doctors if one of does not report to the other."

Jun leaned forward and kissed Bao. It led to another round of lovemaking.

TUESDAY, MAY 28ᵀᴴ, 2002, 9:36 A.M. LOCAL TIME, SAN DIEGO

Adrian sensed a fair amount of infidelity in the squadron and that it was on both sides. Some HSC-8 husbands were not faithful nor were some of the squadron's wives.

Juanita Huerta warned Adrian that this was a sensitive topic and to broach it with care since either side might not want to hear the answer. Ultimately, Adrian decided that what other spouses did while their husbands were on cruise was none of her business.

In their daily emails back and forth, Derek had given her what he called "air cover" for not participating in every one of the squadron wives club events. He agreed that good grades in law school were more important but also asked that she make an appearance "at least once a month to the weekly squadron wives' lunch."

At the end of the year, Adrian finished #2 in her class and had registered for the summer session, eager to complete more courses and finish law school as fast as she could. Driving to NAS North Island to await the fly-in of the squadron's helicopters, she welcomed the thought of no longer being a "cruise wife" and having someone to talk to in the evening and weekends. Maybe, it was Derek's skill and knowing what buttons to push that made her body and mind miss him so. Only time, she thought, would tell.

The wives along with the base commander and a man Juanita Huerta pointed out was Commander, Helicopter Wing Pacific, stood in the shade of the hangar. The 12 helicopters, including the one shot up, had launched 150 miles out and were due any minute.

"Excuse me, are you Adrian Almer?"

Adrian turned to see an attractive woman in uniform wearing a pair of wings. She nodded not quite knowing what to say.

"Hi, my name is Vera Hotchkiss. I was Derek's co-pilot when we took down *Hibiscus*."

Bells went off in Adrian's head. This was the woman who Derek was circumspect in giving her details from the operation, but somewhat graphic about the aftermath. He did say she was very attractive and Derek was right. Adrian held out her hand. "So, you're Tapper!!! I am so glad to meet you and am glad you are all right."

Vera took the offered hand. "I'm on the mend and hope to get back to flying. Racer always talks about you. How is law school?"

Adrian noticed that Vera used Derek's call sign, not his first name. The pilots all did it and she thought it was odd, but in a way, very cool. Call signs were assigned and when they were awarded, it was another indication that you were a member of a very exclusive club. "Good. I managed to survive the first year."

"I hear there is lots of memorization."

The sound of helicopters stopped conversations as the women and children searched the sky to the west. HSC-8 arrived in three flights of four, with the four HH-60Hs last. Each helicopter peeled off, landed and taxied in. Juanita had asked that the women and children wait until the helicopters shut down their rotors before running out to meet their loved ones.

That was a pipe dream. Before the rotors stopped and the shutdown checklists were completed, wives and children were running across the concrete ramp. Thankfully, all were smart enough to stay outside of the slowing rotors.

Adrian thought Derek was going to crush her ribs because he held her so tight. "God, I missed you so much."

"Me too."

They rode home in her Volvo S80 that was a graduation present from her father. Derek only had a few things in a bag since he planned to go aboard *Stennis* after it docked at North Island and bring his "stuff" home.

Clothes were needed until he closed the door to the apartment and they started kissing and pawing each other. Sex, raw, hungry sex was in the air. Talk about what to do next, i.e. buy a house, law school, and their life together would come later.

SUNDAY, JUNE 2ND, 2002, 10:02 A.M. LOCAL TIME, GUANGZHOU

Liang Lín inserted the key in the lock to her daughter's apartment hoping to surprise her with a box of her favorite breakfast pastries. She stepped inside and didn't hear any sounds. Knowing her daughter's preference to sleep in on Sundays, Liang put the pastries on the table before walking toward the bedroom.

Before pushing the partially closed bedroom door open, Liang softly called out. "Jun?"

Fearing the worst, she said her daughter's name a second time, a little more loudly. Still no answer. Fear rose in her gut thinking that maybe Jun was seriously ill or had been robbed and injured or worse, had committed suicide, she pushed open the door.

The scene in front of her made her stop, speechless. Her daughter and a man were sound asleep, with their arms and legs entwined and their naked bodies partly covered by a sheet.

Liang started to back out of the room, surprised but not shocked. Jun was young, beautiful, smart, well-educated and being a young widow, very eligible.

Jun lifted her head, using her hand to shield her eyes, "Mother what are you doing here?"

"I brought you some pastries, but I see you have another dessert."

Jun nodded and then let her throbbing head plop down on the pillow. Bao and she had gone out to a new club in Guangzhou. They drank and danced, sometimes apart, but mostly holding each other close, enjoying being what they were, lovers. Then, when they returned, they made love and Jun remembered glancing at the clock after the last time. The numbers said it was 3:34.

"Mother, I'll be right out."

Jun kissed Bao on the forehead saying, "We have a visitor. You can stay here, I'll get up."

"Who is it?"

"My mother."

"Does she know?"

"Yes. I told her that I was dating someone, just not who."

"Jun, my head is pounding."

"Mine too. Too much baijiu."

Bao nodded and then made a face. The bright sunlight added to the pain of moving his head. "Do you have aspirin?"

"Yes. We both need some."

Jun tossed a robe around her shoulders and tied the belt. It did little to hide her naked breasts.

In the kitchen, Liang was making tea and instead of cheongsam with a flowered print, she was wearing a dark gray skirt that ended just above her knees. Ever since Liang started seeing An, Jun though her 55-year-old mother looked and acted years younger.

Liang served the tea and put the pillow shaped buns on a plate. Jun could smell the mix of garlic and hot red peppers as it was handed to her.

Bao padded out in his bare feet as Jun as shook out white aspirin – two for her, two for Bao who had pulled on his shirt and underpants. He groaned as he sat down.

"Mother Lín, this is Dr. Bao Gu."

"I think we have met before."

"We have. Jun and I work together. I am the head of the immunology department at the institute."

Liang served a glass of tea and a bun to Bao. "Eat, eat. Sex makes you hungry."

Jun exclaimed. "Mother!!!"

"Well, it does. How long have you been lovers?" Not dating but fucking. Liang always got to the most important point first.

"March 30th of this year." Meaning almost three months after Bojing was killed.

"Who seduced who?"

Bao, who was holding his head in a futile attempt to mitigate the pounding, raised his hand. "I wanted to date Jun as soon as I saw her the first time when she reported to the institute." Nothing more was said while the doctors sipped their tea and swallowed the aspirin.

Liang walked around the table to pour more tea into Bao's cup and to get the box with the remaining three buns. Sitting back down, Liang looked at her daughter and then at Bao, nodding before speaking. "I am glad you now have a social life."

CHAPTER 13

HEROES

From the living room window of Bao's apartment, Jun pointed to the column of black smoke in the general direction of the institute. Bao thought the column came from one of the businesses near where they worked. They were, he said, always catching fire.

Neither worried where fire might be until they were a kilometer from the Guangzhou Institute of Biomedicine and Health complex. The stench from burning chemicals, wood, paint, and other materials became stronger the closer they came. Two hundred meters from the institute's entrance, they were stopped by policemen who had set up a barricade to keep spectators a safe distance. They showed their badges to the policemen who let them through.

Jun became more anxious when she saw the fire was in the building where the new Level 3 lab was located. Despite the water being poured into the building, flames and smoke were still coming out of the sixth floor and the structure from the third floor up was darkened by smoke.

Seeing Jun and Bao, Dr. Ng stopped them. "Stay here, you can't go any farther and there is nothing you can do."

"The lab?"

"Gone. Destroyed."

"What about all the records?"

"Gone. I've already checked. The back-ups were kept in a cabinet in the basement because the Ministry of State Security didn't want anyone outside the lab to have access to the lab's files."

Bao slipped his arms around Jun and pulled her close as he whispered in her ear. "This is not your fault. The lab can be rebuilt. It just takes time and money. You have the time and this country has the money."

She watched as firefighters set up pumps with pick-ups in the basement to start "dewatering" the building. Out of the hoses, dirty black water flowed onto the grounds and then into the street. Horrified, Jun turned to Dr. Ng.

"We don't know what is in that water. There are virus and bacteriological samples that could have morphed into lord knows what! That water could contaminate everything around here."

Dr. Ng grabbed her by the shoulders. "That, Dr. Lín, is not your concern. If anyone is to blame, it is the fire chief who ordered the pumps put in place not knowing what is in the water. I suggest, at least for the moment, you keep quiet. Without records to document what was in the lab, it will be very difficult to convince anyone to do anything."

Clenching her teeth, Jun hissed. "Mark my words, Dr. Ng, soon, those who touch this water or were downwind will soon be at the institute's doors."

The head of the virology lab glared at his deputy. "Dr. Lín, again, this is not your concern. This is not the United States where people are held accountable. This is China where the Party cannot be made to look bad or be blamed for anything. Doing so causes our leaders to lose face and challenges the party's supremacy. So, remember the Chinese proverb, he who cheats the earth will be cheated by the earth."

Translation, screw with Mother Nature or in this case the CCP and she will bite you back, even kill you.

By noon, the fire was proclaimed out and the firemen were coiling their hoses. Their job was done. Seeing Dr. Ng and Senior Administrator Siew together, Jun approached the two men. "Senior Administrator, may I recommend something in the aftermath of this fire."

Siew nodded as if to say continue.

"Sir, I strongly suggest that you recommend to the head inspector who will look for a cause of this fire, to wear heavy rubber boots and not touch or pick up anything unless they are wearing thick rubber gloves."

Siew glanced at Dr. Ng who Jun saw nod slightly. "Good idea doctor, I will do that. Do you have any other recommendations?"

"Yes, allow Dr. Ng and I onto the lab floor as soon as possible. We will dress in suits so we do not breathe any of the fumes."

"Would you suggest that to the fire inspectors as well."

"I would."

"Do we have any of those suits?"

"We do. Dr. Gu has some in the immunology lab."

Siew walked toward the fire chief. From a distance, Jun watched the animated dialogue and Siew came back. "The fire chief understands your concerns and he will take his normal precautions. No one other than his men will be allowed in the building until it is declared safe."

"Does he know what was on the fourth, fifth, and sixth floors?"

"No and I didn't tell him since he is not cleared."

Jun's eyes got wide and she felt a man's hand slip into hers and squeeze hard. "Then, Senior Administrator Siew, we wait. Dr. Ng and I will tell our staff to stay at home until we sort out where they will work."

Siew nodded once. Her recommendation saved him from a decision that could come back to haunt him. "Approved."

Drs. Lín and Gu walked back to Jun's apartment. As soon as they were inside, she looped her arms around Bao's neck and whispered, "We have all afternoon and I want to show you how much I like you."

Exhausted, Jun fell asleep and didn't hear Bao making phone calls. When she came out, Jun asked who he was calling as she hugged Bao from behind. He smiled when she said, "No one you would want to meet."

Jun slid her hand down Bao's chest to his groin as she kissed the back of her lover's neck. Bao turned around, stood up, and led the woman he wanted to the bedroom. He had no idea what to tell Senior Investigator Lieu about the fire and the chance that Dr. Lín could be re-assigned outside Guangzhou.

FRIDAY, JUNE 28ᵀᴴ, 2002, 9:46 A.M. LOCAL TIME, NAS NORTH ISLAND

Derek knew it was a big ask for Adrian to come to the ceremony, but he insisted. Her finals for the two courses she was taking in summer school were Monday and Tuesday and she didn't want to take a morning away from studying.

When he described the event as one part inspection, one part awards ceremony, and one part change of command, Adrian realized its importance and asked, since this was the first of its kind she would attend, what to wear. All Derek could say was wear something presentable, so Adrian called Gavin Ritchie's wife Quy who said wear a dress, but don't overdo it with jewelry.

On the way over, Adrian asked if Derek was receiving a medal. Truthfully, he said, "I don't know. Normally, the outgoing CO is given a medal, usually a Legion of Merit if he had a good tour."

For the officers and chief petty officers of HSC-8, the uniform was Full Dress White, a.k.a. chokers with gloves, swords, and large medals. For E-6 (petty officer first class and below) the uniform was known as "cracker jack white" because it and the blue version was on the box of the molasses flavored popcorn from 1919 until the beginning of the 21ˢᵗ Century.

Adrian was ushered to a seat directly in front of the platform in HSC-8s hangar. Behind the platform, a washed and polished HH-60H and an SH-60F were parked nose to nose with their cabin doors closed. The pamphlet handed to Adrian as she sat next to Quy Ritchie gave the sequence of events. She was surprised that there was only one speech and according to the program, the Commander, Naval Air Forces, Pacific – a three-star admiral – was going to speak for only 10 minutes.

Quy Ritchie was one of the few wives with whom Adrian became friends. Her grandparents were "boat people" who escaped from Vietnam in the aftermath of the U.S. withdrawal in 1974 and Quy was in her second year of dental school. Since Derek's return, the Almers and Ritchies had gone out to dinner four times. Adrian liked Quy who graduated from Purdue in the same class as her husband, Gavin.

The three-star walked to the podium. His gold shoulder boards with white stars were noticeably different than the black ones with a wide and thin stripe and gold star that Derek wore. She had no idea what the medals on his uniform were, other than he had a lot.

The admiral started by saying that the men and women of HSC-8 distinguished themselves during their last deployment and it was his pleasure to award Commander Huerta the Legion of Merit in recognition of his leadership. Then he started reading off names and one by one, the men and women filed up onto the stage. The admiral announced the award, pinned the medal on the man or woman's uniform and saluted. The individual returned the salute, was given the box for the medal and the folder with the citation and certificate.

Still no Derek.

The admiral looked over the squadron. Then he read off five names – Lieutenant Gavin Ritchie; Lieutenant Junior Grade Derek Almer; Lieutenant Junior Grade Vera Hotchkiss; Helicopter Rescue Swimmer First Class Anthony Grayson; and Helicopter Rescue Swimmer Third Class Donald Hambleton, front and center.

"It is my pleasure to present the Distinguished Flying Cross to Lieutenant Ritchie for the medical evacuation flight that saved the lives of sixteen French sailors. Lieutenant Ritchie and his crew, three of whom are on this platform, were in the air for eleven hours. Not only did they carry the injured sailors to *Stennis*, but Petty Officer Grayson assisted Doctor David Zelen in a makeshift operating room, saving the life of a French sailor. Congratulations Lieutenant Ritchie. Petty Officer Grayson is being awarded a Navy Commendation Medal and Petty Officer Hambleton, a Navy Achievement Medal for their roles in the mission." The admiral paused and waited until the applause ended before saying, "Lieutenant Ritchie, dismissed."

Ritchie left the platform and Lieutenant Junior Grade Vera Hotchkiss replaced him and joined Derek and the crew that helped the SEALS seize *M. V. Hibiscus* standing in front of the three-star admiral.

"Distinguished guests, I am about present awards to these individuals who represent the finest traditions of the naval service. Crew of Hammer Nine, about FACE." In unison, the four turned 180° to face the audience and their squadron mates.

The admiral then summarized the seizure of *Hibiscus*, mostly for the civilians in the audience. Starting with the most junior person, Hambleton was awarded an Air Medal with a Single Combat V for the seizure of the freighter and a Navy-Marine Corps Life Saving Medal for the MEDEVAC of the wounded. Grayson was awarded an Air Medal with a Single Action Combat V and the Navy-Marine Corps Medal for saving Vera Hotchkiss' life.

Vera Hotchkiss was awarded an Air Medal with a combat V along with a Purple Heart. The admiral asked Vera about her recovery and she said it was going well and she hoped to remain on active duty.

"So, Lieutenant Junior Grade Almer, I'll bet you are wondering what awards you are about to receive?"

There was a murmur of chuckles and laughter from the audience. The admiral waited until the noise died down.

"It is my pleasure to present Lieutenant Junior Grade Derek Almer with the Distinguished Flying Cross for the MEDEVAC from the French frigate *Dreyfus*." He pinned the medal above the left pocket on Derek's service dress whites. The admiral waited a few seconds before saying, "It is my distinct pleasure to award Lieutenant Almer the Silver Star for his airmanship, leadership, and courage during the seizure of the merchant vessel *Hibiscus*. If it were not for him, the operation would have been more costly. He flew his helicopter which was repeatedly hit with machine gun fire close enough so that his gunners could suppress the enemy trying to stop the SEALs from seizing the ship. In the middle of the action, he saw that his co-pilot, Lieutenant Veera Hotchkiss was severely wounded. His crew pulled Lieutenant Hotchkiss into the cabin so Petty Officer Grayson could stabilize her while Petty Officer Hambleton maintained suppressive fire. Lieutenant Almer then flew his bullet-riddled helicopter back to the cruiser San Jacinto and landed safely. Bravo Zulu, Mr. Almer, and Well Done. Your actions were in keeping with the highest traditions of the naval service."

The officers and civilians who knew the Silver Star was the nation's third highest award for bravery stood up and started clapping. Adrian followed and cheered. For her, the rest was a blur. At the reception and cake-cutting ceremony, she stood next to Derek squeezing his hand as men and women came up to him to offer their congratulations. The admiral pulled him aside and said, "Racer, if you don't get the orders you want after HSC-8, call me."

As Adrian was buckling her seat belt in the GTI 16V, she turned to her husband. She found it hard to call her husband by his call sign but found herself doing it more and more. "I didn't know I was married to a real hero named Racer. I gather a Silver Star is a big deal."

Derek nodded. "Yes, Adrian, it is, especially in the Navy."

"Your emails didn't make it sound as dangerous as it was."

Derek smiled, "I didn't want to worry you."

Adrian decided Derek needed a hero's welcome as soon as they walked into their apartment. For a second, she remembered what Juanita Huerta said and wondered if this was raw sex or fucking? It was clearly above "normal" sex.

MONDAY, JULY 15TH, 2002, 2:36 P.M. LOCAL TIME, GUANGZHOU

The large meeting room in the Institute of Biomedicine and Health designed to seat 500 was unofficially called the "propaganda hall" and had extensive audio-visual equipment for presentations. Every month, the institute's staff was required to attend a lecture by a commissar on the benefits of communism. Attendance was mandatory unless one was verifiably sick. If you could not attend, one had to watch it on tape and sign a log saying you had seen it.

Those who worked in Building 4 and the Level 3 Biosafety Lab were called to a meeting by Senior Administrator Siew. The lab staff sat in a small group towards the front and apart from the others in the room.

Building 4 – the six-story structure that housed the lab - was now a smoke-stained wreck. Few windows remained and its doorways were now blocked by sheets of wood to prevent entry.

In Jun's mind, the government should demolish the building, carry away the soil and build a Level 4 lab in its place. It was an opinion she shared with Senior Administrator Siew and Senior Colonel Sun.

Right after the fire, she called Sun. He asked for a written report and recommendations so she wrote a document she classified as Top Secret since it outlined what work had been done as well as what samples, to the best of her and the staff's memory, had been lost in the fire that also destroyed the lab's records.

When it was ready, Senior Colonel Sun had a military courier pick up the report the day she called. The courier, a young captain, gave her a receipt dated July 2nd and that was the last Dr. Lín had heard.

Since the fire, Senior Administrator Siew would not provide information on where the staff who worked in Building 4 would be sent. Each day, the staff gathered in the "propaganda hall" so that attendance could be taken. There, they waited until lunch before being dismissed by Siew.

Today, the staff expected to be dismissed. However, when Siew entered, he was carried two stacks of envelopes bound by rubber bands. "Good afternoon. Finally, I have some news. The Academy of Sciences and the Party has decided to demolish Building 4. What will be built in its place has not yet been decided. What has been decided is that you will either be assigned elsewhere in the institute or to another healthcare facility or lab in Guangzhou. So, as I read your name, come get the envelope with your new assignment and instructions on how to proceed. Then you may leave."

When Siew gave the last envelope to a lab technician, the only two left in the theater were Dr. Ng and Dr. Lín. Smiling like a cat about to pounce, Siew addressed the two doctors. "There is a gentleman in my conference room waiting to tell you what the Party has decided."

Neither Jun Lín nor Jian Ng were surprised when Senior Colonel Sun stood as they entered. Siew closed the door as the PLA officer waved to the seats on the other side of the conference table.

"Well, doctors, your short vacation is over. First, Dr. Ng, you are being transferred to Beijing to a special unit on the General Staff that works for me. There are several projects on which I will be asking for your input. I want you in Beijing by the end of this month. Suitable quarters for you and your family are being located and the PLA will take care of moving your possessions. You will be promoted two levels but will not be required to wear a uniform. We have a nursing assignment in a hospital near where we believe your new apartment will be for your wife. Your wife will also receive a promotion. Printed orders and other needed documents will be delivered on Wednesday."

Jun sensed Ng tense up, but he remained passive and said nothing other than a slight nod signaling his acceptance of his new assignment. He had two boys, one four and the other six years old. His wife was a surgical nurse at the Institute. When not in school, the boys spent the day in the facilities' daycare center. Both Ng and his wife Xue were born and raised in Guangzhou and Jun suspected Xue would not like the move.

Turning to the woman at the table. "Dr. Lín, you too are going to be on my staff, but will stay here in Guangzhou since I have several tasks for you to perform. The first will be to visit Zhanjiang in Guangxi province. There has been a recent outbreak of a strain of poliomyelitis that we have not seen before. Both vaccinated and unvaccinated have become sick. Based on your doctoral thesis, this is a disease with which you are very familiar. Therefore, you are to travel to Zhanjiang, meet with the local health authorities and then determine what has happened. You are to make recommendations on what research needs to be done."

"May I ask why the PLA is involved, not the local health authorities?"

Senior Colonel Sun forced himself not to be annoyed that his order was not receiving unquestioned acceptance. "They are doing the best that they can, but I believe you have the necessary knowledge and expertise. Plus, we have many sensitive military installations in the province. A portable lab used to detect pathogens that may be used by our enemies is being deployed to an air force base outside of Zhanjiang by the PLA's biological warfare regiment. These men will be told to follow your orders. The air base commander will be instructed to support you in any way he can. He will be very interested in your work because several his airmen or their families have been affected by this outbreak."

"Senior Colonel, I thank you for your confidence in me, but I will need a full lab to isolate and identify the strain."

"I understand. Gather samples, do what you can. This is a matter of national security."

"I will do my best, but I would like to bring Doctor Gu who is an immunologist to help. He was trained as an infectious disease doctor at Sun Yat-Sen University and has taken advanced training in immunology. He would be a great help."

"Can he be trusted?"

"His files are here at the institute and I am sure Senior Administrator Siew can vouch for him as will I."

"Are you related?"

"No. He was orphaned during the Cultural Revolution and does not know of any living relatives."

"What is your relationship with Dr. Gu?"

"We are good friends. More importantly, in my view, he is a very, very competent infectious disease doctor and immunologist."

Senior Colonel Sun was tempted to as what Dr. Lín meant by "good friends," but didn't. By taking her answer at face value, it wouldn't have to go into his report and could affect her clearance for the next stages of Insidious Dragon."

He made a note on his pad. "I will consider your recommendation. In a day or so, after I review Dr. Gu's file, you will receive your travel documents, orders, and a package of information on what has been reported from Zhanjiang by both the health authorities and the Air Force and Navy."

The meeting was over and Jun looked at the clock on the wall which said it was almost two. Dr. Ng hurried home to break the news to his wife, leaving Jun alone. Bao had his last appointment at four so she decided to wait at the clinic for him to finish.

SATURDAY, JULY 20TH, 2002, 6:33 P.M. LOCAL TIME, GUANGZHOU

When Jun invited her mother for dinner, she was very circumspect about the topic, but indicated that it was about her work. Like many citizens of the PRC, Jun assumed that the Ministry of State Security could listen into any telephone conversation. Liang knew about the fire and assumed that her daughter would be reassigned to a local medical facility.

Liang stepped through the open door and, after hugging her daughter, she stepped back and spun around to give her daughter the full view of the dark green dress with gold trim around the neck, sleeves, and bottom which came to just above her knees.

"Mother, you look lovely."

"Thank you…. I'm going out after dinner. Where's Bao?"

"He'll be back soon; he is getting dessert."

Seeing the two bottles on the table, Liang picked one up, "Where did you get these?"

"They are from the Xinjiang Autonomous Region who make their wine the traditional way the Ughurs did it centuries ago. The grapes were strained through silk and then boiling water and sugar was added. The wine is fermented in clay urns until it is bottled. I tried some and it is quite nice, but a bit potent. It has a high alcohol content."

Liang pointed to the candles on the table, but no dishes or chopsticks were in front of the chairs. Normally, her daughter would have had the table set by now.

"What's for dinner? I'll set the table."

Jun took a deep breath and hoped Bao was not going to be much longer. "Chicken and shrimp in a black bean sauce. Everything is cut up; all I need to do is cook! You didn't answer my question, with whom?"

Liang feigned being cross. "Are you suddenly my mother?"

"No, mother, but I am interested in your well-being and safety."

"Let's have some wine and I'll tell you."

Jun opened the bottle and poured two glasses before handing one to her mother. Liang headed to the living room and sat on the corner of the couch. Jun sat at the opposite end as they had on many occasions when they talked.

"Jun, please listen and then ask questions."

"This is not bad news, I hope."

"No, my daughter, it is not. It is wonderful news." Liang took a sip and then a deep breath. What came out was not rehearsed, but something she'd been wanting to tell her daughter for years but didn't have the courage. Now, in a steady relationship with An Wu, she was ready.

Liang described how Ai treated her in the last decade and a half of their marriage. While she didn't gloss over the beatings, Liang didn't dwell on them. She admitted that she hoped and prayed that Ai would meet an early end and finally, her prayers were answered.

Ai had a series of affairs that Liang knew about and suspected there were more one-night flings she didn't. Liang told her daughter she could smell the other women when he made her kneel. While Ai was thinking he was humiliating Liang, she was thinking as she swallowed his seed that she was lessening the chance he would father another child.

The older woman then said she had always been curious as to what it would be like to make love to another woman. Yet, Liang didn't act for three reasons. One, she was afraid what Ai would do to her physically if he found out. Second, since homosexuality was illegal in the PRC, she was afraid he'd have her arrested and sent to a re-education camp, so she waited until he was gone. Third, she didn't know any lesbians and was afraid to ask those she thought might be gay. Now that she had been dating An Wu since last fall, she didn't think she could ever sleep with a man again.

"Mother, why didn't you tell me before?"

"You were busy. First with the lab, then the wedding, then Bojing's death. I didn't want to bother you and was afraid you would be upset."

It was time for Jun to be the parent. "Mother, one this is important and no, I am not upset. In fact, I am happy for you. Father, from what I saw when I was in high school and college, was not a nice man. I saw the bruises and you should have told me he was beating you. Maybe together we could have done something."

"No, if we tried something, you would have never been allowed to go to America."

Jun nodded and then asked, "When can I meet An?"

"How about Sunday dinner at my apartment. Bring Bao."

Jun slid across the couch and hugged her mother. "Mother, I am happy for you and love you. In the future, do not hold things like this from me."

Liang nodded and the two women embraced again.

CHAPTER 14

FIELD WORK

Derek put the top on the can of paint, covered it with a paper towel and used a mallet to tap the lid in place. The stirrer and roller he'd taken off the frame were dropped into a plastic bag.

"Done. All that is left is staining the floor and putting the three coats of polyurethane on the floors. Once it dries, we can move in."

The house they bought in Oceanside needed a major upgrade so the price was affordable to a newly promoted lieutenant. Derek insisted they buy a house they can afford on his salary and fix-it up themselves. He convinced Adrian that after she was a member of the California bar and making millions, they can either sell or rent the house if they want something bigger.

Adrian's father had offered to match whatever Derek was putting up for the down payment, but he politely refused. He was adamant that they do not accept money from either Adrian's father or take it from her trust fund. The money for the down payment on the 1,550-square-foot, three-bedroom home came from his college fund that was never spent since his ROTC scholarship covered his tuition, books, fees and room and board.

They contracted for the new cabinets and countertops in the kitchen and bathrooms which were gutted. Contractors did the work that had to be signed off certifying it met code. Everything else, Derek did in the afternoons, evenings and on weekends.

He had lots of free time to work on the house because HSC-8 was in its post-deployment standdown. Eight of the squadron's helicopters were going through major maintenance checks while four were towed across the air station to the rework facility. Flying would begin on October 1st, the first day of the new fiscal year and the beginning the pre-deployment training cycle.

In an AOM (all-officers meeting) Friday morning Commander Stan Richardson, HSC-8's new CO, said that they would deploy sometime in January 2003 again as part of Air Wing 9, but this time on the *U.S.S. Carl Vinson* (CVN-70) as part of Carrier Group Three. Richardson made Derek the squadron training officer to ensure that the lessons learned from the last cruise were incorporated in the syllabus. Richardson also wanted him to think about cross-training so that pilots would be qualified to fly both the SH-60F and the HH-60H.

Derek's well-reasoned argument that flying CSAR, special operations, and ASW required totally different mind-sets and training fell on deaf ears. Richardson wanted his aircraft commanders to be able to fly both types of missions.

"Here, you deserve this for all your good work!" Adrian interrupted his musings and handed Derek an opened bottle of Modelo Especial she took from the cooler. They tapped the bottles together, "to our new house."

"Once the polyurethane is dry, we're going to have the house professionally cleaned to get all the dust off the walls and ceilings."

Derek looked around and then sat in the folding chair next to the card table. "Good idea."

Their voices echoed in the empty house. Adrian had a written schedule of when the drapes would be hung and when the furniture and appliances would arrive. Most of the furniture in their apartment was rented and the few pieces they bought were in a storage area.

"Let's go back to the apartment, clean up, and go out for dinner. I don't feel like cooking."

Derek often kidded his wife that she had "JAP like" tendencies. By that he meant "Jewish American Princess." This time was one, and the joke flashed through his mind, "What does a JAP make for dinner? Answer, "reservations."

He was dog-tired and needed a break. At home, after a shower, Derek was toweling off when Adrian walked into the bathroom wearing nothing but a t-shirt that barely came down to her crotch, "How about a pizza delivered?"

Derek grabbed her hand and pulled her to him. Before he smothered her mouth with a kiss, he said, "Good choice."

"Pepperoni with extra cheese will be delivered in about forty minutes."

He scooped a giggling Adrian up in his arms and carried her to their bed. Derek knew what turned Adrian on and went to work.

Adrian had thick, luxurious hair that also populated her groin. When they were dating, she asked him if she should shave it, and Derek said, it was her choice. Living in California and occasionally going to the beach wearing a bikini to show of her figure, her mound of hair was, in her mind, unsightly. So, after Derek left on *Stennis*, she started shaving it and using depilatory creams to keep it hairless. Creams and lotions kept the skin soft.

Derek hurriedly pulled on a pair of running shorts and a t-shirt when he heard the doorbell ring. As he was headed for the door, Adrian called out, "I want more!!!"

He put the pizza box on the kitchen counter and was naked when he returned to the bedroom. Later, the pizza was heated in the oven and Adrian sat cross-legged on a chair at the kitchen table wearing the same Middlebury College t-shirt she had on when she came into the bathroom.

"Derek, do you like San Diego?"

"I do. Why?"

"I have mixed emotions. It is not Brookline or Boston. There's no winter, no fall with the trees changing color. Skiing is seven hours away. I can't find a deli with decent pastrami and corned beef. The bagels are average. I don't think the San Diego law school is as good as those at home, but a law degree is a law degree."

Derek had heard bits and pieces of this conversation before. "And you miss your family."

"Some of them. Ilana not so much, but the rest, yes. San Diego seems so, so …"

"New…"

"Yeah. It doesn't have the colonial charm of Boston."

"San Diego is our home. I have leave approved so we can fly to Boston for the week of Thanksgiving."

"Yeah, that will be fun." Adrian led Derek over to the couch and pushed him down so she could sit in his lap. She gently kissed him and rested her forehead on his. "My love, I don't know if I can take another deployment. It is not that you are gone, that is hard enough, but it is the fear in my gut that something bad will happen to you never goes away. At the squadron Hail and Farewell last weekend, I talked to Vera. She knows she was very lucky to have you as her HAC. But it could have been you, not her. Bullets hit your seat and you are very lucky not to have been killed."

Derek held Adrian tight and whispered. "I know…" There was not a day that went by that some aspect of that mission didn't pass through his head. "Deployments are hard on both of us. I miss you terribly when I am gone."

"Likewise. Those toys you left me aren't the real thing."

"That should make you appreciate me even more." His hand found her groin and gently caressed the smooth, soft skin. "I love this."

Adrian let one of her legs fall on the floor. "I know."

Derek leaned her back on the sofa so he could make love to Adrian again. The rationale that he was more likely to die in a car accident than in a helicopter didn't resonate with Adrian. His brain, however, did hear the alarm bells about her unhappiness in San Diego. He just didn't know what he could do about it.

MONDAY, AUGUST 19TH, 2002, 1:49 P.M. LOCAL TIME, SUIXI, GUANGDONG PROVINCE

On Saturday, the 18th, Jun and Bao went out to dinner with An and her mother. Sunday the 19th was spent finishing packing followed by a dinner at Liang's flat with An. They collapsed into bed around ten, dreading the alarm that would wake them at six a.m.

At eight a.m. sharp on Monday, again true to Senior Colonel Sun's words, a driver with a staff car took them to Baiyun Airport that had been open since the 1930s. It had been revamped several times, but according to a sign in the terminal, the old airport would be closed and the new Baiyun would open in 2004.

This was all new to Bao who had never been in an airport nor flown in an airplane before. Jun had to keep moving him along as he stopped and gawked at a world totally new to him.

Once their bags were checked, an Air China agent inspected their new internal documents and escorted them directly to the gate. Both were surprised by the special treatment but in their last call with Senior Colonel Sun, he said the PLA was now involved because the Academy of Sciences had not delivered an answer that satisfied the country's leaders. The ongoing outbreaks of polio, Senior Colonel Sun said, was now considered a threat to national security.

Also true to his word, the driver brought a package of Top-Secret documents that Senior Colonel Sun wanted them to review and a list of names they should contact once in Zhanjiang. On top of the list was Senior Colonel Aiguo Zheng, Commander of the 6th Air Brigade that flew J-11 fighters from their airfield in Suixi, a small town about 25 miles north-northwest of Zhanjiang.

The facility they were supposed visit was located about halfway between Zhanjiang and Suixi and Senior Colonel Sun was kind enough to find Jun and Bao a small, two-bedroom, furnished flat in Zhanjiang. How he managed to do that, neither knew, but they were most grateful.

The Air Force sergeant whose name tag said his last name was Pan bowed slightly as he held the door open to the staff car. It was, Jun noted, just after ten in the morning.

"Doctors, Senior Colonel General Zheng has instructed me to bring you to the airbase. There you will meet Lieutenant Colonel You Yichen, the commander of the 215th Special Services Support battalion who will explain the capabilities of his unit. After which, you will have lunch with Senior Colonel Zheng and his wife, Senior Administrator and Doctor Ting Zheng."

To move quickly through traffic, Pan occasionally turned on the blue and white lights on the dash and behind his passengers. Once out in the country, Pan cruised at 120 kilometers an hour, slowing to get around carts pulled by water buffaloes. On either side of the road, there were rice paddies and fields filled with plants. Having never been in the countryside of the People's Republic, Jun had no idea what was being grown.

Major Yichen's brief was conducted around the cluster of trucks that were on a concrete ramp located in the southeast corner of the airfield. Their labs, which were mounted on truck chassis were, Jun concluded, good enough to identify a pathogen, but not much else. What the unit did have was an inventory of protective gear and the capability to sterilize protective gear with ultraviolet light and wash off their clothing and equipment with purified water.

Next stop was the officer's mess where Senior Colonel Zheng and his wife were waiting at a table. To provide privacy, the table was set away from the others.

The Senior Colonel stood when the two doctors entered the dining room. "Dr. Gu, Dr. Lín, I am Senior Colonel Zheng, thank you for coming. This is my wife, Dr. Ting Zheng, who is the administrator of what is officially known as Special Hospital #326 which is a very well-equipped hospital and rehabilitation center."

Ting used her right hand and pushed herself awkwardly to her feet. Her left arm hung limply down and screamed polio survivor to Bao and Jun. Tea was served and Ting started on the history of what was, in her mind, a polio epidemic in southern Guangdong and neighboring Guangxi province. She described how every summer hundreds of people were stricken and the number of cases increased every year.

Twice, Dr. Zheng said, the Academy of Sciences sent teams down to investigate. Each time, the recommendation was the same, vaccinate more people. Yet, since, the number of cases grew every year at an ever-increasing rate, she was convinced vaccinations weren't the only answer.

To Jun, Dr. Zheng's words were replays of the filmed interviews she'd watched of doctors describing the polio epidemics of the 1930s, 40s and 50s. Finding an answer was why she became a microbiologist and virologist.

Conversation stopped while a waiter cleared away their appetizers and served the main courses. Dr. Zheng said that when her husband was stationed at Bailian Air Base in Guanxi province

10 years before, polio left her with a paralyzed arm and left leg that ended her career as a surgeon. When he became the commander of the 6th Fighter Regiment and stationed at Suixi, Dr. Zheng was asked if she would take over the specialized hospital.

The PRC's government, she explained, doesn't want the world to know that polio is alive and well in the republic's southern provinces so Special Hospital #326 is not on any official list of hospitals. On the 100-hectare (about 250 acres) facility, there is a 600-bed hospital along with apartments and rooms to house another 1,500. The facility has everything for those who need assistance in their daily lives, including a dining hall, a large rehabilitation facility with an indoor Olympic-size pool, an orthotics facility, a fully equipped machine shop, and a school for patients who are children.

Jun waited until Ting was finished. "How many of the hospital's patients have been vaccinated and how many have had a booster?"

"I have a team of patients working on gathering the data. My predecessor was encouraged not to keep accurate records, so we, or they, are going through every patient file. By the end of the week, they should have preliminary results so your visit is timely."

Bao asked. "Do you know if the victims are in clusters?"

Ting smiled. "That would, of course, require a map and as you know, in the People's Republic, maps are considered a state secret. So no, we have not been able to conduct an analysis to determine if the victims are in clusters."

"Are most of the patients from Zhanjiang?"

"No, we have them from all over Guangxi and southern Guangdong province."

TUESDAY, AUGUST 20TH, 2002, 10:36 A.M. LOCAL TIME, SPECIAL HOSPITAL #326

The documents given to them by Senior Colonel Sun came mostly from the National Academy of Sciences. All had been endorsed by Toghon Tang. Given the contradictions in the reports, both Bao and Jun wondered if Tang really read them.

Sergeant Pan was waiting when Bao and Jun walked out of the lobby of the apartment building in Zhanjiang. Within half an hour, he stopped at the entrance to Special Hospital #326 where the guard let the BJ212 four-wheel drive vehicle through the gate.

Pan parked the olive green BJ212 that looked like Jeeps Jun had seen in the U.S. in front of the main administration building. A guard ushered Bao to a conference room on the first floor. Until Dr. Zheng limped into the room, they had seen no one else.

Jun thought it odd no patients were shown in Dr. Zheng's presentation on Special Hospital #326. She wondered if this was Dr. Zheng's decision; or a political one, i.e. she was told not to by some party hack; or cultural in that many Chinese think that if a person is disabled, it brings shame and a loss of face to their family. Therefore, the disabled individual is to be shielded from others and society in general. When she asked, Dr. Zheng said after she showed a version to several Central Committee members, they ordered her not to show patients since it would show the country, hence the party, in bad light.

Special Hospital #326 was, even by American standards, an extremely well-equipped rehab facility. Then Dr. Zheng pushed herself to her feet. She pointed to the door with the forearm crutch she used to help provide balance when she walked. "Now that you have seen the official presentation, come, allow me show you reality."

Nothing prepared Jun or Bao for what they saw next. About a third of the patients were children under 15 and crippled for life. Most, Dr. Zheng said some would spend a year or more here before returning to their families.

All the teachers in the school were polio survivors, some had the non-paralytic variant, most had some sort of disability. The government refused to order regular teachers to teach in the hospital, so Dr. Zheng and her predecessor offered those sent here as patients to become part of her staff. Others were family members who passed Ministry of Education tests and stayed. The school was started so the children didn't fall behind those of the same age who were not afflicted.

Dr. Zheng stopped before a set of double doors. "This room will take you back to the 1940s and 1950s." With that, she pushed a button and both doors opened, revealing a room with two dozen iron lungs, four of which were occupied, two with children, two with adults.

Special Hospital #326 had two floors on which 50 iron lungs could be set up. Dr. Zheng thought that the hospital had about 95% of the iron lungs left in the PRC. Plus, through the country's Institute of Health in Beijing, the country bought complete sets of drawings for the iron lungs they had. The facility's machine shop had the tools to make parts to keep the iron lungs operating and fabricate parts for the orthotics and braces worn by the facility's patients.

She noted with a twinkle in her eye, that a friend in Zhanjiang owned a business that "bought" things for the People's Republic and he found iron lung parts all over the world, where polio outbreaks were rare and iron lungs were no longer needed.

Dr. Zheng led Bao and Jun to the large, indoor Olympic size pool where they watched children and adults undergoing physical therapy. Along the side of the pool, braces and crutches were neatly stacked against the wall to keep them out of the way.

Back in her office, Dr. Zheng sat down heavily and unlocked the knee on her brace to let her foot down to the floor. "Now you know my world."

Jun looked at her lover, who nodded as if to say, you go first. They both had a hypothesis. "Dr. Zheng, I would like to start by testing the water near the homes of the most recent victims. I would also like to take blood from those in the hospital who still have symptoms."

"What do you plan to do with the samples?"

"Have them packed in ice and flown to a lab in Wuhan where we can run some tests and grow some cultures."

"When do you want to draw the blood?"

Jun answered, "I need to call Senior Colonel Sun first, but probably tomorrow or the next day."

Dr. Ting Zheng pulled her chair toward the desk and repositioned her paralyzed left arm so her hand was in her lap. It had been hanging down over the side of the chair.

Bao was looking through a patient file that Dr. Zheng had given him. "Do you know who made the vaccines given to those in Zhanjiang where most of the cases occurred?"

"We have some records, why?"

Dr. Gu ignored the question, "Do you have any vaccines here? Or are there clinics in Zhanjiang that can give us samples?"

"We have a small inventory. The clinics in Zhanjiang may be reluctant to part with theirs. What are you thinking?"

Jun interjected, "We can change their opinion. In the United States and most western countries, vaccine batches are tested to make sure they meet specific efficacy standards. I think what Dr. Gu is suggesting is that the victims may not have received an effective vaccine. We would like to draw blood from those who have been vaccinated as well as those who have not."

Dr. Zheng pushed her chair back. "That's what I thought." She pulled a folder out from a drawer and put it on her desk. She opened it and used her limp hand as a paperweight as she paged through the contents.

"When I first took over, I asked two clinics in Zhanjiang to give me the data on their vaccines." She slid a sheet of paper with the labels taped to the page. "I cut these two labels from the box in which the bottles came in."

Bao looked at the label and nodded. "Jun, I think we need to call Senior Colonel Sun now."

Once he was on the phone, Sun agreed to have a plane on the ramp tomorrow evening. Dr. Lín and Dr. Gu would accompany the samples to Wuhan where they would supervise the testing to see if the victims' blood of those who had not become sick but who had been vaccinated contained polio antibodies. He said the plane would bring street maps of Zhanjiang.

Before they left, Jun gave instructions to Dr. Zheng's team on how she would like the data organized, i.e. polio victims to clinics and to vaccine data to the forthcoming maps. On the way back to the seaport, Bao gave their driver addresses of two clinics opened in the last year. It was just before five when Bao got out of the car and said, "Jun, let me lead. We are about to find out if these passes Senior Colonel Sun gave us work. If they don't, we may wind up in jail."

Dr. Gu strode up to the desk and placed his new identity book that said he was an inspector from the Ministry of Health working for the Ministry of State Security. And whomever was shown the plastic card, was to provide whatever information he requested without question.

The receptionist looked at Jun. Bao said, impatiently, "Dr. Lín has the same credentials" which convinced the woman to dial a number. A man in a white coat came out. "Good afternoon, I am Dr. Tham, what do you need?"

"I am Dr. Bao Gu and this is Dr. Jun Lín. We need your records of all the shipments of polio vaccines this clinic received in the past five years."

Tham's face was an impassive mask. "That could take hours to put together."

"It shouldn't. You should have them in notebooks as per Ministry of Health procedures."

The doctor said please follow me and led the two doctors to a small conference room. "It will take a few minutes to get them."

Before Dr. Tham walked out, Bao showed the plastic card and showed him his ID booklet. "If you don't believe me, I suggest you call the number on the card. You might find someone on the other end who is annoyed you are not giving us the records we request. It could lead to a Ministry of State Security investigation into why you are (a) not cooperating and (b) why you don't have the records."

Tham slapped the card and ID booklet on his hand as he debated what he should do. Discretion, he decided, is the better part of valor.

He walked out and a few minutes later, a clerk placed two notebooks on the table and left.

Bao knew exactly what records were required. As the head of the Guangzhou Institute of Biomedicine and Health immunology practice, he was responsible for the institute's vaccine shipment records. Each shipment record was required to have the institute's order number, vaccine batch number, the number of bottles ordered versus those arrived, a completed chain of custody document showing each time the vaccine changed hands enroute from the factory to the clinic. The records should also show the vaccine's manufacturer and date the vaccine was put in the bottle.

Dr. Tham opened the door. "Is that what you needed?"

"Yes. I need to make copies."

"You will have to sign our log."

Bao's impatience was showing. "Of course. How often do you reorder?"

Tham took a deep breath. "Normally, we try to keep at least six bottles on hand, except in July during the summer break when we have the highest demand. Is this about the outbreak of polio around Zhanjiang?"

"Yes. How many cases of polio have you treated in the past year?"

"At least two dozen, I don't know the exact number. If they need hospitalization, or special care, we call a number and an ambulance picks up the patient. That's all I know other than some come back healthy, others come back...." Tham's voice tapered off.

Jun finished his sentence, "... wearing braces or in a wheelchair."

Tham nodded and said, softly, "Yes. It is quite sad."

Bao said, "I need the files on all the patients you treated for polio, do you have that data?"

"Yes, strangely enough we do. Earlier this year, officials from the Ministry of Heath went through all our cases. They were doing some sort of survey. I have the report in my office."

"Excellent doctor, we'll need a copy of that as well."

"Are there any clinics around that have had an unusually large number of polio cases or were subjects of this study?"

"Six others in Zhanjiang were part of the survey. I only have our data and can give you the list of the others."

Back in the furnished flat, Bao spread out the information given to them by Dr. Tham. Tomorrow, they would have the driver take them to the other clinics on the way to the Special Hospital #326.

THURSDAY, AUGUST 22ND, 2002, 4:03 P.M. LOCAL TIME, WUHAN

The twin-engine turboprop, a Y-7 built by Xian under license from the Soviet aircraft manufacturer Antonov took almost three hours to fly to Wuhan from Suixi Air Base. Bao and Jun, along with the two coolers, were the only passengers. In Wuhan, a staff car brought Bao,

Jun, and the 40 samples of blood to the front door of the Wuhan Institute for Virology which had been alerted by Senior Colonel Sun on exactly what tests they wanted run.

Bao and Jun waited in an office while the lab work on 20 samples from those who were vaccinated and 20 from those who were not was performed. In each group there were five samples from individuals who still had a fever, headache, nausea, muscle weakness, or back stiffness so the two doctors thought they had a good sample mix.

While they were at the Wuhan Institute of Virology, the senior administrator visited with them and proudly told them that the Academy of Sciences had recommended to the State Council and the Politburo that the first Level 4 Biosafety lab in the People's Republic would be part his facility. A dozen members of his staff were going to France and the United States for training.

Bao and Jun didn't say that Senior Colonel Sun was planning on building a second lab Level 4 Biosafety lab under the auspices of the PLA and suspected Sun didn't bother to inform the Academy of Sciences.

After a quick dinner, the pair started looking at the lab results. From what they could tell, there was no difference in the blood work between those who had been vaccinated and those who had not. There were some individual oddities, but each person's blood had what one would expect of someone sick with polio.

Exhausted, they crawled into bed after making reservations to fly via Air China from Wuhan to Zhanjiang. Bao was propped up against the headboard and was caressing Jun's back and neck as his lover rested her head on his chest.

"Bao, I think the vaccines were bad. In the West, The People's Republic has a reputation of producing medicines that do not have the specified efficacy. Whether it is to keep costs down, poor manufacturing processes, or some other reason, manufacturers who contract with Chinese companies go to great expense to ensure that the drugs manufactured in the People's Republic are effective. It is a constant battle so it wouldn't surprise me if the vaccines were ineffective."

"Jun, why are you so sure?"

"Well, if Dr. Zheng's team can identify where the individuals were vaccinated and the date, then we can determine who made the vaccine."

"That doesn't prove that the vaccines were weak. Sometimes the vaccine doesn't take or the patient gets a milder case of the disease."

"True. However, in less than one half of one percent of the time, the body doesn't develop some sort of immunity to polio. So, I think we start with the records of a manufacturer. I'll bet money that when all data is in front of us, an arrow will point to at least one."

Bao lifted his lover's chin so he could kiss her. "I think you are right."

Jun responded as she normally did, letting Bao be the aggressor and sending waves of pleasure through her body.

CHAPTER 15

NEW PROJECTS

MONDAY, AUGUST 26TH, 2002, 8:14 A.M. LOCAL TIME, FORT MEADE

Yan had just finished briefing Captain Ellis on the latest letter from Jun. The coded message said Jun was headed to Zhanjiang to learn why the number of polio cases in the southern provinces of the People's Republic increased every year. Her note said the number was alarming enough to get the PLA involved and if possible, stamp it out.

Ellis, who knew who Yan's source was did not want the CIA involved. At least not yet. He, like Yan, were afraid the agency would push for more information, even at the risk of compromising the source or want to control the asset. Jun's information confirmed other intelligence gleaned from other sources, mostly intercepts.

Yan gave Captain Ellis a translation and her analysis to put in "the Jun folder" to which DIA had access to the information, but not the source. Captain Ellis looking over Yan's shoulder as she typed when the telephone rang.

"Ellis." The captain never used where he was within NSA or his rank even though every piece of intelligence collected by NSA on the People's Republic of China came to his team of analysts and linguists.

"Good morning, sir. This is Commander Hensley and I'm the O-4 and O-5 intelligence officer detailer. I have tried to reach Lieutenant

Commander Young several times but she has not returned my calls. I understand she works for you and I need to speak with her urgently."

"Wait one." Ellis handed Yan the phone. "It is your detailer, Commander Hensley." In U.S. Navy terms, detailers in the Bureau of Naval Personnel marry officer qualifications with career needs to open command or unit billets. If you piss off one's detailer, he or she could easily arrange for an assignment that could end one's chances for promotion.

Yan nodded and took the handset. "Lieutenant Commander Yang. May I help you, sir?"

"This will take a minute. A two star at DIA is asking for you by name to run the PLA's Navy surface combatants desk beginning next fiscal year. More I can't say because I don't know the details. You're due for a new set of orders and this slot would normally be filled by a junior O-5. Interested?"

"Yes, sir."

"How soon can you be out of NSA?"

Yan made a face. "May I get back to you later today. I'm in a meeting." Yan hung up. "Sir, you know the question."

"I do and I'll miss you. When do they want you?"

"Right after the fiscal year."

Ellis nodded. "Good, that gives me time to call Commander Hensley to find a replacement with similar quals since you are not due to rotate until February. So, Lieutenant Commander Huáng, my advice is accept the assignment and I'll flounder around with someone not as good. However, before you leave, we need to sort out how you handle future intel from your cousin."

Yan gave him a perfunctory hug and said thanks. The new billet meant she would not have to move.

TUESDAY, AUGUST 27ᵀᴴ, 2002, 10:07 A.M. LOCAL TIME, ZHANJIANG

Rain poured down in sheets. On their drive to Special Hospital #326 from Zhanjiang, the visibility was so bad, Sergeant Pan slowed to 10

– 15 kilometers an hour. Either he couldn't see the road or the four-wheel drive BJ212 was creeping through hub-deep water.

At Special Hospital #326, they were closeted in a classroom that Dr. Zheng gave them to use as an office. Reports and data from patient files were taped to the wall. Geming Huoran, who taught math at the hospital's school, had a doctorate in statistics. Once he was stricken, he spent six months in an iron lung before he learned how to breathe on his own. He was paralyzed from the chest down yet volunteered to teach math at the hospital's school.

Houran pointed to the blackboard on which he had written several calculations. "Dr. Lín, based just on the data we have at the hospital, I can tell you with close to ninety percent certainty that the culprit is a vaccine that did not work. It could have been what you call a placebo that was accidently sent, or a manufacturer who produced a sub-standard vaccine."

"Why?"

"We have associated vaccines by manufacturer to batch numbers delivered by clinics to patients. We know who was vaccinated and got sick and those who weren't. Effective vaccines already exist, so logic says start there."

"I agree, but you have discounted one other possibility which is ..."

Sergeant Pan opened the door. "Doctors Zheng, Gu, and Lín, I have orders to drive you to Suixi without delay. Senior Colonel Zheng says there are senior officials coming from Beijing who want to meet with you immediately. If you have a preliminary report, please bring it."

The rain had lessened to a drizzle making it easier for Sergeant Pan to drive the olive-drab vehicle. When they reached the Suixi Air Base, Pan was directed straight to a four-engine turboprop in PLA Air Force markings parked on the ramp. A small canvas shelter had been rigged over the passenger door just aft of the cockpit. Pan braked the four-wheel drive vehicle under the shelter.

Conscious that Dr. Zheng might need help negotiating the air stair, Sergeant Pan stood by her side as she limped to the door. She waived him off and pulled herself up using her right arm and leg, step by step. Once Dr. Zheng was in the airplane, Dr. Gu and Dr. Lín climbed on board. Jun had expected that they would be walking into an empty cargo plane or one full of seats. It was neither. She was standing in a nicely finished conference room with a table that was, she guessed, about five meters long and had chairs along each side and one at each end. At both ends of the room, there was a door, one she presumed led to the cockpit.

The door on the aft end of the room opened and Senior Colonel Sun emerged with two other men none of the three had ever met. Sun waved to the chairs and said, "Doctors, please sit down. Would you like some refreshments?"

They all nodded. A woman dressed in civilian clothes brought a tray of tea and bottles of water. She placed two plates with an assortment of Chinese cookies within easy reach of any of the six sitting at the table, bowed and backed out of the room.

"Doctors, may I introduce Senior Director Jie Kong from the National Health Commission. He runs the fraud investigation department. Sitting next to him is Senior Director and Inspector Yong Mao from the Ministry of Public Security criminal investigations department. Given the gravity of what you are learning, I thought it best we meet as soon as possible. I have briefed both men on your areas of expertise. So, with that introduction, Dr. Lin, since you are leading the research, the floor is yours."

Jun nodded. "Thank you." She bent over and pulled a sheaf of papers that she had hurriedly shoved into her briefcase. One was the folded map showing the clinics and addresses of the polio victims.

"Let me start with what a comedian would call the punchline. We, and that's the three of us, suspect SinoPharma, headquartered in Guangzhou, manufactured vaccines that did not have the level of potency needed to prevent a person from contracting polio. We have copies of the records showing the batch numbers sent to these six clinics."

She slid the map across the conference table and tapped the locations of the clinics. Surrounding them were dots indicating the victims.

"Conclusion two is that the water supply feeding these apartment complexes is very likely contaminated by feces from animals carrying the polio virus. We think that the National Heath Commission should conduct tests to find the source and then take the proper steps to eliminate the contamination. At the same time, everyone in these areas should be revaccinated with doses we know have the proper level of efficacy. I suggest the commission acquire a Western, preferably American, batch of vaccines to use as a comparison to what the People's Republic has been using as a standard."

Senior Director Kong took in a sharp breath. "You do know what you are proposing is politically difficult." Translation – it would be an admission that the People's Republic's vaccines were not as good as those used in the West. This would cause many in the Institute of Health to lose much face.

Dr. Zheng spoke before Jun could respond. She put her useless hand on the table. "Senior Director, how many more of our citizens do you want to become crippled by this disease? The number of cases is not going down, it is going up at an ever-increasing rate of over ten point three per cent per year in Zhanjiang. I suspect other cities along the South China Sea have similar outbreaks and trends. Dr. Lín, do you have the chart?"

Jun slid the chart showing the asymptotic rate of growth for just where they had data.

"So Dr. Lín, where would you start an investigation?" Senior Director Kong put down the chart.

"First, I would issue a recall of SinoPharma's polio vaccines and test them for efficacy. At the same time, I would do more research into the stricken population in Zhanjiang. Dr. Gu and I agree with Dr. Zheng that if we look, we will find other outbreaks in other cities in Guangdong and Guanxi provinces."

Jun took a cookie but did not take a bite. "Then, I would go back through SinoPharma's manufacturing records for every batch. We need to compare the ingredients list with what they bought; when they bought it; and from whom they purchased the ingredient. Assuming they are following the processes and protocols used in pharmaceutical countries around the world, they and their suppliers should have meticulous records. A trained investigator should be able to find anomalies."

Yong Mao was listening intently. "How far would you go back?"

"Five, maybe seven years."

Mao had worked his way up through the ranks based on his reputation as a thorough investigator. Financial fraud was his specialty but he could see the parallels. He would need a forensic accounting or manufacturing data specialist to lead this case.

The experienced investigator sat back and clasped his hands and rested his forearms on the table. "Dr. Lín, I presume that Dr. Gu and you would be able to assist in an investigation, assuming we open one."

Senior Colonel Sun answered for both doctors. "Yes, and I will make sure that Dr. Bao and Dr. Lín along with the data they have collected and analyzed will be made available to the Ministry of Public Security. Dr. Zheng's Special Hospital will also support a thorough investigation only on the condition it is performed by the Ministry of Public Security. The National Military Commission will lend its support and provide resources."

Jie Kong spoke slowly. "Senior Colonel Sun and Senior Director and Investigator Mao, I have a recommendation and two questions for Dr. Lín."

The PLA senior colonel nodded as if to say proceed to Kong. "I agree that the Ministry of Public Security should lead this investigation. It has far more authority than my organization, which will be happy to assist."

Translation – There will be resistance within the National Health Commission since many will lose face and/or their jobs, and/or their lives.

Senior Colonel Sun tapped his index finger on the table. "Agreed. I think that is wise." Translation - The National Health Commission will do its best to avoid blame even though this is its area of responsibility. "And your questions are?"

"One, Dr. Lín, do you think this is a localized outbreak?"

"No. I think if we broadened our investigation to where SinoPharma shipped vaccines, we will find more cases. Our challenge is to keep it from expanding."

Kong nodded thinking that containment of the information will be the order of the day at the National Health Commission and more important than preventing the disease from spreading. Careers of senior members of the organization will be at risk along with their lives. If the investigation became "public," it would be another reason to distrust the government and the party.

"Dr. Lín, have you looked at other alternatives besides a weak or ineffective vaccine?"

"Yes, however, the data supporting the ineffective vaccine hypothesis is very convincing. It is a place to start."

"Understood, however, there must be other possibilities."

Bao put her hand on Jun's arm. "Senior Director Kong, our data shows a mix of paralytic and non-paralytic strains among the patients at Special Hospital #326 are within the range of the data from India, Indonesia, and other countries in Africa where polio has not been eradicated. The percentage of those at the hospital who have permanent paralysis or other long-term effects also matches the data from the World Health Organization. The warm, humid climate of southern China makes the region a petri dish for new diseases or strains for other ones. If our weak vaccine theory is wrong, then sir, we have a new, stronger strain of polio on our hands. Dr. Lín and I believe the possibility of an ineffective vaccine and a mutation are both possible. And that, Senior Director Kong, is frightening."

Senior Colonel Sun looked at the two men he brought with him. Neither had anything more to say. "Senior Investigator and Director Mao, will the Ministry of Public Security open an investigation?"

"Yes. However, I will need to assign a team. Where should we have our first meeting to go over your information."

Dr. Zheng said what was on both Dr. Lín's and Dr. Gu's mind. "My facility, Special Hospital #326. We have the data plus we are close to Zhanjiang. It is a perfectly good place to start."

On the way back to the hospital, each of the doctors stared out the windows, saying nothing. Dr. Zheng broke the silence. "I think a celebration is order. Two in fact. One at the hospital for all those who helped. Thanks to the two of you, there is now hope that our government will do something. Senior Colonel Sun is a man of his word. I trust him to keep the fire lit under the Ministry of Public Security. The second will be a nice dinner in Zhanjiang and introduce you to a friend who can help, off the record, of course."

Jun, who had been sitting in the back seat holding Bao's hand, was curious. "Dr. Zheng, how do you know Senior Colonel Sun?"

Dr. Zheng twisted in the front passenger's seat awkwardly so she could face the rear seat. "My husband and Senior Colonel Sun were classmates and became very good friends at the National Defense University. When I was stricken, Senior Colonel Sun's wife came to our flat and the rehab center in Beijing every day to help me so she as well as her husband has seen firsthand what polio can do to a human being."

That was not the answer Dr. Lín was expecting. It made her more curious as to why Senior Colonel Sun was interested in creating new strains of polio and other diseases in a lab. Or maybe, that was the reason.

CHAPTER 16

A CRIME AGAINST HIS PEOPLE

MONDAY, SEPTEMBER 23RD, 2002, 11:07 A.M. LOCAL TIME, NEAR YINGXIONG RESERVOIR

Senior Colonel Sun stood on a small wooden platform and watched the front-loaders and backhoes grade the land where the vehicle shed would be built. The plans for his new lab showed that the existing dirt road from Route X569 was being improved to crushed gravel to ensure it would be passable during the monsoon. Later, it would be paved. Much of the dirt being dug out at the new lab site was being trucked to fill in gullies so the road wouldn't be washed out during the rainy season, which ran from late May to the middle of August.

Northwest of where Sun was standing, there was a tree-covered ridge rising 213 meters above the plateau where he was standing. The Army engineer who picked this place, Senior Colonel Sun thought, chose well.

When the new lab was finished, there would be a 4-meter-tall wall around the compound which sat on 15 hectares (~37 acres) of land.

When the new lab was finished, there would be a 4-meter-tall wall around the compound which sat on 15 hectares (~37 acres) of land. The complex would house a three-story lab building built to Level 4 standards, but not certified.

To house the guard contingent, a barracks large enough to house a company of biological warfare and chemical troughs as well as two companies of soldiers to provide security. In addition, there would be large sheds for the guard contingent's and the chemical and biological warfare troops. These would hide them from the prying cameras of satellites as well as to provide shelter from the elements.

The facility would have separate buildings for offices, conference, and classrooms and, a cafeteria. All would be connected to the lab via a enclosed passageway.

This would be, Sun believed, equal to any facility in the West except that it would be operated by the PLA. He could see where the forms for the foundations for the three main buildings – lab, barracks, and administration – were being laid.

Satisfied, Senior Colonel Sun thanked the construction manager, a lieutenant colonel in the PLA's military engineering corps, who said this was a welcome challenge. Most of his unit's work in the past had been building hangars and fortified structures, but since the facility was being constructed to commercial finish-out standards, it was a chance to improve his unit's skills.

Once he was in the back seat of the BJ212, Sun's thoughts turned to the other issue that arose from this project. The investigation into the vaccines was a blessing in that it enabled him to gainfully employ both Dr. Lín and Dr. Gu while the facility is being built while at the same time, sort out a pressing problem that the PLA will take credit for solving. He figured the investigation would take months and if needed, he'd find another project for the two doctors to keep them occupied.

However, there was a wrinkle with Dr. Gu. Sun's brother, who was a deputy minister in the Ministry of State Security, said that Ministry of Public Security had interest in Dr. Gu but would or could not elaborate. All his brother would say was that Senior Investigator Lieu was using Dr. Gu for male "honeypot" roles to gather incriminating evidence. So the question in his mind was did Lieu order Dr. Gu to gather evidence on Dr. Lín?

What cast Sun's doubts on Lieu's effort to use Dr. Gu was that anyone who has seen Dr. Gu and Dr. Lín together, would conclude that they are in love. Or at least Dr. Lín was in love with Dr. Gu. Which led to another set of questions. Was Dr. Gu faking it or did he share Jun's feelings? Was Dr. Gu sent by Lieu to seduce Dr. Lín after her husband was killed? What hold did Lieu have over Dr. Gu? And what did Dr. Lín reveal about her work if anything? All he believed, would sort itself out in time.

WEDNESDAY, SEPTEMBER 25ᵀᴴ, 2002, 10:19 A.M. LOCAL TIME, GUANGZHOU

Bao and Jun were neither on leave, nor were they employed. They were in limbo ever since they presented their formal report to Senior Director and Senior Inspector Yong Mao. He urged them to be patient until he called. In the meantime, there was little for the two doctors to do.

An investigation, Mao said, is like medical research. One takes one small step at a time and sees where it leads. Sometimes you go backward; sometimes you go forward.

That was until they were summoned this morning. Mao's assistant said a car would bring them to the Ministry of Public Security office in Guangzhou.

After presenting their credentials to the guard, they were given visitors badges and escorted through the maze of halls to a room on the second floor. There, Yong Mao was waiting for them.

"Please," He waived to the chairs. "For security purposes, I have chosen not to introduce you to my team, but that may change in a few days."

Mao lifted a small cooler from the floor and put it on the table. "This arrived today. In it are two dozen vials of polio vaccine made in the U.S. by Sanofi-Pasteur. The vaccine is certified to meet the WHO standards for an effective polio vaccine. Which lab can compare the Sanofi-Pasteur vaccine to the Sino Pharma samples you collected from the clinics in Zhanjiang?"

Jun looked at Bao before answering, "Are you looking for absolute accuracy or an answer that will stand up in a People's Court?"

"Both would be preferable."

"I would take it to any immunology or virology lab in the United States that could provide an unbiased comparison. There would be some paperwork involved."

Bao then spoke up when Jun hesitated, "We could test them in the Guangzhou Biomedicine lab. I would supervise the test using people I know and whose skills I trust. Then, I could testify in court."

Mao made a note. "I like that answer better. But, Dr. Lín, if you were to take it to a country closer, where would you go?"

"Japan or Australia. You would have the same issues in terms of permits to bring the vaccine in, have it tested, etc. But it could be done. We did it at the San Diego State University as part of our lab courses."

"So, Dr. Lin, you know the procedures as well?"

"I do."

"Dr. Gu, can the Guangzhou Biomedicine lab store these samples and keep them secure?"

"Yes. I can arrange with Senior Administrator Siew to have a separate cooler for all our samples to which I will have the only key."

"Excellent. I will have the samples from Special Hospital #326 and delivered by courier to you at the institute. I will have one of my men guide you through the custody process to ensure there are no mistakes. He will also explain the documents that must be attached to the lab reports. Once you have the samples, conduct the necessary tests."

Both doctors nodded.

Mao went to his next item. "Did you know that the manufacturers are required by the state to retain a specific number of samples, twelve bottles to be exact, of each batch of vaccine for at least twenty years?"

Both doctors shook their heads.

"After twenty years, the samples cannot be destroyed without approval from the National Health Commission. The State Council issued an order signed by Jiang Zemin to the National Health Commission forbidding it from ordering any samples destroyed."

Zemin, who is the General Secretary of the Communist Party of China signed the order. His signature meant that the leadership of the CCP took matters such as this seriously.

"How long, once you have the samples from Zhanjiang, will it take to have results?"

Bao looked at his lover. "We have six different batches from Sino-Pharma. I would test three samples from each batch from SinoPharma and compare them to one Sanofi-Pasteur vaccine. Then Dr. Lín and I will compare the results. We may get lucky, or we may have to test all six. Or worse, get more from the manufacturer or clinics in the hot spots where there are clusters of polio cases."

Yong Mao made another note. "Excellent. Expect the samples there by tomorrow morning. Dr. Zheng will supervise the packing. I suggest you go make arrangements with the Biomedicine Lab. If you run into any resistance, use those plastic cards, or call me. Senior Colonel Sun has done an excellent job of gaining support for this investigation at the highest level of our government."

FRIDAY, SEPTEMBER 27ᵀᴴ, 2002, 3:18 P.M. LOCAL TIME, GUANGZHOU

Senior Administrator Siew ordered one section of the lab used to test tissue samples, cordoned off for the tests. This lab was in another building of the Institute. Only two of Dr. Gu's former technicians and Dr. Lín were allowed in and everyone was dressed in full protective gear.

The first round of tests was inconclusive. Yes, the vaccines were weak, but as they were taking samples from the bottles, Jun noticed subtle differences in the markings and data stamped on the first bottle. Curious, she slid the bottle under a microscope to examine the label.

Forgetting lab protocol and formalities, Jun yelled, "You bastards!!!"

Bao came over and touched Jun on the shoulder. "What are you looking at?"

"Someone has altered the markings. Hand me another bottle from the same batch."

They could see where someone had used a very fine pencil or pen to change numbers. "I am going to call Senior Inspector Mao. Meanwhile, we need to figure out which bottles have been altered - which begs the question: Why?"

Jun looked at the bottle again. "I think the seal has been tampered with."

An hour later, Senior Inspector and Director Mao and a member of his staff arrived with a device that could take a magnified picture of the label. To protect the lab, each bottle was brought to a separate room and photographed. Before it was allowed back in the lab, it was sterilized again by UV light.

On a hunch, Jun put a sample on a slide taken from the bottle that should have been manufactured using the live, attenuated polio vaccine method developed by Dr. Albert Sabin. She dabbed a tiny drop of ammonium molybdate onto the liquid, transferred it to an electromagnetic grid, and blotted it with a piece of sterile paper. From there, she slid the sample into the slot under the transmission electron microscope.

Jun waited impatiently while the machine scanned the sample. If there were molecules of the virus in the sample, the microscope would show them. The green light illuminated indicating that the scan was finished and Jun pressed her forehead against the rubber eyepiece as she studied the image. There were some impurities from the solution, but no virus molecules in view. She pushed the button to record the image.

The printouts from the tests of the liquid's composition showed that the bottles with the modified manufacturing data contained a sterile, saline solution, not vaccines. Senior Inspector and Director Mao asked Bao and Jun to bring the results to the Ministry of Public Security Office in the morning.

MONDAY, SEPTEMBER 30TH, 2002, 9:03 A.M. LOCAL TIME, GUANGZHOU

At 6:30 a.m., a police car picked Bao and Jun up at their apartment complex so they could attend the pre-raid briefing. Each four-man arrest team was given a map and an objective.

Dr. Gu's and Dr. Lín's participation started when Senior Director and Senior Inspector Mao called Saturday, the 28th, asking if they wanted to witness the arrests. Four SinoPharma executives – Xiu Bai, the chief executive officer; Lim Cao, the chief operating officer; Wei Ruan, the chief financial officer; and Kuo Lee, the senior vice president of manufacturing – were in Mao's crosshairs along with the firm's financial and manufacturing records. Mao initially wanted Jun and Bao to accompany him to the Xiu Bai's office, but they suggested that Kuo Lee might have more information.

Mao's plan was to have the targeted records brought to a large conference room where they would be guarded while they were reviewed. This way if, during questioning, his investigators wanted more records, they were in the building and could seize them right away.

Jun and Bao rode in the lead car of the caravan with Senior Inspector Mao as his driver worked its way through the streets of Guangzhou toward what the road signs said was the city of Zhongshan. Unlike what was portrayed in movies in which the police arrive with sirens blaring, lights flashing, and guns drawn, the policemen did neither. Maybe, Jun thought, the guns will come out later.

Mao presented his badge and warrants to the receptionist and ordered. "No one is to leave the building until we are finished here. You are not to use the phone."

A wave and the policemen entered the building in teams of four, each headed to a different office. As planned, Jun and Bao went to the conference room just off the entrance lobby of the company traded on the Shanghai Stock Exchange. Its 2001 revenue was close to 2.5 billion yuan (about $300 million).

Just before they left the Ministry of Public Security offices, Mao handed Jun a folder with an analysis of SinoPharma's financials and the current reports filed with the state; biographies of each executive; and a brief overview of SinoPharma products. He said that trading of SinoPharma's stock would be suspended this morning.

On the third floor Zihan Deng, one of Mao's senior investigators, walked past a surprised administrative assistant and stood in front of the manufacturing vice president's desk. "Citizen Kuo Lee, you are under arrest for manufacturing and selling polio vaccines that did not meet WHO standards." He placed the warrant on Lee's desk and two policemen moved to each side of the executive to handcuff him.

Lee stood up and put both his hands on his desk. "I tried to stop Xiu, but he overruled me. We had a failure that ruined most of our virus cultures for the Sabin vaccines. Rather than shut down and tell our customers we couldn't meet our delivery schedules, Xiu ordered me to fill the bottles with sterilized water. Bai and Cao were worried about explaining why the company did not meet earnings expectations during a quarterly analyst call."

Deng motioned to the two policemen who were about to handcuff Lee to stop. "Can you prove this?"

Lee nodded vigorously and pointed to a horizontal file cabinet. "If you will open the top drawer, taped to the bottom of the top drawer are envelopes with my notes along with the list of batch numbers that were just water."

One of Deng's men found the two envelopes, one about two centimeters thick, the other only a centimeter. Before Deng opened them, Lee continued. "I called the National Health Commission to report this crime and spoke with two men who asked me to send them my notes. Later in 1998, they interviewed me and told me that if my accusations were true, there would be arrests."

"What happened?"

"Nothing."

"Do you remember their names?"

"One was a doctor by the name of Toghon Tang. He smelled like an ash tray and smoked the entire time he talked to me. The other was an investigator by the name of Jie Kong. I remember their faces and names as if it was yesterday."

Deng asked, "Where are the stored samples?"

"Destroyed. Bai and Cao did it themselves and replaced them with batches made a year later. Our labeling machinery does not let one change dates or batch numbers, so they hired outsiders to use pencils to modify the labels."

"You have proof?"

"Of the modified labels, you can see them for yourself. But, if you will accompany me to my home, I have a box in my refrigerator with three samples from each of the batches that went out that were not vaccines. I have been saving them, hoping this day will come."

"Did you follow up with Tang or Kong?"

"I did and Tang said my accusations were false. He warned me to be careful before I accuse a reputable company such as SinoPharma of selling fraudulent vaccines to the state again."

"So what did you do?"

"Nothing. What could I do? Bai and Cao could have fired me but they needed my expertise so they kept me as the vice president saying that if I did this again, they would kill me."

"So you think Tang and Kong just filed away your information and did nothing?"

"I do."

Investigator Deng ordered, "Will you allow us to record your statement and testify against these men?"

"I will."

Lee led Investigator Deng to the refrigerated storage lockers where the required samples were kept. He found the batches that he said Bai had put there. They were taken to the conference room where Deng's team had set up shop and placed them in a cooler filled with ice. Before they brought Lee into the room, Deng told Mao about his conversation and asked Bao and Jun to follow him.

Xiu Bai was handcuffed and sitting at the table in his spacious office with a mock putting green on one side. Deng had a different folder in his hand when he entered and asked the two policemen guarding him to step outside.

"Citizen Bai, do you understand the charges?"

"I do and they are nonsense. SinoPharma is a publicly traded company and we would never commit such an act that would endanger my fellow citizens."

Deng opened the folder and began placing photographs of children crippled by polio taken by Dr. Zheng at Special Hospital #326. Bai turned his head away from the photos of boys and girls in wheelchairs and wearing leg braces.

"Look carefully at the pictures. This is what your greed has done."

Bai tried to look out the window. Deng slammed the palm of his hand on the table hard enough to cause the photos to move. Bai stood up defiantly. "How dare you accuse me of selling fraudulent vaccines."

Enraged, Jun, who had met and talked to almost every one of the children in the photos, grabbed the putter and swung it as fast as she could. The clubhead slammed into the side of Xiu Bai's knee hard enough so it flew off the club and banged into the wall.

Bai slumped to the ground screaming in pain, grabbing his knee. X-rays later showed his kneecap dislocated by the blow and the top of his tibia fractured.

Jun took a different putter and pressed it into Bai's neck, making it hard for him to breathe. "I just want to give you a sample of what these children went through as they struggled to breathe. Some spent months in an iron lung so they would not suffocate. Forty percent of them learned that parts of their bodies were permanently paralyzed. So Citizen Bai, when you are convicted, if I was the judge, my sentence would be to infect you with enough live polio virus to ensure you become sick so you can experience what these children went through. Then, when your body is crippled, you would be assigned to change the leg bags and soiled diapers of those whom the disease robbed of their ability to control their bodily functions."

Bai moaned and said he will press charges against Jun for assault. Deng lifted Bai into a chair and said, "My sworn report, attested by Doctors Bao and Lín, will say you were hurt resisting arrest and tripped over your putting green."

As he watched the prisoners being led out of the building, Mao asked Jun, "Would you really infect Bai, Cao, and Ruan with polio as punishment?"

Jun nodded. "If the disease didn't paralyze them sufficiently, I would have it done surgically. My guess is that they will only serve five or ten years in prison, so for the rest of their lives I want them reminded daily of what they did to their fellow citizens."

Mao's brain and heart agreed with Jun's idea of punishment and made a mental note to add that to his report. With that, Mao ordered Xiu Bai, Lim Cao, and Wei Ruan to be put in separate vans and taken to Guangzhou for their formal interrogation. With the prisoners off to jail, Mao, Jun, and Bao went with Kuo Lee to his apartment where he gave Mao the samples and documents he had taken from SinoPharma to be entered in evidence.

CHAPTER 17

UPPING THE INFO ANTE

FRIDAY, OCTOBER 11TH, 2002, 10:21 A.M. LOCAL TIME, SHENZHEN

The four naturalized Americans stood quietly in the entry line for non-citizens of the People's Republic of China. Slung over Zimo Huáng's shoulder was a Sony DCRTRV950 camcorder and his briefcase. There were six blank tapes along with recorded ones from Yan for Jun to watch and one from his grandson Qing, his wife, and children for Liang. He had no idea how the officers from the PRC's Immigration section of the Ministry of Public Security would view the camcorder he suspected may not be available in the People's Republic.

An officer not wearing a nametag walked down the line and motioned Zimo to follow him. He led Zimo through a closed door to a windowless room with two tables and two chairs and pointed to one of the chairs. He spoke Mandarin in a cold, emotionless voice. "Put your bag, briefcase, and camera case on the table and sit there."

A second officer entered, unzipped Zimo's roller bag, and dumped the contents on the table. He rummaged around through the clothes, not caring what he unfolded. He picked up the six tapes still in their original cellophane wrapper and the roller bag and disappeared out the same door. No explanation was given as to why they were taken. Zimo forced himself not to react and remain calm.

"Passport and entry card." The words were in the same cold voice. Zimo slid them across the table.

"When did you arrive in Hong Kong?"

"Wednesday."

"Why are you coming to the People's Republic?"

"To see my daughter and granddaughter."

"Where were you born?"

"Guangzhou."

The immigration officer flipped through Zimo's passport and saw the stamps from his last visit. There were also entry stamps to Canada, the United Kingdom and France. "When did you leave the People's Republic?"

Before Zimo could answer, the second officer came in, tossed the tapes that had been removed from the cellophane wrapper and his roller bag on the table and left with the case holding his Sony camcorder. Suspecting that the inspectors would want to open it, he'd put hairs on the compartment where the battery and memory cards were located. He also had the serial and chip numbers written down on a piece of paper folded in his briefcase that contained his Apple Titanium PowerBook G4. So far, the nameless officer had not looked at his computer.

"1971."

"So you defected which means you are a traitor."

Zimo replied quietly, "I am an American citizen who has been granted a visa by the People's Republic of China to visit his daughter and granddaughter in Guangzhou. We are staying at the White Swan in Guangzhou. I object to this harassment …"

The immigration officer slammed his hand on the table. "And you'll do what!!!"

Zimo said nothing realizing that anything he said would just antagonize the officer.

The man leaned across the table and from his breath, Zimo could tell he was a smoker. "You are a traitor and defector and may be a spy carrying a video camera. I could have you arrested!"

Zimo was not going to argue with the man. He stood up after the second officer came in and shook his head as he put the camcorder case on the table next to Zimo's clothes. Zimo took a step toward the table to repack his bag.

The immigration officer again slammed his hand down on the table. "Sit back down. This interview is not over."

Zimo turned around and placed both hands on the table. "We are done here. This is harassment of a U.S. citizen."

The immigration officer tried to insert himself between Zimo and the table, but Zimo pressed his hips against the table so there was no gap and started folding a shirt. Frustrated that if he tried to force Zimo away from the table, it could wind up in an incident, the officer grabbed the shirt and flung it on the floor.

Ignoring the angry immigration officer, Zimo picked up the shirt, held it up so it could hang out and began to fold it again. The immigration officer swiped at all the clothes, sending them to the floor.

Zimo who was slightly taller, even at 62, glared at the immigration officer and then smiled. "If you wish, we can continue this intimidation game which you will not win. Or you can let me leave and please yourself irritating other foreigners and thereby convincing them that the People's Republic is not a pleasant place to live."

The immigration officer took a step back and went to the door. "Turn left when you leave where an officer will stamp your entry card."

Zimo's wife Shi and his son Tao and his wife Mei were waiting for Zimo on the train platform. There he opened the case with the camcorder and popped open the back. Both gray hair telltales were gone, but the chip and memory cards had the same numbers.

The White Swan Hotel was a landmark in Guangzhou. Built and funded by Fok Ying-tung from Hong Kong, it opened in February 1983. The white building rose 28 stories, had 520 rooms, and was located on Shamian Island in the middle of what the Communists called the Xi Hangadao River. Before 1948, it was known as the Pearl River.

When Guangzhou was a British and French enclave, Shamian Island was in the middle of the Pearl River and, to get to the hotel, Yin-tung built a special causeway. Inside the facility, there were five restaurants, all of which served five-star Cantonese cuisine, and two separate bars.

Now that they had checked in, Shi called Liang and a celebratory dinner was planned at the hotel's Jade River Restaurant. When Liang called her daughter to tell her to bring Bao, she said she had invited An.

The last time Jun's grandfather came to Guangzhou, Jun and Yan were teenagers. So much had changed and yet their letters had brought them closer together. Yan's poignant letter that tried to console Jun over Bojing's death was one she saved.

Jun held Bao's hand tightly as they approached the maître d's podium. Initially, Bao didn't want to come, saying he could meet Jun's grandparents later, but Jun insisted he meet her American family.

The real reason Bao didn't want to come was that he would have to report who he met, what they talked about, and other details to Senior Investigator Lieu. It would not be a pleasant conversation.

Grandmother Shi, seeing Jun and Bao, walked quickly toward her granddaughter, not wanting to wait for Jun to reach the table. They hugged tightly in silence before Shi pushed Jun gently to arm's length. "My god, you are even more stunning than I remember." Turning to the man standing next to Jun, "You must be the handsome Bao?"

The ever-proper Bao, except in bed as Jun often kidded her lover, bowed slightly to acknowledge the comment. Before Bao could speak, Shi said, "Both of you could be models."

Liang and An were late and the delay allowed Jun's grandparents time to ask Bao the usual questions. Jun noticed that her grandmother looked at her quizzically for a few seconds when Bao said they were roommates.

When Liang and An arrived, it was a non-event. Shi looked at her daughter and seeing that she was genuinely happy and healthy, made An feel comfortable.

Dinner was, as they expected, fabulous. All ate too much and Zimo suggested they take a walk around the grounds and then come back for an after-dinner drink.

Shi slid between Bao and Jun as they walked arm and arm. Behind them, Liang walked with An, her brother, and father. At a pond with large orange goldfish, they stopped. Shi pushed herself up onto the waist high pond coaming and faced her daughter and Bao, and said, "You two are in love, aren't you?"

Jun flushed noticeably and Bao nodded. Neither said anything, until Jun, said yes.

Shi, "There is nothing to be ashamed of. So, when is the wedding?"

Taking a deep breath, Jun answered, "Not for a while. We are both involved in a project and when it is done, we will marry. But right now, we're just lovers."

That caused Shi's eyebrows to rise. Looking at her granddaughter, "You need a ring on your finger." Then she looked at Bao, "You need to make a commitment to my granddaughter, and the sooner the better."

Zimo overhearing what he thought was an uncomfortable conversation for his granddaughter and pointed to Jun and then himself as if to say, can we talk privately? Well away from the others, Zimo spoke softly, "Yan thanks you for the information. What you sent is very, very informative. She does not want you to take any unnecessary risks. She also misses you."

"Grandfather, before you leave, I will tell you about the work I have been doing. It will be of great interest to Yan."

Before parting, they agreed to meet at Liang's apartment for lunch tomorrow. Zimo said he would hook up his video camera so they could watch the tapes he brought.

TUESDAY, OCTOBER 15TH, 2002, 9:06 A.M. LOCAL TIME, GUANGZHOU

Yong Mao read the documents on his desk a second time. The plea agreements for Sino Pharma's senior executive team, CEO Xiu Bao, COO Lim Cao, and CFO Wei Ruan would put them in prison for 15 years and require them to give back their stock without compensation as their fine for their crimes.

Whether the board would sell the company or find new executives was not Mao's problem. What was his problem was what to do with the information Kuo Lee gave him about Dr. Tang and Senior Inspector Kong. He checked all three's phone records and Lee's information was accurate. This was enough to assign a member of his team to look through SinoPharma's financial records to see if payments were made to either Kong or Tang.

If there were, then Dr. Tang and Senior Inspector Kong should be prosecuted. But this is the People's Republic of China where connections and power counts. If the evidence Mao and his team uncovered doesn't win in court, he could find himself being prosecuted.

As he thought about Tang and Kong, Mao wondered if Kong decided after the meeting in Suixi to say nothing based on assurances from Xiu Bai that an investigation would not lead to him. Since Bai and Cao were still in cells in the Ministry of Public Safety office in Guangzhou awaiting transfer to a prison, he asked that they be brought to separate interrogation rooms.

Mao chose to speak to Bai first since he thought he had the most to gain or lose. Bai was in a chair and manacled to the table with his left leg encased in a cast from his groin to his ankle.

As he walked into the interrogation room, Mao placed a folder with the information Luo Lee had provided before he acknowledged the prisoner's existence. He wasn't interested in Bai's health and made a show of opening the folder and sifting through the documents.

"So, Prisoner Bai, have you ever met with or spoken on the phone Senior Inspector Jie Kong or Senior Director and Doctor Toghan Tang of the National Health Commission?"

"About what?"

"About the quality of SinoPharma's polio vaccine."

Bai said nothing. Mao noted on his pad that Bai did not answer the question before asking his next one. "While you are contemplating what lie you are going to tell me, I will ask you my second question. Did SinoPharma ever make a payment to either one or both these men?"

"Payment for what?"

Mao didn't want to fence. "Prisoner Bai, you have already agreed to a fifteen-year sentence. If you bribed either of these two men not to perform their duty, then the People's Republic will add bribery of a public official to the charges and your time in prison will increase by at least five years for each person bribed or, in your case, since there were two men, ten more years."

Bai looked down at the table and then at Mao. "The National Health Commission knew SinoPharma had polio vaccine production problems but decided to do nothing. I suggest you ask Dr. Tang and Senior Inspector Kong why."

"So you know these two men."

Bai nodded.

"I'll take your nod as a yes answer. How often have you spoken with them?"

There was a knock on the door and one of Mao's inspectors motioned for him to leave the interrogation room. Zilan Deng was waiting down the hall with a sheaf of papers.

"I have a bank statement showing two separate withdrawals of two hundred thousand Yuan each listed in SinoPharma's financial records as "consulting on vaccine problems." The money was deposited in two banks in Beijing. I called the banks in question and the money was deposited in accounts owned by Toghon Tang and Jie Kong. Payments of fifty thousand yuan were made to each man ten days after Kuo Lee's first call to Jie Kong about production quality problems. A second payment fifty thousand yuan was made after his second call to each man and the funds went into the same banks."

"Can you give me the information the banks faxed to you?"

"Yes sir, I have them here."

Mao held out his hand. "Please, give the documents to me."

With the additional information in his hand, Mao settled in his chair and looked at Bai who was stone-faced. He shifted through the paperwork again. "Prisoner Bai, would you like to avoid staying in prison for more than your sentence?"

"I would."

"Excellent. So I am going to ask you this question one time. If I don't like the answer, I will walk out of the room and you will be charged with bribery of a state official and I will ask the prosecutors to add the time to your existing sentence so you will spend twenty-five years in prison. If you survive, you will be close to seventy when your sentence ends."

Bai stared at Mao; his face was impassive.

"Did you give money to Dr. Tang and Senior Inspector Kong to look the other way? And how much did you give them?"

"Yes. If I paid them, both said they could make SinoPharma's problem go away."

"How much did they want?"

Bai took a deep breath. "Tang and Kong asked for half a million yuan each. We settled for one hundred thousand each. Wei Ruan authorized the money transfer. He was new and I told him if he didn't take care of this, I would fire him for cause and he would never work as a chief financial officer in the People's Republic again. If he refused, I had a vendor willing to testify that Ruan was taking kickbacks."

"What was Lim Cao's role?"

"Lim and I agreed that the payment would buy us time to fix our production processes and still meet our revenue forecast."

"Will you sign a deposition and testify if needed?"

Bai nodded. "Yes, if it means my sentence stays at fifteen years."

"I will agree to that on the condition that you convince Cao and Ruan to testify fully against Kong and Tang."

"Bring them up here and I will do that."

While a prosecutor was taking the written statements from the SinoPharma executives and recording their testimony, Mao went to his office and asked for a secure line. The operator connected him to Senior Colonel Sun. After explaining what he had just learned, the PLA officer simply said, "Continue the investigation to see where it leads. When you are ready to arrest Tang and Kong or if you run into roadblocks, contact me on this, my private line. It is secure."

Senior Colonel Sun had another reason for Mao to continue. If he could force changes in the leadership of the National Health Commission and the National Academy of Science, it may make the organizations more agreeable to future requests for personnel and facilities.

Mao now had another problem. He needed a prosecutor in Beijing willing to handle the case discretely.

CHAPTER 18

TWO DIFFERENT MISSIONS

THURSDAY, OCTOBER 24ᵀᴴ, 2002, 5:46 A.M. LOCAL TIME, NAS NORTH ISLAND

The two matte-gray HH-60Hs, call signs Lancer Five and Lancer Nine, were flying at 120 knots, 50 feet above the water headed west, toward San Clemente Island. Behind them, the sun was just making its presence known but not enough to create shadows.

Both helicopters carried eight Navy SEALS from SEAL Team Three's first platoon. The objective was a small building on the north end of San Clemente, approximately 50 miles from NAS North Island.

The HSC-8 helicopters were part of a live fire training exercise in which the SEALs would be inserted, "raid" a building, capture a "high value target," and then be extracted by the HH-60Hs.

Derek "Racer" Almer was leading the mission in Lancer Five. At the last minute, the squadron's operations officer, Lieutenant Commander Blanchard decided to fly as the HAC in Lancer Nine. Originally, the plan was to put Vera "Tapper" Hotchkiss in the right seat and use this exercise as her HAC check.

Hotchkiss had been cleared by a medical board to return to flying and while Blanchard had over 1,000 hours in the SH-60B and F, he had less than 20 hours in the H model. Even though he was the operations officer, he was not authorized to conduct a HAC check ride in the HH-60H. Blanchard's rationale supporting his decision was that he wanted more special operations flying experience. The HAC check could be flown later.

Behind closed doors, Derek tried to convince Blanchard, Naval Academy class of 1992, that he would be better off flying several HH-60H syllabus hops before flying as a HAC on a live fire training mission with eight SEALs and two crewmen in the back. Blanchard was adamant and said the squadron's skipper supported his decision.

Their AN/PVS-7 night-vision goggles turned the black sky and water into shades of black and green. The monocular gave the wearer a circular view of the world in front of the helicopter to about 500 yards. Depth perception was not as good as the naked eye but with practice, wearers learned the limits of the marriage of night vision googles and their eyes. The training plan was to fly using NVGs during the transition from night to dawn on the way in and, on the way back to NAS North Island, fly using the naked eye. Chris Blanchard had his head down monitoring the flight instruments displayed on the flat panel screen on the instrument panel. Occasionally he would glance at the engine instruments and the torque and rotor rpm.

Squadron practice was that one pilot would fly while the other would navigate, monitor the engine and transmission instruments, and look outside the cockpit. Doctrine suggested the crew switch roles every 15 – 20 minutes. Blanchard had insisted on flying the insertion so Vera was responsible for navigating, helping him maintain position on the lead helicopter using the formation lights and looking for hazards.

Her timeline listed on her kneeboard agreed with the GPS which suggested they were five minutes from the insertion landing zone (LZ). Vera keyed the intercom, "Ops Oh, five minutes out."

She didn't need an acknowledgement and expected Blanchard to slow slightly so Lancer Nine would arrive over the LZ seconds after the SEALs finished fast roping from Lancer Five. Blanchard, who was flying in a loose left echelon hadn't slowed to give Lancer Five time and space to flare, let the SEALs out and then depart the landing zone. If Blanchard gets the timing right, he would be flaring Lancer Nine just as Lancer Five cleared the LZ.

Vera Hotchkiss, now a full lieutenant, keyed the intercom. "Ops Oh, don't you think you should slide back a little. Lancer Five will need fifteen seconds over the LZ to get his men out."

Blanchard nodded as he clicked the mike and moved Lancer Nine a quarter a mile from Lancer Five, which was much too far. "Sir, suggest you speed up because our timing will be off. The SEALs want both helicopters in and out of the LZ in less than a minute."

"Got it." Blanchard dumped the nose abruptly and pulled power to accelerate.

Lancer Nine arrived 40 seconds late. As he flared the helicopter, instead of coming to a hover at 40 feet, the needle on the radar altimeter indicated they were at 50.

Below the helicopter, green tracers filled the air as the SEALs executed their assault. The brief noted the aircrewmen on both helicopters to expect to engage targets with their M-60s during both the insertion and the extraction. The targets would be, as the SEAL team briefer said, easily identifiable by their green tracers fired from remotely controlled machine guns aimed at the sky.

While there was enough rope to reach the ground, the insertion was briefed to be at 40 not 50 feet. Two SEALS were still on the ropes when Blanchard shouted, "What the hell is all that? We need to get out of here."

Calmly, Vera gripped the cyclic and the collective so Blanchard couldn't fly out of the hover before the last SEAL was on the ground. "Sir, those are tracers. Ours are red, the enemies are green."

"Ropes away." The call from the aircrewman meant all the SEALs were on the ground and the ropes were released.

Blanchard dumped the nose of the helicopter by pushing the cyclic stick between his legs forward and then yanked up on the collective. The helicopter groaned, lost four per cent of its rotor rpm before the engines responded. It also settled slightly toward the ground as Blanchard executed his ham-handed departure.

The briefing said that Lancer Five and Nine would depart to the right, orbit at 200 feet three miles away over the water. When called by the SEALs, land in a nearby clearing and extract the SEALs and their prisoner.

Vera keyed the mike as they were climbing out. "Pop Up, why don't you let me fly for a bit to give you a break."

Blanchard acknowledged the use of his call sign and raised his hands and took his feet off the rudder pedals. He'd gotten the call sign of Pop Up because he was the starting center fielder on the academy's baseball team. But, when he checked into his first squadron, he bragged about his .300 plus batting average in NCAA competition. It took him almost a full season of playing slow pitch softball team to master the art of hitting a softball coming at him in an arc. He did, however, hit some monstrous pop ups for easy outs, hence the call sign Pop Up.

The training exercise called for minimizing radio communication between the helicopters unless there was an emergency or the exercise commander wanted to change the sequence of events. No calls meant no change in plans, so Vera slid Lancer Nine into a loose left echelon on Lancer so she didn't have to look across the cockpit at her flight leader. It was also, she hoped, a signal to Derek as to who was flying Lancer Nine.

"Pop Up, remember, when they call, we're going to come in low and fast, scissoring behind Lancer Five to clear each other's tail. We will probably get a smokey SAM or two fired at us, so be ready with the flares. We're supposed to touch down within seconds of Lancer Five and less than a hundred feet from the SEALs. Look for their light signal. Our spot will be marked by green chem lights, Lancer Five's by red. We want to be on the ground less than thirty seconds."

"Got it."

Smokey SAMs were rockets that simulated a shoulder-fired, surface-to-air missile. The exhaust plume was designed to set off the helicopter sensors and the pilots would fire at least three pairs of flares from launchers on each side of the helicopter designed to decoy a heat-seeking missile.

Glancing at Blanchard, Vera could see he was staring straight ahead, not scanning the instruments. "Pop Up, how are we on fuel?"

Her own math said they had about 120 minutes of gas left. It took them 30 to reach the island. The mission plan included 30 to get back. Subtract 30 for a reserve from the 3.5 hours of fuel they had when they took off leaving at least two hours of fuel. Orbiting at 100 knots for 20 minutes will eat into the margin, but not enough to make it unsafe.

Rule of thumb said that at their HH-60H's weight which was about 20,000 lbs. the helicopter burned 950 pounds of jet fuel per hour at 90 knots. For each 10 knots of added airspeed, the fuel burn increased by about 100 pounds. So, at 120 knots, they were burning fuel at about 1,250 pounds per hour.

Blanchard glanced at the instrument panel and keyed the intercom, "We've got plenty." And went back to staring at the sky.

"Lancers, this is Gimbel Actual. Alpha and Bravo moving to the LZ. Two casualties on stretchers."

Vera recognized Derek's response on the radio. "Lancer's inbound, if possible, have one stretcher with each load."

Two clicks of the transmitter acknowledged Derek's response. Gimbel was the platoon's call sign and Gimbel Actual meant it was the raid commander. Alpha and Bravo were the two eight-man squads brought in by the HH-60Hs. In their brief, they covered bringing a stretcher on board.

Lancer Five had turned toward San Clemente Island and dropped down to 40 feet above the water. Vera eased off some power to let Lancer Five get about 500 feet in front of her. She keyed the intercom, "Crossing aft of Lancer Five."

Vera smoothly rolled the HH-60H into a 30-degree left bank to pass behind Lancer Five. Right after she started turning, Lancer Five rolled to the right. When they had about 1,000 feet of separation, almost in unison, they reversed their turns.

"Tapper, I've got it."

Vera let go of the controls and let Blanchard take over. His first cross was acceptable but in his second, Blanch climbed to 150 feet. If there was an enemy radar, the rotor disc would have alerted the enemy to their location or worse, let them target the helicopters with missiles or gunfire. Without looking, she made another note on her kneeboard.

Lancer Nine was crossing behind Lancer Five as they crossed the shoreline. A crewman in the back keyed the intercom. "SAM, SAM, three o'clock low."

Vera repeated the warning over the UHF radio. Rather than steepen the turn and pump out flares, Blanchard eased up the angle of bank and let the HH-60H climb. The helicopter ballooned to almost 300 feet before Blanchard reversed direction and dove for the deck, now way out of position. Vera held her tongue rather than saying anything. The crewmen in the back knew what happened and within hours after the exercise, Blanchard's performance will be known by all the rescue aircrewmen. As the aircrew training officer, Vera made a mental note to speak with the air crewmen after the mission.

"Lancer Nine, Lancer Nine, this is exercise control, you are considered shot down. Lancer Five, say intentions."

As per the exercise rules, Blanchard rolled the helicopter wings level and climbed to 1,000 feet over the island and entered a lazy orbit. Vera said nothing and scribbled notes for the debrief as they listened on the radio to Derek's improvised plan to extract 16 SEALs plus one prisoner. When Derek was finished, an empty Lancer Nine flew back toward NAS North Island in formation with Lancer Five.

Blanchard didn't wait until they finished the shutdown checklist to start unstrapping, a clear violation of squadron procedures. Vera looked over her shoulder to make sure that the aircrewmen were unplugged from the intercom before she keyed the intercom, "Sir, with all due respect, you are a clusterfuck of a special ops helicopter pilot. That was embarrassing to me, the aircrewmen, and Mr. Almer. I hope you are good at ASW because if you are, stay there. There's no way in hell any of the rescue aircrewmen will ever fly with you again, nor will I."

Blanchard glared at Vera but said nothing and headed for the debriefing room alone. Once she had her helmet and flight bag in hand, she walked around the HH-60H with the aircrewmen to finish their postflight inspection. "AW2 Thornburg and AW3 Nicholson, please join me on the way to the debrief."

Thornburg had been in the squadron long enough to know what was about to happen. Nicholson had just reported from rescue swimmer school and the combat corpsman course and didn't.

As they walked, Vera looking straight ahead wondered for a second what it looked like from the hangar. She was 5'2" standing between Nicholson who was a six foot and 180 pounds and Thornburg who was 6' 4" and 220.

"Mr. Blanchard's performance was not up to snuff and Mr. Almer will deal with that in a private conversation. However, I do not want rumors flying around the aircrewmen about Mr. Blanchard's unsatisfactory performance. Do I make myself clear?"

She heard two, "Yes ma'am's." Then Thornburg spoke. "Ma'am, the rescue aircrewmen hope the skipper will return to the two det concept that worked well. We do our thing and the ASW guys do theirs."

"Thornburg, we're working on it. Mr. Blanchard's performance today just gave it another endorsement. There is something in the works that may force the issue, but you did not hear that from the Aircrew Training Officer."

That afternoon, Derek was called into the CO's office. With him was LCDR Blanchard who, rightly so, took it on the chin, during the pilots only debrief.

Commander Richardson spoke evenly in a measured tone since he was trying to hide his annoyance. "Mr. Almer, don't you think you were a bit hard on the Ops Oh?"

"No sir, I don't. If this exercise was a HAC check for the HH-60H, Lieutenant Commander Blanchard would have failed. He made enough mistakes that would have put the mission at risk and endangered the lives of his crew and the SEALs on board his helicopter."

Richardson's jaw set. Three pilots witnessed Blanchard's poor performance so trying to defend the operations officer would cost the CO credibility. Instead, he decided to switch topics and snatched a piece of paper off the table, "Where did this come from?"

The CO held out his hand and Derek read the message from the Commander, Navy Special Warfare Group 1, outlining the type of training exercises he would like to conduct with HSC-8 and other Navy squadrons flying the HH-60H.

"Sir, he wants our helos regularly participating in their training evolutions. It will be good for our crews."

"We don't have the training hours to support this."

"Sir, he is offering to fund the exercises from Navy Special Warfare training and readiness accounts."

"How'd this come about?"

"Sir, I went to school with the training officer on the SEAL group's staff. Today's exercise was the first of many. May I remind you that when you made me the squadron's training officer, you instructed me to make the training as tough and as realistic as possible. That's what we are doing for the 60H's and why we have hops where the SH-60F crews get to ping on real submarines."

"How come I didn't know about this?"

Derek decided to stay formal. "Sir, I briefed the training plan to Mr. Blanchard when he checked in."

Richardson glared at his operations officer. The squadron's training plan was their blueprint to getting ready for their deployment to support operations in Iraq and Afghanistan.

Wanting to keep the initiative, Derek asked, "May I make a suggestion, sir?"

The CO hoped Derek was going to give him a way out with his dilemma with Blanchard who needed an ass chewing.

"Skipper, I would like to suggest an all-officers meeting during which the pilots choose whether they want to fly the F or the H. If there are not enough for one group or the other, then you can allocate officers. This way we can focus each aviator's training accordingly."

"Is this another way of splitting the squadron into two dets as per my predecessor?"

"Yes sir. I also believe as does the safety and NATOPS officers that this is the best approach. All we need is one accident in which one of the contributing causes is …."

Richardson waved his hand dismissively, "Yeah, yeah, yeah, lieutenant. I know, it will reflect on the CO, the XO, Ops Oh, and yes, even the training officer."

The CO looked at his operations officer who was standing as if he was made of stone. "Make the meeting happen, Racer. If it doesn't work out, it is your ass."

"Aye, aye, sir."

Derek walked out of the CO's office and as soon as he spotted Vera Hotchkiss, he called out. "Miss Hotchkiss, find AW1 Grayson and both of you come to my office ASAP!!!"

While Grayson was not the senior air crewman in the squadron, he had the most SAR and special ops experience. After Derek told the pair what the skipper agreed to, he said, "Start recruiting ASAP. Grayson, you know who you want in the back, and Ms. Hotchkiss and I will do the same with the pilots. We want at least six full crews, eight if possible."

When they left, Derek called his friend from Norwich. His friend was right, his CO had no choice but to agree.

TUESDAY, OCTOBER 29TH, 2002, 1:38 P.M. LOCAL TIME, BEIJING

Over the years, Senior Inspector Yong Mao learned that in the People's Republic, nothing was what it appeared to be. Corruption was everywhere, even in the Ministry of Public Security. He had his own moments when he was less than ethical but had never crossed that line from white to completely black. Experience had taught him that the higher in the organization, the greater the corruption. Power which begets control and money, he believed, was the source of men straying from what they should do legally, ethically, and morally.

When Mao was first assigned this case, i.e. investigate the possibility a pharmaceutical company had delivered bottles filled with sterile water instead of a polio vaccine, it appeared mundane. His visit to Special Hospital #326 flipped an internal switch. Mao was now angry and could not get the sight of his fellow citizens crippled by SinoPharma's greed out of his mind. The pictures of children who would never walk again or had limbs distorted by the disease were forever imprinted in his brain and were with him every step of the investigation.

Yong Mao was determined to arrest and prosecute everyone associated with the decision to allow SinoPharma to sell its fake vaccines. The company's senior executives were already in prison and it was now time to arrest those who failed to do their regulatory duty.

He needed a prosecutor willing to take on the powerful and well-connected Academy of Sciences. What Mao did not know was how far beyond Tang and Kong the corruption went. Or worse, how many other companies did Tang let go unpunished?

Senior Colonel Sun, who had the support of the Central Military Commission and the General Staff, had been a resource. So other than the obvious national security issue, why the PLA was involved? It was a question that begged an answer but Mao was not going to ask unless the evidence pointed in the army's direction.

Mao waited patiently in the fourth-floor conference room in the Ministry of Public Safety headquarters in Beijing. The table was made from polished bamboo sandwiched together, glued, sanded, and finished; the chairs padded; and curtains hung down the sides of the windows through which he could see Tiananmen Square. All of which contrasted with the steel-topped tables and unpadded chairs in the field offices.

Waiting let Mao make sure that his three folders, one with the chronology of the investigation; another with the list of the evidence he had collected along with some of the more damaging documents; and the third contained photos of Special Hospital #326 patients.

Yong Mao stood up when Ghoshi Haoyu entered followed by a younger woman he guessed was in her mid-30s. Haoyu had gray hair and wore glasses with heavy dark gray frames and a noticeable gray tint. Mao's peers referred to Haoyu as the "man with two first names." Behind his back, they called him the "man with two faces."

Haoyu's attitude as he sat down at the head of the table was "show me what you have and it better worth my time. Haoyu, who Mao guessed was in is 50s, nodded to Mao as if to say, "speak to me."

As a courtesy, Mao said to the woman, "I am Senior Director and Investigator Yong Mao. I specialize in financial fraud crimes and now, pharmaceutical fraud."

Grateful that she was not being ignored, the woman nodded and said, "I am Prosecutor Chyou Hu and I am both a physician and a lawyer and I work in Senior Prosecutor Haoyu's office."

Hu had a round, but attractive face. He also thought it odd that she wore no jewelry.

Mao started by noting that he had written statements and video recordings from three witnesses saying that two members of the National Academy of Sciences were told about the fraud and did nothing.

Before he could continue, Haoyu interrupted, saying, "That's hearsay and won't hold up in court."

Mao nodded and was unfazed, "We have bank records showing Kong and Tang were paid a quarter million Yuan each for consulting services. While we don't have recordings of the calls between Xiu Bai and Wei Ruan and Tang, we have the telephone records along with the time of the calls that corroborate what my witnesses said. And the SinoPharma executives are willing to testify against Kong and Tang."

The senior prosecutor leaned forward and put his hands flat on the table, palms down. "So you want an arrest warrant for a Senior Director of the National Academy and then have me take him to trial for bribery?"

"Yes, I do, Comrade Senior Prosecutor. However, before we arrest them, I want to dig deeper since I suspect there may be others. For that, I need search warrants signed by a judge here in Beijing."

"Do you know what you are looking for?"

"Yes. Here is a list of what I would like to examine."

Haoyu looked at the list and shook his head. "No judge will sign off on this list."

Alarm bells went off in Mao's head. Rather than argue, he asked, "To what will a judge agree?"

Haoyu looked at the list and then took a pen from his pocket and checked off three items. "Bring me a warrant request for these three items. You need to catch them in the act or plotting a crime before I will take the case on."

The senior prosecutor left the room. Chyou Hu pulled the list toward her so she could read it. "Senior Investigator Mao, I must apologize for Senior Prosecutor Haoyu's rudeness, but he has many demands for his time. Would you please show me all the evidence you have?"

When he was finished, Mao laid out the photographs saying these are the victims of SinoPharma's crimes. Chyou Hu face changed expression as she looked at a little girl wearing braces from her mid-section down and leaning on a pair of crutches. She had a wan smile on her face. When the photo was taken two years ago, Chyou's daughter Ah Lam was six. She was now eight.

"This pains me." Chyou forced herself to not cry. Ah Lam was five when she was diagnosed with polio and spent a year at Special Hospital #326. Chyou took official leave to visit her every month before An Lam returned home.

"It is not just children, there are adults as well." Mao slid more photos across the table of male and female polio victims. "If you want to really understand, I suggest you pay Special Hospital #326 a visit. I am sure Dr. Zheng will be happy to give you a tour. As of last month, she has eight hundred and seventy-two patients who are residents. More arrive every month. The last time I spoke to her, she told me that the People's Republic was about to double the size of the facility. I think there are more victims of SinoPharma out there, we just don' t know where they are."

Chyou Hu stood up and handed Mao her card. "If Senior Prosecutor Haoyu cannot help, my father works in the Ministry of State Security. I am sure he would be interested."

He would, Mao said, have his formal requests for warrants on Senior Prosecutor's desk by this evening. As a life-long bachelor, Mao had nothing to do in the evening but to work on this case.

Back in his 6th floor office, Senior Prosecutor Haoyu spun his chair to look through the window at the monument that is at one entrance to Beijing's Forbidden City. That was ancient China, and today it is the People's Republic of China. Communism had changed the outer layer of the culture, Haoyu mused, but not the core ways its society functioned. Satisfied he knew what he would do, he dialed a number from heart.

The phone rang once "Jie Kong."

"If you are free this evening, meet me in the bar at the Zhaolong Hotel on the main floor at six-thirty."

"I'll be there.

When Jie Kong slid onto the bar stool next to Ghoshi Haoyu, the prosecutor had put enough yuan on the table to cover his almost finished glass of whiskey. Since foreigners often had drinks at the bar, Haoyu assumed it was wired. "Let's take a walk."

Kong had been Haoyu's lead investigator for five years before taking his current position, one that Haoyu had used his contacts to ensure Kong was selected. Sure they were in an area where the ambient noise made it difficult for a microphone to record his words, Haoyu said, "I presume you know senior investigator Mao?"

"I do."

"You are now a target of his investigation."

Kong's head went up and down slowly. Mao was one of those investigators who were like a shark. Once they got their teeth into you, they didn't let go until they had consumed you.

"How close is Mao?"

"He has enough to charge you right now, but I told him I need more before I issue a warrant that lets him expand his investigation. Given his reputation, he will find every scrap of evidence there is and his work will be done legally."

Haoyu said nothing for a few meters before adding. "Mao's assistant is Zilan Deng from Guangzhou. I believe if Mao is removed, Deng may be persuaded to take on other cases and let this one will die."

Kong nodded two times. "How much time before Mao decides to move?"

"I suspect documents will be on my desk in the morning asking for a warrant to expand the scope of his investigation. I can sit on the warrants for a day or so, but eventually, I must issue them."

"So I have days, maybe a week or two."

Haoyu said nothing. His silence was confirmation of Jie Kong's assumption.

THURSDAY, OCTOBER 31ST, 2002, 2:22 P.M. LOCAL TIME, BEIJING

Dr. Ting Zheng needed a nap. Her flight from Zhanjiang was late and arrived at two a.m. She only had four hours of sleep before she left for an 8:30 a.m. meeting with officials at the Ministry of Health who showed her the plans to triple the size of Special Hospital #326.

While she was grateful, she asked what the ministry's plans were to deal with the root causes of why her facility needed a major expansion. Their answer was that water quality was a matter for the Ministry of Ecology and the Environment.

Her contacts at the provincial offices of the Ministry of Ecology and Environment had set up this meeting with Senior Director Bolin Xiao that would begin in a few minutes. Dr. Zheng believed the two studies commissioned by the Ministry of Health and endorsed by the regional office of the Guangdong and Guangxi provinces offices of the Ministry of Ecology and the Environment would or should have led to some action.

When Xiao entered the conference room, two members of his staff accompanied him. Dr. Zheng awkwardly pushed herself to her feet to greet the visitors. She sensed the knee lock on her brace drop into position so when she sat down, she pulled the lock back letting her foot fell to the carpeted floor with a soft thump.

Arrayed in front of Dr. Zheng were the studies and a folder full of pictures of Special Hospital #326's patients. Xiao clasped his hands in front of him and spoke in a condescending tone. "Dr. Zheng, it is so kind of you to come to Beijing. We are very aware of the projects recommended by our offices in Guangdong and Guangxi. However, you must understand that in the People's Republic, we do not have unlimited budget and must make choices based on the greater good of our citizens."

Before Bolin Xiao could continue, Dr. Zheng erupted and forced herself to her feet. She leaned over the table and glared at Xiao as she placed her paralyzed hand on the table palm down. "Look at my left hand. Touch it."

All three men found something else to look at in the room. "By God, look at me and touch my hand so you understand what eight hundred and seventy-two of my patients and thousands more live with every day."

Xiao finally looked Ting in the eye, but she was not finished. "The Ministry of Health has found the money to triple the size of Special Hospital #326. Why? Because the number of polio patients who need long-term rehabilitation in southern Guangdong and eastern Guangxi provinces grows by several hundred every year. So, if you want to do something for the greater good of our citizens, you can clean-up the water in Zhanjiang and other cities so I don't have to ask the Ministry of Health for another expansion."

One of the assistants piped up. "But what about polio vaccines for the people who live there? Our research suggests they are effective."

Dr. Zheng took a deep breath. "One, the vaccine is not one hundred percent effective. Two, not all our citizens are vaccinated." She started to say that at least one manufacturer didn't make vaccines that were effective but didn't. Instead she said, "The Ministry of Health has instituted a program to re-inoculate our citizens in the area with a newer, more potent vaccine. We are facing an infection rate bordering on an epidemic. Already our Ministry of Health is debating what it will report to the World Health Organization since it is getting harder and harder to hide the truth. So, if the Ministry of Ecology and Environment doesn't do its part, I will ensure the finger of blame points at this office."

The silence that came over the conference room was palpable. Dr. Zheng sat back down leaving her paralyzed hand on the table and spread out the photos on the table. "These are photos of patients in my hospital. Maybe you should keep them as reminders of why the projects proposed by your Zhanjiang office should be combined with similar ones in Yunnan, Guangxi, and Guangdong provinces where most of the polio cases occur. Maybe then, you might have a project worthy of your consideration."

Bolin Xiao stood up, clearly upset at being treated like a child. "My office will review the proposals. Good day, Dr. Zheng." He left and the other two asked where they could find the proposals. She pushed a folder across the table that contained the executive summaries of the proposals. It, along with her folder of pictures, was picked up by Xiao's assistants as they left the room.

Exasperated, Dr. Zheng decided to wait before she called her father who was the country's Minister of Science and Technology. Her mother, who was a Central Committee member who sat on the National Defense and the National Heath Committees would soon hear a report they would not like.

CHAPTER 19

PLANS YOU CANNOT HIDE

Coming into his apartment complex, one of the men at the security desk waved at Yong Mao as he walked through the doors. They were there, Mao was sure, to record who came in and who left rather than as protection for the residents. Mao heard his name and saw Dr. Chyou Hu walking quickly toward him.

Suddenly, her eyes went wide and someone yelled "Gun!!! Look out."

Mao turned and saw a man wearing a hood covering his face except for his eyes and mouth. He was pointing a suppressed pistol at him not five meters away. The man jerked the trigger for what Mao thought was the second time. Again, the gun didn't fire. Mao charged at the gunman while he was racking the slide to free the jammed round.

Mao grabbed the man's wrist above the pistol with his left hand and kneed his attacker in the groin. The pistol made a soft pop as it fired when Mao slammed the palm of his hand into the side of the gunman's head. The blow was hard enough to stun the shooter but not hard enough for him to release the pistol.

Mao twisted his grip and swung underneath the arm with the gun to try to wrench it free and gain leverage. Mao failed to achieve the second goal as the Chinese-made version of the Tokarev TT-33 known as the Type 54 clattered to the floor. Mao kicked it to the side rather than allow himself to become vulnerable by attempting to pick it up. The two men traded a series of blows. Mao avoided one to the face but took one in the chest, staggering him. He dropped back and waited for his attacker to charge. It had been months since he'd practiced fighting in a dojo, but he was confident he could defend himself long enough for help to arrive.

His attacker drew a knife with a long black blade and tried to intimidate Mao by moving it back and forth between hands. He waited until the man lunged at him and grabbed the man's wrist, just above the knife with both of his hands. Using his legs and torso, he forced it up and to the side as he twisted the assassin's arm. As he torqued the man's arm, Mao smashed his forehead into the attacker's nose.

The man staggered, trying to get away but Mao twisted his arm farther and the man screamed in pain as his shoulder dislocated. Mao again smashed his forehead into the man's nose. The knife clanged when it hit the floor. Now that he had control of his attacker, Mao tried to slam his foot into the man's knee but missed. His shoe slid down the man's shin.

While he didn't have complete control of the attacker, he did have enough to enable two policemen to force Mao's assailant face down on the terrazzo floor. As they did, Mao looked outside and saw a green Honda Accord speed away. He managed to memorize three digits of the license plate.

Mao flashed his badge. "I want to talk to this man before you take him away."

The policemen searched the man and found no identification. Mao pulled off the ski mask revealing a man in his twenties with short hair. He pointed to a small couch where visitors were asked to wait. "Take him over there."

Breathing heavily, one of the policemen showed Mao the two plastic bags that contained the pistol and the knife, now in its sheath and two spare magazines for the Type 54 pistol.

The man sat with his hands handcuffed behind his back and glaring at Mao. "You are going to tell me who hired you. It is your choice whether you do it here or I get the name at police headquarters where you won't like my methods."

"I received a phone call offering me 20,000 yuan to kill you. After I accepted the job, they sent me to a dead drop in a park that had an envelope with your photo and address and half the fee. More I don't know."

"Yes, you do. The caller knew how to reach you. What number did he call?"

The man said nothing. One of the policemen came over to Mao to tell him the van to transport the prisoner was outside the front door. He gave him the address of where he wanted the man taken and asked if he could ride in a car that followed the van to the Ministry of Public Security headquarters.

As Mao turned to go, Chyou Hu asked. "Senior Inspector Mao, I want to come with you. I witnessed the assault and I have information I need to tell you."

On the way to the Ministry of People's Security headquarters, Senior Investigator Mao asked the driver to radio headquarters to contact Investigator Zilan Deng to meet him in his office immediately.

While the assassin was being fingerprinted, photographed, and booked, Chyou Hu reminded Mao that neither of them could question the attacker. Mao was the intended victim and she was a witness. His response was simple, "This is why Investigator Deng is coming. He will conduct the interrogation."

"There is a protocol to follow in that attempted murder cases are assigned in a rotation."

He showed her a plastic card emblazoned with the logo of the Ministry of Public Security that he kept with his badge. It told the reader that they were to provide whatever resources or support requested. "I was given this card to use in my investigation into SinoPharma. If needed, I will use it to ensure my deputy, Zilan Deng, be assigned to this case which I believe, is connected to SinoPharma."

With the assassin in an interrogation room and yet to be examined by a doctor, Mao went back to his small office that had a desk, two vertical file cabinets and two chairs, one in front and one behind the desk. It didn't matter to Mao because he tried to spend as little time as possible in the office. Crimes were solved by gathering evidence and interviewing witnesses, not sitting at a desk.

"So, Prosecutor Hu, what did you want to tell me?"

"Jie Kong worked for Senior Prosecutor Haoyu for five years as his lead investigator. He owes his current position to Haoyu."

Mao looked at the ceiling and then at the young woman. "I did not know that. Thank you for telling me." To Mao, that explained why Senior Prosecutor Haoyu wanted to delay issuing arrest warrants for Tang and Kong.

"I took the liberty of preparing the documents for Senior Prosecutor Haoyu to sign authorizing the warrants. Now, since he may be implicated, we need to find another Senior Prosecutor and I know who to ask."

"Thank you, but why did you do this?"

Chyou Hu took a deep breath and fished one of the photos she had taken from their earlier meeting from her briefcase. She put it on the table. "This is my daughter. I will do everything in my power as a prosecutor to see all those responsible go to prison."

He was saved from saying something by a ringing phone. Investigator Deng was waiting for him and had an identity for his assassin.

Kong Mao started toward the door and Chyou put her hand on his arm. "Senior Investigator, show me that card again?"

"Why?"

"Please do. You'll understand after you do."

Mao obliged.

Chyou smiled. "Excellent. Now I can issue the search warrants you requested, assuming I receive the paperwork that justifies issuing the warrants."

"You are a woman after my own heart and will go a long way in this world. Investigator Deng has already sent a team to search the assassin's flat. What I will need is a warrant to get copies of Senior Investigator Jie Kong's and Dr. Toghon Tang's bank and phone records for the past five years. I think they will be most informative because I don't think SinoPharma is the only company that paid Tang."

Hu nodded and headed to her office while Yong Mao walked down to the basement where the assassin was sitting in a room, manacled, handcuffed, and chained to the floor. "Investigator Deng, what do you know about this man?"

"He is a former policeman who was fired for taking bribes. Since then, he has been arrested several times for extortion and robbery but in each case, the charges were dropped. I have requested the case files to learn why."

Deng handed Mao the card that showed the man's identity and address. "The searchers found 43,250 yuan in his apartment along with papers showing he has an account at the Bank of China and his address book. They also found another Type 54 pistol with a suppressor and two and half boxes of ammunition. All of those should be here in a few minutes. What do you suggest?"

Mao shook his head. "Tell him what you have found and give him a chance to tell us who hired him. I am willing to recommend a light sentence if he tells us. But he must cooperate now or we send him away for the rest of his life for attempted murder, resisting arrest, illegal possession of a firearm and illegal possession of a suppressor. That adds up to around thirty years in prison."

Deng nodded and entered the room with another officer who stood by the door. Mao dialed a number and told Chyou Hu that he may have another bank account number shortly to put on a search warrant and then settled into a chair behind the one-way glass to watch Deng work.

At first, the assassin was stoic and sat stone-faced, not wanting to speak or confess. Deng then started building the number of years the man would spend in prison. Ten years for the attack on Mao, another five years for owning a second firearm illegally. An additional five years for two boxes of ammunition, also owned illegally. The suppressor could add another five to ten years. And that was, Deng said, just the beginning. Once they have all the evidence, an aggressive prosecutor could ask for life because of his history of arrests.

A policeman stuck his head in the observation room to say he had the case files on the assassin's arrests. Mao asked him to put them on the table while he watched Deng. While the assassin was contemplating his future, Mao glanced at the first folder and learned the arresting officer was Jie Kong. In fact, in each arrest, Jie Kong was either the arresting officer or authorized his release because there was insufficient evidence to hold the man. The prosecutor who signed off on the decision not to press charges was Ghoshi Haoyu.

That was enough. He walked around and knocked on the door to ask Deng to come into the observation room. While he was looking over the files, two police officers came in with the assassin's bank book, his internal passport, and personal phone book.

Chyou copied down the bank account while Deng flipped through the phone book. The assassin wasn't smart enough to use some sort of code to disguise the names. Under Jie Kong, he had his phone in his flat, his direct dial number for his office along with Kong's direct number for his office.

Back in the interrogation room, Deng placed the assassin's phone book on the table. "In a few days, we will speak with everyone you called within the past year. Some will be questioned, some may be arrested, all thanks to you. So, are you willing to cooperate and help us?"

The assassin clasped his hands and leaned forward. "If I tell you everything, what can you do for me?"

Deng exited and came into the room with the one-way glass. "Prosecutor Hu, you cannot approve any bargain, but what do you think a senior prosecutor will accept?"

"Assuming everything he tells us can be used as evidence, then I think we can get him five years in a minimum-security prison."

"I'll tell him we can get a prosecutor to allow seven years in a minimum-security prison, but there is no guarantee unless he gives us Kong and Tang. Then, let's see what he says. If he cooperates, we will tape-record his statement."

WEDNESDAY, NOVEMBER 13TH, 2002, 11:07 A.M. LOCAL TIME, ANACOSTIA

Once Yan was back at DIA, what she suspected was true. Commander Lansing, who was the intel officer when she was on the Seventh Fleet staff, was now at DIA. A captain and head of the PLA Navy desk had gotten the head of DIA to ask for her by name. He remembered her analysis and its predictions and said to Yan on the day she checked in, "Your job is to lay out the growth plan of the PLA Navy. If you don't have the data, ask, and my job is to move heaven and earth to get it."

Yan started with the PLA Navy's carrier plans. She believed the PLA Navy a.k.a. PLAN wanted to create at least three carrier task forces, each of which could take on a U.S. Navy carrier battle or strike group.

Beginning with the PRC's acquisition of the Australian carrier *Melbourne*, which was supposed to have been bought for scrapping, Yan found a sequence of satellite images of Guangzhou showing the flight deck and the catapult and arresting gear being lifted out. On photos of Cangxian, the airfield that the PLA Air Force used for flight tests, Yan found a taxiway where trenches were dug into which the *Melbourne's* catapult were installed.

The Soviets sold their small carriers - *Minsk, Kiev,* and *Novosibirsk* - to the South Koreans, but environmentalists protested their contract to turn the ships into scrap metal so the ships went back on the market. The PRC gladly purchased all three and only *Novosibirsk* was scrapped. *Minsk* was turned into a theme park tied to a pier in Shenzhen and *Kiev* became a luxury hotel docked in Tianjin.

Yan was sure that the PLA Navy inspected *Kiev* and *Minsk* in detail and determined, as the Russian's did before them, that while the ships may look formidable, they were not vessels a navy could build task forces around to successfully fight a U.S. Navy carrier battle group.

Varyag, the Russian Navy's successor to the *Kiev*-class was acquired by the PLAN when it was less than 70% completed. The cover story was that it would be a theme park in Macau, but Yan found a succession of companies through which the PLAN purchased the vessel. *Varyag* was towed to Dalian where imagery showed it was being refurbished. A hole had been cut in her flight deck and satellite photos over time showed equipment being lowered into what marine architects suspected were its engine rooms.

In addition to the photos, Yan pored over PLA Navy as well as PRC strategy documents in their original Mandarin to see what she could glean about the PLA Navy's intentions for *Varyag*. She became convinced that the PRC was turning the Soviet-era carrier into an improved and more capable version.

By sorting through stacks of documents, Yan found orders for long lead items intended for the *Varyag* not available in the PRC.

She discovered references, albeit sometimes oblique, that the PLA Navy was building a new version from the keel up that would make improvements not possible in the original Soviet design. This improved version would give the PLA Navy two aircraft carriers, each displacing about 65,000 tons, or about 5,000 tons larger than a U.S. *Kitty Hawk*-class carriers but much smaller than 100,000-ton, nuclear-powered *Nimitz*-class.

Excited, she started looking for new designs for ships with ASW and anti-air warfare capabilities that would become the carrier's escorts in a battle group. Yan concluded that the PRC was focusing on large, multi-mission destroyers based on pirated Western designs. Comparing the PLAN's designs with those of the U.S. and NATO Navies, the similarities were alarming.

On charts showing PLAN ship designs, she notated their similarities to Western naval vessels. When she finished, she took the results to Captain Lansing who had her brief the head of the DIA. After the briefing, she was thanked for her work.

Frustrated at the lukewarm response to a clear long-term threat to the U.S. Navy's dominance in the Western Pacific, Yan went to Lansing for advice. His answer was that the shiny object attracting intelligence community's attention now was the war in Afghanistan and Iraq. Any and everything else took second fiddle. Eventually, Lansing said, they will wake up.

Yan wrote a cover note to the analysis that went into the file implying that if the U.S. does not counter the PRC's espionage and respond to this threat, the country may wake up 10 - 15 years from now and find itself with the second strongest Navy in the Pacific. If that happens, it will, she wrote, be hard to maintain the alliances the U.S. spent the Cold War building.

MONDAY, NOVEMBER 18ᵀᴴ, 2002, 3:22 P.M. LOCAL TIME, BEIJING

Senior Colonel Sun sat back in his chair, turned around and looked outside. One could tell winter was coming to Beijing because the smoke from all the coal furnaces hung a gray pall over the city. One could taste the acrid smoke and, if one walked outside for any length of time, ash would accumulate on one's clothing.

But today was a day to celebrate, quietly of course. Sun liked playing kingmaker and building a network that would, he was sure, be useful when, not if, he was promoted to major general, the next rank up from senior colonel.

Unlike others in the PLA, he started with a good foundation. His father was a lieutenant general on the General Staff. His twin brother ran Division 13 in the Ministry of State Security which was responsible for inspecting mail and telecommunications. His mother was the daughter of a Politburo member. Each had a network that he could tap into.

Why should Senior Colonel Sun celebrate?

Senior Prosecutor Haoyu was now simply citizen Haoyu awaiting trial which created an opening for a position to which Senior Colonel Sun could recommend a more honest prosecutor to fill. Mao said he was impressed with Choyu Hu so Sun asked his brother to recommend that she be considered. His recommendation was seconded by Senior Director and Senior Inspector Yong Mao whose recent successes added weight to the promotion of Prosecutor Hu.

Mao's arrest of Dr. Tang and Senior Investigator Kong created another opening he could use his influence to fill with someone beholden to him. Dr. Hang Ng was the perfect replacement for Dr. Toghan Tang who was now in prison for a long stay.

If Tang and Kong didn't know it, they would soon be contracted out to companies as cheap labor. In the PRC, the country doesn't pay for the full upkeep of the prison. Prisoners earned money by working as laborers in factories to pay for the food they eat, the clothes they wear, and the roof over their heads. Living in a Chinese prison, Senior Colonel Sun knew, was not pleasant.

With Dr. Ng now head of the Life Sciences department at the Academy of Sciences, Sun now had an ally to get more funds and highly qualified people to implement the next stage of *Insidious Dragon*.

Technically, Doctors Bao Gu and Jun Lín didn't work for him, although they were temporarily assigned to his staff. Now, the good doctor Ng was about to officially acknowledge his request.

While the Wuhan Institute of Virology was building its Level Four Biosafety lab, the PLA's lab was nearing completion. Like Special Hospital #326, it would be "off the books" but for a different reason. It was close to Nanning where there were two prisons full of subjects for tests of any diseases developed in his new Level 4 lab.

TUESDAY, DECEMBER 3RD, 2002, 9:22 A.M. LOCAL TIME, BEIJING

Neither Bao nor Jun were surprised when Senior Colonel Sun summoned them to Beijing. When they boarded the plane in Guangzhou on Monday afternoon, they believed that what they called their vacation was now over. While they could speculate on where they would be assigned, neither knew what Sun had planned.

Both were conservatively dressed in Western-style clothes when they were ushered into a well-appointed conference room at PLA headquarters. They felt out of place as they followed the young Army captain through the halls because almost every person they saw wore a uniform. They were led to a room with a table made from laminated bamboo, pressed, and glued together before being varnished and polished. Around the table were 12 high-backed leather chairs. A plate of cookies, a large pitcher of hot tea, cups and saucers, and bottles of mineral and purified water were in the center of the table. The furnishings were far nicer than those in the conference rooms at the Guangzhou Institute for Biomedicine and Health.

When Senior Administrator Siew handed them their vouchers for tickets, he wished them well and said, "Enjoy Beijing." He admitted that he had no idea why they were summoned. He did say if they saw Dr. Ng, please wish him well.

At the small hotel, Senior Colonel Sun's assistant handed them keys for separate rooms - a subtle reminder that in the People's Republic, co-habitation of unmarried men and women was still frowned upon.

She put her bag on the stand and didn't unpack. Instead, Jun opened the door to go down the hall to Bao's room and found him about to knock on her door. They started laughing and went out for a drink and dinner. Back in the hotel, Jun messed up the sheets and waved to where she thought the cameras might be placed and went to Bao's room.

The pair made love and, before they drifted off to sleep naked, Bao said, "I hope those from the Ministry of Internal Security who look at the recordings enjoyed the show."

Dr. Ng was the next person to walk into the conference room. After warmly greeting his former co-workers, he sat at the table next to where Jun presumed Senior Colonel Sun would sit. The Senior Colonel was prompt as was his custom. The first time a meeting with the PLA officer was scheduled, Jun was told by Senior Colonel Sun's administrative assistant that the colonel believed that promptness was both a courtesy to the others in the meeting and a sign of respect. Members of his staff were always at their places at least five minutes before a meeting when Senior Colonel Sun was scheduled to begin.

Greetings took only a few seconds before Senior Colonel Sun began to describe his plans for Doctors Gu and Lín. There was no, "How was your flight?" or, "Were the accommodations comfortable?"

Senior Colonel Sun assumed they were or his administrative assistant would have let him know. Hence, the agenda began almost immediately. Anything else would be, in Senior Colonel Sun's mind, a waste of time.

"Doctors, the discussion we are about to have is classified Top Secret and has the code word *Insidious Dragon*. The Ministry of State Security has recently conducted background investigations on each of you and has granted you access to this program. The Politburo has agreed with the PLA's assessment that in the People's Republic's two southernmost provinces – Guangxi and Guangdong – at least four diseases – dengue fever, malaria, typhoid, and polio – still plague our citizens. Just as important, many of the personnel on PLA Air Force Army and Navy's bases in this region are at risk from these diseases."

Everyone at the table knew that Sun wasn't finished.

"A new laboratory should be finished by the end of this month. This new lab will conduct research into these four diseases and determine if new variants exist. If possible, you are to test existing vaccines or medicines to see if they cure or prevent these new mutations."

Senior Colonel Sun consulted his notes. "Dr. Gu will lead the research into immunology and Dr. Lín will focus on virology. Anyone assigned to this lab must be approved by the three of you. The senior administrator for the facility will report to both of you and help you with the administrative work needed to transfer them to this facility. It is up to the three of you to decide if this person will be allowed to provide input on any candidate. Later today, Dr. Ng will bring the resumes to this conference room for the senior administrator candidates for the three of you to interview and ultimately choose."

Both Jun and Bao sat impassively waiting for Senior Colonel Sun to finish. He was, as they suspected, not finished with his briefing.

"This new facility will be known as Special Laboratory #62 and is funded and controlled by the PLA since the work is required for national security. The Academy of Sciences will be responsible for providing the research staff, the PLA will provide security, use our access to overseas procurement when needed, and funding. The entire 215th Special Support Force battalion which has expertise in dealing with chemical spills and biological waste will be stationed on the grounds along with a company of military police for security. Dr. Gu and Dr. Lín, I believe you have met the 215th's commander, Major You Yichen."

Senior Colonel Sun checked off another note and then looked at the two doctors who would lead the research. "Dr. Gu and Dr. Lín, immediately after this meeting, you will be escorted by one of my staff to have your internal passports stamped, new national ID cards issued along with PLA cards that will give you access to this building and Special Lab #62. From a military protocol perspective, you will have the privileges of colonels."

Unfolding a map, Senior Colonel Sun spread it out so that the others at the table could see. He pointed to a small circle on the map. "Special Laboratory #62 is located here, south-southeast of Nanning. The research staff will live in Nanning. We have reserved enough one-, two-, and three-bedroom apartments in a building near the Nanning Medical University to accommodate the entire staff. The guard detail for the apartment building will be provided by the security company whose commander will report to Major Yichen. Dr. Gu and Dr. Lín, you will be driven to and from the lab each day by car. The drive should take you about twenty minutes. The others will travel by vans. The road is, unfortunately, crushed rock. Once the lab is operational, we will begin paving the road."

Senior Colonel Sun looked at the two doctors. "Questions?"

Bao, always the practical one, asked, "When do we have to move to Nanning?"

"After March 1st, the Army will help you pack and transport your possessions to Nanning by truck. While they are enroute, the Army will provide hotel rooms."

Jun was still trying to understand the scope of the research she was expected to perform. "Senior Colonel Sun, you mentioned four diseases. They are already controlled in most of the People's Republic provinces. Malaria and dengue fever are spread by mosquitos which can be controlled by spraying pesticides not harmful to humans. Polio and typhoid are spread by contaminated water. It is my understanding that the only contaminated water is near Zhanjiang. Are you suggesting this is a bigger problem?"

Senior Colonel Sun had a thick neck and large biceps that were the result of hours in the weight room. He nodded noticeably, "Dr. Lín, I gather you have not seen Dr. Zheng's latest report, but the number of polio cases in Zhanjiang and all along the People's Republic's southern coast is increasing exponentially. The Ministry of Health believes it is an epidemic but will not say so because of the international implications. The Ministry of Environment and Ecology project to fix the water supply in Zhanjiang where the largest cluster of cases is located will take several years, as in three or four, before it is completed. Dr. Zheng's facility is being tripled in size and she does not think that it will be enough. She is concerned that the poliomyelitis virus in these provinces may have mutated. Already she is seeing permanent paralysis rates in the ten to twelve percent rates in children under twelve and higher in adults. Worse, Dr. Zheng believes, based on her limited sample, the fatality rate amongst children and adults are higher than norms."

"So, Senior Colonel, is polio in all its forms going to be the focus of our research?"

"Yes. We also need to look at the other diseases, but all forms of polio should be the first target."

Sun said what he said with a straight face. There were enough facts to support his words, but it was his emphasis that was a lie. He really wanted Dr. Lín to isolate either the current or mutated poliomyelitis virus to use as a biological weapon.

Their discussion on roles and responsibilities went on until it ended when a member of Senior Colonel Sun's staff came into escort Bao and Jun to the security office. Dr. Ng left for a meeting and would return at one with the resumés.

Back in the conference room, Senior Colonel Sun came in and closed the door. He did not sit down. "Doctors, there is something I must say. First, both Dr. Ng and I know you are not married and therefore it is party and PLA policy we should assign you separate apartments. However, given the shortage of apartments, we are assigning you a two-bedroom unit. If you end your relationship, it will be complicated since I will have to explain why."

Neither Bao nor Jun said anything.

"Second, Dr. Lín, I appreciate that you have kept me apprised of your family that lives in the United States. Again, you are not the only citizen of the People's Republic with relatives living abroad. I trust you will be circumspect in what you say about your new assignment. Officially, Special Lab #62 doesn't exist on paper. You may tell them that the party has assigned you as a professor of virology at the Nanning Medical School where Dr. Gu will be a professor of immunology."

Sun did not mention that he had read all the reports filed by Bao about his relationship with Jun. Senior Investigator Lieu will be told that Dr. Gu has been transferred and he is no longer the senior investigator's asset. His file was being transferred to the Ministry of State Security office in Nanning and an officer will contact Dr. Gu after he arrives.

By the end of the afternoon, the staff, or at least the list of individuals whom they wanted to interview, was set. They would return to

Guangzhou and then, once the interviews were scheduled, they would return to Beijing where they would be held.

WEDNESDAY, DECEMBER 11ᵀᴴ, 2002, 1:22 P.M. LOCAL TIME, ANACOSTIA

Shi Huáng called Yan the moment the letter arrived. As she did with Jun's previous letters, it went into a Federal Express envelope marked for next-day delivery. Knowing that it was coming, Yan waited for it to arrive and then alerted the administrative assistant who supported Captain Lansing's team. At DIA headquarters, the envelope was scanned for a bomb and checked for chemicals before Yan was allowed to bring it to her office.

She went into a secure conference room and decoded the message written on the aerogram form letter postmarked from Beijing. After Yan read it the first, time, she didn't believe her eyes. Then Yan read the terse text again.

> Polio – both non-paralytic and paralytic, bulbar, spinal bulbospinal – epidemic in Guangxi and Guangdong. PRC not reporting cases to the WHO since number in the 1000s. Am being assigned to Special Laboratory #62 approx. 20 km SSE of Nanning on March 1. Tasking is to evaluate potential of polio virus to mutate through gain of function research. Suspect biowarfare project due to TS classification and code name Insidious Dragon. MTK.

Yan swallowed hard. Before, all Jun's notes provided insight into the state of the PRC's healthcare system. This, however, was a game changer. Yan wondered if Jun thought she was in danger, but the letter didn't indicate she was and the MTK – more to come – meant that Jun thought she would have other opportunities to send more.

On the way to Captain Lansing's office, Yan tried to script what she should say. Her biggest fear was that the DIA or CIA would want to control Jun as their agent. If that was the case, she would not cooperate and, if needed, resign her commission. She took a deep breath and knocked on Captain Lansing's door.

Within minutes of Yan finishing her description of her relationship with Jun and the contents of the note, the head of the epidemiology department at the National Center for Medical Intelligence was sitting in Captain Lansing's office. The delay gave her time to call up her prior reports.

Captain Eagan Rainbow listened, almost without emotion, to Yan's short briefing. At the end, he asked one question. "How sure are you that your cousin is telling the truth?"

"Very. I would bet my life on it."

Rainbow tented his hands under his chin as he thought about what he would say next. "What Dr. Lín has told you is consistent with reports we have received and are receiving from other sources. Since you are not cleared for that intelligence, I cannot say more."

There was a pause before Captain Rainbow continued. "Lieutenant Commander Huáng, what do you want to do as the next step? It is clear Dr. Lín has an interest in keeping you, a Naval Intelligence Officer, informed."

Yan looked at Captain Rainbow, then at her direct superior, Captain Lansing, and explained what she wanted to do and why.

Rainbow's reaction was, "That's high risk but maybe worth the effort. I will run it by the agency's Clandestine Service and the Defense Cover Office and see what they think."

After Captain Rainbow left, Yan went back to her desk wondering if she did the right thing. Jun had stuck her neck way out in her note. Would she be able to help?

CHAPTER 28

DAMNING INFO

Jun and Bao returned to their apartment building from the Institute of Biomedicine and Health where they signed forms that documented their change in status. Officially, they were still assigned to the institute through which they were paid and apartments were assigned until February 1st when they would become officers in the PLA.

When they entered, the security guard handed Jun a DHL envelope. The return address was her grandfather's. From what she could tell, the bright yellow and red envelop had not been tampered with.

Beginning in 1980, Zimo Huáng set up a brokerage account in Jun's name into which he deposited $10,000 per year that would go into mutual funds. The funds were selected based on their ability to return eight to 10% per year, post-tax. The money would give Jun, if she ever decided to emigrate to the U.S., a nest egg. Zimo was paying the taxes on the income as the co-signee so the total would continue to grow. In the years since he set it up, the mutual funds were averaging a 12% post-tax growth.

Jun tossed the bright yellow envelope on the table and opened the door to their small balcony. Bao followed Jun her and stood stroking her lower back. "Aren't you going to see what is in the envelope. It is not every day that you get something from your grandparents."

His reason behind the question was more than curiosity. Its contents were something Bao could tell Senior Investigator Lieu. He did not know that Lieu was about to be told that Dr. Gu and Dr. Lín were about to be transferred and Lieu was not, repeat not, to attempt to contact Dr. Gu ever again.

Jun turned to face her lover and placed her arms around Bao's neck. "My lover, you are about to learn something you cannot share with anyone. My grandfather has been very generous to me."

"As grandfathers should."

Jun stood on her toes and kissed Bao. "Promise me you will tell no one, including my mother?"

"I promise."

"Go sit on the couch and we will open the package together."

"So you know what is in it?"

Jun nodded and let her hands drop and caress both Bao's sides and the top of his rear before she took one of his hands in hers. "I do. Come…"

They sat shoulder to shoulder while Bao caressed Jun's thigh. Bao's touch made concentrating on what she was doing difficult. Jun put her hand on his as if to say, stop, and pulled the tab to open the envelope.

Taped to the cover letter from the broker that described the contents of the folder, there was a short note from her grandfather that said, "Someday, you can enjoy this." Then he wrote, US$1 = CN¥8.47

In the folder was a copy of an Ameriprise end-of-year statement. The front page showed the fund's growth and the value of her shares which was $601,099 as of December 31st, 2002. The other pages were the summaries of the transactions.

Bao looked at Jun as her brain tried to make the calculation to convert dollars into yuan but couldn't. Jun put the folder on the armrest of the couch and turned to Bao whose hand was still between her legs. She put her hands on Bao's cheeks and pulled his face toward her so she could kiss him.

"My love, it is about five million yuan which in the People's Republic is a lot of money."

Bao took a deep breath, surprised by the amount. His head pulled back.

The implication was that if she ever went to the United States, she would have some money. The account in a brokerage firm in the U.S. kept funds away from the prying eyes of the Ministry of People's Security. He was sure investigators would interpret that she was, at some time, planning to defect.

"So, my lover is a rich capitalist?"

Nodding, Jun put her hand on Bao's arm and then slid her fingers into his hand that had been working its way up her inner thigh. "By capitalist standards, I am far from rich. Someday, I may be able to spend this money. Now that I have seen the annual statement, I will destroy it by burning them in a pan and then flushing the ashes down the sink."

At the stove, Jun lit the sheets on fire with the gas and then dropped them in a large pot to finish burning. Then she used a wooden spoon to break up any pieces which were then flushed down the drain.

Changing the subject, Bao asked. "Would you leave the People's Republic?"

This was, Jun knew, a loaded question. If Bao ever was interrogated by the Ministry of State Security or People's Security, one expected to be beaten and tortured and he would reveal her answer. "I have a duty to take care of my mother. When she leaves this earth, then I will decide."

Bao leaned over and kissed Jun. "That was a very political answer. You are all I have and care about. Until I met you, this country brought me nothing but pain."

Jun leaned forward and French kissed Bao. "I love you and I will never do anything to hurt you."

Breathing heavily because she understood the implications of their conversation, Bao responded. "I would die before I would betray you."

The pair sat with their foreheads touching, breathing deeply. They were savoring the moment in which they shared a fear deep inside their brains that they may soon be pawns in a game they do not like. Any misstep could lead to torture, prison, and/or death.

SUNDAY, JANUARY 12TH, 2003, 9:36 A.M. LOCAL TIME, MAMMOTH LAKES, CA

From where she stood on the second floor, Adrian Almer could barely see the trees across the street through the heavy snow. On the local TV station, the weatherman announced a "Dump Alert" meaning the anticipated snowfall at the ski area for the next few days would be measured in feet, not inches.

With Derek's blessing, Adrian used money from her trust fund to rent a two-story, three-bedroom, three-bath house on the corner of Canyon Lodge and Warming Hut #2 Road. From the front door, Adrian could walk across the street to a gap in the trees, put her skis on and ski down to the Canyon Express chairlift.

About halfway through summer school, Adrian decided she needed a break. She'd always wanted to be a ski bum and this was her opportunity. The owner was willing to rent the house at a substantial discount if she would take it until the area closed on the July 4th weekend.

Derek went along on the condition Adrian would host the wives and children of HSC-8 who wanted to come to Mammoth for a vacation. Adrian readily agreed since over the summer she'd become friends with several cruise wives. And, on one of her visits, Adrian spoke with Mammoth's management who sold her a half dozen adult season guest passes and a dozen for skiers under 12 at a 50% discount. The only expense for squadron members would be food and ski rentals.

In the first week, after trying several different ski brands and models, she treated herself to a new pair of 178-centimeter-long Dynastar Course Giant Slalom Skis with Marker M10.0 bindings. Derek raced on Dynastars and recommended them. He was right and she fell in love with how they held their edges in round, carved turns on hard, packed snow and were easy to handle when it got deeper.

Before driving to Mammoth, Adrian had bought a small library at Mercury. The books, along with her regular clothes, and the small box of toys Derek gave her were packed into her Volvo S70.

With the snow floating down, the house was eerily quiet now that the last of the Christmas and New Year's holiday guests had departed. Adrian held her mug of coffee in cupped hands, thinking the upper part of the mountain would be closed given all the snow that was falling. Today, she thought, would be a great day to curl up with a book.

A snowplow drove past the window as Adrian looked at the falling snow. Overnight, almost a foot had fallen and Adrian wondered if Lea Ann Scranton and Betsy Schroeder, two HSC-8 wives with whom Derek and she were friendly, would make it up from San Diego. They said they were leaving San Diego about nine in the morning. With luck and good roads, they would make the 400-mile trip in about seven hours.

Betsy, whose husband Eric was the squadron's administration officer, was planning to drive their 2001 Toyota 4Runner Limited with all-wheel drive. She grew up in Aspen, Colorado, and met her husband when they were students at the University of Colorado in Boulder.

Lea Ann Scranton was, like Adrian, a New Englander. She grew up in Springfield, Massachusetts and was a graduate of Bennington College. She'd dated Matt off and on while they were in high school and then she started seeing him regularly when he was at Rensselaer Polytechnic in Troy, New York. Bennington was less than an hour away from Rensselaer.

While the Almers, Schroeders, and Scrantons weren't the only couples in the squadron who did not have children, the three women gravitated together at parties which drew the husbands in. Matt Scranton was in the unofficial HH-60H detachment led by the squadron's maintenance officer-in-charge (OinC), Lieutenant Commander Gus, short for Gustav, Johansson.

Johansson volunteered to fly the HH-60Hs at the all-officers meeting where the pilots chose which aircraft. This was his first experience in the CSAR and special operations world and he jumped in with both feet. In their first private meeting, Johansson admitted he didn't know "shit from shinolah" about the HH-60H mission but was willing to learn.

Adrian went to the master bedroom, showered, and dressed before pulling a book from the box. She had fallen in love with Rosa de la Cruz's series that started with *The Pair, The Racers, The Grinders, The Champions* and ended with *The Repeaters*. Now de la Cruz had another work published called *The Shell Project*. She'd read her favorite, *Lotus Bloom* several times and was thinking of reading it again.

The crunch of potato chips and concentrating on reading *The Grinders* almost caused her to ignore her ringing Nokia 3560 phone.

"Adrian, hi, it's Betsy. We're just turning onto Davidson."

She looked at her Rolex. It was not even two. *Where had the morning gone?* "Wow, you made good time?"

"Well, we saw the weather report and left at about seven instead of nine."

"Did you have to put on chains?"

"No, we've got all-season tires and Betsy shifted into four-wheel drive at one of the stations where the state police check for chains."

"I'll open the garage. The driveway hasn't been plowed yet."

"How much snow is the mountain going to get?"

"Don't know, Betsy. At least a foot and it's supposed to keep snowing tonight. They're talking two and a half feet at the base and three or four at the top."

"Fantastic. See you in a few minutes."

FRIDAY, JANUARY 24TH, 2002, 4:18 P.M. LOCAL TIME, GUANGZHOU

Yan could feel the tension rise inside her as she inched closer to the PRC immigration booth for foreigners. She pushed whatever self-doubts she had about meeting with Jun out of her mind. It was, she believed, the only way they could figure out how to keep communicating.

Her mental debate about the wisdom of a Naval Intelligence Officer with access to some of the most sensitive intelligence on the PRC's navy continued. Her cover - Yan was visiting a cousin and an aunt – wasn't a cover, it was the truth. Her visa application said she was an employee of San Diego Real Estate Investments owned by her Uncle Tao. Should someone call the telephone number on the application, it would ring on her Aunt Mei's desk. The trip was approved by the head of the DIA that she was a civilian visiting a relative. Before Yan left, she was given a two-week crash course in spy craft at what she assumed was a CIA facility in Virginia.

Four days after she left the CIA facility, Yan walked off the

Cathay Pacific flight and checked into Mandarin Hotel on Hong Kong Island. She walked around the city, practicing her Mandarin and forcing her body to adjust to the 12-hour time change.

When she hugged her three-year-old daughter Min before she left, Yan hoped it would not be for the last time. Her grandparents had moved into Yan's house in Glenn Dale after Glenn was tossed out so her absence for a week or more wouldn't be too much of a shock for her daughter.

At the kiosk, Yan presented her U.S. passport and her entry card. The officer looked at her and said, in English, "Welcome to China. Enjoy your stay." He stamped her passport and entry card and Yan walked into the People's Republic of China.

Her grandfather said that the only hotel worth staying at in Guangzhou was the White Swan. After unpacking her bag, Yan wanted to appear as a rich American and hailed a taxi to take her to Lianhe. From what she remembered from her trip as a teenager, the city hadn't changed much. Yan walked from the street into the complex and found the building where Bao and Jun lived.

She waited outside until two families walked into the building and followed closely. The guard waved at them as they passed by his desk. Inside the elevator, the other couples pushed the buttons for floors six and eight, she pushed the one for 10.

Jun's apartment was at the end of the corridor. Yan took a deep breath and knocked. No answer. She tried the doorbell, again no answer.

After debating what she should do, Yan sat on the floor and took out a book in Chinese. A couple came out of the elevator and said, "Do you want to see their apartment. It will be available in March?"

Yan wasn't quite sure what to say. "No, I am waiting for my cousin Dr. Lín. She said to wait and she'd be back soon.

If the couple was suspicious, the security guard would be here shortly and then the fun would begin. Yan was engrossed in her book when she heard the clump of boots on the tile floor made by a security guard.

"Miss, if you are waiting for someone, you must wait in the lobby and meet Dr. Lín there. Please, may I see your identification?"

Yan was prepared for that question. She had an internal Chinese passport and national ID card saying she was from Nanning in her purse. She found them in her purse and was about to hand both documents to the guard when Jun and Bao came out of the elevator carrying net bags full of groceries. "There she is!"

Yan ran to her cousin who put her bags on the floor so the two could hug. Jun blurted out, "Yan, this is a wonderful surprise. It is so good to see you. You look wonderful!!!"

The guard stood off to one side. Yan, not wanting her Chinese IDs to be entered in a log, asked for them back. The guard smiled and handed the red booklet with the plastic Resident Identity Card to Yan.

As soon as the elevator doors closed with the guard inside, Jun put a hand on Yan's arm. "This is my lover, Bao."

Yan bowed slightly. "I have heard about you from our grandparents. The video tapes my grandfather showed do not show you as handsome as you are." While her grandparents didn't approve of Jun living with Bao, they accepted it since it was common in Southern California.

"You are much too kind. Jun, keeps me young."

Yan remembered Aunt Liang as strict, formal, even stodgy, and very traditional. The aunt she hugged when Liang came for dinner was attractive and was wearing a mid-thigh dress that was tight enough to show off her figure but was not overly suggestive.

Later that evening, Liang and Bao hung back to let Jun and Yan talk as they walked around the Lianhe Residential District. Yan was sure they were out of earshot of the two women behind them when she asked how much they knew about the letters. She was gratified to learn that Liang knew nothing and all Bao knew was Jun was writing letters to her relatives in the U.S.

Yan asked when she could talk to Jun about what the work in Nanning and she said tonight, after Liang left, and they would have to do it away from their apartment.

"I prefer to speak with you alone."

Jun asked, "Do you not trust Bao?"

Yan replied, "I know you love each other, but right now, you shouldn't trust anyone with this secret, including Bao."

"Agreed but it's hard."

"Jun, you live in the People's Republic of China. Neither the Ministry of State Security nor the Ministry of Public Safety care whose lives they destroy. They will do whatever is necessary to get whatever secrets you are keeping out of you."

Jun didn't say anything because she knew her cousin was right.

SATURDAY, JANUARY 25TH, 2003, 4:29 P.M. LOCAL TIME, MAMMOTH LAKES

The snow finally stopped around four, Friday afternoon. Even though the upper part of the mountain was not open, the three women spent the day yo-yoing off the runs off the Gold Rush, Canyon Express, and Chair 22 lifts. The trails were groomed, but the snow kept coming down. On each run, they found untracked powder, usually about six inches to a foot deep.

Saturday's weather was, as Lea Ann stated when she stepped into her bindings, glorious. The sun was out, the temperature in the low 20s, and the entire mountain was open. Earlier in the morning, they heard the booms from the explosions knocking down the cornices where avalanches started.

They all hoped that the snow would have delayed many of the skiers from Los Angeles who would have to slog up U.S. 395, but it didn't. By lunch, the area was crowded and getting more so. Spoiled by short lines, the three women decided to return to the house.

This was the second week Betsy and Lea Ann had come to Mammoth and Adrian welcomed their company. Skiing alone, while fun, was O.K. Skiing with good friends was better.

Rather than go out for dinner, they agreed to "eat in" so they went first to Von's and then to the Meat Market. Besides a large hot tub, the house had a propane-powered grill on which Lea Ann offered to grill the flank steak.

While the steak marinated in the bowl, the three changed into bathing suits and slid into the hot tub's 102^0 F water, each with a glass of wine to, as Lea Ann said, marinate their tired muscles. After dinner, the three were working on finishing their second bottle of wine when Lea Ann, who was the youngest of the three, asked, "How do you manage to get through these cruises?"

For Betsy, HSC-8 was her third squadron since Eric was designated a Naval Aviator. After three years in HSL-43, Eric was assigned as an instructor at HS-10. Three years later, he was in HSC-8. This was, by Betsy's count, Eric's fourth long cruise, three in HSL-43 and now one in HSC-8.

Adrian had managed to live through her first and now this was her second. The first was an academic success and an emotional disaster. She was, she believed, handling this one much better. Now she knew what to expect.

Betsy sipped her wine before saying, "You need to have something to do that you like or you'll lose your mind. I got my teaching license in California and substitute teach when I am not hanging out with the wives in the squadron that I like." She tilted her glass toward the other women. "Adrian got two semesters of law school out of the way."

Shaking her head, Lea Ann meant something else. Giggling, she said, "I'm not a nun!!! What do you do for sex? Eric left me a bunch of toys, but let's face it, they are not a substitute for the real thing!"

Lea Ann's comment generated a round of giggles which stopped when Betsy Schroeder spoke in a serious tone. "Remember, the guys have a saying that what goes on during a cruise stays on the cruise. It's a way to tell each other that if a guy or his wife decides to fool around while they are deployed, no one says anything. Well, that goes the same for us with two caveats. One, if you are a woman, you better not get pregnant or if you are a guy, you better not impregnate someone who is not your wife. Two, if you fool around, be very discrete because you have no idea who may spot you. All it takes is someone to say something to his significant other and it will be all over the world. We had that happen in Eric's first squadron, HSL-43. One of the wives was carrying on and when someone showed her husband a photo of his wife kissing a guy, the shit hit the fan. I believe that about ten percent of the couples in the squadron have one partner screwing around."

Betsy took a long sip of her wine and then continued. "My point is, if one wants to screw around, do it outside of San Diego. And, if it is a wife, do it the Bennington Way."

Adrian started laughing and new what it meant. "I've never heard that before."

Betsy Schroeder who grew up in Aspen looked at Adrian and then Lea Ann quizzically. "O.K., I'll bite, what is so funny?"

Lea Ann said that Bennington started as a liberal arts college for women and had a reputation for being very accepting of lesbians. She guessed that when she was at Bennington, maybe a third or more of the female students were either bi or lesbians.

Each woman sipped their wine, not wanting to continue the discussion, at least to where it was headed. Both Adrian and Derek had heard that expression before and knew Bennington's reputation. At Middlebury, Adrian's first roommate was gay and tried to seduce her. That led to a change in dorm rooms and roommates.

Adrian decided not to mention her collection of sex toys and what Derek referred to as "fuck books" and "fuck movies." Instead, she said, "I've had way too much wine and am going to bed. See you in the morning."

SUNDAY, JANUARY 26ᵀᴴ, 2003, 9:28 A.M. LOCAL TIME, GUANGZHOU

When Jun knocked on Yan's hotel room door, her cousin had just come out of the shower. They waited until room service had delivered breakfast before Jun began placing the documents she brought with her on the coffee table. Last night, Yan said she had a device that scanned her room for listening devices and had looked for cameras and found none.

When Jun was finished, there was a stack of information 15-centimeters tall on the table. One document was the transcript of Jun's and Bao's depositions in which they explained their analysis of the vaccines made by SinoPharma. Another was Dr. Zheng's 1998, 1999, 2000 and 2001 reports to the Ministry of Health documenting the expanding number of polio cases in both Guangxi and southern Guangdong. Dr. Zheng's justification for expanding Special Hospital #326 and her request to clean-up of the water north of Zhanjiang was in the pile that included Dr. Zheng's briefing on Special Hospital #326. Last was a centimeter-thick folder of photos of the patients.

Yan picked up one of Dr. Zheng's reports "What am I supposed to do with these?"

"Give them to someone who can stop this epidemic. Our Ministry of Health is not interested. And what I am about to be asked to do may make things worse and I cannot stop it."

Jun reiterated her conversation with Senior Colonel Sun and her suspicions that led to her letter.

"I can't carry these with me on a plane. What do you propose I do?"

Jun handed Yan three large envelopes that could be sealed. "There is a DHL office in the international terminal at Baiyun International airport. Bring them there to send to Aunt Mei. I'll give you a fake return address so they cannot be traced. I am sure the front desk has some packing tape."

"Has that worked before?"

Jun nodded.

Yan was very serious when she spoke. "Going forward, here is how we will communicate. If you are anywhere in the People's Republic, memorize this number that the Ministry of State Security cannot trace. I don't understand all the telephone technology, but it will ring a number in Guangzhou, then the call will be switched to a number in Hong Kong and then a number in the U.S. When someone answers, in English or Mandarin, ask if this is Cousin Shan. The person on the other end of the phone will then connect you to me."

"That is not a name I have heard before."

"Shan is your mother's and my father's brother who died of typhoid in 1948. When I come on the line, we will ask each other questions for which only you and I know the answers. It is simple and should work. In fact, we are going to test it tonight from either your apartment or from a phone at the post office. My Nokia mobile phone should ring."

Jun nodded and memorized the number and left to go back to her apartment. When Jun left, Yan sealed the envelopes and hailed a taxi to take her to Baiyun airport. The woman at the DHL kiosk asked her for identification, she handed the woman her Chinese ID card along with the cash needed to pay for the shipment. The clerk made a note on the waybills that the fees had been paid and tossed them into the bin that almost overflowed with other packages. The packages, the clerk said, should be delivered in three days to her father's real estate development firm in San Diego.

At about 4:15 p.m., Yan was in her room, waiting to meet Aunt Liang for dinner when her Nokia phone started ringing. "Is this Cousin Shan?"

CHAPTER 21

COLD RESCUE

Walking down the passageway, Derek could feel the 100,000-ton *U.S.S. Carl Vinson* (CVN-70) pitch up and down. How much, he couldn't tell until he walked out on the flight deck that was wet from rain. The ship had just emerged from a squall line leaving small puddles of water dotting the flight deck. In the light from the quarter-moon moonlight, Derek estimated the deck was moving up and down about five or six feet.

Vinson was running downwind between launches and recoveries to let the ship's speed and the wind come close to canceling each other out. Derek shivered in the 40⁰ Fahrenheit air despite wearing a turtleneck under his flight suit and leather flight jacket.

Derek pulled on his helmet specifically designed for helicopter pilots as he stood just off the white stripe that marked the port side of the angled deck's runway. He and his crew were waiting for the HH-60H they were about to fly to return from delivering mail to the cruisers and destroyers of Strike Group Three. The pilots braked the rotor to a stop and left both engines running. The co-pilot climbed out and Derek's co-pilot, Lieutenant Junior Grade Matt Scranton, climbed into the left seat while the helicopter was being refueled.

Derek walked around to look for leaks before he climbed into the right or helicopter commander's seat.

As he buckled his shoulder harness, Matt Scranton pointed to the fuel totalizer that showed the helicopter's internal fuel tanks and the single external tank on the starboard side were full. With 4,015 pounds (~590.4 gallons) of fuel in the fuselage tanks and 815 pounds (~119.9 gallons) in the starboard external tank, the helicopter had four and a half hours of fuel on board; more than enough for the 40 minutes needed for the launch and recovery.

"Ready in the back, Mr. Almer." It was AW1 Tony Grayson. Derek turned around and counted noses. Grayson sat behind him on the cabin deck and AW3 Hambleton sat on the left side. The cabin doors were open and both men rested their feet on the sponsons.

"Scrawny, let's do it."

Scranton was skinny as a rail. In Adrian's words, he needed to eat bagels every day with an inch of cream cheese. On a good day, Derek thought his 5' 8" frame might weigh 135 pounds, hence the call sign "Scrawny. Matt waved a thumb's up so Derek could see and keyed the mike. "Gold Eagle, Angel Zero Three is ready to engage and take-off."

Derek keyed the intercom after the rotors were spinning at 102%. "Check the power once I pull it into a hover. We're close to max gross weight."

Two clicks of the mike told Derek that Matt understood who signaled the two linemen to pull the chocks and tiedown chains, starting by pointing his thumbs together and then rotating his wrists as he moved his hands out. Two linemen ran to stand beside the enlisted man known as the Landing Signal Enlisted (LSE). Each held a tiedown chain and a chock.

The LSE twirled the flashlight with a conical lens screwed on the front over his head. AW1 Grayson keyed his mike, "All clear aft, chocks and tie downs are out."

Grayson's transmission was confirmation that the tie-downs were removed so when Derek added power, the HH-60H wouldn't try to lift the 100,000-ton aircraft carrier. The call became mandatory because when helicopters started flying from ships, the pilots tried to lift the ship more than once. And, despite the precautions, it still happened.

By adding power with the collective and a little forward cyclic to keep the helicopter in position over the deck, Derek eased the HH-60H into a hover 10 feet off the deck.

Matt reported, "Racer, power looks good, gauges are all green."

With Matt's call, Derek eased forward on the cyclic and increased power. By the time the helicopter was at the end of the angled deck, it was passing 20 knots. Derek waited until the airspeed indicator passed 60 knots, and a glance to the right told him to maintain his present course since the carrier had already begun its turn into the wind. Once it passed behind the helicopter, Derek smoothly rolled the HH-60H into a 20⁰ right bank as he leveled off at 500 feet. At the end of the maneuver, the helicopter was on *Vinson's* starboard side at 70 knots.

Matt keyed the mike. "Gold Eagle, Angel Zero Three, in starboard delta."

The carrier's air boss acknowledged the radio call. Angel Zero Three would now maintain an orbit at 500 feet about one-quarter mile from the *Vinson's* island. Unless otherwise directed, the helicopter would maintain that position until the last airplane was recovered and then land.

As Derek pointed out to the new pilots of HSC-8, when they are flying plane guard, there's no one to rescue them if they must ditch. If the plane guard helicopter went into the water, the flight deck crew would have to pull the stand-by helicopter out of what was known as "the pack" by the island and launch. On a good day, it could take 10 minutes to pull the helicopter onto the angle, spread the rotor blades, start the engines, and take off.

As standard operating procedures, Derek insisted that whenever they flew at night, the aircrews flew the helicopter while using their AN/PVS-7 night-vision goggles. Since the HH-60H crews needed to be ready for a CSAR and special ops support mission, he wanted the HH-60H crews comfortable flying with them. Once airborne, both pilots turned on the goggles that turned their view of the world into a circle of green and black images.

Flying plane guard is boring. Most of the time, the helicopter flies in circles for hours on end. To gain training value from each flight, as soon as Derek had the helicopter on station, he began a manual approach to a 50-foot hover. After staying in position for about a minute, he eased the nose forward, climbed to 200 feet and came around again. This time, he engaged the auto approach to a hover system. With his hands not touching the controls, both he and Matt watched the system control the descent at 130 feet per minute, slowing from 70 knots to less than 10 when it flared the helicopter in a 50-foot hover.

With the HH-60H in a steady hover, Derek rocked the mike switch to intercom position. "Grayson, when you are ready, I'll give you control."

In the auto-hover mode, the pilots could give the aircrewman manning the hoist limited control of the helicopter to move it left or right, forward, or backward to put it in a better position over the survivor.

"Ready, sir."

Derek pushed the button on the center console on the automatic flight control system panel that initiated the crew hover mode. A green light on his panel said Grayson had control.

"Green light, sir. Easing forward." The helicopter moved forward at about two knots and then stopped.

"Moving right." The HH-60H slid to Derek's side.

The process was repeated in each direction. "Sir, system checks out, we're good to go."

"Roger that. Am taking control." Matt turned off the capability that gave the aircrewmen control as Derek beeped the nose forward using the electric trim on the cyclic and increased power. As he leveled off at 200 feet, Derek keyed the intercom. "Scrawny, you've got the helicopter. Make a couple of manual approaches, hold it in a hover at 50 for two minutes each time and then wave off."

Two clicks on the intercom and Derek said, "You've got control."

They were waving off from Matt's second hover when the radio crackled. "Angel Zero Three, Gold Eagle, say fuel state."

Derek looked at the fuel totalizer number and then added the numbers next to the tapes indicating the amount of fuel in the left and right tanks together. They were within 100 pounds.

"Angel Zero Three's state is 2.9." They took off with 4,800 pounds and had burned 1,100. Derek anticipated the controller's next question with his next transmission. "We've got about 3.25 hours of fuel which means we can fly about 120 nautical one way with a reserve."

"Angel Zero Three, Gold Eagle, fly three-four-eight, for seventy-three nautical. Blue Diamond Three Zero Six has a fire and is headed back to home plate."

"Matt, I have the helicopter." Derek heard the cabin doors shut as he pushed the nose forward and began to climb to 1,000 feet. At 140 knots, the helicopter began to vibrate so he eased back to 135.

"Crew, rig for rescue. Matt, did you talk to Moses about the electrical problem the guys before us encountered."

Moses was the last name of the copilot who Matt replaced. "All he said was the number one generator dropped off the line twice. Each time they pulled the circuit breaker, waited about five minutes before pushing the breaker in and pushing the reset button. Moses said Mr. Johansson was going to write it up."

"O.K. let's be prepared for losing the number one generator. If we do, light off the APU. Call off each item as you touch them, I'll either nod or approve."

"Got it."

"Angel Zero Three, this is Roundtop Seven Zero Two. Blue Diamond Three Zero Six is planning to eject once he gets below the overcast. Blue Diamond Three Zero Eight is on his wing."

No one on the crew of Angel Zero Three saw the flash of the explosion that destroyed the F/A-18C. They did hear the beeper on the UHF guard channel signifying that the pilot had ejected. With the high-pitched warbling tone in their headsets, they saw the burning wreckage falling toward the sea.

Matt's hand was turning a knob on the AN/ARC-182 radio so that the number 1 needle on the visual display unit would give Derek a heading toward the beeper. "Racer, turn right to three-five-five. DARS has got a lock on the beeper."

DARS stood for Downed Aircrew Recovery System. Once the survivor started using his handheld survival radio, it would give the helicopter crew bearing and distance to the survivor.

"Turning." Derek made a gentle correction and when he looked up, he noticed that it was raining heavily.

The beeper suddenly stopped. "Angel Zero Three, Round Top Seven Zero Two. Blue Diamond Three Zero Eight reported a good chute. Estimate the survivor is on your nose at five miles."

Matt acknowledged the call from the controller on board the E-2C Hawkeye. The carrier-based, airborne early warning aircraft had a crew of five, two pilots and three controllers who manned the radar scopes in the fuselage.

Keying the intercom, Derek forced himself to sound calm although he could feel the excitement of making a rescue and adrenalin starting to flow through his body. "Descending to 500 feet, everyone look for flares or a reflection from his helmet. Matt, wait a minute or two and then try to contact Blue Diamond Three Zero Six. Hopefully he'll be in his raft and have his survival radio out."

As he descended, Derek slowed the helicopter to 70 knots and heard the doors open. "Gents, briefed water temperature was forty-nine degrees Fahrenheit. Hambleton, I presume you have your wet suit on?"

"Yes sir, I do. I wear it under my flight suit."

"Keep a sharp eye out. He will be hard to spot this rain."

Matt looked at the visual display unit in front of him. "Derek, we should be marking on top, but I think the wind may have blown Blue Diamond Three Zero Six to the west a bit."

Derek looked down. The sea was black as slate, but there was enough ambient light to see white caps. Wind, rain, and waves could make it hard for a pilot to get into his raft. If he was injured, damned near impossible.

"Sir, this is Grayson, I just saw a glint off what I think is a helmet. Come starboard about thirty degrees."

Derek rolled the helicopter into a 10-degree angle of bank and slowed to 60 knots while he kept the helicopter at 500 feet.

"Sir, I've got the pilot. One o'clock, about a mile."

"Descending to two hundred feet. Grayson, mark me on top and toss a flare out."

Two clicks of the mike told Derek that Grayson understood. He lowered the collective and eased back on the cyclic to descend at 500 feet per minute at 60 knots.

"Racer, survivor is less than half a mile at eleven thirty." Derek could hear the excitement in Matt's voice.

Derek forced himself not to look up and try to spot the survivor. He was flying the helicopter on instruments. It was Matt's job to spot the survivor from the cockpit.

"Three hundred yards."

Matt could see the helmet and the arms of the pilot who had not separated from his parachute.

Grayson's voice was calm and cool as if they made rescues every night. "Mark, mark, MARK!!! Flare's out and looks like the wind is coming from our three o'clock. The pilot looks injured and is not out of his chute so we're going to have to put Hambleton in the water."

Derek clicked the mike twice and then said, "I am going to come around and manually fly the approach. Once we're in a hover, lower Hambleton into the water and we'll slide off and wait. I do not want to lose sight of the survivor or Hambleton."

"Roger that, sir. Hambleton is already in the sling. He's taking his radio so we'll have comms with him assuming the damn thing works."

"Everyone take off their NVGs. If we need to, we'll turn on the flood lights."

Still flying on instruments, Derek glanced outside to make sure that he had the survivor in sight. When lined up about half a mile downwind, he began a slow descent to a 50' foot hover 100 feet short of the survivor.

Grayson keyed his mike. "Boss, easy forward."

Derek used the trim to move the cyclic forward and the HH-60H crept toward the man in the water. "Stop. Steady hover."

"Grayson, I'm going to engage the auto hover and then once it is engaged, I'll give you control."

Two clicks. "Swimmer is going out the door."

Matt pushed the auto hover coupler engage button and a green light said it was working properly. On Derek's visual display unit, the crossbars were centered as he maintained a hover. "Giving you control."

"Got a green light. Swimmer is halfway down...."

"Swimmer is in the water and getting out of the horse collar."

The horse collar was a yellow, kapok-filled sling used to hoist survivors out of the water.

"Swimmer is with the survivor. Sir, take control and move us away."

Matt pushed the button that gave control to the hoist operator to take back control. The light went out. Derek disengaged the hover coupler and eased the helicopter away from the two men in the water.

"Boss, I could see shroud lines all over the place. Blue Diamond Three Zero Six was only moving one arm so it will take Hambleton a few minutes to get Three Zero Six ready for pick-up."

Two clicks of the mike. The most immediate danger was freeing the pilot from his parachute. Until that was done, they couldn't hoist him into the helicopter. It was now a matter of waiting for Hambleton to work his magic. There was nothing that any of them could do until the pilot was in the helicopter. In 49⁰ Fahrenheit water, the pilot's hands would go numb in 10 or 15 minutes. If he wasn't wearing an exposure suit, within half an hour, the pilot's body would start shutting down from the cold.

"Scrawny, how's our gas?"

"Plenty. We've got eighteen hundred pounds, good for an hour and a half."

"Angel Zero Three, Roundtop Seven Zero Two. Confirm you are in a hover."

Matt nodded, then he keyed the intercom first. "Racer, my bad. I forgot to let Roundtop know we found Blue Diamond Three Zero Six. I'll let him know."

Derek keyed the intercom. "Don't worry about it."

"Roundtop Seven Zero Two, Angel Zero Three. We have a swimmer in the water with Blue Diamond Three Zero Six. Swimmer is working to free Blue Diamond Three Zero Six from his parachute."

Derek glanced out the window and saw the glint from the reflective tape on Hambleton's helmet as he pulled the pilot away from his chute.

"Angel Zero Three, say status of Blue Diamond Three Zero Six."

Derek didn't wait for Matt to key the mike. "Roundtop Seven Zero Two, this is Angel Zero Three. When we know, you'll be the first we tell."

In other words, shut up and let us do our job. Matt broke into a broad smile.

"Swimmer is clear of the chute and pulling pilot to safe distance."

Derek flexed his hands to keep them loose on the controls. While his hands were on both the cyclic and collective, he moved them with his fingertips.

"Hambleton has signaled that he is ready and has the survivor hooked to his harness. Ready for pick-up."

"Roger that. Grayson guide me to them."

"Easy starboard."

With a touch of the conical switch on the top of the cyclic known as the coolie hat, Derek started the HH-60H to the right. The HH-60H responded.

"Stop right. Easy forward."

Again, Derek moved the controls to move the helicopter as Grayson guided him into position. The radar altimeter barely flickered as the helicopter flew sideways and showed the helicopter was still at 50 feet.

"Stop forward. We're on top of Hambleton and the survivor. Request control."

Again, Matt engaged the coupler that would keep the helicopter over a spot in the ocean. The green light said it was working so he pushed the button to give Grayson limited control. Almost immediately, the button flashed red.

"Mr. Almer, I got a flash and smell electrical fire smoke."

A yellow light caught Derek's attention. The master caution light lit the cockpit "Roger that. We'll leave the system off and I'll fly the helo manually."

"Roger that." Grayson paused to gauge the helicopter's position relative to the two men in the water. "Easy forward." A pause. "Stop. Easy right…." Another pause. "Stop. Horse collar going down." Another pause.

Matt held his arm across the center console with a thumbs up. Derek nodded noticeably to his signal that the gauges looked good. He went back to his scan, the two needles that showed fore and aft and left and right horizontal movement, the radar altimeter, rotor rpm, and torque. The needles showing drift were centered and not moving.

Out of the corner of his eye, Derek saw yellow lights come on. He stayed with his scan to keep the helicopter in position. "Racer, we've got both a number one generator and number one generator bearing warning lights."

"Scrawny, reset the generator. If it doesn't come back online, light off the APU."

"Roger that."

"Sir, we got hoist problems." Grayson didn't need to tell Derek who was speaking. "The hoist won't go down much beyond about twenty-five feet. It comes up O.K., but when I tried to bring it up and then lower the collar, it will only go down about twenty-five feet."

"Angel Zero Three, Roundtop Seven Zero Two, say status of rescue."

This time Matt keyed the mike first. "Roundtop Seven Zero Two Attempting pick up. Standby for status when we can report. Right now, we're busy."

Derek keyed his mike. "Scrawny, the flag is probably asking for info.. Ignore them. Break, break, Grayson, help me down. When the collar is in the water, let me know. Scrawny, we're going to ingest salt spray so watch the gauges for signs of compressor stall. If an engine starts to wind down, initiate a restart immediately. Don't shut an engine down."

The danger was that as the air entered the engine, the heat and pressure would separate the salt from the seawater. Salt build-up on the turbine blades changed their shape and made them less efficient which in turn, reduced the power available. Add in the humidity from the rain and the fuel control changes the air/fuel mix. If the particle separator in the intake of each engine doesn't take enough water out, the engine could shut down.

Compressor stalls announce themselves with loud bangs. Depending on how the engine is affected, it could shut down completely, produce less power or keep running normally. Matt knew to watch for a rise in either Ng (gas generator turbine speed) or TGT (turbine gas temperature) that could indicate an impending compressor stall.

"Easy down."

Derek forced the problems with the helicopter out of his mind. There were three things one does in an airplane. Aviate is always the priority, i.e. keep flying the airplane or helicopter. Then one can navigate and last, communicate. He eased the collective down, keeping the helicopter in position over the survivor with the cyclic.

"Angel Zero Three, Roundtop Seven Zero Two, Bulldog Actual wants a status report."

Bulldog Actual meant that the Commander, Carrier Group Three was on the radio. Derek, not wanting to get into a pissing contest over the radio with a two-star, said, "Tell Bulldog Actual that we will report when we have finished the rescue or if we need assistance."

He couldn't see the smile on Tony Grayson's or Matt Scranton's face. Their HAC had not so politely told a two-star admiral to bugger off.

"Ten feet…" "Five feet…" "Stop down. Horse collar in the water…"

It seemed like minutes but was only seconds. "Swimmer is hooking his harness to the hoist…" Then, "Survivor and swimmer coming up."

Derek added a skoosh, that's a technical naval aviation term for just a bit, of power with the collective to compensate for the weight of two waterlogged men on the hoist.

"Survivor out of the water."

"Grayson, I am going to ease back up to fifty feet and then stay in a hover until you have them in the cabin."

Two clicks.

Derek added more power and the helicopter rose accompanied by four bangs in rapid succession. "Racer, Ng speed on number one is fluctuating and TGT is rising."

Decision time. Adding more power now to fly out of the over was the prudent thing to do and might cause another series of compressor stalls. Climbing would make it more difficult for Grayson to get both Hambleton and the survivor into the helicopter. Derek stayed in the hover now that the helicopter was at 50 feet.

"Survivor is halfway up…" a few seconds passed. "Survivor and the swimmer are at the door and am pulling them into the cabin." Finally, "Survivor and swimmer are in the cabin, am closing the doors."

"Scrawny, watch the power, am going to start a gentle climb to 1,000 feet. Once we are past 70 knots and climbing and Grayson tells us about the health of our passenger, call Roundtop and get us a vector to Gold Eagle."

Derek eased the nose down as he slowly pulled up on the collective, expecting compressor stalls to announce themselves with either a single or a series of loud bangs. He wasn't disappointed.

A very loud bang was easily heard by everyone on board as the number one engine lost power. The gauges showed a rapid change in Ng and the turbine gas temperature went way down and then flashed over the red line before settling down. The gauges showed that the number one engine was producing about 80 percent of the torque the number two was putting out.

The HH-60H continued to climb. Passing 500 feet, AW1 Grayson keyed the intercom. "Boss, Blue Diamond Three Zero Six has a dislocated left shoulder and left arm is broken in at least two places. His helmet is also split which leads me to believe he probably has a concussion. He's got burns on his hands and face and his flight suit shows that he probably ejected through the fireball. Hambleton and I are splinting the arm and have him wrapped in a thermal blanket. He swallowed a lot of water and is suffering from exposure. He didn't have an exposure suit on so if we didn't get here when we did, we'd be bringing back a body."

"Scrawny, do us the honor and call Roundtop. Then, you can fly us home. While you do, try not to fly us into the water or cause us to shut an engine down. I need a break and have had enough entertainment for the night."

Derek waited until Blue Diamond Three Zero Six had been gently helped onto a stretcher and carried away before he and Matt began the shutdown checklist. They were the last to land and with flight operations for the night over, the flight deck was quiet save for the sound of tractors moving airplanes.

In the back of the squadron's ready room, the four men huddled together for a mission debrief. While everyone was interested, no one interrupted the crew as they made notes of every detail so what went well and what went wrong. When finished, they would share the info with the rest of HSC-8's crews, particularly those who flew the H model H-60s.

Matt was writing the formal mission report and Grayson went back to sickbay to learn what the prognosis was on Lieutenant Thomas Jamison, the pilot of Blue Diamond Three Zero Six. Derek didn't hear the phone in the ready room ring, nor did he notice Commander Richardson standing behind him, waiting for the crew to finish. A look from AW1 Grayson told Derek to look up. "Admiral wants to see you ASAP as in right now."

"Do I have time to take a piss?"

"Don't be a wise ass, Mr. Almer."

The tile in the port passageway on the 03-level changed from green to blue telling Derek he was in the spaces of the Commander, Carrier Group Three. The 03 (pronounced "oh three") level meant that the deck or floor in civilian terms was the third deck above the main or 0 deck. On the starboard fore and aft passageway that ran the length of the 03 level, the tile was green it's entire length. On the port side, it changed to blue which was a reminder to the rest of the crew that the individual was in the flag spaces. Unless one was a member of the admiral's staff, one was supposed to use the starboard passageway in this section of the carrier.

The admiral's aide, a.k.a. "the rope" spotted Derek as he entered the flag spaces. The lieutenant was easily identified as the aide by the gold and blue braided cord known as an aiguilette worn on her left shoulder. The officer, a woman wearing the insignia of a surface warfare officer over her two rows of ribbons, pointed to the bulkhead, as if to say, you wait there. Her name tag said her last name was Briscoe. "Lieutenant Almer, I'll tell Admiral Castle that you are here."

Lieutenant Briscoe who had brown, closely cropped hair and was almost as tall as Derek, emerged a few second later. "The Admiral will see you now."

Derek walked past a conference table, a couch and lounge chairs and came to attention in front of the admiral's desk. He started to say Lieutenant Almer reporting as ordered but didn't get the chance. Admiral Castle spoke first. "Close the door lieutenant."

The voice was commanding and not friendly and Derek did as told. The door closed with an audible click and he returned to stand at attention in front of the man who was just promoted to rear admiral, upper half meaning he now wore two stars on his collar. Derek knew from reading his bio before the cruise that the admiral flew F-14s, F/A-18s and was a graduate of the Navy's Test Pilot School.

The man who spoke was sitting at a large steel desk. Behind him was a portrait of Senator John C. Stennis and framed photos of the ship when it was christened on December 9th, 1995, and at sea.

RADM Castle finished the document he was editing and tossed his pen on the desk. "Do you always tell admirals to fuck off?"

"No sir." No good job, or well done, or thanks for Hambleton's quick work that probably saved Lieutenant Jamison's life. No, the two star is pissed because I told him to wait. "Sir, we were in the middle a difficult rescue. Besides the weather, we were dealing with a helicopter with only one generator, a balky hoist, and time was of the essence. As it turned out, Lieutenant Jamison wasn't wearing his wet suit."

Castle's jaw worked, his face flushed as he stood and leaned on his desk. "Goddamn you, Lieutenant. When your commanding officer asks for information, you provide it, do you understand?"

"I do sir." Derek waited a few seconds for the tension to ease. "Sir, may I provide an analogy." He didn't wait for an answer before opening his mouth. "Sir, if the roles were reversed and you were in the middle of a dogfight with a Flanker and I was in CIC asking for a status report, what would you do?"

Castle's face turned redder. "You know lieutenant, I could have you grounded, order Commander Richardson to yank your quals and write a fitness report that would ensure you will never make lieutenant commander."

Derek wanted to say, "For what? Doing my job?" But he didn't – he stood at attention and said nothing. He'd made his point and was confident that when the admiral calmed down, he would see his side.

Castle sat back down, "Dismissed."

Derek started speaking before his brain could stop his mouth. "Sir, for the record, Lieutenant Jamison, the pilot of Blue Diamond Three Zero Six has a dislocated left shoulder, his left arm was broken in two places, second-degree burns on his face and both hands and a moderate concussion. He was not wearing an exposure suit and was entangled in his parachute lines. Had he been in the water another five minutes, he would have died."

He did a smart about face and walked out of Admiral Castle's office figuring that by the time he reached HSC-8's ready room, he would be grounded and orders would be cut sending him home. Instead, he found all HSC-8s pilots seated in the ready room standing and clapping when he walked into the room.

Commander Richardson said, "Racer, Mr. Scranton and Petty Officer Grayson have been singing your praises for the past ten minutes as they described the rescue. You're just in time to answer their questions."

SUNDAY, MARCH 16ᵀᴴ, 2003, 10:46 A.M. LOCAL TIME, NANNING

Rain pelted the windows of the 8th-floor apartment. The storms had been going on for two days. Unlike the flat Jun and Bao had in Guangzhou, this one didn't have a porch, not that they would have ventured onto it this morning. From what they could tell, the building in the Zhongshan residential district had been gutted and rebuilt after a major fire. There were still soot stains in the concrete on the halls inside the building and the outside walls that had not been removed.

From their top-floor apartment, they could look out over a U-shaped bend in the Yongjian River that snaked through Nanning. Zhongshan was only a short walk from the Nanning Medical School and the Qingxiuan Scenic Park.

Since Jun and Bao had been in Nanning, they went to a different part of the city on Sundays. Today, they were planning to walk around Qingxiuan.

Thunder woke Bao up and he propped himself on his side to look at the woman sleeping next to him. As he traced Jun's breasts with his index finger, tears started to flow down Bao's cheeks. He used a finger to spread a tear that dropped on Jun's side as Jun stirred. Bao's finger circled Jun's nipples which hardened.

"Hmmmm, keep doing that and you know where that will lead." Jun reached out with her hand and touched Bao's cheek. When her finger touched a tear, her eyes opened wide with alarm. "Bao, my love what is wrong?"

Bao lost it. He started to sob and couldn't speak for a few seconds. "They made me do it."

"Who? And what?"

"The week after your cousin Yan visited us, I was called into a meeting at the institute. There were two men from the Ministry of State Security in the room and they threatened to charge me for crimes for which I was cleared back when I was a medical student. A man who raped several of my friends was killed and investigators from the Ministry of People's Security thought I may have committed the murders. Then, someone reported after I started living with Daiyu that I had been living in a bathroom. They found no evidence, but again, I was interrogated."

Bao pushed himself up so he was sitting cross-legged. Taking a deep breath for what was a painful and could be a life-threatening conversation, Bao continued. "The investigators told me that if I didn't cooperate, they would charge me."

"So what did they want?"

"To report on who you see, what you say and do. Anything that would be a threat to the People's Republic. They wanted to know details about your family in America."

"What did you tell them?"

"I never met them." Both knew that was a lie.

"Did you tell them that I write to them?"

Bao's hair flung back and forth as he shook his head violently.

"Did they say why I was a threat?"

"Not exactly…. They did mention the study we did that exposed SinoPharma."

"Do they want to meet with you regularly?"

"No, they said my control from the Ministry of State Security office in Nanning would contact me after we moved here. No one has contacted me yet and I dread the moment they do."

Jun held out her arms and pulled Bao toward her. Neither person said anything for a few minutes. "We'll get through this together." Inside, Jun was terrified. Since they started sleeping with each other, Jun held nothing back other than she was sending Yan information on her work. His words meant that now her lover Bao could no longer be trusted. She didn't know if she was telling him a cover story or the truth or both. If Bao knew what she was sending Yan he would either tip off the Ministry of State Security or, if arrested, break under torture. More than ever, Jun wondered if their apartment was bugged.

TUESDAY, MARCH 25ᵀᴴ, 2003, 6:10 P.M. LOCAL TIME, MAMMOTH LAKES

Along Davison Road, the wall of the snow had settled down to about eight feet above the road surface. So far this winter, Mother Nature had been generous to Mammoth Mountain and almost 20 feet of snow had fallen so far this year.

After their first ski trip together, Adrian, Betsy and Lea Ann agreed to come back for week each month. Like the earlier trips, they arrived Sunday afternoon.

Monday was great skiing and then it began snowing. By Tuesday, the falling snow and flat light reduced visibility so the women came in. After time in the spa, they started making dinner.

Neither Lea Ann nor Adrian paid attention when Betsy's phone rang. Their attitude changed when they heard, "Oh, my God!!!!"

Betsy went to the table, pulled out a chair, sat, and listened. "Dad, I love you. I'll be home as soon as I can. I'll call you as soon as I have my flight booked."

"What happened?" The words came out of Betsy's friends almost simultaneously.

"My mother's Yukon skidded off into a ditch then rolled before hitting a tree. She's in intensive care in a hospital in Glenwood Springs."

Adrian picked up her phone and started dialing.

Betsy asked, "Who are you calling?"

"My family's travel agent. They're available 24 hours a day. Reno is the closest airport. Do you want to fly to Denver and then into Aspen or direct into Glenwood Springs?"

Adrian told the woman who answered to help Betsy and charge the flight to her credit card. Then she handed Betsy the phone. "Make your reservations. Lea Ann and I will make sure you make the flight, whenever it is."

After speaking to the travel agent for several minutes, Betsy handed Adrian her phone. "I'm on a direct flight to Denver tomorrow that leaves Reno tomorrow at one-thirty and connects to a United flight from Denver into Aspen."

"Good. The snow should end sometime tonight. Reno is about two and a half to three hours away on a dry road. So, we'll leave after an early breakfast."

Lea Ann added, "I'll drive, my CR-V is all-wheel drive."

WEDNESDAY, MARCH 26ᵀᴴ, 2003, 2:23 P.M. LOCAL TIME

U.S. 395 was relatively clear. As soon as they descended to about 6,000 feet, the road was dry. After a lunch in a restaurant near the airport,

Betsy checked in at 12:30 and Lea Ann and Adrian headed back to Mammoth. Neither woman said much as Lea Ann worked her way down through the traffic in Silver City and Carson.

Passing through Sonara Junction, Lea Ann pulled the gear shift lever into fifth. She was looking straight ahead when she spoke. "Adrian, may I share a secret with you? Before I do, you must promise me that you will never tell Derek."

"I promise."

Lea Ann took a deep breath. "Matt has a man-crush on Derek. It is not romantic, but he adores your husband. Every email has some tidbit about your husband. Matt and many of the squadron's pilots and aircrew think Derek is the best pilot in the squadron and its best leader. If Derek asked Matt to unlock the gates of hell, he would try to do it gladly."

Adrian nodded. Derek was very circumspect in what he put in his emails, afraid that someone else will read them. Also, he didn't want to bother her about internal squadron issues. "Why are you telling me this?"

"I'm hearing rumblings that some of the wives are hearing comments from their husbands who are jealous of Derek and you. Matt hasn't said anything directly, but I can tell, he's overheard some ugly conversations."

"Why are they jealous?"

"One is how Commander Richardson and Lieutenant Commander Johansson are always asking Derek for his input. Another is that you've rented a big house in Mammoth for the winter."

"I did because I can afford it."

"I understand and those who know you understand. I think the real reason behind the jealousy is because you come from money."

"Well, I can't help it that I have a trust fund. By offering it to the squadron's families, I am trying to improve the morale of the spouses left behind." *Wait until Derek starts driving the Porsche 911 Turbo I have on order. It should arrive sometime in August and should start some tongues wagging. Sorry, money is to be enjoyed.*

"Oh Adrian, you are, but you know there are always those who will bitch to get attention."

Adrian looked at Lea Ann, "Well, they can go fuck themselves. I did the right thing. In Judaism, we call what I am doing Tzedakah which is the Hebrew word for charity and philanthropy."

Quiet filled the 2000 Honda CR-V as Lea Ann rowed through the gears as the small all-wheel drive SUV passed Mono Lake and started the climb up to where they would turn off U.S. 395 onto California Route 203 and the ski area.

CHAPTER 22

MUTATIONS

At the first door inside the building, Jun held out her right wrist, on which there was a thick black band the size of a large watch, next to a panel on the wall. All the individuals who worked at Special Lab #62 were required to wear the black rubberized band that, according to where one was assigned, gave one access.

The door unlocked with a click and she pulled it open. The device on her wrist gave Jun access to the building and all the labs. The wristband also unlocked the door to the lobby of their apartment building and allowed the wearer to use the elevator.

Everyone assigned to the lab also wore a badge that hung from a lanyard around their necks. The badge was color coded to their work area and had a large photo, their name, and title on the front.

On their first visit to Special Lab #62, each staff member was ushered into a room where they were 'fitted' with the band. Once the metal clasp was in place, a rubberized material was slipped over the device before a heat gun melted the material in place.

They were told never to remove the bands under any circumstances. If one did without authorization, they would be arrested. Jun and Bao suspected that the wristbands contained a geolocation device. Workers at the lab were instructed that they could not leave Nanning without special travel permits issued by the lab's Senior Administrator Baozhi Ming after being approved by Senior Colonel Sun. Ming was selected by Dr. Ng and Bao and Jun before the lab opened.

Visitors were not allowed into the Level 4 lab building. Everywhere around the Special Lab #62 complex there were security cameras. Those who worked there understood that any violation of the lab's security or safety protocols would be punished.

A week earlier, Senior Colonel Sun sent word that he wanted a complete tour now that the lab was functional and the entire staff in place. The call came to Senior Administrator Baozhi Ming who passed the request on to Doctors Gu and Lín.

Senior Colonel Sun listened carefully to Ming's description of the security protocols. As Dr. Lín led him around the lab, it was clear that he paid attention to Senior Administrator Ming, who was in her 50s. Her gray-black hair that came down to the middle of her back was in a braided ponytail that was reminiscent of the Manchu people and the Qing Dynasty.

Jun's conclusion about Baozhi Ming was that she was a competent administrator who knew her way around a chemistry and biology lab. She was, however, devoid of any sense of humor and never smiled nor did she talk about her family. She lived alone on the same floor as the two lovers. In private, Bao and Jun wondered if Baozhi Ming ever had a lover of any kind.

Senior Colonel Sun, Bao, and Jun were trailed by Ming and an Army captain who took notes when directed. When the PLA officer arrived, Jun said that at the end of his tour, both Bao and she wanted to discuss how the lab was going to achieve the goals Senior Colonel Sun had established.

Smiling, the PLA senior colonel said, "I would expect nothing less."

Lunch was in the facilities cafeteria, then the four went to one of the three small conference rooms. The PLA captain note taker to whom neither Jun nor Bao was introduced sat in a chair against the wall, not at the table.

With everyone seated, Jun was in research director mode. She planned to hand Senior Colonel Sun her presentation one sheet at a time.

"Senior Colonel Sun, I want to start with what we know as facts. As you know, Senior Hospital Director Dr. Zheng has provided us with a large amount of accurate data." What Jun didn't say was the information sent to them by the Ministry of Health was inconsistent, inaccurate, misleading and, therefore, worthless.

Jun described what they knew about the polio outbreaks in the southern provinces of the People's Republic. Her first chart was based on data from the World Health Organization. She noted that the data was worldwide and varied from country to country.

Location	Spinal cases by %	Bulbar cases by %	Bulbospinal cases by %
Outside the PRC	79%	2%	19%
Inside the PRC	71%	3%	26%

Jun explained that there were three types of polio. Spinal polio was the most common but still could result in paralysis because it attacks the nerves in the spine. Approximately 2% of the cases are bulbar polio which destroys nerves in the bulbar region of the brain and affects the individual's ability to breathe, swallow, and chew.

Bulbospinal polio makes up about 19% of the cases and has the highest death rate of the three types of poliomyelitis. It is a combination of both spinal and bulbar polio. Victims of this form are usually paralyzed from the chest down and need external help to breathe, i.e. an iron lung or a respirator. Jun noted after her description of the three serotypes of polio that any of them could cause the full range of symptoms.

Her second chart was a description of how the disease runs its course. Paralysis with either of the three types of polio usually begins within 10 days of first symptoms and is complete by the time the fever breaks. However, the paralysis sometimes recedes over time, but after six months, whatever paralysis remains is usually permanent.

The older the victim is, the higher the chances of permanent paralysis of more portions of the body. Children under five usually lose the use of one or both legs. Above the age of 40, quadriplegia occurs in one out of every 75 cases. However, most polio survivors of all ages who suffer paralysis lose the use of an arm or leg, one side of the body (an arm or leg, i.e. hemiplegic) or both legs. On rare occasions, the patient loses the use of both arms while the rest of his/her body remains normal.

Jun slid her third chart across the table to Senior Colonel Sun. It contained numbers based on geography as well. As she did so, she said the analysis completed at Special Hospital #326 was based on data from all the patients treated at the hospital. Jun noted that Statistician Houran adjusted the figures so they reflect the population of Guangxi and Guangdong provinces based on the occurrence of other infectious diseases in the population. She was confident that the numbers were accurate enough to support Dr. Gu's, Dr. Zheng's, and her conclusions.

Chart number four compared the paralytic and mortality rates from all types of polio in the People's Republic with the rest of the world where polio still occurs.

Age Range of Victims	Paralytic Rate Outside PRC	Paralytic Rate inside PRC	Death Rate Outside PRC	Death Rate Inside PRC
Under 5 years old	Under 1%	3%	2 – 5%*	5 – 6%
6 – 20 years old	~1.5 - 2%	5%	~15%*	~18%
Older than 20 years	2 - 5%	8%	25 - 30%*	25%+

* If the victim contracts bulbospinal polio, the death rate increases with age from 25% to 75% for senior citizens.

Dr. Lín noted that these numbers were for the most common of the three paralytic polios known as spinal polio. The death rates for bulbar polio and bulbospinal approach 75% in adults because the disease affects the nerves that control a human's breathing. Unless the person is on a ventilator in using a respirator or an iron lung, the victim suffocates.

The next chart she slid in front of Senior Colonel Sun was #5. On it, she had a summary from their research in Guangxi and Guangdong provinces and was based on a very small sample. Special Hospital #326 provided five years of data gathered and analyzed by Dr. Zheng's staff to Jun.

Unfortunately, she said, without going through the records of all the hospitals in the provinces and counting the number of paralytic and non-paralytic cases the facilities treated, there was no way to determine the total number of cases. She pointed out that Dr. Zheng estimated that only about 25% of the most severe paralytic cases were sent to Special Hospital #326. Dr. Zheng, Dr. Gu, and Jun suspected that many of those who contracted bulbar or spinobulbar polio died. Where the 75% who survived were, she did not know. If the country wanted a more precise estimate, then a team would have to scour hospital and rehab center records.

What was clear, Jun said, was that polio, in both the paralytic and non-paralytic forms, was affecting not hundreds, not thousands, but probably tens of thousands of citizens of the People's Republic living in its two southern provinces. The disease was an epidemic, whether the country wanted to admit it or not.

Chart #6 showed data only from patients at Special Hospital #326 from all types of polio.

Victim's Age	Paralytic Rate	Death Rate
Under 5 years old	8 – 10%	<4%
6 – 20 years old	12 – 15%	12%
Older than 20 years	25 – 30%	20%

Dr. Lín watched as the army officer compared the two charts. "Senior Colonel Sun, at the risk of stating the obvious, the strain of the polio virus we have here in the People's Republic may be different from that found around the rest of the world. The differences may be in the treatment, the immune system and health of the victim when infected, or we could be looking at an unknown mutation of the disease that vaccines do not prevent."

Jun slid the seventh slide across the table which had only three bullets. The title said they were the primary ways the polio virus was transmitted. She read them aloud to emphasize the danger starting with the first cause of infection – was microscopic droplets expelled from the lungs when a person breathes or coughs and are inhaled by the victim.

Second way the virus gets into the body is through fecal matter that contains the polio virus that is in water used to wash one's hands, food, or cooking utensils. It gets into the body through cuts in the skin, or if it is splashed into one's mouth or eyes.

The third is that someone who is a polio carrier touches food which is eaten by a healthy individual or touches their plates, glasses, chopsticks, spoons and even cooking utensils. Infection occurs after the food is ingested.

Dr. Lín looked directly at Senior Colonel Sun. "We know that areas of Zhanjiang have poor sanitation, not enough clinics, or were given a vaccine that was less than full strength in a high population density of polio hotspots. These areas also have higher than normal instances of diarrhea that require medication and, if severe enough, hospitalization."

The PLA officer let the last sheet fall to the table. "This information is in Dr. Zheng's reports to the Health Ministry, correct?"

"Yes."

Senior Colonel Sun held his hand up as if to say stop. "Did you just tell me a few minutes ago that there was no way of knowing how many cases of polio we had in Guangdong and Guangxi provinces?"

"Yes sir, I did. Statistician Huoran made statistically valid projections based on what data we know is accurate. To make them more precise, we would have to collect data from every clinic, hospital, and rehab center in the two provinces. This assumes the clinic correctly diagnosed the disease. As I said before, we know only of the individuals who suffered from a paralytic strain and who were referred to Special Hospital #326. We are confident that probably only about twenty-five percent of the cases were."

"I think this is a wonderful project for Dr. Ng in his new role. I will encourage him to make it one of his highest priorities." Senior Colonel Sun waved his hand. "Please, Dr. Lín, continue."

Jun nodded and began speaking in a flat, emotionless voice. "I think this is a good time to point out that there is a disease called post-polio syndrome. About forty percent of the polio survivors who suffer from some paralysis that goes away find it returns about forty years later. Sometimes, the paralysis that returns is mild, sometimes it is worse than originally experienced. Any paralysis that returns is usually permanent. At this time, we cannot predict if or when post-polio syndrome will occur or how severe its effects will be or the number of citizens who will be affected."

The PLA colonel made a note on a sheet before he looked at the American-trained virologist. "So, Dr. Lín, what do you propose?"

"We need to determine if we have a new strain here in the People's Republic or just that our citizens had other underlying health conditions that made them more susceptible. To do that, we need samples of the spinal polio virus found outside the People's Republic. At the same time, we take samples in Zhanjiang and compare the viral isolates by growth in a tissue culture which we will examine with a scanning electron microscope."

"And, if you determine we have a new strain?"

Jun hesitated, and then decided not to sugarcoat her answer. "If that is the case, the People's Republic is faced with a medically and politically difficult decision. We should share our findings with the World Health Organization so the world can begin research on an effective vaccine or we say nothing and try to find an answer internally..."

Jun paused for a few seconds. "We can test the strain of poliomyelitis we have here on live tissue samples and compare them to what we know occurs outside the People's Republic. This will tell us if we have a new strain. What this will not tell us is the paralytic and death rate by age, sex, and underlying health conditions such as whether the individual has been vaccinated."

She took a deep breath for what Jun was about to say went against her training. "However, there is only one way to know with certainty the effect of the polio here in the People's Republic. To gather that data, we need to test the strain in a controlled environment on three groups of humans who are in good health. One group will have been vaccinated with the Sabin oral vaccine made outside the People's Republic. A second group of volunteers will get what I will call the Chinese version and the third will not be vaccinated at all. We expose them all to the strain we have here in southern China and watch what happens. I am not sure you will get many volunteers, even if they are offered a fortune."

Sun's mind was working overtime. This was better than he hoped for, and faster. He already knew where he was going to get the "volunteers." The Nanning Machinery and the Nanning Yibin Motorcycle plants were just outside the city. Both held, if he remembered correctly, about 5,000 inmates."

"Do you recommend testing on both men and women?"

Dr. Lín nodded.

"How many volunteers do you need?"

"Two hundred and fifty in each group between the age of twenty and fifty and split evenly between men and women. You may need more because we intend to give each a thorough physical so we understand their health before we start. No children, please."

Senior Colonel Sun quickly did the math in his head. If he provided 500 prisoners who passed their physicals, about 100 would die and another 150 or so would be crippled in some way for life. He would offer the survivors a commuted sentence and 50,000 yuan to each survivor. For what he wanted to do, this was a small price. "How long before you could be ready for a human test?"

"Six months, maybe a year. It depends on what we find. There is a chance our hypothesis is wrong."

"Dr. Lín, I must ask. Assuming we have a new strain of polio on our hands, how long before an effective vaccine could be developed?"

"If it is developed inside the People's Republic. I would plan on two or three years. Outside, less."

Sun nodded, not in agreement, but from excitement. Dr. Lín just told him that soon he would have a weapon that could panic the People's Republic's enemies and take them a year to counter. If Dr. Lín is correct, he can report to the National Military Commission that his plan is ahead of schedule.

"How would you plan to infect the volunteers?"

"We are not sure yet. Let us prove or disprove our hypothesis on the strain first. That research will tell us a lot about how the virus is transmitted."

"So, what do you need to begin?"

"Samples of the polio virus from a lab in Europe or America and enough doses of the American oral polio vaccine to run a viral neutralization test."

Senior Colonel Sun asked, "What is a viral neutralization test?"

"Sir, in this type of test, we determine whether the antibodies produced by a vaccine can neutralize an introduced virus and prevent infection or re-infection. In other words, we would expose individuals whom we know have been vaccinated to see if they develop polio."

The senior colonel nodded and issued an instruction to his aide. With that, Senior Colonel Sun thanked Dr. Gu and Dr. Lín and left.

FRIDAY, APRIL 18TH, 2003, 11:07 A.M. LOCAL TIME, APRA, GUAM

With the ship on the way to Guam, Derek picked 11 a.m., Friday, April 18th for his time slot for calling home. When he called it would be 5 p.m. Thursday, April 17th in California and he figured Adrian would be off the mountain and preparing dinner.

Stennis moored at what was known as Kilo Wharf on the south side of the harbor in the U.S. Territory of Guam. Banks of portable phone booths were set up on the pier so crew members could call home on the government's dime provided the call lasted less than 30 minutes. At 29 minutes, an operator interrupted with a warning that time was running out. Extra minutes were be billed $5/minute to the caller's credit card.

He dialed Adrian's mobile phone and a familiar voice answered. "Hello?"

Given the distance, he waited until he was sure that was all Adrian said. "Hi lover, Happy Pesach!" Derek used the Hebrew word for the Jewish holiday of Passover.

"Derek!!!!"

"'Tis me. Sweetheart. Don't forget, you must wait a few seconds for your voice to travel out into space and then back to the island paradise where I am standing."

Adrian giggled. "Happy Pesach to you. Did you have a seder?"

"We did on the ship. There were twenty-nine of us from the strike group and I had to run it as the senior Jewish officer."

"Good for you. I went to the community seder here in Mammoth. Was fun. How's the cruise going?"

"We'll be back on schedule." Derek was careful not to mention the date and where he was. Theoretically, it was a violation of security, but every husbanding agent in the ports knew when *Stennis* was scheduled to visit. "How's the skiing?"

"Awesome. Mammoth is having a record year and now I am a competent powder skier."

"Great. How's the house working out?"

"I love it. Toward the end of the lease, I am going ask the owner if he is willing to sell it. However, it does need some updating that I would expect the owner to pay for."

"Do I get a voice in this?"

"You do. I'll let the real estate development group in my father's company handle the negotiations. I love Mammoth. If buying this one doesn't work out, I may have them look for one for us when you're back."

"Are you planning to go back to law school?"

"Yes. I'm going down to San Diego in two weeks for a couple of days and will register for the first summer session and the fall."

"Great. Different subject. What do you have planned for the middle of August?"

"Nothing, why?"

"Wanna come to Hong Kong? The navy can get us, or you a good deal on an airfare from LA to Hong Kong. Not sure of the hotel yet, but the skipper's wife should have the details."

"I'm coming. Would they get pissed if I made my own hotel reservations and flew first class?"

If she did, some jealous asshole would make a snide remark. Derek no longer cared. "FYI, I'm pretty sure Betsy and Lea Ann are coming, or at least that's what their husbands are saying."

"I'll find out. Count on me being there and…" Adrian started to say, *fucking your brains out*, but didn't. Instead, she said, "spending time in bed with you."

"Or on the chair, or the couch…"

Adrian started giggling. In the background, Derek heard the doorbell ring and Adrian asked Derek to hang on as she went to the door. It was Commander Richardson's wife Erin and their two kids. They and Lieutenant Commander Johansson's wife and boys were spending the week at Chez Almer in Mammoth.

"Hey lover, I gotta go. Its Skipper Richardson's wife and kids and Lieutenant Commander Johansson's family. I love you and miss you!!!"

"Me too." And then Derek was holding a phone listening to a dial tone. At least in a few months, he'd get laid.

WEDNESDAY, APRIL 23ᴿᴰ, 2003, 9:26 A.M. LOCAL TIME, SPECIAL HOSPITAL #326

A week earlier, Jun walked into Senior Administrator Baozhi Ming's office to tell her that she needed travel permits to drive to Special Hospital #326 and asked if the older woman wanted to come.

"How long are you planning to stay?"

"Assuming we leave on Tuesday, April 22ⁿᵈ, we'll spend the night in one of the rooms at the hospital. Dr. Gu and I will meet with Dr. Zheng and some of her staff for a few hours and then the driver will bring us back to Nanning either that night or on the morning of the 24ᵗʰ. From what I understand, it is about a four-hour drive. I am sure Dr. Zheng or a member of her staff will be happy to give you a tour. I must warn you, when you see the children, it will tear your heart out."

Ming nodded. "I want to see what this polio scourge has done to my fellow citizens, so I will go with you."

After a thorough tour of the facility, Ming was with Bao who was meeting with Statistician Geming Huoran. This let Jun speak with Dr. Zheng alone. Sensing that the topic might be sensitive, Dr. Zheng suggested they take a walk around the grounds.

Once clear of the office, Dr. Zheng said, "I have been living at the hospital full time for over a year now that my husband is in Beijing at Air Force headquarters. His assignment was the excuse to file for divorce and his excuse is my disability turns him off. Now, he is free to play with his girlfriends who are usually thirty or younger."

"Dr. Zheng, I am sorry to hear that."

The older woman stopped and turned to Jun with a twinkle in her eye, "I, on the other hand, have a male friend in Zhanjiang who thinks I am the sexiest woman alive. My friend runs an import and export business that finds things needed by his customers inside the People's Republic. We met several years ago when the hospital was looking for parts for our iron lungs and equipment for our machine shop. If you ever need something or must call someone outside the people's paradise without government ears listening, please ask. My friend's satellite phone does not go through the People's Republic's phone system."

Sure they were out of earshot, Jun asked, "How well do you know Senior Colonel Sun?"

"Why are you asking?"

"He has been very supportive of me, but I keep asking myself the question of why would the army be so interested in the polio virus? Preventing the disease and helping those afflicted is a medical problem. I keep coming back to the only reason why and that is he wants to use it as a weapon."

Dr. Zheng pointed to a bench in a U-shaped area surrounded by chest-high hedges that provided a modicum of privacy. She used her right hand to help lower herself to the bench. Once seated, she released the knee lock on her leg brace and used her hand to lower her foot to the concrete. She put her paralyzed hand in her lap and looked at the sky as if asking God where do I begin?

"Senior Colonel Sun is a very, very powerful and influential officer. His wife's father is on the Politburo. His father is a member of the general staff and his brother is the head of a department in the Ministry of State Security. I am sure there are many more in his network. Senior Colonel Sun is dedicated to this country and prefers to operate in back rooms and the shadows. In other words, he prefers to be a maker of emperors than be the emperor."

Dr. Zheng reached out and put her hand on Jun's thigh. The gesture was motherly, not erotic. "My family also has powerful connections, which is why Sun is very careful not to cross me. My father is the Minister of Science and Technology; my oldest brother is a lieutenant general in the Air Force and he likes my ex-husband. Another of my brothers is the Deputy Minister of Public Security and my youngest sibling is a rear admiral. In other words, Senior Colonel Sun sees his friendship with my husband and I as an opportunity to expand his network."

Jun said nothing as she absorbed the meaning of Dr. Zheng's words.

The older women looked directly at Jun. "Be very careful and do not cross him. He uses people like paper. When he has no use for someone, Senior Colonel Sun tosses the person in the trash without a second thought. Remember, I too have powerful friends and through my friend I can communicate with the rest of the world and if needed, can cause important people to lose face. I will give you my friend's card when we return to my office and tell him about you."

Translation – if you should leave the PRC, this is how we can communicate. And, she has the means to tell the world the truth about polio in the People's Republic.

The dark clouds in the sky signaled heavy rain. Jun stood and held out her hand, "Dr. Zheng, we must get back inside before we get soaked."

As Dr. Zheng used Jun's hand to pull herself to her feet, she made a face, "So, I get chilled and sick. I've already had polio. A cold or a little pneumonia is nothing."

On the way back to the complex's headquarters, Dr. Zheng said Special Hospital #326 and its patients are now her life's work.

FRIDAY, APRIL 25ᵀᴴ, 2003, 6:25 P.M. LOCAL TIME, NANNING

Just before Bao left to go to a local market to buy ingredients for dinner, Jun wrapped her arms around her lover and pulled him close. After kissing him passionately, Jun said, "I love you so much."

"And I love you. Tonight, we will spend the night pleasing each other."

With that, Bao left the apartment with a smile on his face. Jun had become a very accomplished lover who loved both oral and vaginal sex. With her mouth, she could stimulate Bao to the point he felt as if he was about to pass out from the intense pleasure. Bao was still thinking about what the night might bring as he left the building.

Two men, both smelling of garlic, grabbed an arm. One waved a Ministry of State Security badge in front of Bao's face and said, "Bao Gu, please come with us."

Fearful of what might happen next, he said as calmly as he could, "Am I under arrest?"

One of the men said, "No, but we must talk. You are about to meet your new control."

The van entered a building that Bao assumed was the local office of the Ministry of State Security. One of the men opened the van's door and pointed to the entrance. He was led to a windowless room in which there were three chairs. The one he sat in was bolted to the floor where there were rings connected to posts set in the concrete. In front of Bao was a railing to which one could be chained. The meaning of his position was not lost on Dr. Gu.

Bao had been in one of these rooms before. The interrogation game, he thought, had begun. One of the Ministry of State Security's tactics was to leave one in a room like this for hours hoping the person would rack their brains thinking of what crimes they may have committed. Wanting to get out, they could confess to a minor crime not knowing it was a trap to continue the interrogation and intimidation.

He assumed that while he waited, they were looking through his wallet and accessing his new Nokia mobile phone to see whom he called. Bao smiled thinking that the only people he called was Jun when she was out shopping to ask her a question or to make reservations at a restaurant. The Ministry of State Security officers took his watch so he would lose track of time and fiddled with the black, rubberized armband around his left wrist looking for a latch. When they couldn't figure out how to take it off, a man brought a pair of bolt cutters.

Bao laughed and said, "Don't do that or you will be sitting in my chair." The bolt cutter was put on the floor and one of the men said, "We'll deal with it later."

He put his head down on his forearms and closed his eyes, forcing himself to relax. He had no idea how long he had been in the room when the door opened and two different men entered. One sat down, the other stood in the corner.

"Comrade Gu, I am Captain Chung, your new control." The man brought two folders into the room. Both were about 10 centimeters thick. Bao guessed one was his file and the other Jun's.

Chung addressed him as comrade by choice and ignored his title of doctor to show his power. It was, he learned when he had his prior run-in with the Ministry of Public Security, an interrogation tactic to annoy or anger the detainee. Also, as a doctor, he was, in the PRC's classless society, considered more highly educated than a captain in the Ministry of State Security and had more status. If this session was held during the Cultural Revolution, he could be one of the many targets du jour of the fanatical Red Guards. Bao let the insult pass and said nothing.

Flipping open the top folder, Chung looked at several pages and then slid a pad to a position where he could make notes. "What can you tell me about Citizen Lín?"

"Nothing you don't already know." Bao had learned the hard way to keep his answers short. The less said, the less they could twist.

"By that, what do you mean?"

Bao said nothing and pointed to the folder.

"Citizen Bao, we know Citizen Lín along with Senior Administrator Ming and you visited Special Hospital #326 this week. She met with Dr. Zheng alone for an extended period. What did they discuss?"

So, they have a plant in the hospital which is precisely why Jun and Dr. Zheng went for a walk. In public, they were very careful in what they said.

"The People's Republic's expansion plan for the hospital, where Dr. Zheng thinks there are more clusters of polio cases, and a data collection plan for those who had non-paralytic polio."

"Why did Citizen Ming go with you?"

"She had not been to the facility before."

"Why?"

"You are not cleared for our research. Until you are, I cannot give you more details."

Chung's mouth opened slightly in surprise. "So all three of you needed to visit the hospital?" Chung tried to sound incredulous but failed.

"Yes. Senior Administrator Ming wanted to visit the facility. Dr. Lín and I needed to speak with Statistician Huoran."

"Why?"

"It is a vital part of our research."

"What kind of research?"

Bao leaned across the table and smiled. "Again, research for which you, Comrade Chung, are not cleared."

"I am cleared for everything you do in Special Lab #62."

Bao was not going to rise to the bait. "I think not."

"So you are not going to tell me what Citizens Lín and Zheng discussed privately?"

Jun did not tell him so Bao shook his head. He didn't see the blow coming, but the man who had been standing in the corner slapped the side of his head hard enough for him to see stars.

Leaning across the table, Captain Chung smiled. "You will tell me everything you know about Citizen Lín, her work, and her conversations with Dr. Zheng."

Again, Bao shook his head. Again, the other man hit him. This time it was a slap on his cheek and Bao's skin felt like it was on fire.

"She has relatives in America. Do they work for the CIA?"

Bao shook his head. "You do know, that if I report to Senior Colonel Sun that you are asking about the work of Special Lab #62, you will be in this chair being beaten."

Chung ignored his comment, thinking it a bluff. "Who do Citizen Lín's relatives work for?"

"Themselves. They own houses for rent, apartment, and office buildings."

Chung yelled, "She is a spy stealing our secrets!!!"

"No, she is not."

His assailant yanked his shoulders back so the chair scraped across the floor. No longer next to the table, he slapped Bao's right cheek and followed it with a blow to his abdomen.

Bao had been here before. They were going to beat him until he said something incriminating. He would die first.

Chung came around the table and put his hand under his chin to lift it. "You are going to tell me everything you know about Comrade Lín and her work or we will charge you."

"With what?"

"Not cooperating with the Ministry of State Security, for one. We can always charge you for the crimes you committed in college."

Oh that again! You have no evidence I killed those two boys. And later, I was living in a bathroom because the government would not provide housing and I could not afford a dorm room. I did what I had to do to survive as an orphan.

"Before you charge me, I suggest you call Senior Colonel Fang Sun on the People's Liberation Army's general staff and ask him for clearance. Once we have his authorization in writing, Dr. Lín and I will be happy to show you the lab and everything we do. Until then, it is a state secret that I am duty bound to protect. Now, may I go? If you don't allow me to leave, I am sure Dr. Lín will report me missing. You wouldn't want that to happen, now, would you?"

Bao held up his arm, "This band has, among other things, a tracker and soon, the security detail at Special Lab #62 will start looking for me. When they report to Senior Colonel Sun that I am here for no other reason than you want to find out about the lab, it will not go well for you."

Chung stood up and opened the door. He'd delivered the message he had intended. Now, he had to find out who and what Dr. Gu was protecting.

When Bao walked into the apartment, Jun was horrified when she saw the bruises on his face. At first, she thought Bao was beaten and robbed. Then, when she heard the story, she was horrified and afraid. Horrified at the unnecessary beating of her lover. Terrified that Ministry of State Security may suspect she was sending information to her cousin. It was time to take the offensive.

SATURDAY, APRIL 26ᵀᴴ, 2003, 8:06 A.M. LOCAL TIME, BEIJING

Senior Colonel Sun did not expect a call on his direct line. Only a few knew his private number and those who did were on a list less than a page long that he kept in his desk drawer. He picked up the handset and said one word, "Sun."

"Senior Colonel, this is Dr. Lín. I need five minutes, maybe ten. It is important."

"I'm listening."

"Last night, Dr. Gu was interrogated in the Ministry of State Security office here in Nanning. A Captain Chung wanted Dr. Gu to tell him about what we are doing in Special Lab #62. When he refused, Dr. Gu was beaten. Captain Chung said he was his control and he must report to him on my activities and the work we are performing in the lab."

The unasked question – Are we under investigation?

Jun didn't want to tell him that the Ministry of State Security had accosted Bao in Guangzhou and wanted him to spy on her. She assumed Sun already knew that fact.

"If the Ministry of State Security believes there is a spy in Special Laboratory #62, then they should have contacted me. I'll check into it."

Senior Colonel Sun hung up and asked himself why the Ministry of State Security would want to investigate the lab? They just cleared Dr. Gu and Dr. Lín. He spun his chair around and ran scenarios through his mind as he looked out the window. The one most likely is that someone at either the Academy of Sciences or the Ministry of Health wants to find a source in the lab in retaliation to the abrupt and deserved removal of Dr. Toghon Tang. Before he acted, Sun decided to call his brother who could give him the source of the Ministry of State Security's inquiry.

CHAPTER 23

DISCOVERIES

When they arrived at each sewage treatment plant, they found streaks of raw sewage spilling over the sides of the pen and into the river. Bao suspected that sewage from these pens may be contaminating the water being treated and piped to residential areas along with the water in Wulishan Harbor.

When Jun started taking pictures of the site, the representative from the Ministry of Ecology and the Environment tried to grab her camera, saying that this was a government facility and photographing it was forbidden. Defiantly, Jun kept taking pictures and the representative went back to the truck, muttering that he must report this.

Even with the rubberized canvas suit, knee-high boots and a tank of air feeding a mask under the hood, the stench of the human waste was enough to make Jun gag. With each step, she sank calf-deep into the muck where the sewage emptied into a large concrete pen.

The heavy rubber gloves made her feel clumsy as she scooped samples and dropped them into a sample jar. Screwing the lid on was even harder. Residue from their gloves stuck to the outside of the jars that were already marked.

The jars were placed into steel racks that held 12 samples. Once the rack was filled, it was handed to a member of the 215th Special Services Battalion who took it to a portable decontamination station. There, the sealed bottles were sprayed with soapy water, then a bleach solution before being put in a containment locker in a truck.

Back in the lab, the sample jars were washed again with a bleach solution and then wiped down with alcohol. No one touched the samples unless they wore a complete set of protective gear.

There were four - Jun, Bao, and two members of the lab's staff – taking samples. The treatment plants and effluent were picked based on information Dr. Zheng's staff and patients provided where residential areas had high instances of polio.

The team had been in Zhanjiang since Monday and this was the last day of sample gathering. Twice between plants, Bao asked the driver to stop and Bao donned his protective gear and collected a sample from what he suspected might contain raw sewage.

Just as they did at the treatment plants, Bao walked from the sewage stream to the 215th's decontamination truck. There, in a temporary tent, his suit was sprayed with a disinfectant before being washed a second time. Unfortunately, Jun noted, no effort was made to collect the water from the washing of their protective gear. Instead, the team used hoses to wash it into the storm drains in the street.

TUESDAY, MAY 13TH, 2003, 1:22 P.M. LOCAL TIME, ON U.S. 395

Adrian had the cruise control set at 75 as she hustled down U.S. 395 from Mammoth. The car was packed and she was planning to spend a few days in San Diego before returning to Mammoth to collect another load, hoping it was the last one.

She was listening to Celine Dion's album from 2002 called "A New Day Has Come" when her new Nokia 7650 mobile phone rang. She pushed the green button on the handset to accept the call.

"Hi lover…"

"Derek, where are you?"

It took six seconds for the electronic signal that was her words to travel from California to a satellite 25,000 miles above the earth and then back down to Guam. "Can't tell you. Am waiting to pick up a VIP to take out to the boat. You in the car?"

"Uh huh."

"When you get home read my latest email. I don't have much time and need a favor."

"Sure, what?" History said when Derek asked for a favor, it was important.

"Vera Hotchkiss invited Evan Klinghoff – that's her boyfriend – to come to Hong Kong with the wives. His family, from what she said, owns a couple of car dealerships in San Diego, including the VW place where I buy parts. Anyway, I'd like you, Vera, Evan, and I to go out to dinner a couple of times while we are in Hong Kong. Also, please include him in whatever you're planning you are doing so he doesn't feel left out."

"Will do. Can you send me his phone number?"

"It is in the email. Matt is asking Lea Ann as well and I am pretty sure that Scott is asking Betsy the same thing. Evan has never been in the military but has a private pilot's license and an instrument rating and owns a Mooney 252. Gotta go. Love you and see you in Hong Kong."

A smiling Adrian was left with a dial tone. She started to toss the phone onto the passenger seat and then held onto it. Derek, what you don't know is that I have had several conversations with Evan Klinghoff when I was ordering your anniversary present.

Finished reminiscing, she glanced down at the color screen, paged down through the directory, and called Lea Ann Scranton. She got voicemail so she called Betsy Schroeder whose mother was out of the hospital but still recovering from her injuries. Same thing. Frustrated, Adrian dropped the phone into a well on the center console.

Adrian figured that she would be back in San Diego by about three, unload the car, take a shower, and look at Derek's email. It would, now that he had called to alert her, require a response before she would join Betsy at Lea Ann's for dinner. The email from their spouses would give them something new to discuss.

THURSDAY, MAY 15ᵀᴴ, 2003, 10:06 A.M. LOCAL TIME, SPECIAL LAB #62

From the field trip to Zhanjiang, they had nine sets of samples, seven from sanitation plants and two that Bao collected on the street. The samples now were divided in half. One would be put in petri dishes and allowed to grow.

Samples were taken from the other half and dried using a chemical called glutaraldehyde, a disinfectant and fixing agent that prevents any further decay. From these, they would be able to search for signs of polio under a scanning electron microscope. In a week, they would start looking at samples from the cultures to see if there were any polio cells.

If they had new polio virus, these would be added to blood samples from those who have had polio and those who have been vaccinated. In a matter of hours, they would be able to see if polio virus destroyed the cells in the American samples which had antibodies from U.S. vaccines. If this happened, they would know that they had a new strain of polio.

Those preparing the samples for examination were in separate rooms. One for the samples being dried, the other for the live cultures. All the technicians wore suits with hoods, gloves, boots, and breathed purified air to protect them from inhaling any pathogens.

Entry into the clean room was a three-step process. Step one required stripping down to one's underwear. In step two, the technician entered a special room where he or she donned a previously sanitized suit. For step three, the technician walked into a smaller room, fully kitted out, and stood for two minutes while exposed to ultraviolet light that would, hopefully, kill any bacteria on the outside of the suit. Then, and only then, was one allowed into the clean room that had four workstations.

Earlier in the week, the samples of the three polio viruses – paralytic, spinal, and bulbar - from the Center for Disease Control – arrived along with anti-polio-virus anti-body samples from U.S. vaccines. They were packed with dry ice in a sealed and locked cooler. A courier accompanied the container from Houston to LA, to

Hong Kong, to Nanning where a driver brought the courier and the container to the lab. There, Senior Administrator Ming signed for the cooler that was now stored in one of the lab's refrigeration units.

The courier also brought an envelope with images of the polio virus contained in the vials. These would be compared to any polio cells found in the Zhanjiang samples.

With what they needed in hand, Jun directed the lab technicians to create two sets of cultures. In one set of tissue culture flasks they would put the viruses from the CDC. In the other, they would place the Zhanjiang samples.

Once the virus had grown, they would introduce it into new tissue culture flasks with healthy cells along with antibodies derived from American and Chinese vaccines. They estimated that in two or three days they would know if the polio viruses collected from Zhanjiang destroyed the healthy cells. If they did, then they would know if their hypothesis that they had discovered a new strain was correct.

To create redundancy, each set was further divided in two and stored in different containers in different incubators. Now it was just a matter of waiting two or three days. Until the Zhanjiang samples were compared to those from the CDC, they would not know if the People's Republic had a different strain or just more cases caused by poor sanitation.

Preparing the samples was a painstakingly slow process that only those who have worked in a biosafety lab would understand. Everything had to be sterile. Neither Jun nor Bao trusted what they could get from suppliers, so the used Dr. Zheng's friend to procure what they needed most: dehydrated nutrient sugar that she could trust was free of contaminants from a supplier in Australia. The mixture, or agar, was stirred as it was boiled before being placed in sterilized dishes whose covers were already labeled. Then the samples of material that they thought carried the polio virus were added.

While she didn't do the actual work, Jun closely supervised the technicians who understood the importance of what they were doing. With the samples in the incubator, there was nothing for Jun, Bao, and their team to do for several days, maybe even a week. Then, they could use their Hitachi FE-SEM-S4800 scanning electron microscope to take pictures of what they found.

Four members of the staff spent three weeks at a Hitachi facility in Japan learning how to set up and use their FE-SEM-S4800. With a resolution as small as two nanometers, the device should be able to provide images of any polio virus cells that are 25 – 30 nanometers in size.

If the cells were markedly different, then Jun and Bao would have to decide whether they want to split the cells to see if the RNA inside them is different. That capability, however, was beyond the capabilities of Special Lab #62. Those laboratories were in Europe and the U.S.

Bao was visibly excited when he opened the door to Jun's office. "Come, Dr. Lín, I think we have found something."

The lab had a small conference room in which there were two large, high-resolution monitors on a table so, if one was sitting in a chair, the 36" wide screens were at eye level.

Jun and Bao took the seats directly in front of the monitors while a technician whose name tag said her name was Shu Liu slid a CD into the drive. She tapped on the keyboard and slowly an image was revealed on the right screen. "Comrade Doctors Gu and Lín, the image on the right is from the sample sent to us by the Americans. Note its hexagonal shape of its outer shell or capsid. It is a pure sample and if cells like this one enter the human body, there is a high likelihood the person will become ill with polio."

Liu tapped on the keys and then pushed the return key that would enter her commands. Slowly another image began to appear. "We believe this is the polio virus from our samples. We've found it in three of the four we have studied. Look at its shape in which the outer layer, the glycoprotein shell, is almost a perfect sphere and noticeably larger. In the American sample, most are twenty-two to twenty-five nanometers in diameter. The smallest ones taken from Zhanjiang are all at least twenty-nine nanometers in diameter and most are between thirty-five and forty, plus they are polygons rather than being round like the American ones."

Both doctors leaned forward and studied the image in front of them. Liu added, "We've isolated these from the other fecal samples collected from patients with polio so we are ninety-five per cent sure that this a poliovirus, which if true, means we have found a new, mutated strain of the poliovirus."

Jun turned around and saw the entire staff crowded into the conference room. "Lab Technician Liu, can you compare these to the cultures made from the blood samples we have from victims at Special Hospital #326. We should have some from patients who were still showing symptoms as well as those who are in the rehab center."

"Comrade Doctor Lín, we have those specimens already imaged. Please allow me to recall them."

More taps at the keys and the image of the American lab's poliomyclitis virus disappeared and another one slowly started to come into view. "Comrade doctors, this is one of a dozen samples from patients at Special Hospital #326. The notes show they were taken when the patient was running a fever of between thirty-eight (100.4^0 F) thirty-nine degrees Celsius (102.2^0 F)."

The shape and size were identical to the ones they took from the sewage treatment plants. It too was bluer than the American sample.

Jun stood up and faced those packed in the room. "We may be looking at a new strain of the polio virus. I emphasize, may. You will not talk about what you have seen in this room outside of this laboratory to anyone who is not a member of this team. This is a state secret."

Training and experience told Jun that what was on the screen and in her lab was a mutation of the polio virus. Turning to Bao, she said, "Dr. Gu, please test samples from our live cultures that have antibodies to prevent polio to determine if they are neutralized by a polio vaccine manufactured in the People's Republic."

FRIDAY, MAY 23RD, 2003, 10:11 A.M. LOCAL TIME, SPECIAL LAB #62

Unlike the last time Senior Colonel Sun came to Nanning and the lab, Jun and Bao had little to show him other than the facility. This time was different. Jun placed a single chair in front of the monitors and showed him the two viruses. Senior Administrator Ming stood in the back of the room while Lab Technician Shu Liu took her seat by the keyboard, ready to call up additional images.

Jun explained the significance of the two different shapes and of the resistance of the new strain to being neutralized by a poliovirus made in the People's Republic. Their tests suggested that the current polio vaccines made in the PRC were about 40 – 50% effective against what they initially called the Zhanjiang strain. The American ones about 60 – 70% effective.

If one goes by the World Health Organization standard for desired vaccine efficacy of 50%, then those produced in the PRC do not meet this standard to prevent this new strain. The American vaccines are better, but to reduce the number of cases, we would need a new vaccine.

Hearing that news, Senior Colonel Sun asked both Senior Administrator Ming and Lab Technician Liu to leave the room. Looking at Jun, he asked, "Are you sure this is a new strain?"

Jun looked at Bao and gave Senior Colonel Sun the answer they agreed upon. "Ninety-five percent sure. It is resistant to vaccines made in America as well as our country. The only way to be one hundred percent sure would be to test it on humans, some of whom were vaccinated by American vaccines and some by those made in the People's Republic."

They had scripted the likely questions from Senior Colonel Sun and had ready answers. The senior colonel's next question was, "How would you conduct a test and how many volunteers are needed?"

Neither Jun nor Bao believed that anyone would volunteer to be given a virus with a mortality rate of 20 - 30% in adults and would probably permanently paralyze parts of their bodies.

"Do you want to measure the infection rate or do you just want to see if the individuals become sick?"

Senior Colonel Sun didn't hesitate. "Both. How would you recommend we carry out this test?"

Jun swallowed hard. While she was not a medical doctor who had taken the Hippocratic oath, she believed in its principles to do no harm to a patient. Bao had taken the oath but had, in several private moments, said that he and others were often asked to treat patients in a way that violated the oath.

Bao, as the immunologist had their prepared answer. "We have several choices…." Senior Colonel Sun made notes on his pad as Bao explained before asking, "Do you have to conduct the physicals?"

"No, we would provide the desired age range and the requirements for the physicals and lab work. We would need the results to make the selections."

"How soon could you provide the requirements?"

Dr. Gu was ready with the answer. "I can give them to you now."

Senior Colonel Sun held up his pen as if to say, tell me.

"Half men, half women, ideally between thirty and forty." He rattled off the need for each candidate for the test to have an EKG and what type of blood tests to create a baseline against which to base the results. Some would be vaccinated by Chinese vaccines, some by American and some not at all. Then Bao described the type of facility needed. It must be, he emphasized, secluded from others to ensure the test is not compromised and others outside the test group are not infected.

When Bao finished, Jun added. "The ideal place would be on the grounds of Special Hospital #326. They have the space and the knowledge of how to treat polio. There, we can isolate each test individual in a separate room in a separate building. And, they can have the capabilities to deal with the results."

Senior Colonel Sun sat back in his chair. He hadn't thought of that. He was planning to use a local prison and keep the prisoners in a separate building once they were selected. Special Hospital #326 would separate them from the general prison population in case they needed to conduct a separate test.

In Sun's mind, Dr. Zheng was a wild card. While he respected her and she was the wife of a good friend, he was afraid her principles would cause her to object and protest to the Ministry of Health. No, he thought, this must remain within the Army's control. Sun was confident that he could arrange for the Ministry of Justice to turn over a section of the Guangxi woman's prison or the newer Nanning prison to him.

Whether or not Dr. Gu and Dr. Lín created a vaccine for this new strain mattered not. Senior Colonel Sun had what he wanted and now he needed some data.

"We will run this test. As you can imagine, I need to make some arrangements. However, I do not like the name Zhanjiang strain. Come up with another one that does not implicate the People Republic's good name."

Jun blurted out the name they were using internally as a code for the mutated strain. "Oilop-03."

Senior Colonel Sun smiled as he realized the source of the name. "I like it."

He pushed himself to his feet and glared malevolently at Jun and Bao. It was not a look of hate but threatening. "Our conversation today is a state secret as is your work here. Make sure everyone knows that if there is a leak, the penalty will be severe."

Once the senior colonel left, Bao and Jun sat at the table holding hands with tears welling in their eyes. Senior Colonel Sun's plan made them sick to their stomach and they were sure it would haunt them for the rest of their lives.

WEDNESDAY, AUGUST 6ᵀᴴ, 2003, 2:39 P.M. LOCAL TIME, NANNING

When Bao and Jun took their seats in the back of the staff car, their driver informed them that they were not going to Special Lab #62 today. Instead, their driver said the two doctors were going to the prison that supports the Yibin Motorcycle Plant and the Nanning Machinery Plant.

Two weeks earlier, Jun and Bao were brought to the prison to review inmate medical records. Neither knew which inmate would be placed in each group and both were convinced they would be the scapegoats if anything went wrong with the test.

On this visit, Senior Colonel Sun met them at the front door and handed them surgical masks with an extra layer of filtration before leading them to a building just outside the prison. The prison doctor, Dr. Donhai Pingying, was waiting, also wearing a mask.

Pingying was, Jun guessed, in his fifties and was so thin, he looked emaciated. They had met him on their first visit when he gave them a tour of the modifications to the two barracks buildings that were now fenced off from the main prison.

The prison doctor was amiable and helpful on the first visit. This time, he was grim faced when he entered the room. "Senior Colonel Sun has asked me to brief you on the progress of the test."

Jun fought the bile rising in her throat. Bao's eyes suggested that his hidden face was an emotionless mask. Her lover's hands were so tightly clasped, Jun could see the flesh was white as he squeezed his hands together. Both had been dreading this visit and those to this prison that might come later.

Pingying began to talk in an emotionless drone that, if Jun was not careful, would put her to sleep. "Doctors Gu and Lín, as per your instructions, we have two groups, evenly divided between men and women. One group of fifty ate contaminated food during their morning, noon, and evening meals on the 21st. The other group was exposed to an aerosol spray containing Oilop-03 on the evenings of the 21st and 22nd as they slept."

Pingying stopped and looked at Jun and Bao who were doing their best to remain and appear emotionless. Bao didn't like what was being done, but in his mind, these were prisoners and the state owed them nothing. If they die, so be it. If they live through their prison term, then what waited for them as former criminals wasn't pleasant either. After the test, those who survived unharmed would stay in this prison to serve out their sentences. Those whose suffered paralysis would have their sentences commuted and given menial jobs at military bases but would never know the cause of their illness.

Jun, on the other hand, having lived in the U.S. for six years and having been trained in American and Western medical practices, was horrified. If someone contemplated this in the U.S., she was sure he or she would be locked up.

The prison doctor continued in his monotone voice. "It is becoming clear that the incubation period for those who ate the contaminated food is shorter, about six to ten days. For those exposed to the aerosol, the incubation period is averaging ten to twelve days."

Pingying slid a chart across the table so that Senior Colonel Sun and Doctors Gu and Lín each had a copy. The papers were marked *Top Secret/Insidious Dragon.* "This is what we know so far based on the subjects. We need until the end of September to determine which subject's paralysis is temporary and which is permanent. And some of the sicker may still die."

Preliminary Results		
Relevant Data	Food	Aerosol
Number in each group	52 men	51 men
	48 women	49 women
Illness rate	40% - percentages same for each sex	30% - percentages same for each sex
Days ill	6 – 12	6 – 10
Paralysis rate	5%	4%
Death rate	28%	25%

The prison doctor continued to speak. "My preliminary conclusion is that infecting a population through the food they eat is more effective than aerosol sprays. However, aerosol is easier to employ. And last, contracting Oilop-03 is much more dangerous than the other strains of poliomyelitis. We have collected blood samples to be delivered to Special Lab #62 to, if we can, determine what type of polio – spinal, bulbar or bulbospinal – each victim has."

Jun was afraid to pick up the sheet because her hands might show they were shaking in anger. What she saw made her sick to her stomach. Once you were exposed, an individual was going to become ill. Oilop-03 had a much higher paralytic rate than other strains and about the same death rate.

The doctor's monotone brought Jun back to reality. "There was one unplanned result from this test...."

Neither Bao nor Jun said anything, confident Dr. Pingying was about to tell them. "We divided our staff so that one doctor and four nurses were assigned to each group. Unfortunately, four of the nurses came down with Oilop-03 despite wearing double masks. None died, but all have paralysis that I think will be permanent. This tells me that the virus is highly contagious."

Jun blurted out, "We knew that!"

Dr. Pingying continued. "By September 30th, we should know how many of the subjects' paralysis is permanent and how many died. If you have any questions, I will do my best to answer them."

Neither Jun nor Bao had any questions. Both wanted to leave the prison as fast as possible.

FRIDAY, AUGUST 8TH, 2003, 4:26 P.M. LOCAL TIME, HONG KONG

Derek lay against the headrest of the king-sized bed with Adrian's head resting on his chest. He was spent and both were totally naked. They'd interrupted a shopping trip when it started to rain. Outside, the sky was dark and the heavy rain prevented him from seeing *Vinson* anchored about a mile from the landing where he'd come ashore.

The four – Adrian, Betsy, Lea Ann, and Evan Klinghoff – had arrived on the 4th and the ship anchored on the morning of the 6th. It was not scheduled to leave until the morning of the 11th.

Through Adrian's parents' connections in the hotel industry, she booked rooms for any of the wives who wanted to stay at the Mandarin at the same rate that the JW Marriott was charging the other wives. About a half dozen took Adrian up on her offer.

Derek was running his fingers up and down Adrian's side, occasionally caressing her breast. "Thank you for taking care of Evan."

"It was my pleasure." Evan knew that Adrian would cut off his balls if he mentioned that she was buying him a 911 Turbo.

"Word is that you made a lot of the wives' events which meant you came down off the mountain."

Adrian giggled. "It was if I was Moses coming down from Mount Sinai with the ski report. The events were on weekends so who wanted to stand in lift lines?"

"Before I forget, after this cruise, I get a month or so off and then I am going to HS-10 as an HH-60H instructor. No more long cruises for a couple of years."

Adrian perked up. "Really."

"Yup. The message orders should arrive right after we leave Hong Kong."

Adrian sat up suddenly and crossed her legs. Gently, she poked him. "I just want you to know that I got my NASTAR handicap down under ten, so next winter, we're gonna race!"

Laughing, Derek shook his head. "And you're going to lose."

Determined and proud of her improved racing skills, she poked him in the chest. "No, Racer I am not."

Derek grabbed Adrian, and before he kissed her, he said, "Yes you will, but I'll still love you."

Adrian wrapped her arms around her husband. They had time before getting dressed for dinner with their friends to have what Derek referred to as a quickie.

CHAPTER 24

REAL FEARS

The captain that appeared at his administrative assistant's office insisted that only Senior Colonel Sun could sign for the envelope and the sealed container he was carrying. The officer was from the 215th Special Services Support Battalion.

Hearing the man's unit, Senior Colonel Sun exited his office to sign for the document and the case. Before he opened the case, he slit open the envelope and put the two sheets marked Top Secret/ Insidious Dragon Final Report on his desk.

He pulled the report from August and compared the two charts. The only difference was that the death rate for Oilop-03 transmitted through food was five percent higher than those infected through an aerosol spray.

On the second sheet, Doctor Pingying noted that a nurse died, one doctor and two nurses have permanent paralysis and have been sent to Special Hospital #326 for treatment. Their medical records show they were treated in a small clinic north of Zhanjiang.

Pingying also mentioned that the aerosol spray reached the barracks next to where the test was being held. Eleven prisoners, including Lim Cao, the SinoPharma's COO and its CEO, Xiu Bai contracted Oilop-03. They were in different sections of the barracks and did not know the other was there. Cao died and Bai survived but was paralyzed from the chest down.

Inside the canister was a spray bottle commonly used for spray paint and insecticides. A note said that the 215th Battalion could fill these with a liquid in which the live Oilop-03 virus would survive and a propellant. On the outside, they could attach any label for a product made in the People's Republic for sale in the west. The battalion had enough bottles, propellant, and liquid with the virus from the test at the prison to fill 50 bottles.

Senior Colonel Sun now had a weapon the PRC could use. Now, he had to decide if when and where it should be used.

This left Senior Colonel Sun with the decision about Doctors Lín and Gu. Neither needed to know the results from the test. They gave him what he really wanted and now were at Special Lab #62 to create a vaccine to prevent Oliop-03. They were, he guessed, years away.

The question in Sun's mind was what to do with Doctors Gu and Lín. They were extremely competent, resourceful, and therefore, valuable. However, Senior Colonel Sun believed they suspected he was weaponizing Oilop-03. Should he leave them in place where he can watch them? Or should he send them into the prison system where they will disappear and lose their talent?

While he debated their fate, Senior Colonel Sun had a cup of tea. Looking out the window at the bright blue sky that, for a change, was not muted by Beijing's pollution, he decided that right now, he will do nothing. His task now was to get the National Military Commission and the Politburo to agree to a test Oilop-03 in a Western country.

TUESDAY, OCTOBER 7TH, 2003, 10:08 A.M. LOCAL TIME, NAS NORTH ISLAND

Derek dropped Adrian off at the Naval Exchange, promising he would only spend a few minutes at HS-10. His official reporting date was Monday, October 20th, and thought he might learn what billet he would be assigned besides an instructor.

Seeing Derek in the passageway headed to the admin office, Ray Nicholson, HS-10's CO, asked his administrative assistant to bring Derek to his office. After introducing himself, "Lieutenant Almer, you saved me a phone call."

Derek followed the CO into his office. "Racer, please close the door and stand easy."

With the door closed behind him, Derek approached the CO's desk wondering what the commander wanted. "We received a request from the powers that be to send a top-notch HH-60H driver TAD to some super-secret outfit. Both your CO's say you're the perfect fit. So, I gave this outfit your phone number. Expect a call this week and yes, they know you are on leave. I'm not, nor is anyone in HS-10 cleared for what they do or want or if you will still be on HS-10's roster. So, once you find out, please let me know."

Derek tried not to look or sound confused. "Yes, sir. I will." He started to open the door.

Nicholson said with a grin, "Racer, do me a favor. Don't embarrass the Navy's helo community."

His metallic Forest Green Porsche 911 Turbo grumbled to life. It was barely above idle in second gear as he drove to the Navy Exchange's parking lot, wondering what the call would be about. And then, what was he going to tell Adrian?

He let the Porsche idle for a few seconds before he turned it off just in time to hear his new Nokia 7650 mobile phone ring.

"Almer."

"Derek, this is Don Sanderson, a person from your deep dark past. Do you have time for a beer tonight?"

"Why don't you come over to the house? I'll grill some steaks."

"Done but call me on this number if Adrian objects. We can meet for breakfast tomorrow if that works better."

No Don, that won't work because it will interfere with my morning lovemaking session with my wife. We're trying to make up for all the days we missed while I was out on the Vinson.

"Cool, I am about to see her so I'll call you back if it is a no go."

"Look forward to seeing you."

Dial tone.

Derek was on the patio behind their house grilling corn and steaks. In one hand, he had a set of tongs and in the other, a cold bottle of Modelo Especial. Don Sanderson was standing next to him sipping from his beer. "The unit to which you've been assigned is a mix of Navy, Air Force, and Army pilots. Officially, it came into existence on October 1st, but the pilots, aircrew, and maintainers have been filtering in since August. You will be flying a highly modified version of the H-60 and testing tactics that will get the helicopter in and out of highly defended airspace. Eventually, three more Naval Aviators will join you in the squadron."

"Cool, sounds like fun."

"Here's the bad news. Every Monday morning at 0730, you will board an unmarked 737 and fly back Thursday afternoon. Where you are going is in the Nevada desert to a place officially called Area 51. More I can't tell you."

"Don, what's your role in this?"

Sanderson was two years ahead of Derek at Norwich and was from Portland, Maine. He had an Army ROTC scholarship and became a Green Beret. Then, from what Derek could tell, he disappeared for a few years and now, he was with the CIA.

"Y'all work for me and let's leave it at that for now."

Later that night, when they were curled up next to each other, Adrian said she could live with him being gone three or four nights a week. She just wanted to be assured that it would be worth it and the deployments would be short and few and far between.

TUESDAY, OCTOBER 28TH, 2003, 9:11 P.M. LOCAL TIME, GROOM LAKE, NV, A.K.A. AREA 51

A sergeant from the flight line crew stuck his head into the room where the officers of the 4007th Joint Special Operations Squadron were waiting, "Show time gents. The C-5 just touched down."

Derek along with the 4007th's CO, XO, operations officer, four other pilots, and two maintenance officers filed out of the room to watch the C-5 taxi to a stop where the 4007th already had four MH-60Ls from the Army's 160th Special Operations Aviation Regiment.

"Racer, so these are our new toys?" Derek heard the soft voice of Vera Hotchkiss whom he found out was also asked to join the 4007th when he saw her checking in for the 737 flight on Monday, October 20th. Grinning, she said, "Whither thou goeth, so shall I."

"I guess so. Supposedly these new H-60s are special but no one knows how special."

Tapper giggled, "Yeah, special means more pages in the NATOPS manual to learn."

The C-5 stopped and the loudest sound was the cargo airplane's auxiliary power unit as the rear doors of the giant airlifter opened and the ramp at the rear began to extend.

The Air Force captain assigned as the assistant maintenance officer watched as the crew of the C-5 untied the helicopter farthest aft in the fuselage. Once the tow bar was attached, the matte black MH-60 was pulled out. Under the yellow Klieg lights, they could tell the shape of the helicopter was different. Conversation stopped as the pilots realized how much different as it passed in front of them and into the hangar.

Three more helicopters were pulled out of the C-5 along with ten pallets on which large wooden boxes were strapped. Once forklifts had moved the boxes into the hangar, the C-5's pilots started its engines and taxied into the darkness.

With the hangar door closed, Air Force Colonel Lionel Hollingsworth waved the pilots and mechanics to gather round. Behind him was one of the new H-60s.

"Ladies and gentlemen, these are our new helicopters. With a full set of panels installed, they will be stealthy, at least for a helicopter.

Tests show they have about a quarter as in twenty-five percent of the radar signature of a regular Blackhawk. One of our jobs is to validate that analysis and develop the tactics to take advantage of their stealthy features. We are also on call for any special tasking our leaders in Washington might decide we should carry out. We will only fly these versions at night, and as far as the world knows, they are *Top Secret* code-named *Have Circle* and therefore do not exist. The 4007th's call sign is Dragonfly."

The flight schedule of the 4007th began at three in the afternoon and ended 12 hours later. Hollingsworth had those from the same service flying together, but eventually he wanted to mix and match cockpit and cabin crews from each of the services.

Another familiar face arrived alongside Derek in the form of AW1 Grayson. He said that Hambleton, who left *Vinson* while it was in Hong Kong to attend the combat paramedic course, would report around the 1st of November. The two other Navy air crewmen who came from East coast helicopter squadrons had also completed the full Air Force PJ course and would soon be in the 4007th.

Derek and Vera flew two, three-hour sorties each day. They had to catch up to the others because the Army MH-60Ls had more sensors than the HH-60Hs flown by HSC-8. And they had to learn a new skill - tanking from a C-130.

The Naval Aviators were the only ones who hadn't tanked before. To do so, they had to learn how to take on fuel from a C-130 flying with its flaps down, level at 3,000 feet at 130 knots. The baskets into which the refueling probes were inserted streamed down aft from pods outboard of the C-130's engines. When the refueling hoses were fully extended and in position, the basket was about 50 feet aft of the tail of the C-130 and 20 feet below.

To catch the tanker, the MH-60s flew almost as fast as they could. The refueling probe extended about 20 feet in front of the nose of the helicopter. Derek found that by flying into a position about 10 feet above and aft of the basket, he could make a quick dive and stick the hose in the basket. A little aft cyclic and a little extra power from raising the collective seated the hose. The orange light would turn to green, saying fuel was transferring which would be confirmed by the fuel totalizer showing an increase.

As the pilot, all he had to do was maintain a constant position relative to the basket and stay in the proper spot relative to the C-130. The transfer rate was 1,200 pounds (~185 gallons) a minute. In just a few minutes on the basket, the helicopter could take on enough fuel to fill the MH-60L's tanks with 4,000 pounds (~615 gallons) of JP-4.

JP-4 was the standard fuel used by the Army and Air Force. The Navy and Marine Corps used JP-5 which had a lower flash point. One can drop a match into a bucket of JP-5 and it will not burn while JP-4 will quickly flame. As a practical matter, JP-4 burned hotter and gave the helicopter more power and range. JP-5 in the tanks reduced the chance of a catastrophic fire from a fuel leak.

When in position, the tips of the rotor blades passed about 10 feet above the hose. If the air was turbulent, then the hose and the helicopter were moving up and down. If one got out of sync, the blade could hit the hose with catastrophic consequences for the helicopter.

After two or three hops during the day, they practiced getting the probe into the basket, taking on about 500 pounds, and then pulling off and doing it again. Once they became proficient, they started tanking at night wearing night vision goggles. The process was the same, it was just dark. Every training sortie involved taking on fuel from a tanker at least twice.

SATURDAY, NOVEMBER 15ᵀᴴ, 2003, 7:18 P.M. LOCAL TIME, NANNING

Jun waited five minutes after Bao went out the door. Then, she ran down the stairwell and emerged just after Bao walked out the door of their apartment building. She stayed about 50 meters back in the mass of people. His height made following the man she loved easy.

Since they returned from the trip where they were shown the preliminary results at the Yibin Motorcycle factory, Bao took much longer to complete his food shopping trips. The delays and excuses made Jun suspicious so she decided to follow her lover. At first, Jun thought she was just being paranoid. She was living in the People's

Republic and its citizens were encouraged if not forced to spy on their friends, co-workers, and relatives.

At the edge of the market, Bao met two men, one of whom Jun recognized. She had seen him in Senior Administrator Ming's office at Special Lab #62 show his Ministry of State Security badge and ID.

She followed the three individuals across Liusha Road and into the paths along the banks of the Yong Jiang River. Here, the crowds thinned out and Jun hung back. When the two men broke off, Jun hurried back to their apartment, not quite sure what to believe.

Ever since the test at the prison, Jun decided that she could no longer live in the People's Republic. She hadn't called Yan because she was afraid the Ministry of State Security would learn of the conversation. Or, that Yan would say there was nothing she could do.

However, now was the time. Given what Dr. Zheng said, Jun believed Senior Colonel Sun would soon decide he didn't need either Bao or her. Better she rationalized, that she was caught trying to escape than not trying at all.

Back in her apartment, she didn't know what time it was in Washington, D.C., but didn't care. Jun figured she had about half an hour before Bao returned. She dialed the number from memory and the call went from her apartment to an exchange in Nanning and then to one in Shenzhen where the switch recorded the call as ending. Now that the call had ended, the switch sent it to another device in Hong Kong. From there the signal went to a satellite in a stationary orbit that covered the southeastern provinces of the People's Republic, Vietnam, Hong Kong, and the Philippines.

Enroute to the satellite, the call was encrypted and transferred to another satellite over the eastern U.S. where it was sent to a ground station at Fort Meade, Maryland. When it entered the switch at NSA, it was decrypted and rang at a call center.

"Allo."

Jun spoke in Mandarin. "Is Cousin Shan there?"

The woman checked the roster for call-in IDs and responded in perfect Mandarin. "Just one moment please. I will connect you." She pressed a switch which sent the call to Yan's mobile phone.

"Lieutenant Commander Huáng?"

Yan recognized the number as coming from NSA's switchboard and her mind raced as to why someone from NSA was calling her at

0718 on a Friday. "I have a caller asking for Cousin Shan. Should I connect you?"

"Yes, please do." Yan's heart started racing and she pulled into a convenience store parking lot so she could concentrate and, if needed, make notes. She heard a click and spoke. "Jun, this is Yan."

Jun just started speaking in rapid Mandarin as her mind gave Yan a dump of the summer. When she finished, Yan asked, "Do you want out?"

"Yes."

"What about Bao?"

"I am not sure. I am not going to ask him until I am walking out the door. He has been talking with the Ministry of State Security who has been blackmailing him."

"Do you think you will be arrested soon?"

"No, but I am afraid that I may be by the end of the year. Can you help me get out?"

Yan answered before her brain had time to process the answer. "Yes. Give me your new phone number."

Jun rattled off the number that started with 86, the country code for the People's Republic of China, then the city code for Nanning, 771 and then the eight digits of the phone in the apartment. "I will find a way to get you out, trust me. Be calm, trust no one, including Bao."

"I don't want to leave him behind to face the goons in the Ministry of State Security unless I think he will or has betrayed me."

"We cannot kidnap him, so he must come willingly."

Jun bobbed her head. "I understand." This was something that she would have to sort out.

When she hung up, Yan dialed her boss who answered on the second ring with one word. "Lansing."

"Boss, this is Yan. I just talked to my cousin. She wants out as soon as possible."

"How soon will you be here?"

"Thirty minutes. I need to spend a few minutes in my office converting my notes from what she said into something that resembles intelligence. Then we can talk."

"When you are ready, come see me. I'll alert Captain Rainbow."

After listening to Yan, Captain Rainbow summarized the situation by saying, "These are the bullet points. One, the PRC just tested a mutated strain of polio as a biological warfare weapon. Two, the strain has a significantly higher rate of paralysis and mortality among adults. Three, American vaccines are only at best 50% effective at preventing the disease. Fourth, Dr. Lín wants to defect. And fifth, you want to bring her out. Is this correct?"

Yan nodded and said, "Yes sir. Time, I believe, based on what Dr. Lín said, is of the essence."

Captain Rainbow took a deep breath. "Lieutenant Commander Huáng, the National Center for Medical Intelligence found Dr. Lín's information to be a treasure trove. We have used other sources to corroborate both the sources and the content. So, I can assure you that my organization would love to debrief Dr. Lín. However, please understand that within the intelligence community, there are conflicting priorities. Nonetheless, I believe extracting Dr. Lín should be of national importance and I will do my level best to convince my boss that bringing Dr. Lín to the United States is in its national interest and should be a priority. I presume Captain Lansing will part with you if needed to help in this endeavor."

Laughing, Captain Lansing said, "Not letting Ms. Huáng do her part is not one of my options."

THE SAME DAY, 9:50 P.M. LOCAL TIME, GUANGZHOU

Along the wall in the back of the club Blind Maiden, Liang found a padded bench seat with small tables for drinks and purses. It was also as far from the speakers as she could find where one didn't have to yell to converse.

The club, which catered to lesbians and transgenders was slowly filling up. Already, the tables lining the dance floor were all occupied.

Her date, Ya Teow, was a programmer at the Guangzhou office of the Indian technology company Infosys. She'd been working there for three years and they were giving her time off to take courses to earn a doctorate in computer science at Guangzhou University. They'd met two weeks ago at what was a formal lesbian club at Sun Yat-Sen University. It was a far cry from the first time she went with An Wu. Now, it was out in the open, and on the first Saturday of each month it met in one of the student dining rooms after it stopped serving dinner. Admission was modest five yuan to cover the food, beer, wine, and soft drinks.

The large dining room was partitioned off so that the gay men had their own party and the women theirs. The standing joke at the gathering was how many of the women and transgenders who were really lesbians and were members of the Ministry of Public Security or State Security. And, if they were there, were they straight or gay?

The relationship began when Ya and Liang started talking while waiting in line for a glass of wine. She wasn't sure who asked out who first, but Ya spent that night at Liang's apartment. Since then, they'd been sleeping together several nights a week.

They'd decided to come to Blind Maiden after dinner and Ya, who was wearing a micro mini skirt that came down just below her groin had the figure of a model and the face to match. She stroked Liang's thigh as she finished her beer saying she had to go to the ladies' room.

Leaning back against the backrest, Liang sipped her glass of Shaoxing wine, enjoying the nutty aroma as it warmed her throat on its way to her stomach. She could drink several glasses and not wind up with a hangover in the morning. Liang watched a woman she guessed was in her forties dance provocatively in front of her lover. Her interest in the dancing couple meant she didn't pay attention to the couple sliding onto the bench next to her.

"Liang?"

The senior professor of finance turned to the voice and in the dim light, she thought she recognized the woman. "Daiyu?"

The woman who was the head of Sun Yat-Sen University's library smiled and her hand was entwined with that of another woman. "Liang, This is a pleasant surprise."

Translation – I didn't know you were a lesbian.

"Have you been here before?"

Liang smiled. "Many times. They play songs so us old people can dance."

Daiyu laughed heartily. Ya came back and was introduced to Daiyu and her date, Li Mei. She held out her hands to Liang as if to say, let's dance. Daiyu looked up and said, "Ya, would you mind dancing with Li Mei for a few minutes."

Translation – I need to talk to Liang privately.

Li Mei stood up and towered over Ya who said, "One song, then I want Liang."

Daiyu nodded and turned to Liang. "I need to tell you something that is very, very important." She summarized her arrangement with the Ministry of People's Security and the Ministry of State Security in that the ministry looks the other way when she imports banned books. In return, she identifies students they may want to recruit. She recounted about how she came to know Bao Gu saying that she heard that Liang's daughter was in love with him.

As she listened, the knot in Liang's stomach grew tighter and larger. This explains why, she believed, Bao hasn't proposed. It also meant that Jun was in danger.

Ya's return let Liang stand up and gather her thoughts. As she danced with Ya in her arms, scenarios in how to warn Jun ran through her mind. He would come up with a way to warn her daughter tomorrow.

The couple sat down when the tempo of the music changed. Ya took Liang's hand and placed it between her legs so she could feel the wetness. That was when Liang stopped thinking about what Daiyu said.

TUESDAY, NOVEMBER 18ᵀᴴ, 2003, 1:26 P.M. LOCAL TIME, ANACOSTIA

Yan was engrossed in studying a photo of the PRC Navy's base in Baihai in southern Guangxi province when Captain Lansing tapped on the door frame to her office. Yan put the image of the frigate down and looked up.

He handed her a slip of paper. "Yan, you have a meeting in this location at two. It is about getting Dr. Lín out of the PRC."

"Are you coming, sir."

The retired Navy Captain shook his head. "Nope, I'm not cleared. Good luck."

The only person in the room that Yan knew was Captain Rainbow. Seated at the head of the table was a two-star admiral she recognized as the Deputy Director of the DIA. There were three other men, all in civilian clothes.

When she entered, Captain Rainbow said, "Yan, please tell these gentlemen what you know that is fact about your cousin. Then tell them what you can interpret with at least a seventy-to-eighty percent confidence level. I know this will be hard but try to be unemotional. These gentlemen are very interested in what you have to say. Our boss is here as window dressing to show how important we think this mission is."

"Who are they?"

"Friends from Langley. They have the assets and stroke to get your cousin out."

When the questions began, she could tell the men from the CIA were skeptical at first. Still, the more she spoke about Dr. Lin and showed the documents she'd provided, the more interested they became. The gentleman who Yan believed to be the most senior, asked, "So, assuming we agree to extract Dr. Lín, how do we convince her the cavalry has arrived?"

"Simple, sir. I go into the PRC, meet my cousin, and take her to the extraction point."

"What do you mean by extraction point?"

Yan then described the bracelets. "This means she can't get on a plane at the airport or take a train to Guangzhou to cross into Hong Kong. Once the bracelet leaves Nanning, the Ministry of State Security will start searching for her. And, if she doesn't show up for work, the same thing will happen. So, suggest we get her out by helicopter that lands either on the road to the lab or on the outskirts of Nanning. Just before boarding the helicopter, the bracelets are cut off and left in the rental car."

"Rental car?"

"Yes, sir. Here's what I suggest. I go to Nanning, rent a car, stay in a hotel, and contact Jun. On the night of the extraction, I drive Jun to where the helicopter will land. By the way, this isn't the first time our helicopters have visited Nanning. I found in the archives that a Lieutenant by the name of Josh Haman dropped off a SEAL team that spent several days on the ground during the Vietnam War and then he went back to get them."

Don Sanderson leaned forward. He still hadn't introduced himself. "Miss Huáng, do you have any experience in planning special operations?"

"No, sir."

Sanderson turned to the others. "Please give Lieutenant Commander Huáng and I a few hours to develop a plan that I think we can get blessed."

When the others left, Don turned to Yan and held out his hand. "I'm Don Sanderson and spent a few years as a Green Beret before joining the agency. I have the assets we need to pull this off if we can solve a few communication issues."

FRIDAY, NOVEMBER 21ˢᵀ, 7:26 P.M. LOCAL TIME, NANNING

Bao had just finished dicing two small chicken thighs into small chunks. All the other vegetables – scallions, snap peas, shallot, and a Sichuan pepper – were all in their little dishes so all Jun had to do was toss them into the wok and cook them.

Jun was waiting for the noodles to be cooked so that they still had some texture. Once they were ready, she would drain them before putting them into the wok where the meat and vegetables were almost finished cooking. Once the dish was plated, each would sprinkle chili oil, peanuts, and the green ends on the scallions on the top as their version of Dan Dan noodles.

Halfway across the apartment, Jun heard the phone ring. Bao, who was checking the noodles, waved at Jun as if to say, you answer.

"Allo…"

"Jun, this is your Cousin Shan. Listen and do not react. We are coming to get you. Plan needs final approval. See you soon."

Dial tone. Into the phone, Jun said, "I am sorry, you have the wrong number."

"Jun, who was that?"

"Wrong number."

"O.K. the noodles are ready."

While they were eating, Jun looked at the man she loved wondering what his reaction would be when she told him and asked, if he wants to go to America, pack a backpack with what he wants to take and be ready to go in five minutes.

Twelve time zones to the east, Yan hoped she didn't lie to her cousin. Tomorrow, supposedly, the head of the CIA would approve the mission.

TUESDAY, NOVEMBER 25TH, 2003, 10:26 A.M. LOCAL TIME, NAVAL BASE, CORONADO, SAN DIEGO, CA

Rather than dash off to Boston for a hurried four or five days, Adrian suggested that Derek take leave in late December and come back in early January. Hollingsworth agreed since he was about to tell the unit that it was standing down beginning on December 18th and not resuming flight operations until January 12th, 2004. Unless of course, there was some sort of national emergency.

With that schedule in his mind, Derek was puzzled why Don Sanderson wanted him to bring Vera Hotchkiss to the office of the Commander, Navy Special Warfare at the Coronado Naval Base. It meant only one thing, there was an op in the offing.

Sitting outside the door, AW1 Grayson was sipping a coke with now AW2 Hambleton. "Sir, Ms. Hotchkiss is already inside. Apparently, we're meeting in the SCIF. Do you know what's up?"

Derek shook his head. "You know as much as I do, but I suspect we're about to find out."

After introductions, Yan Huáng stood at the end of the table in the facility known as a Sensitive Compartmented Information Facility a.k.a. SCIF pronounced like the small rowboat skiff. "Everything you hear from this moment on is classified as *Top Secret/Specially Compartmented Information/Code Word Killer Brace*. Here's the op. We're going into the PRC to extract one, maybe two scientists who have knowledge of a biological weapon the Chinese have developed and may test on the U.S."

Derek looked at Vera whose eyes were wide open. Neither said anything and LCDR Huáng continued. "In the next twenty-four hours, we must finalize an extraction plan so when I go into the PRC to meet these individuals, I know when and where to go to be picked up with the defectors."

Derek looked at Don Sanderson who grinned. "You and Ms. Hotchkiss have been picked to fly the mission by Colonel Hollingsworth. If you don't want to go, speak now or forever hold your peace and we'll pick the next crew on the list, which is, by the way, from the Air Force."

Derek knew the last comment was a matter of pride. He'd never hear the end of it if he turned down a mission that the Air Force successfully carried out. "Before I say yes, where are we picking the three of you up?"

"Near Nanning. It is a city about seventy-nautical from the northern tip of the Gulf of Tonkin."

"When?"

"Preferred date is December 6th; back-up is the 13th." Derek turned to Don Sanderson. "Don, how do we get the helicopter or helicopters in position?"

"My problem. That's what they make C-5s and C-17s for."

Derek tilted his head thinking the CIA obviously has the stroke to dictate to the Military Air Lift Command. "Where are we launching from?"

Sanderson quickly said. "Your choice."

"What kind of cover can you provide to focus the PLA Air Force's attention someone other than us?"

"Derek, before I answer are you and your crew in or out?"

Derek looked at Vera who said, "Racer, if you're the HAC and we can do it our way, I'm in."

He swiveled his chair so he could look at his two aircrewmen. Grayson answered first. "Sir, if you are going, I am too. Just promise me that you'll do everything in your power to keep me from having to eat Chinese food for the rest of my life."

"Hambleton?"

"Ditto what Grayson said."

Derek turned to Sanderson. "You've got your crew. Now, I need to see an old-fashioned chart."

"I thought you would never ask." The former Green Beret tossed a folded J11B Tactical Pilotage Chart (TPC) from 1972 and an Operational Navigation Chart (ONC) J11 from the same era on the table.

Derek opened the ONC first to familiarize himself with the area. "Don, to do this, we either must ask the Vietnamese to use one of their airfields or we sail a ship with a helicopter deck big enough to launch and recover an H-60 up into the Tonkin Gulf. The PRC is not going to like it, but if it stays outside the twelve-mile limit, the PRC can scream, but the noise will fall on deaf ears."

"The agency would prefer not to ask the Vietnamese for help."

"O.K., so let me lay this out. We sail up to about here, launch, fly to a field southeast of Nanning, pick-up Ms. Huáng and her friends and take a slightly different route south back to the boat. What would really make this easier would be if you could have a carrier strike group or an amphibious group conducting flight operations in this area."

Derek pointed to the area between Hainan Island and the Vietnamese Coast at 18^0 North, 108^0 West. "Again, Don, it will focus the PRC's attention on them and help us sneak in and out. We need to plan the route, but my guess is it is about a three-hour round trip assuming we are on the ground for less than ten minutes."

"How many helos?"

"Good question. We only need one for the mission."

"You don't want a wingman?"

Derek took a deep breath. "Two helicopters mean twice the radar and noise signature. Plus, if this goes in the crapper, its four more U.S. servicemen or women who will get to enjoy the hospitality of the Ministry of People's Security. If we are only picking up three people, then we've got plenty of room." He turned to Vera, "Tapper, your thoughts?"

"If we can't prepare an H-60 to fly for three hours without a major problem, we've got other problems."

Derek looked at Yan. "Look, you're taking most of the risk, so what's your take."

"I like *one*."

Before they started the detailed route planning, Derek asked, "How do we communicate with you?"

She slid a mobile phone and a satcom phone across the table. "The SATCOM phone is secure, the mobile isn't. I've been told that the SATCOM phone has coverage in Nanning, the mobile phone is from the PRC and is compatible with their system. This one is yours. I have another."

Derek looked at the slight and beautiful Chinese-born woman. "When do you leave?"

"The first flight I can get on once the mission is approved. I'm planning to call you once we are enroute to the pick-up point."

Quickly, one issue after another was resolved, and by 8 p.m. they had a plan. Sanderson said that tomorrow, they may have to defend their plan to those in the CIA who conduct red team evaluations on ops such as this one. He was confident they would have problems punching holes in the plan and it would be approved.

CHAPTER 25

NO DOUBTS

SATURDAY, NOVEMBER 29ᵀᴴ, 2003, 1:07 P.M. LOCAL TIME, BEIJING

Senior Colonel Sun was almost, he thought, almost caught up with the documents on which he had to make comments. This would let him leave at 1:30 versus the normal time of 3 p.m. He was wondering what he would do with the extra 90 minutes when the direct line on his desk jangled. He was not expecting any calls on this line, so rather than letting its annoying ring continue, he picked up the handset. "Sun."

"Senior Colonel, turn on the encryption." He turned a dial and listened to the hissing and static as the two phones synchronized. Fang Sun hated talking using the encrypted mode. The distortions made it impossible to discern the tone and the mood of the other individual on the line.

"You may execute the second phase of *Insidious Dragon*. Please advise when the teams will leave."

Sun nodded even though no one could see his head move. "They are already in place and they will be contacted. We should see the impact before the new year."

"Excellent. We will watch for the news."

Dial tone. Sun dialed a phone number for a hotel in Barcelona. When he was connected to the room, he used the code phrase "It is cold but the sun is bright."

The speaker at the other end said, "It will be sad to leave this beautiful city."

Sun's next call was to a number in Cancun. When the individual answered, he stated unemotionally, "I hope the weather is warmer where you are."

The male at the other end said, "I am sure it is."

Satisfied that his plan was in motion. There was nothing more that Senior Colonel Sun could do other than wait, confident his plan would be successful. If the two teams contracted polio, so be it. And, if they infected passengers on the plane as they travel back home to the People's Republic, so much the better.

With his thoughts about *Insidious Dragon* back in its proper compartment in his mind, Senior Colonel Sun went back to what he was doing when the phone rang – reading a memo from Dr. Ng. In it, he wrote a strong argument in favor of transferring Dr. Gu and Dr. Lín to the Wuhan Virology Lab. There, they can be trained on the latest bio medical techniques which could be later employed by the PLA.

That, Senior Colonel Sun thought, was an interesting idea. There, they could be watched, monitored and if they stepped out of line, dealt with. He would decide what he would do with them after he saw the effect of *Insidious Dragon Phase II*. If it fails, then he can have Dr. Gu and Dr. Lín charged with sabotage.

MONDAY, DECEMBER 1ST, 2003, 2:07 P.M. LOCAL TIME, SINGAPORE

Derek was dog-tired when he walked up the gangway of the *U.S.S. Cushing* (DD-985). It took the C-17 cargo plane almost 20 hours to make the trip from Groom Lake to Changi Air Base in Singapore. The four-engine aircraft flew non-stop, refueling three times on the 12-hour flight before landing at Anderson Air Force Base in Guam for two hours to change crews and refuel. It was enough time for a bus to take the 16 officers and men of Det 11 of the 4007th Joint Special Operations Squadron to a dining hall to eat before they reboarded the cargo plane for the 5.7-hour flight to Singapore.

Even though he slept for about half the trip, Derek didn't feel rested. His body was out of synch, having advanced 15 time zones and lost a day he'd never get back.

Fatigue, Derek kept telling himself, was mental, and forced himself to look and act awake when he walked up the destroyer's gangway. Stopping at the top where it crossed the edge of the deck, he saluted the flag at the stern and then saluted the officer of the deck. "Sir, Lieutenant Derek Almer requests permission to come aboard. Lieutenant Hotchkiss and I have a meeting with Captain Wilcox."

The ensign who was the officer of the deck (OOD) returned the salute. When he came on watch at noon, there was a turnover item in the log stating that when Lieutenant Almer and Lieutenant Hotchkiss arrived, they were to be escorted to the captain's in-port cabin. The OOD assigned one of his enlisted men to do just that.

Brianna Wilcox barely made it into the Naval Academy. She was a gymnast in high school and, while not skilled enough to compete at the Olympic level, the coaches at the Naval Academy believed Brianna would be an excellent collegiate gymnast. Brianna, who grew up in Plano, Texas, had all the tickets needed for an appointment to the Naval Academy. She was in the top five percent in a class of 1,100 students, had a 4.0 GPA, scored 1,510 on the SAT, was a member of the National Honor Society, and the president of her class.

There was one minor problem holding up her acceptance. Brianna was 4' 9.5" tall, and therefore, a half an inch short of the height requirement. While she applied for a waiver, Brianna was not counting on it to gain entrance to the naval Academy. To ensure she met the height requirement, Brianna spent hours at a chiropractor's office on what she referred to as "the rack." The pain and suffering paid off. She measured exactly 4' 10" when she took her Naval Academy physical.

Cushing was Wilcox's second command. As a lieutenant, she commanded *Patriot*, (MCM-7), an Avenger Class mine countermeasures ship. Many thought that after *Cushing* she'd command a cruiser, make captain, and would probably be selected for promotion to admiral.

Vera Hotchkiss thought she was short at 5' 3" until she met Captain Wilcox who was three inches shorter. With the door closed,

Wilcox asked in a soft, but commanding voice, "Would you please tell me what in God's green earth is going on? Four hours ago, the Commander Seventh Fleet himself tells me to cancel all liberty, get my sailors on board and expect you who will explain to me when and where I am to take my ship."

Derek wanted to be diplomatic, "Captain, right now, I can only say that *Cushing* is to get underway tonight after my detachment brings our cargo and equipment on board. Then, after dark, *Cushing* will go to flight quarters and launch its SH-60 so we can bring our helicopter on board and pull it into the hangar. Then *Cushing* needs to sail north, northeast at twenty knots. Once back on board, ma'am, I will explain to your operations officer, XO, and you what comes next."

"What squadron are you from?"

"We're Det 11 of the 4007th Joint Special Operations Squadron."

"How come I have never heard of your unit."

"Ma'am, that's because officially we don't exist."

Wilcox shook her head. "How many people are you bringing on board?"

"Including Ms. Hotchkiss and me, one Senior Chief and 14 others. About half are Navy, the rest are a mix of Army and Air Force. For the Army and Air Force men and women, this will be their first time living on board a Navy ship, so some education will be needed."

THE SAME DAY, 3:26 P.M. LOCAL TIME, EAST OF TAIWAN

The commander of Carrier Group Five put down the satellite phone. He still couldn't believe what he had heard. He pushed the intercom and his aide answered. "Get CAG, my chief of staff, the staff's operations, and intelligence officers in the flag conference room ASAP."

When he hung up, the Rear Admiral (upper half) turned around to the rack of charts behind his desk. He quickly found an ONC-11 and rolled it out. Empty cut-down 30mm brass cases were used to hold down the corners.

Looking at the chart, he was smiling. *Kitty Hawk* and her escorts were about to go into waters where the ship had not operated since the Vietnam War. Why was Carrier Group Five to conduct flight operations on the evenings of December 5th, 6th, 7th, and 8th in an area southwest of Hainan Island? He was not given any instructions other than to "make enough noise to capture the PRC's attention but not enough to start World War III."

TUESDAY, DECEMBER 2ND, 2003, 4:30 P.M. LOCAL TIME, SOUTH CHINA SEA

No one from the *Cushing*'s crew was allowed in the hangar deck as the mechanics transformed the MH-60L from its original "as built" shape into a stealth helicopter. The cargo they brought on board were the panels and struts that would make the helicopter stealthy along with a few spares and tools. Now that it was done, it was time for a quick test flight on which they would also test their M-60 machine guns.

Just before they left, Derek told Colonel Hollingsworth that he didn't want to carry any weapons on board the helicopter. The Air Force colonel insisted, in fact, ordered him to ensure the helicopter crew would be fully armed. If he had his way, Derek hoped they would not have to fire a round.

Communications with the Commander Carrier Group Five were all via encrypted satellite phone conversations. Just before *Cushing* entered the Gulf of Tonkin, the destroyer would refuel from a tanker. Once that was completed, *Cushing* would turn off all its radars and not transmit any electronic signals. Her SLQ-32 version 2 suite of electronic sensors would provide Wilcox enough warning to know if the ship were targeted. At its closest point of approach, the destroyer would be in 50 meters of water, 25 nautical miles from the Chinese coast.

Theoretically, no one on *Cushing* was supposed to see the MH-60L with the panels on, so its SH-60B was ordered to look for ships 20 miles ahead of the destroyer. Meanwhile, Derek eased up on the collective and the MH-60L took off like any other H-60. Once airborne, he turned south and west and accelerated to 140 knots first at 500 feet, but began to ease it down to 100 feet, then to 50.

He let Vera fly and she made another series of steep turns and even several quick stops in which she pulled back on the cyclic at the same time reducing power with the collective, finishing with the helicopter in a 50-foot hover. Nothing seemed out of the ordinary, so Grayson tossed a smoke flare out and the aircrewmen emptied a 250-round belt from each gun. Satisfied, Derek radioed the destroyer, "Golden Lion, Flechette Seven returning for landing."

"Flechette Seven, you'll have a ready deck in five mikes and wind will be thirty degrees port."

SHANGHAI, THE SAME DAY, 4:43 P.M. LOCAL TIME

About the time Derek was landing on *Cushing*, Yan was boarding a flight in Shanghai for Nanning. The immigration officer said, seeing the stamp in her passport from her last visit, said, "Welcome back to China" and waved her through. No one looked through her bags. If they did, they would have found her Globalstar FAU-200 satellite phone modified to allow both encrypted and non-encrypted calls. And, if an immigration official asked her to turn it on, he would have found a directory of U.S. companies, each with offices in the People's Republic.

At Nanning's Wuxu International Airport, Yan towed her bag to where the taxis waited. The 45-kilometer drive from the airport to the Yongjiang Luxury Hotel took an hour. Once there, Yan took a bath and went to sleep. Work would begin tomorrow.

WEDNESDAY, DECEMBER 3ᴿᴰ, 2003, 1:46 A.M. LOCAL TIME, NANNING

Jun looked at the sleeping form next to her. As usual, Bao went right to sleep, but Jun couldn't. She loved the man next to her with all her heart, but just didn't know if she could trust him. So, she decided to force her lover into a decision at the last minute.

What if Bao said no? Could he be trusted not to call the Ministry of State Security? Jun reasoned that if Bao had betrayed her to the authorities, then it was only a matter of time before she was arrested and tortured until she confessed before being executed. Or worse, sent to a Chinese prison for the rest of her life.

The only option, she concluded, was that if Bao said no, he had to be killed. Not incapacitated, but dead. Could she kill the man she loved? And if she could, how?

Complicating her "departure" was that her mother called earlier in the week saying she was attending a conference in Nanning. After it was over on Thursday, she wanted to stay with her daughter until she took a Sunday evening train back to Guangzhou.

What would she do with her mother? In private moments, Liang said there was nothing left in the People's Republic but Jun. So, she presumed that meant she would come if asked.

Liang's torrid relationship with An had ended. It had, Liang said, served its purpose and now her mother was having what she said were flings with other, often much younger, women. Variety, Liang told her daughter was fun. When Jun asked how much younger, Liang laughed and said, young enough to be her daughter, maybe even granddaughter.

Jun smiled at the thought of her mother with a younger woman. Bao stirred bringing Jun back to the decision that was keeping her awake. She asked herself: Bao, what choice will you make?

THE SAME DAY, 10:19 A.M. LOCAL TIME, CARTAGENA, SPAIN

M.S. Rotterdam's repositioning voyage back to Fort Lauderdale was delayed by a month when one of its Azipods jammed at about 30 degrees off the centerline. The Azipod is a streamlined pod beneath the ship that swivels 360^0 and allows its propeller to push the ship in any direction. Without a functioning Azipod, *Rotterdam* would need tugs to push it alongside piers and limited the ports it could visit. Holland America, the ship's owner, decided to postpone the repositioning voyage from the Mediterranean to Fort Lauderdale and send the ship to Genoa where the offending Azipod could be replaced or repaired.

Passengers booked on the ship's original schedule were either rebooked on different cruises, or on this voyage, or given a refund. To fill the cabins, Holland America offered a 40% discount on the 14-day cruise that would begin in Barcelona, stop in Cartagena, Malaga, Cadiz, Lisbon, and Madeira before crossing the Atlantic. For Senior Colonel Sun, the cruise fit his purposes perfectly.

A verandah cabin was booked for a couple traveling as Mr. Hop and Mrs. Yanlin Yuhang who had arrived in Barcelona a week before they boarded the ship. In their checked luggage, both Yuhang's had three aerosol bottles tightly wrapped in three layers of plastic wrap.

Just after two a.m. with the ship at sea, the Yuhang's left their staterooms, each carrying two of their aerosol bottles and headed for public restrooms. Yanlin emptied a bottle into the return vents on the floor that pulled air out of the women's bathroom on the main deck. The can, marked with a popular brand of suntan lotion, went into a trashcan in the hall. Her next stop was the woman's restroom on the Promenade deck where she did the same thing.

Hop, a captain in the PLA's special forces, took his cans to the Upper Promenade Deck and sprayed one into an air conditioning vent at the forward end and the other into one at the aft end of the deck.

Back in their rooms, the couple climbed into their bed and went to sleep. Their alarm was set for 0730. Room service was scheduled to deliver their breakfast at eight. They ate leisurely, dressed, and showered. Before they left their room, they emptied the last two aerosol cans into their stateroom's return air vents and dropped them in the trashcan.

Mr. and Mrs. Yuhang walked off *Rotterdam* into Cartagena. Posing as tourists shopping, each bought two sets of clothes, toiletries, and two small bags before hiring a cab to take them to Murcia San Javier airport.

Rotterdam's captain delayed *Rotterdam's* departure for an hour while the ship waited for the Chinese couple. While *Rotterdam* and its other 1,206 passengers were tied to the pier, the Yuhangs were boarding an Air China Flight to Beijing at Madrid's Adolfo Suarez International Airport.

THE SAME DAY, 2:08 P.M. LOCAL TIME, CANCUN, MEXICO

Guzhi Tsao stood outside the cabana on the beach at the Krystal Grand Cancun. As he dried himself off, Guzhi looked at the three towers he and his wife Xue had reconnoitered. Now, back in their room, they unwrapped six aerosol bottles. Before leaving Beijing, each bottle had been wrapped in plastic wrap before being vacuum sealed.

A researcher on Senior Colonel Sun's staff had picked the complex popular with Americans and where the Tsao's could move around relatively unnoticed. They were posing as a Canadian couple of Chinese descent escaping Toronto's cold weather and would be one of several hundred other guests enjoying the hotel's amenities.

The Krystal Grand Cancun complex consisted of three large buildings. No one was in the stairway nor were there any cameras Guzhi could see. The lock on the 14th floor that provided access to the roof of the tallest building gave up its security in seconds. Once on the roof, he removed the access panel downwind of the fans and put on latex gloves and a surgical mask before emptying his two bottles of spray into the conduit.

Guzhi dropped the two empty bottles into a trashcan in the lobby and walked to the eight-story building next to the one he'd just visited. His remaining two bottles and lock picks were in a cream-colored canvas bag he held in his hand. It took him only a few minutes to empty the cans into the air conditioning vent and return downstairs on the elevator. Along the way, he doffed the second set of latex gloves and mask and dropped them along with the empty aerosol cans into a trash can.

Xue was folding their receipt that documented their expenses on a credit card whose charges were paid by the PLA. Outside the entrance lobby, a valet gladly called them a cab. The couple left Cancun on a four o'clock flight to Mexico City. Later that night, the Tsaos boarded an Air China flight to Beijing.

CHAPTER 26

ONE BY LAND, ONE BY AIR

THURSDAY, DECEMBER 4ᵀᴴ, 2003, 2:36 P.M. LOCAL TIME, SOUTH CHINA SEA

From where Derek stood on the bow forward of the 5" 38-caliber gun mount, the 55,000-ton, 796-foot-long replenishment ship *U.S.S. Sacramento* (AOE-1) dwarfed the 8,000-ton, 585-foot-long destroyer *Cushing*. At lunch today, the executive officer who served on *Sacramento* when he was a lieutenant said the ship's powerplant came from what would have been the sixth Iowa-class battleship, the *U.S.S. Kentucky* (BB-66).

When WWII ended, *Kentucky* was about half built when the decision was made to scrap the hull. Half of its steam turbine powerplant found its way into *Sacramento* while it was under construction. The other half went into *Camden* (AOE-2), the second ship in the class. The 100,000-shaft horsepower drove two large, 23-foot diameter screws and made it one of the fastest ships in the U.S. Navy.

Derek was watching *Sacramento's* H-46s transfer pallets of food to the destroyer when the Globalstar FAU-200 he was holding started ringing. He was wondering when Yan Huáng might call and was paranoid that he might miss her call if he was inside the ship.

Once underway, he called Don Sanderson from the stateroom he was sharing with another officer just to see if the call would go through. It didn't, and he assumed that being in what he referred to as the "bowels" of the ship attenuated the signal. He tried again in the helicopter hangar and spent five minutes giving Sanderson an update. Yan had arrived safely in Nanning and Derek didn't ask how he knew.

If Derek had to go below the main deck, the phone was handed to the detachment's chief petty officer or the petty officer on watch. If it rang, the holder of the phone would answer and then find Derek.

He pushed the green button to accept the call. As he did, he saw Vera Hotchkiss walking toward him.

"Good afternoon."

"Lieutenant Almer?"

"'Tis I. Where may you be?"

"I am standing on the road next to the primary LZ. It is very muddy and looks as if it had been recently flooded. I suggest we move to the first back-up. Its dry as a bone and there are no power lines around it."

As she spoke, it was clear that Yan wasn't worried about being overheard or seen. If someone was watching, all they would have seen was a woman standing by the side of the road leaning against a car and talking on a mobile phone.

"Back-up number one it is. When do you contact our passengers?"

"Tonight."

"Anything else change?"

"No. Will call if they do."

Yang ended the call and Derek did as well. Turning to his co-pilot for the mission, he said, "We're a go unless we hear something different."

THE SAME DAY, 3:27 P.M. LOCAL TIME, BEIJING

Now that both the Tsao's and the Yuhang's were back in Beijing, they gave Senior Colonel Sun the times and days they released their aerosol sprays. He marked a calendar thinking that the countdown to learning if the Oilop-03 spray works was underway. Based on what Drs. Gu and Lín told him, within five days, people should be coming down with polio on board *Rotterdam* and guests who stayed at Krystal Grand Cancun should start getting sick. Sun thought it will be interesting to see how many others become ill.

Sun understood accurate data on the number who contracted polio will be hard to acquire, but, since in the U.S. polio was believed to be eradicated, new cases will be newsworthy. So, he rationalized that if there are news stories about new polio cases, he will consider the project a success. Bureau 3 of the Ministry of State Security that gathered intelligence political, economic, and scientific intelligence had been alerted. Senior Colonel Sun was told it would take weeks, more likely months before Bureau 3 could give him an accurate report.

THE SAME DAY, 6:48 P.M. LOCAL TIME, NANNING

Rather than use her phone in her room, Yan went to the large fountain in the courtyard of the Yongjiang Luxury Hotel so it could provide background noise. Leaning against the concrete rim, she could see if anyone was around her and if there was any surveillance. So far, she'd detected none and was staying in the hotel under an American passport. Traveling as an American in the PRC made her even more paranoid.

Taking a deep breath, she dialed Jun's apartment number. "Allo."

"Jun, this is Cousin Shan. Are you alone?" Cousin Shan was Jun's mother's sister who died in 1948.

"No, my mother is in the bathroom. She's here until Sunday night."

"Can you talk?"

Jun nodded as she said yes.

"Did she know about the trip in advance?"

"No, mother said that she was filling in at the last minute for someone who was ill. I believe her."

"Will she come?"

"Yes." Jun hadn't asked. When Jun asked her mother about the conference, she said, once you peeled away the party's bullshit, there was some good accounting information. Her disdain for the CCP and the PRC was out in the open when she spoke with her daughter and Jun believed her mother would leave the PRC if given the opportunity. Liang said was she was "counseled" by the senior political officer at the conference not to be so direct in her criticism of the Party and its policies when she spoke in public.

"Bao?"

"I don't know yet. I will give him a choice just before we leave."

"What if he says no?"

"Then I will deal with it. When do I see you?"

"Saturday evening. I will be a surprise guest for dinner."

"And then?"

"You'll be free."

Yan heard Liang in the background ask who was on the phone. Jun said someone from work and hung up.

SATURDAY, DECEMBER 6TH, 4:39 P.M. LOCAL TIME, NANNING

To minimize any questions that might be raised, Yan asked for a late check out which let her stay in her room until three. The valet brought her rental car from the car park and put her roller bag into the back of the small 2003 model Changhe Haitun. In the U.S., the vehicle would be called a microvan. The engine was a one liter, four-cylinder engine connected to a five-speed transmission. For what Yan needed, it was perfect – inconspicuous and could carry four people.

Now that she was out of the hotel, Yan was now Yan Kuang of Shanghai. Her U.S. passport was tucked away in a compartment at the bottom of her roller bag, between the two metal bottom panels that would make it hard to see in an X-ray machine. The address on her People's Republic national identity card, driver's license and internal passport were all fictitious. She was confident that the only way her cover would be blown was if she was arrested and interrogated. If that happened, she would have bigger problems and would never see her daughter again.

At the entrance to Jun's apartment building, she asked the guard to call Jun to tell her that she had a visitor. The guard nodded, made a note of her name and national ID card number in his log and call Jun's apartment. When he hung up, the guard said Comrade Doctor Lín would be down in a few minutes.

Jun ran toward her cousin and they hugged before walking toward the elevator. "What did you tell them?"

"Only that we have a surprise guest."

When Yan walked into the apartment, she couldn't tell who was surprised more, her Aunt Liang or Bao. Both gave her tight, emotional hugs.

Yan gave a vague answer as to why she was in Nanning and noticed that Bao kept looking at Jun as if to say, what is going on? Liang knew nothing of Jun and Bao's underlying fear that Senior Colonel Sun could have them arrested on trumped-up charges. Liang was eager to hear about her relatives in San Diego.

At a pause in the conversation, Jun looked at her mother and asked, "Mother, would you like to live in San Diego?"

"You mean leave the people's paradise they call China?"

Yan nodded.

"When?"

"Tonight. You can join Bao and me."

Bao stepped in front of Jun with his face showing his surprise. "Are you defecting?"

"Bao, I prefer to call it leaving, but yes. I am. Bao, do you want to come?" Jun felt a coldness in her tone of voice that she never used when talking to Bao. The immunologist looked at Liang and then at Jun. His eyes were wide open his face flushed with anger. "Traitors!!! The both of you. I am going have all three of you arrested!"

Bao reached for his briefcase and took out his mobile phone and a Type 64 pistol that fired a 7.62 x 17mm round (~.32 caliber). He pointed the gun first at Jun and then at Liang while he started to dial a number. Liang moved off to the side. When Bao turned to see where Liang was, he yelled, "Stop!!!"

The distraction gave Jun the moment she needed. She took a stride forward and grabbed the top of the compact pistol that had many features borrowed from the Walther PPK and twisted at the same time she lashed out with her foot, aimed at Bao's knee.

Bao, who hadn't practiced martial arts in years, managed to dodge the strike. He launched a series of blows aimed at Jun as his training returned. Jun, who practiced several times a week, managed to parry them all and landed a blow with her balled fist in the center of Bao's chest, driving him back.

Wanting to regain the initiative, Bao launched several attacks using kicks aimed at Jun's body. Some landed but didn't faze Jun who was at least three inches shorter and 50 pounds lighter than Bao. She wanted to end this fight quickly without objects being thrown and loud sounds that might bring unwelcome attention to the flat.

As Bao circled, he didn't watch his back and didn't see Liang sneak up behind him. She hit him on the side of the head with a steel wok. Bao went down in a heap and Liang hit him again on the head before stepping back. "This bastard is not going to keep me from leaving!!!"

Liang looked up. "Jun, two weeks ago I was warned that Bao was an agent of the Ministry of People's Security. I came to Nanning to warn you. The conference was a convenient excuse."

Jun was stunned. She did not know whether to cry, grieving for the man she loved or be angry at him for threatening to shoot her or turn her into the police.

Yan bent down and felt for a pulse. There was none. "Bao is dead." She flipped a mental switch. Jun and Liang were now defectors and she was a foreign agent. Murder had just been committed.

Yan disconnected the phone. "Both of you pack what you want to take but it must fit in a backpack that you can carry easily."

Jun stuffed her Apple PowerBook along with cases of CDs containing her research and info from Special Hospital #326 in a zipper pouch into a backpack. In the bedroom, she found the small boxes with Bao's diamond and ruby-encrusted broach along with the diamond ring. They went into her backpack thinking that someday, she might wear them or sell them.

Liang said that other than her phone which had the numbers of her friends in the PRC, she could buy better things in America and her backpack was the lightest. If Jun needed more space, she could put things in hers. Jun took a photo of Bao and she together along with another of Bojing and she right after they were married. She looked around the apartment and decided there was nothing else worth taking.

Yan saw Liang and Jun were finished. She was in Naval officer mode. "From this point on, you must follow my instructions without question."

THE SAME DAY, 8:26 P.M. LOCAL TIME, NANNING

After they nervously finished a dinner at a restaurant, the three women walked to where Yan had parked the small van. Before she got in, Yan dialed a number on her cellphone. The phone rang once.

"Go." The time said on the phone indicated the time was 8:26 in the evening.

"Enroute. Three pax."

"Understood. ETD one plus thirty from the time we hang up."

Derek pushed the red button to end the call and placed the satellite phone on the MH-60L's center console and keyed the intercom. "Ladies and gentlemen, it is time to start the engines. We have three passengers to pick up."

THE SAME DAY, 8:52 P.M. LOCAL TIME, ON BOARD FLECHETTE SEVEN

Once airborne, Derek trimmed the MH-60L to fly at 120 knots at 100 feet off the water. Derek watched the water go by through the circular black/green world presented to him through his AN/PNVS-7 night-vision goggles. Vera pointed out sampans she could see on the FLIR several hundred yards in front of the helicopter.

Her main role was as the navigator while Derek was flying. On the mission, they planned to swap roles about every 20 minutes to ease the workload. The first check point after leaving *Cushing* was where they wanted to make landfall at the north end of Quizhou Bay.

The land on the west side of Quizhou Bay was a quarter of a mile to port, just out of range of the FLIR. Off to the east, Vera could see the glow of the lights from the city of Beihai which had a small naval base ringed by surface-to-air missile batteries.

The arrow symbol showing the helicopter's position relative to the planned course was right on the line in the visual display unit. On one screen, Derek had airspeed, altitude, rate of climb or descent, ground speed and heading along with navigation data. He was flying the helicopter on instruments with occasional glances outside.

"Racer, about to go feet dry. Stand by for a turn to three four five for ten."

Derek clicked the mike twice to acknowledge Vera's alert that he was about to turn the helicopter to a new heading he would maintain for ten minutes.

"Racer, feet dry, turn to three four five. Clock started."

When the helicopter went "feet dry" at the north end of Quizhou Bay, Derek banked the helicopter slightly to left and a new course of 345^0. "Feet dry" is a naval aviation term for crossing from flying over the water to flying over land. Going "feet wet" is the opposite, i.e. transitioning from flying over land to flying over water.

Even though the helicopter's navigation system would provide the cues, Derek insisted that they maintain a manual track of their position on a Tactical Pilotage Chart (TPC) J-11B. He wanted to make sure he knew where the helicopter was in case the GPS-driven system malfunctioned. The helicopter crossed over a road noted on their chart as G228 and suddenly there was no ambient light.

Through the AN/PNVS-7s, he could see the dark ribbon that was the Maoling River. Cars and trucks could be seen driving on the next road they would cross, G7511. Past it, they would be in what their satellite imagery showed as mostly uninhabited terrain. Along the way, they would cross a few more roads as they hugged a low mountain ridge.

Unless one was looking out, most people might hear, but not see the blacked-out helicopter. They were flying at 100 feet over the terrain to stay below the Chinese air traffic control and air defense radars. When weighing the mission's risk factors, they decided trade the lack of radar detection for the risk of someone on the ground hearing the helicopter.

"Mr. Almer, we have a problem." It was AW1 Grayson.

"What's up?"

"Sir, the panel just aft of you and just forward of the door is loose. If we keep up at this speed, I think it will come off and then the others will follow."

"What do you suggest?"

"Slow down so I can try to see what's wrong."

"How slow?"

"Fifty knots or less. It'll only take a minute or two."

"Lemme know when you are ready."

"Anytime, sir. As soon as you get below 100 knots, I'll open the door."

"Racer, as soon as we pass the next road, in a minute or two we'll be over trees."

"Copy, ma'am."

Derek waited for Vera to suggest he slow the helicopter. Outside, it was pitch black as they flew along a ridge to their left that rose about 1,000 feet above the helicopter. Below them, Derek could make out the trees as he eased back on the cyclic and lowered the collective. A touch of left rudder kept the MH-60L on course.

"Sir, one of the struts broke at the mount where the bolt holds it in place. It is putting a lot of strain on the other struts for that panel."

One of the lessons from testing the stealth properties around Groom Lake was if a single panel was removed, the helicopter had a radar signal from that side about one and a half times bigger than if it had no panels installed.

"Do you think it will stay on for another thirty-five minutes?"

"Probably. Slowing down would help."

"Tapper, what does slowing to 100 knots do to our ETA?"

She already had the answer. "Five minutes, maybe seven."

"Grayson, while we're enroute, figure out how to get the panels off quickly once we land."

"Already have."

Everyone on the MH-60L heard the slap as two struts on the panel failed and it slammed against the door. Derek pulled back the cyclic to slow the helicopter while Hambleton grabbed one of the struts and used it as a handle to pull the sheet of radar-absorbing material into the helicopter's cabin.

Now down to 80 knots, the panels aft to the one that broke off were fluttering wildly. While Derek was worried that they could come off, he was betting that the rotor wash would blow them down so they would not hit the tail rotor.

"Racer, we're going to be about 10 minutes late."

"Am hoping she'll call if we're not there on time."

"Grayson, how are you planning to get the panels off?"

"With these, sir!" He held out a pair of bolt cutters. "When we land, Hambleton and I will take the panels off and stuff them in the cabin. We've got two of them. Should take us less than five minutes."

THE SAME DAY, 9:56 P.M. LOCAL TIME, SUIXI

The watch officer took the call, the fourth that had come into the Southern Theater Command's air defense center. The earlier calls, like this one, were reports of a helicopter flying low and fast over the countryside. While he didn't have accurate times for the sightings, he plotted the locations he was given on a map. The dots represented a zig zag course headed in the general direction of Nanning.

While no one had reported seeing the helicopter, he suspected there might be an intruder in the People's Republic's air space. Its altitude precluded using any of their surface-to-air missile sites.

He looked at the list of aircraft on alert and picked up the handset. He had two J7H Leopard fighter bombers on alert at Wuxu International Airport and four J-11 interceptors based at Suixi.

He ordered two J-11s, the version of the Sukhoi Su-27 built in the People's Republic to launch. He then called the commander of the Air Defense Center to inform him that there was a possible intruder in their airspace. After the launch was approved, the watch officer notified the tower to clear the jets for takeoff.

If this turns out to be nothing, the officer rationalized that the pilots would get some night flight time. If there was an intruder, he would be commended for his initiative. Once they were airborne, the J-11s would be vectored toward Nanning and he hoped that the powerful radar on the J-11 could spot the low flying helicopter. If so, he would authorize them to shoot it down.

THE SAME DAY, 10:11 P.M. LOCAL TIME, ON BOARD FLECHETTE SEVEN, SOUTH OF ROUTE 569

Vera spotted the short flash followed by a longer flash on the FLIR. "Our passengers are at the LZ, a mile to go on the nose."

"Everyone, search the area around the LZ for bad guys. As soon as we touch down, Vera will get the women. Grayson and Hambleton get the panels off."

Two clicks of the mike.

"Racer, you want me to get out?"

"Yup, Tapper, go earn your keep."

"While I am gone, try not to bend anything."

Derek flared the helicopter and touched down about 100 feet from the white Haitun van. Vera was out and running toward the three women as soon as the wheels touched down. She recognized Yan and pointed to the helicopter yelling that they must stay on the ground to take some panels off. It would be, she thought, about five minutes. As the women approached the helicopter, she pointed to the seats Grayson wanted them to occupy and where they were to slide their backpacks and Yan's roller bag under the crew seats.

Once the women were loaded onto the helicopter, Vera pointed to Jun's wrist and shouted, "Where is your bracelet?"

Yan yelled back. "We cut it off and left it in Jun's apartment."

Vera gave the women a thumbs up and keyed the intercom. "Racer, let's get the fuck out of here."

Grayson was true to his word. Within five minutes, the panels were inside the cabin and said he would have them tied down within minutes after takeoff.

"Sir, we're good to go. We look like a porcupine!"

"Roger that. Lifting."

Vera was still strapping herself in her seat as Derek raised the collective and dumped the nose. The helicopter was soon up to 140 knots and headed south when Derek turned the helicopter over to Vera and gave her a heading to fly.

Skirting the Yingxiong Reservoir, Derek saw the light on the ALE-39 Radar Warning System flash. The small display showed a blip momentarily on the screen but there was no tone in their headset that told them the type of radar tracking the helicopter.

"Racer, was that what I think that was?"

"Yup. No lock, but it tells us someone is searching for us. Stay at 100 feet and go as fast as you think is safe."

Out of the corner of his eye, Derek saw the airspeed indicator showing 145 knots. They continued south using the most direct route to the water. The MH-60L was no longer stealthy and hugging the ground would make the helicopter harder to find visually and with a radar.

THE SAME DAY, 10:33 P.M. LOCAL TIME, ON BOARD DOG FIVE

Dog Five was the lead J-11 fighter in the two-plane section flying at 5,000 meters. Both Dog Five and his wingman, Dog Six were loaded with four R-27 radar-homing missiles based on the Russian AA-10, NATO code name, Alamo. Also under the wings were four infrared homing PL-8 missiles built under a license from the Israeli defense contractor, Elbit.

If these airplanes were in the Russian Air Force, they would be known as Flanker-Bs. In the PLA Air Force, the airframes flown as Dog Five and Six were members of the first production batch of fighters that were produced in the PRC with Russian help.

The pair of J-11s were vectored north of Nanning and then turned south, five miles apart so they could sweep the sky with their powerful radars that were specifically designed to spot low-flying aircraft. The pilot of Dog Five ordered his wingman to slow to 500 kilometers per hour as their pulse-doppler radars scanned the sky for a helicopter.

Twice, Dog Five's radar flashed a blip. But each time, the blip disappeared. The third time, the blip stayed illuminated long enough for him to mark it on his scope. "Nestor, Dog Five has an intermittent contact. Speed two hundred and seventy-five kilometers per hour, course one six five. Distance one hundred and fifty kilometers."

Nestor was the call sign of the Southern Theater Air Defense Center. "Dog Five, close and identify."

"Nestor, Dog Five and Six descending." The pilot pulled the throttles back almost to idle and extended the J-11's speed brake. As he did, he began a series of S-turns to stay behind the contact.

THE SAME DAY, 10:36 P.M. LOCAL TIME, ON BOARD FLECHETTE SEVEN

The radar warning system (RAWS) light came on and the tone in their headsets said that an airborne radar had found the MH-60L. "Tapper, I've got the helicopter."

Once he had his hands on the controls, Derek ordered, "Tapper, arm the chaff and flare launchers and turn on the DIRCM system."

DIRCM stood for directed infrared countermeasures. The system was designed to detect an oncoming missile by the heat signature of its exhaust plume. Then, it would use mirrors to confuse the missile's sensor and cause it to go "stupid." If needed, the system would fire a laser that would blind and then fry the missile's infrared seeker or radar.

Effective as DIRCM was, it could only deal with one missile at a time. If their attacker launched two, as per the PLA Air Force's doctrine, they needed to launch chaff and/or flares and hope they worked.

The RAWS display showed two airplanes at the helicopter's six o'clock position. Derek assumed the jets were well above the helicopter and would dive, launch, and shoot.

"Grayson, are our passengers on the intercom?"

"Negative."

"Get them strapped down tight and tell them we are being chased by two fighters and are about to maneuver abruptly. Then get your heads outside to look for the missiles. I am about to do some of that pilot shit you see in movies. I hope it works."

Two clicks of the mike were followed shortly by the opening of the helicopter's cabin doors. Derek could feel the added drag and added a bit of power to get the helicopter back up past 145 knots. On the RAWS display, the two blips were inside the five-mile range ring.

Grayson saw what he thought was a reflection off a canopy and then he saw the shape of the fighter silhouetted against the moon. The rocket motors ignited with a flash and their spiraling said they were infrared missiles.

"Two IR missiles, four o'clock high."

Derek craned his head around to see the missiles but couldn't. "Lemme know when they are inside three-quarters of a mile."

Grayson saw the flash of the laser and the closest missile pitched down before flying into the ground and exploding. "NOW!!!"

"Tapper, give me four flares." At the same time he spoke, Derek bottomed the collective, pulled back on the cyclic and moved it to the right as he fed in full right rudder. His movements of the controls brought the nose up to 60^0 above the horizon, rolled the MH-60L into 120^0 angle of bank, and then down again as the helicopter reversed course. Once he could see the missile, Derek pulled the collective up to get maximum power from the engines and to get the helicopter climbing almost vertically. Another flash of laser light caused the missile to veer sharply and pass off to the left of the helicopter.

He breathed a sigh of relief. Two missiles dodged. *How many more were coming and could he avoid them?*

THE SAME DAY, 10:38 P.M. LOCAL TIME, ON BOARD DOG FIVE

Seeing no explosion, the pilot of Dog Five armed his 30mm cannon thinking that he could shoot the helicopter down if needed. With the target in his sights, he moved the controls to align the nose of his fighter with the target. By fixating on the helicopter, he ignored his altimeter and discovered much too late that the helicopter was well below 300 feet. Realizing he was about to slam into the ground, he pulled the ejection seat handles, but was a millisecond too slow. The seat fired but the pilot was incinerated in the fireball from the plane slamming into the ground.

Dog Six, seeing the explosion radioed the Southern Theater Air Defense Center saying that he thought the helicopter was shot down. The controller radioed him 30 seconds later saying no, Dog Five crashed and Dog Six was to shoot down the helicopter.

Not wanting to get close to the ground, the pilot of Dog Six leveled off at 3,000 meters, acquired the helicopter on his radar and, at a range of 10 kilometers fired an R-27 missile. He slowed the J-11 to 370 kilometers per hour in a desperate attempt to stay behind the helicopter. He turned to reduce the closure rate and the missile broke lock and flew off into the night sky.

The pilot of Dog Six turned back south and his radar re-acquired the helicopter. He pulled the trigger to fire a second radar-guided missile. As soon as it left the fighter, he lowered his flaps to half and his landing gear and extended the speed brake. The J-11's controls were sloppy, but he managed to keep the nose and the radar beam the missile was following on the helicopter he could not see.

THE SAME DAY, 10:40 P.M. LOCAL TIME, ON BOARD FLECHETTE SEVEN

Derek eased the helicopter down to 70 feet above the ground. Vera was calling out telephone and power lines so he could pop over them.

On the radar warning display, they saw and heard the warbling, high-pitched tones saying they were targeted by a radar-guided missile. Hambleton called out, saying, "Missile, port side, eight o'clock high!"

Derek ballooned the helicopter up to 500 feet and just before it crested, he ordered Vera to pump out four bundles of chaff. At the last pair of bangs signifying the chaff bundles had left the helicopter, Derek pushed the cyclic to roll the helicopter into a 60^0 bank to turn it away from the chaff floating down.

The R-27's guidance system hesitated. It saw the radar blip of the helicopter and then a bigger one caused by the blooming chaff. The software in the guidance system headed the missile toward the chaff and the rocket passed 300 feet from the right side of the helicopter. A mile later, it plunged into the ground and exploded.

"Grayson, how are our passengers doing?"

"Sir, they've got their arms linked together and are green around the gills. They're scared shitless, just like the rest of us. If I may say so, sir, this is better than a roller coaster."

"We're not out of the woods yet, Grayson." For a few minutes, the helicopter was straight and level allowing everyone on board to take a deep breath. Fear was perched on Derek's shoulder. He wondered if his luck would hold and then told himself that luck would not have anything to do with them surviving, his skill, tactics and the helicopter's defensive systems would be needed to carry the day.

THE SAME DAY, 10:43 P.M. LOCAL TIME, ON BOARD DOG SIX

Frustrated, the pilot of Dog Six shoved the throttles for the two Russian-made Saturn AL-31 engines forward after he retracted his speed brake, landing gear, and flaps. The J-11 accelerated and the pilot eased back on the stick to send the fighter into a 60^0 climb. Passing 3,000 meters, he rolled the still-climbing fighter into a 90^0-degree bank and pushed right rudder.

The airplane, still climbing and accelerating, responded by rotating around its vertical axis. When the nose was pointed at the ground, he pulled the throttles back to idle, deployed the speed brake, rolled wings level as he eased back on the stick and waited for his radar to find the fleeing helicopter that he was sure was headed south.

Seconds after his airplane's nose was on a heading of 180^0, a blip appeared on his scope approaching the north end of a large bay. He was determined to shoot the helicopter down before it reached the Gulf of Tonkin.

He was grateful that the controllers were only acknowledging his short reports such as missile missed or when he lost or re-acquired the helicopter. They couldn't see the helicopter on their radar and were non-players in this deadly game in which there was only one acceptable outcome - the helicopter shot down.

The pilot of Dog Six locked the radar beam onto the helicopter which was not turning. He waited until he was inside three miles away and fired two PL-8 missiles.

With the throttles back and the speed brake extended, the J-11 decelerated to 400 kph (~215 knots). It was as slow as he dared to fly the jet and keep his radar on the helicopter.

THE SAME DAY, 10:50 P.M. LOCAL TIME, ON BOARD FLECHETTE SEVEN

The tone in his headset told Derek what was coming at the MH-60L. He flexed his hands so he wasn't holding the cyclic and collective in a death grip. So far, he thought, we've been lucky.

Vera keyed the intercom anticipating what was needed, "Standing by with chaff and flares."

Derek pulled back on the cyclic and raised the collective. "Four bundles of chaff, four flares, NOW."

Inside the cabin, the bangs of the chaff packets and flares fired sounded like a 12-gauge shotgun fired in the next room. In the cockpit, they were muted bangs.

"Here we go." Derek ignored the sweat stinging his eyes or that his undershirt and cotton turtleneck were soaked with sweat generated by sub-conscious fear and tension. He was too busy to be scared.

The MH-60L climbed higher than Derek planned. As he rolled it into a steep turn and then nosed it down, he noticed they had passed 700 feet.

One PL-8 liked one of the flares and followed it down to the earth. The other, confused by the flares and the heat from the MH-60L's exhaust waffled back and forth. For a second it would head toward the flare, then veer toward the helicopter. The second

PL-8 was passing about 80 feet to the right of the helicopter when its proximity fuse set off its blast fragmentation warhead. Shrapnel peppered Derek's side of the cockpit and the right engine. Warning lights came on in the cockpit saying that the fuel flow to right engine was now zero. The red fire warning light burned brightly as the engine started to unwind.

One chunk punched a hole in his calf, burning as much as hurting. Dereck ignored the pain. "Tapper, go through the engine fire checklist, but don't pull the T-handle yet to fire the fire extinguisher bottles."

"Boss, we've got flames around the right engine cowling."

Derek recognized Grayson's voice. "Tapper, pull the T-handle to shut off all fuel. Let's wait a few second to see if the fire goes out. If it doesn't use the fire extinguishers."

With half the power, the helicopter slowed noticeably. With full torque and the left engine at full power, the best the MH-60L would fly was about 110 knots. As he moved his feet, the pain in his right calve increased and his heels slipped on the cockpit floor.

"Boss, I can still see flames and smoke."

Derek didn't need to order Vera. They didn't hear the gas being expelled into the engine compartment, but all could smell it.

"Standing by with the reserve bottle."

"Tapper, hold off, hopefully we won't need it."

Derek's leg really hurt but with the helicopter stable and still flying, he asked, "Anyone hit besides me?"

Jun couldn't hold it in anymore. What was left in her stomach from her dinner a little over two hours earlier, came out. Her vomit splattered on top of the tied-down stealth panels. The wind coming through the cabin from the open doors blew the noxious odor away, but not fast enough so that it made Yan and Liang gag.

"We're all good. The radar-absorbing channels took most of the shrapnel and when we get back, we'll have to clean up some puke. Sir, do you need help?"

Derek could feel the blood oozing down into his boot. "Give me a pressure bandage and some of the stuff you use to stop the bleeding."

Grayson passed it forward and Derek turned over the flying to Vera saying, "After all my hard work, don't get us shot down!"

She flipped him the finger. They were halfway down Qinzhou Bay. In another 15 miles or so, they would be in international waters.

THE SAME DAY, 10:53 P.M. LOCAL TIME, ON BOARD DOG SIX

The pilot of Dog Six saw the flash of the explosion but didn't see a fireball indicating that the helicopter had crashed. He pulled the nose up in a climbing left-hand turn to stay above and behind the helicopter.

Below him, the water of Qinzhou Bay glistened and as he turned south again, he could see the shiny black water of the Gulf of Tonkin in the distance.

Again, he turned Dog Six to the south and his pulse-doppler radar picked out the helicopter from the ground clutter. This time, he fired his last two PL-8s and then his third R-27.

He was cursing when he realized that he misread the range and that the two PL-8s would never catch the helicopter. Never mind, he concentrated on keeping the beam on the helicopter to shoot it down with an R-27.

THE SAME DAY, 10:55 P.M. LOCAL TIME, ON BOARD FLECHETTE SEVEN

A glance at the radar warning receiver, Vera did the same thing Derek did. Change altitude, pump out chaff and flares to decoy the radar guided missile and turn. This time, instead of flying perpendicular to the missile, she again ballooned the helicopter to almost 1,000 feet and had Derek pump out four more bundles of chaff.

This time, the R-27's software decided that its terminal homer was looking at two targets and decided to fly through the middle. Right after flying past the flares, the missile's proximity fuse set off the warhead, 200 feet in front of the MH-60L.

"Racer, call Golden Lion and let them know we're behind schedule, chased, and are, by my guess, less than fifteen minutes out."

"I can do that." Derek rolled his finger so when he pulled back on the switch, he was transmitting on the UHF radio, not the intercom position. "Golden Lion, Golden Lion, this is

Flechette Seven. We're feet wet and over international waters. ETA 15 mikes."

"Flechette Seven, standby for vectors. Squawk 4613 and ident."

"Tapper, I'm going to wait until we are really in international waters before I light off the transponder which will say 'here we are' to every PRC radar controller in the area."

Derek twirled the knobs to set the code in the AN/APX-100 transponder. Then he put his finger on the visual display unit to track the helicopter's progress and noticed his glove was soaked in his blood!

At 12.5 miles from the coast of the People's Republic, Derek pushed the transponder's ident button. At the same time, he heard the tone indicating they were being targeted, again.

THE SAME DAY, 11:00 P.M. LOCAL TIME, ON BOARD DOG SIX

The pilot had one R-27 missile left and he was determined to shoot the helicopter down. He heard the tone of an American air search radar and turned down the volume on his Chinese copy of the Russian radar warning system. He concentrated on the blip representing the helicopter on his radar.

At eight miles, he fired the RL-27. The missile streaked toward the helicopter. When it picked up a larger target, the missile veered off.

THE SAME DAY, 11:04 P.M. LOCAL TIME, ON BOARD U.S.S. CUSHING

The destroyer had been at battle stations ever since Flechette Seven took off. Its SH-60B had spent the past three hours scouting around the destroyer and at 10:38 p.m. landed to top off its fuel tanks.

When Flechette Seven called, Captain Wilcox ordered the SPS-40 air search radar turned on. The ships SH-60B was identified as Track 1. Flechette Seven, Track Two and Dog Six, was labeled Track Three.

In the combat information center, Captain Wilcox recognized what was happening before the ALQ-32 system sounded the alarm. She ordered the chaff decoys be fired as the R-27 headed toward her ship.

"TAO, cleared to engage Track Three with two Sea Sparrows."

The TAO, a male lieutenant grinned and said, "Yes ma'am." The sailor on the console that controlled the eight-cell Sea Sparrow missile launcher, said, "Yes, sir. We have a lock. Firing one."

THE SAME DAY, 11:07 P.M. LOCAL TIME, ON BOARD DOG SIX

The pilot of Dog Six saw his missile head toward the large black object he quickly recognized as a warship. He was horrified when he saw it hit just aft of the bow and explode.

He was wondering if the ship was American or from the PLA Navy as eased back on the stick to climb and turn back to land. Something made him look over his shoulder and was stunned to see the Sea Sparrows coming at his J-11 at 2,600 miles an hour. It was then he realized that he never turned on his radar warning receiver.

The last thing the pilot of Dog Six saw was the closest Sea Sparrow's warhead explode and send its expanding rod ripping through his airplane. The J-11 erupted in a fireball, raining parts onto the Gulf of Tonkin, 15.8 nautical miles from the coast of the People's Republic of China.

CHAPTER 27

FEVER PITCH

After the R-27 easily penetrated the destroyer's hull, the 89 lb. (39 kg.) warhead exploded in a small empty space five hull frames aft of the bow. What was left of the solid fuel rocket motor added fuel to the fire started by the warhead. A plume of gray-white smoke streamed from the hole on the port side of the bow.

With *Cushing* steaming south at 25 knots, one fire-fighting team sprayed a stream of water into the hole while another team unbolted the hatch that provided access to the space. As two sailors wearing oxygen breathing apparatus used a large wrench to work the nuts loose, the bulkhead was sprayed with seawater to keep it cool.

Once through the hatch, the damage control team quickly doused the fire and pumped out the water. As they did, Captain Wilcox had them collect as many pieces of the missile as they could find in the unlit compartment.

The corpsman insisted that they carry Derek to *Cushing's* small dispensary where the doctor numbed his calf muscle before digging out a quarter-sized piece of shrapnel. He closed the wound with a dozen stitches. A corpsman handed Derek a clear plastic bag containing the cleaned, jagged piece of tungsten from the missile's blast fragmentation warhead to keep as a souvenir.

With an envelope of antibiotic pills and another of hydrocodone for the pain, Derek limped to the wardroom where Yan and the two Chinese women were waiting. Each was still a bit pale from riding in the back of a helicopter that by Vera's count, had six heat-seeking and the same number of radar-guided missiles fired at it.

When Derek came in, Captain Wilcox was pouring her favorite bourbon into a row of glasses with the *Cushing's* logo etched on the side. "Ladies and gentlemen, welcome to *Cushing*, and after what I presume was a white-knuckle ride, I think you could use some of Kentucky's finest."

Wilcox held up her glass and then said, "Welcome to the United States." After a swallow, "Lieutenant, well done! What do you plan to do with the helicopter? Is it flyable?"

"Yes, once we get a new fuel line made. It has a bunch of holes, but nothing vital was hit. We're staying on *Cushing* which will be ordered to Singapore where we'll unload and be flown home. Your SH-60B will take our passengers to *Kitty Hawk* where they will be flown back to the U.S. on a military transport."

Derek took a long swig. While he preferred scotch to bourbon, the liquor felt good going down. "Thank you, Captain. I would like my air crewmen to have a taste as well. Without their calls on the missiles, we would not have made it."

Wilcox picked up the phone in the wardroom, dialed a two-digit number. Pausing to make sure someone was on the line, she said, "patch me into the 1 MC – *Cushing's* main communication system. It let her broadcast over speakers positioned throughout the ship. "This is the captain. Would AW1 Grayson and AW2 Hambleton come to the officer's wardroom immediately, repeat, immediately."

The diminutive captain was smiling. When the two enlisted men appeared in the door, Wilcox said, "Gentlemen, please join us."

Two more crystal glasses quickly appeared on the table. She poured four fingers of the amber liquid into each glass and handed them to the aircrewmen. "Well done."

Once each man took a sip, she said, "The only rule is that you cannot leave the wardroom until those glasses are empty. Gentleman, ladies, if you will excuse me, I have a ship to run."

Wilcox's departure gave Derek a chance to apologize to his passengers for the wild ride adding that the rest of the trip to the U.S. should be more comfortable.

MONDAY, DECEMBER 8TH, 2003, 1:13 P.M. LOCAL TIME, NANNING

Senior Administrator Ming stood in the middle of the living area of Jun's apartment holding the bracelet that was on the table. It didn't take an expert to realize how the bracelet was removed. When cut, the wire that would trigger a radio signal that the bracelet had been damaged or removed had been bridged so no signal was sent.

Tossing the bracelet up and down, Ming stared at the sheet covered body of Dr. Gu. She didn't need to walk into each room to discover that Dr. Lín was not there. The bed was made, the apartment was clean and neat and the refrigerator full. The only odd thing were the two empty backpacks on the couch.

Question 1 – how many more defectors were here?

Question 2 – did Dr. Gu try to stop the defection? If so, was he killed in the process? And, who killed him?

Knowing the relationship between Dr. Lín and Dr. Gu, she couldn't believe that Jun killed her lover. So, she wondered who would do it?

As she tossed the bracelet a few centimeters in the air, Ming wondered if the two women were kidnapped. It was possible, but not likely. The women's work at Special Lab #62 made their disappearance a matter of national security.

Baozhi Ming put the bracelet back on the table where she found it along with Jun's access badges. Someone had laid Bao's phone and the pistol on the table next to the badges. She turned to the security guard standing in the doorway. He had not entered the apartment.

"Did Dr. Gu and Dr. Lín have any visitors last night?"

The guard keyed his radio. And had an exchange with the man at the front desk. "Comrade Senior Administrator. The log shows that at 3:23 p.m. on Saturday, her mother Liang Lín arrived. Then, around 4:17 p.m. Dr. Lín signed for a Yan Kuang whose identity document showed she was from Shanghai."

Ming's stomach churned. This meant they may have been gone for two days. "Call the Ministry of State Security and let them know that Doctor Lín is missing. Then, while we are waiting for their investigators to arrive, I will need your office to make a call."

What Ming didn't know was that the rental car company had filed a police report saying that their van that was supposed to be returned Sunday wasn't. A farmer had spotted the white Changhe Haitun on Sunday and reported it to the police. The rental car company sent an employee to drive it back to Nanning. Before Ming entered Jun's apartment, it had been rented. The rental car company said they would need hours to track it down and return it to the rental car facility.

The senior guard on duty cleared the desk where the phone was in their tiny office behind the lobby desk. While he was in another room searching the video recordings of who came and went on Saturday, Ming dreaded the conversation she was about to have.

"Sun."

"Comrade Senior Colonel Sun, this is Senior Administrator Ming. Do you have time to discuss something of importance?"

Few called Sun on his private line. Even fewer called to discuss something frivolous. Those that did, didn't make the same mistake again.

"Go ahead."

"Doctor Gu is dead and Dr. Lín is missing."

"What do you mean by missing?"

"Neither showed up for work on Monday nor did they call in sick. Protocol requires that I send someone to their apartment to check on their welfare. Given their importance to the lab, I took the responsibly personally and entered their apartment at approximately one this afternoon."

Ming recounted what she found and said the Ministry of State Security investigators were on their way. As he listened, Sun instantly regretted not having Dr. Lín arrested. *If she has defected, Phase III of Insidious Dragon may be in danger.*

"Comrade Senior Administrator, do you have a theory of where Dr. Lín is?"

Ming was not going to allow herself to fall into that trap. If she said she thought the woman may have defected, a Ministry of

State Security interrogator will twist that around and suggest that she should have known. "No."

"Explain."

"They liked to go out dancing on Saturday nights. Some of the places in Nanning are in seedy neighborhoods. They also liked to take walks in the Qingxiushan Scenic Area in the early evening. As you know, there is a criminal element that preys on walkers in the park. Normally, all they do is rob people, but Dr. Lín may have gone for a walk by herself and resisted."

"So Senior Administrator Ming, do you think Dr. Lín could have been robbed and may be lying in an alley or a park someplace in Nanning?"

"We cannot discount that possibility, but that would not be my hypothesis."

"What do you think, Senior Administrator Ming?"

"Senior Colonel, Dr. Lín was educated in the U.S. so I suspect she may have defected, or worse, may be a spy."

"Agreed. My hypothesis is that she defected. The question is who helped them and how did they leave? Make sure that when you talk to the investigators, they are aware of my theory and the Ministry of Security tracks down this mysterious Yan Kuang from Shanghai."

"Yes, Comrade senior colonel, I will."

When he hung up the phone, Senior Colonel Sun debated in his mind for a few seconds if Ming was covering up for her own lack of insight. He decided that determination would come later. He dialed a number on his personal phone from memory.

Major General Aigua Zheng picked up the ringing phone. "Senior Colonel Sun, to what do I owe the pleasure." Zheng was being sarcastic. He knew his friend would not call him just to chit chat.

"Have you had any intruders into the Southern Theater in the past few days?"

"Why are you asking?"

"A scientist working for me is missing and I think she may have defected. Their national ID cards and passports prevented them from traveling outside Nanning without special permits."

Zheng took a deep breath. He was leaving for Suixi in the afternoon to attend a ceremony honoring the pilots who died chasing an unknown helicopter. The Air Force was still trying to put all the pieces together and he was about to receive a full briefing when he visited the air defense center at his former base. He could not reveal what he already knew and suspected to Senior Colonel Sun.

The questions asking why the PLA Air Force could not shoot a helicopter had already begun. The finger-pointing and recriminations would lead to arrests and sudden retirements. His primary job was to control the story so he stayed in the Air Force. Therefore, he could not tell Sun much, or at least not yet.

The fact that he was calling meant that Senior Colonel Sun was worried. And if he was worried, then the interservice politics and in-fighting would be off the chart.

"We have had some reports of an unidentified helicopter in that area. I am flying to Suixi this afternoon for a ceremony. While I am there, I will see what I can learn."

"Thank you." Senior Colonel Sun hung up the phone thinking, bullshit. You are the senior air defense officer on the PLA Air Force's general staff. You know what happened.

Sun dialed a number at the Ministry of State Security and was told that his brother, the deputy minister, was in a meeting and would call him back. Now, Senior Colonel Sun, thought was the time to begin executing his plan to point the finger of blame at someone else. Senior Administrator Ming would be high on his list.

THE SAME DAY, 4:38 P.M. LOCAL TIME, 216 NAUTICAL MILES, SSW OF LISBON ON BOARD M.S. ROTTERDAM

Doctor Darin Trenchard's specialty was emergency medicine. After earning his M.D. from the University of Michigan in Ann Arbor, he spent eight years in the Army in return for the government paying for medical school. Most of the time he was on active-duty Trenchard was deployed with special forces units in Africa. After his active-duty commitment, he joined the reserves and returned to his native Detroit. When he retired, Trenchard was running the ER at the Detroit Medical Center's receiving hospital.

Now having retired from the hospital and the Army Reserve as a full colonel, Trenchard signed on with Holland America to be an on-board physician. He hoped life aboard ship would be much less stressful than working in an ER. Tall, fit and with a shock of gray, the fifty-five-year-old Trenchard was a bachelor and loved going to sea.

Trenchard was in his mid-fifties when he went to work for Holland America. His first goal was to bring their shipboard clinics into the 21st Century by convincing the cruise line to install tele-medicine terminals on board its ships. *M.S. Amsterdam* was the first, *M.S. Rotterdam* was the second.

When the first passenger came into his dispensary with a fever, headache, muscle stiffness in his neck, and fatigue, the patient thought he had the flu. Then, when the second one came in with the same symptoms and complained of vomiting, Trenchard became alarmed. What was happening on *Rotterdam* was one of his worst nightmares.

With only six beds in his hospital, Trenchard asked *Rotterdam's* captain if he could move passengers around on the main deck or even give them cabins on the upper decks so he could create a ward which could be quarantined off. Captain Dirk van der Molen quickly agreed as did the passengers who saw the move for what it was, an upgrade.

At first, he thought he might be dealing with an outbreak of meningitis, but the more he spoke with his patients, he realized he'd seen this disease before in Nigeria with a U.S. Special Forces team. *Rotterdam* had an outbreak of polio.

Trenchard hung up from a conference call with the CDC. The conclusion from all on the call confirmed his suspicion. He dialed the bridge and asked to meet with Captain van der Molen as soon as possible.

THE SAME DAY, 5:21 P.M. LOCAL TIME, LEESBURG, VA

After landing at Andrew Air Force Base, Yan, Liang, and Jun were taken to a CIA safe house south of Leesburg. The imposing three-story building was on 150 acres of land. And they could not see the facility's security, the estate was ringed with an electrified fence, sensors, and cameras. Armed guards with dogs who could be reinforced by a quick reaction force patrolled the grounds.

Inside, the CIA had allocated Jun and Liang their own rooms. A full physical, which included urine samples and drawing blood followed along with a body scan to make sure they did not have any chips embedded in their bodies. Then the debriefing began.

Normal procedure would be to interview Jun for two to three hours and compare what she said to what the CIA and DIA already knew. Then, in the next session, ask questions to fill in gaps or clear inconsistencies.

Before the debriefing could begin, Jun, Yan, and Liang were all brought to a separate room to describe why Dr. Gu was not on the flight. Each signed sworn statements on what happened and how Bao died. The determination was that he was killed in self-defense. Had Bao prevailed, then none of the women would have made the rendezvous with the helicopter and Yan and her mother would either be in prison or dead.

Jun was instructed not to refer to Dr. Gu and his demise in any briefings or conversations other than those with the CIA and DIA. For Jun, this made sense as she was still dealing with her emotions. On one hand, she was angry at herself for falling in love with Bao. She now realized their relationship was a sham - he said he was in love with her yet was beholden to the Ministry of State Security.

Bao chose loyalty to the state over freedom and the woman who loved him. If he had come, Bao would now be free of the tenacles of the Ministry of State Security and they could have married. But it was not to be and she would never know if his love was real or faked. This was, Jun believed, her karma.

Jun wanted to begin the debriefings with her work for Senior Colonel Sun and the *Insidious Dragon* program. Instead, CIA debriefer started by going through her life, asking her to start with what she remembered as a little girl. Frustrated because Jun believed there was a bigger threat, and asked where the report she carried with her and the two folders with CDs were?

The answer was that the CDs were being examined and their contents evaluated. The second interrogator left the room and came back in for a few seconds with the document. Jun held out her hand.

Holding it up by its edges as if it was contaminated, she said, "This is what Senior Colonel Sun is planning. It is the report on the test done at Yibin Motorcycle Plant. The only reason for the test was to see if Oilop-03 could be spread and what the infection rate might be. The test, I believe, was his proof of concept for an attack someplace in the world. It confirmed my hypothesis that Oilop-03 is more contagious than earlier strains of poliomyelitis."

There was silence in the room and then the interrogator asked, "Can you translate this?"

Yan, who was sitting off to the side, said, "If Jun can't, I can."

They were partly through the summary when a security guard gently tapped on the door frame to the living room overlooking a well-kept garden. "Lieutenant Commander Huáng, there is a call from a Captain Rainbow, where would you like to take it?"

"In here is fine. Jun, why don't you start the translation."

Yan walked to the back of the room where there was a STU-III that facilitated encrypted conversations as well as those that didn't need the added security. "Lieutenant Commander Huáng, this is not a secure line."

"Yan, how's it going?"

"Dunno. The debriefers keep asking the same questions a different way hoping to get an answer that they can use to trip Jun up. What they get are more details. How are Jun's and Liang's citizenship papers coming?"

"Working on it. Immigration wants a thumbs up from the CIA first. My staff has been reading the debriefs every night and they are a treasure trove of info."

"I don't understand half of it. Thanks for letting me chaperone."

"My pleasure. You deserve it. Back to why I called. Right after we hang up, the debriefers will receive a call to put Dr. Lín on a call with the CDC. It appears a cruise ship may have been infected with Oilop-03."

"Oh my God."

"Yeah, it is already ugly. This will be a great chance for Dr. Lín to win friends and influence people. Gotta go."

Gently, Yan put the phone down and stood looking at it for a few seconds to give her time to think. When she turned to return to where Jun was sitting, the senior debriefer was standing, saying we're going to reconvene in another room and join a video conference call. He wanted Jun to bring the report on the test from the Yibin Motorcycle Works prison.

Jun sat in front of the camera. The doctor at the CDC dialed in Dr. Trenchard who summarized the number of cases and tests he had run and his description convinced Jun someone had introduced Oilop-03 on the ship.

Before entering the room, the CIA officer had asked her not to reveal anything about where she worked before coming to U.S. or the test. She was only allowed to divulge what she knew about the strains of polio found in the People's Republic.

Jun began by saying the PRC's Ministry of Health has known about the polio epidemic in Guangxi and Guangdong provinces for years and has chosen to ignore it. What was recently discovered in Zhanjiang was a new, possibly vaccine-resistant strain with a noticeably higher rate of paralysis and death.

A question came from someone at the CDC. "Why hasn't the People's Republic reported this to the World Health Organization?"

"It would be an embarrassment for the government to admit that their polio vaccine is not as effective and that the disease has not been wiped out, despite its claims to the contrary. If this became common knowledge, many Chinese leaders in the party would lose much face. What I do know is that this epidemic has been getting worse. Several thousand or more contract this strain of polio every year and the number contracting the disease is increasing."

Jun paused and then asked, "Dr. Trenchard, do you have any passengers from the People's Republic on board?"

"Yes. We did leave a Chinese couple behind in Cartagena. They did not report on board at our departure time and Captain van der

Molen decided to leave without them as per the line's policy. They did not return to the ship at our next port. Why?"

"Do you still have their belongings?"

"Yes. Holland America has locked their room with their possessions in it. The room will not be opened until we reach Fort Lauderdale. Again why?"

"One more question, is it possible for someone on the ship to look in their trash for large aerosol bottles the size women buy for hair spray."

Trenchard said yes and picked up a phone in his office. When he finished and was again facing the camera, Jun asked, "While we are waiting to see if anything is found in their stateroom, Dr. Trenchard, can you send blood samples from your patients to America?"

"Yes, why?"

"I will arrange to have photos taken of the cultures grown in the People's Republic sent to the CDC so they can be compared to that which has sickened your passengers."

Dr. Trenchard nodded. While he was on the phone, Captain van der Molen was conferring with Holland America's management. Trenchard answered his ringing phone, listened for a few seconds, before speaking. "We will be in Funchal in the Madeira Islands tomorrow. Holland America will arrange for a private jet to fly them from Funchal to Atlanta."

Someone wearing latex gloves and a surgical mask handed Dr. Trenchard two plastic bags, one had a 16-ounce bottle of a well-known hairspray and the other was the same size sunscreen. Jun felt sick. The bottle of sunscreen looked just like the ones she saw in the prison.

"Doctor Trenchard, are both empty?"

He shook the bags. "My guess would be yes."

"I am willing to bet that if a lab examined those bottles, one of them will contain Oilop-03. Can you triple seal them and put them on the same plane with the samples?"

The CIA interrogator asked for the room at the CDC to be cleared. Angrily, he turned to Jun. "You don't know that."

Jun glared back at him. "Yes, I do. If we had started my debrief with the test at the prison you wouldn't be asking me that. Those are the same bottles used in the Yibin prison. It was clear to me that Senior Colonel Sun was planning an attack to see how the west responded. Why else would you run such a test with live victims?"

Pointing at the screen, Jun said, "I think that man wants to speak with you."

The man was an FBI agent assigned to the CDC who insisted the FBI be allowed to interview Jun. The CIA interrogator said he would check with his superiors.

Jun left the call and was escorted back to the room where she was being debriefed. She described the test at the prison in detail and then paged through the report until she found the chart that summarized the results.

Pointing to the chart, she said, "This is what you are dealing with."

Final Results +90 Days		
	Infection Means – Food	Infection Means - Aerosol
Infection rate, assuming 100% exposure to the disease	Age 20 – 30 - 74%	Age 20 – 30 - 50%
	Age 31 – 40 – 76%	Age 31 – 40 – 60%
	Age 41+ - 78%	Age 41+ - 67%
Days with fever and symptoms	6 – 10	6 – 9
Permanent paralysis rate by age with all three types	Age 20 - 30 – 5%	Age 20 – 30 - 5%
	Age 31 - 40– 6%	Age 31 – 40 – 6%
	Age 41+ - 8%	Age 41+ - 8%
Death rates by age of those with spinal polio**	Age 20 – 30 – 9%	Age 20 – 30 – 8%
	Age 31 – 40 – 10%	Age 31 – 40 – 10%
	Age 41+ - 12%	Age 41+ - 11%

Final Results +90 Days		
	Infection Means – Food	Infection Means - Aerosol
Death rates by age of those with bulbar polio**	Age 20 – 30 – 11%	Age 20 – 30 – 10%
	Age 31 – 40 – 13%	Age 31 – 40 – 12%
	Age 41+ - 15%	Age 41+ - 15%
Death rates by age of those with spinobulbar polio**	Age 20 – 30 – 19%	Age 20 – 30 – 18%
	Age 31 – 40 – 25%	Age 31 – 40 – 24%
	Age 41+ - 28%	Age 41+ - 25%

*Paralytic rates do not appear to vary significantly by strain of Oilop-03.

** Type of polio diagnosed during illness prior to death.

Jun explained that one of the unique attributes of Oilop-03 was that it started as spinal polio but would often become either bulbar or bulbospinal. Their research had not yet figured out why. The rates in the prison test were close to the data provided by Special Hospital #326.

The next chart provided more details in each category. A copy was made of the report that was given to a translator.

WEDNESDAY, DECEMBER 10ᵀᴴ, 2003, 12:01 LOCAL TIME, 50 NAUTICAL MILES NORTH OF FUNCHAL

Dr. Trenchard couldn't wait any longer. Overnight, the president of Carnival Lines, the owner of Holland America, pulled as many strings as he could before he was given a phone number to call. It was Captain Rainbow's government-issued mobile phone, but Trenchard didn't know that. He also didn't know that Rainbow had just left his house to drive to where Jun was being debriefed.

When Captain Rainbow's phone rang, he looked at the time. It was just after six and he figured that the time on *Rotterdam* was probably six hours ahead of DC.

"Rainbow."

"This is Dr. Darin Trenchard, the physician on the Rotterdam. I was told by the president of Holland America that you could put me in touch with Doctor Lín."

"I can and I will. Can you give me an hour? I am driving to where she is. There are some ground rules that I must explain to you before you are allowed to speak to her directly."

"Sir, is she being debriefed? I'm a retired Army 0-6 who spent much of his career supporting the Green Berets in Africa. If so, I know the drill."

"I can't answer that. Please listen carefully." Rainbow explained to Trenchard that he could ask questions about Oilop-03 the disease, but not how Jun knows about it."

An hour later, Rainbow briefed Jun and Yan on what they could say and not say to Dr. Trenchard. She asked Captain Rainbow where her mother was since she had not seen her since they arrived. Liang, she was told, was being debriefed about her knowledge of her husband's work in a separate room. Liang should be finished in a day or and then will be allowed to talk to her brother about resettling in San Diego.

When Trenchard hung up from his call with Dr. Lín, he knew more than he did the day before. Given the ship's ventilation system and filters, Jun said he could expect only about 5 - 8% of the ship's passengers and crew to be infected. He was hoping the ships' air filters, bends in the ducts, and distance may have reduced the number of Oilop-03 cells that made it into the spaces occupied by the passengers.

On a pad, Trenchard created a table based on the 1,208 passengers and 865 crew members. Nonetheless, the numbers on his chart, rounded up if there was a "part person," told him what he could expect was staggering to him as a citizen and a medical professional. He cursed the cynicism of any individual who could unleash such an illness on the world. But then again, it was the PRC, and one never knew what they would do. Human life to the CCP's leaders was not valued.

Passengers	1,208	Crew	865
Average Age	56	Average Age	33
5% Infection	8% Infection	5% Infection	8% Infection
61	96	44	70
Death Rate at #	11%	Death Rate	10%
# of Deaths	11		7
	Estimated max total deaths - Pax & Crew	18	

Trenchard had pieced together many a man and women in the ER, but this was almost beyond his comprehension. Looking at his chart, his eyes welled up with tears and his stomach felt as it was twisted in knots. He could expect between 61 and 96 passengers and between 44 and 70 crew members would be sickened by Oilop-03.

Most of *Rotterdam's* passengers were over 50 which meant that between 7 and 11 passengers and between 5 and 7 crew members might die. He could, if Dr. Lín's estimates are anywhere near correct, have 18 bodies on his hands by the time the ship reaches Fort Lauderdale.

He immediately called the home office and asked them to find a way to acquire 20 respirators and get them out to *Rotterdam*. Any form of polio scared him since any one of the three could either kill or leave the victim with long term paralysis. With only one respirator on board, if any passenger on-board came down with either of those two types, the death rate would skyrocket. So far, none of those who were sick have showed symptoms of bulbar or bulbospinal polio. He didn't believe the ship's good luck would continue.

Trenchard was staring at the sheet with his numbers when his phone rang. It was Captain van der Molen. Holland America had ordered the ship to head for the Azores. Desperately needed medical equipment would be flown out to the ship by helicopter. It would leave with the blood samples and the aerosol bottles.

However, no one was to leave the ship. The ship and its passengers were to be quarantined until further notice. The lower two decks of staterooms were to be considered off-limits and to be used as a hospital. Only ill passengers and his medical staff were allowed in those staterooms. Meals would be served by stewards wearing protective clothing and two layers of surgical masks.

THE SAME DAY, 8:07 A.M. LOCAL TIME, GROOM LAKE

From an operational perspective, the extraction of Dr. Jun Lin and Liang Lin was an unqualified success. The evasive tactics that the 4007th Special Operations and Test Squadron had been practicing worked. How the stealth panels were attached, however, still needed work.

In a ceremony at Groom Lake, Derek was awarded his second Distinguished Flying Cross while the crew members were all given Air Medals. Colonel Hollingsworth's request that Derek be awarded a Purple Heart was turned down by the bureaucrats in the Pentagon because the operation was not conducted in a "combat zone."

FRIDAY, DECEMBER 12TH, 2003, 8:03 A.M. LOCAL TIME, CANCUN

Two-man teams from Mexico's Policía Federal Ministerial (the Mexican equivalent of the FBI) spread out throughout the Krystal Cancun Palace complex. Each man wore a full hazmat suit as they walked out onto the roofs of each building.

On an inspection panel just downwind of the filters, what were known as "torque stripes" were not aligned. These thin lines of paint were put on when the systems were installed and if someone removed the screws, they were impossible to reinstall and keep the lines aligned. Each time the panels were removed for inspection, new screws were put in place, the old paint removed with thinner and new stripes painted.

This suggested to the investigators that someone unscrewed the panel and then replaced it. Swabs on long sticks were used to take samples from inside the vent and smaller ones were used on the area just outside the access panel. Each cotton swab was put in a separate tube marked with its location.

At the front desk, other Policía Federal Ministerial agents and two from the American FBI watched recordings of those who came to the front desk. Three couples who had Chinese passports were identified, two of which were still at the hotel. The third couple, the Tsaos, had checked out on Wednesday, December 3rd.

The senior Mexican agent then called his office to search for any travel records and recordings of Guozhi and Xiu Tsao at Mexico's airports. With copies of the tapes and the samples, the senior Policía Federal Ministerial agent gave one set to the FBI agent and a copy of the security system videotape.

At the Cancun airport, there were two planes waiting. One to take the Mexicans back to their headquarters where the samples would be evaluated at a Mexican Ministry of Health lab. The other was a corporate jet that would bring the FBI agents and the samples to Atlanta where the swabs would be evaluated at the CDC.

THE SAME DAY 1:06 P.M. LOCAL TIME, LEESBURG

Jun's debriefing was again interrupted by a CDC request to speak with her via a video conference. As she walked into the room on the top floor of the house where she was being debriefed, she noticed the room had no windows.

Again, Jun was positioned in front of the camera. The senior researcher and virologist who had been on the last call was in Atlanta along with two other researchers and the same FBI agent.

"Dr. Lin, we have samples taken from the Krystal Cancun Palace and would like to show them to you. We also now have samples taken from patients whom we are pretty sure were stricken with Oilop-03 who have been flown back to the U.S. from Mexico. I know this may be difficult with the resolution given the cameras used for the conference call, but we want to show you the pictures our scanning electron microscopes have taken of what we think is the Oilop-03 virus."

"Please show me."

A very familiar image appeared on the large 80" projection screen. Jun stood and walked closer to the screen. After studying it for a few seconds, Jun stated emphatically. "This sample has the polygon shape of Oilop-03 as opposed to the rounded shape of the other known strains of the poliomyelitis virus."

"So you are sure this is Oilop-03?"

Jun bobbed her head to emphasize her answer. "Yes."

"Did you do anything in the lab in Nanning to alter or change its structure?"

"No. We didn't have the equipment. Once Senior Colonel Sun understood Oilop-03 was more contagious, more deadly, and left more people paralyzed than other known strains, he used our cultures in the Yibin prison test."

"Do you know if there are any cultures left in the lab in Nanning?"

"Yes. Before I left, I recommended in writing that some the samples be given to a virology lab to help us develop a vaccine. How many are still there now, I do not know."

"Do you know where your request went?"

"No. Special Lab #62 was run by the PLA which is why I think Senior Colonel Sun was trying to develop Oilop-03 as a weapon. If it was passed on by the senior administrator of the lab, she would have sent it to Doctor Jiang Ng. He is the head of the Life Sciences department in the People's Republic's Academy of Natural Sciences."

"Thank you, doctor."

The screen went blank before she could add I know Dr. Ng from our days at the Guangzhou Institute of Biomedicine and Health. She would make sure she would note this in her debriefing.

SATURDAY, DECEMBER 13TH, 2008, 9:07 A.M. LOCAL TIME, 228 NAUTICAL MILES EAST OF FORT LAUDERDALE

Dr. Trenchard was back in his little office by his dispensary, having just returned from his daily staff meeting. Captain van der Molen had assigned a crew to go through all the compacted trash kept in large bins. The contents of each bin were laid out on the deck and the contents searched. They found two of the bottles on the first day, a third the second and today, bottles four and five.

When it came Trenchard's time to speak, he said that as far as he could tell, Oilop-03 had infected all those that it would on *Rotterdam*. The butcher's bill, as old Royal Navy doctors referred to the casualty list, was not as bad as it could have been, but it was still ugly.

The food freezer turned into a morgue and held 12 bodies – eight passengers, four crew members. The ship only had a dozen plastic body bags so his staff wrapped the corpses in sheets that were sewn together and then in plastic wrap. It was gruesome work that never seemed to end.

The final tally was that 104 - 81 passengers and 23 crew members - became ill, which was below Dr. Lín's estimate of between 5 and 8 percent. Of those who survived, seven passengers and two crew members suffered some form of limb paralysis, which matched Dr. Lín's prediction. He attributed the lower numbers to the filters in the ship's ventilation system which caused the viruses to die as they traveled inside the ship's system.

Captain van der Molen warned his officers to ensure their staffs knew not to discuss how the line would compensate the families of the loved ones who died, or those who became ill, or any other passengers on board *Rotterdam*. Those discussions would be held by a team from the corporate office. They were, however, allowed to reassure those affected that the company would cover any legitimate long-term medical expenses. Everyone on the staff and most passengers believed lawsuits would be filed soon after *Rotterdam* docked.

CHAPTER 28

THE PERFECT PUNISHMENT

MONDAY, DECEMBER 29ᵀᴴ, 2003, 3:17 P.M. LOCAL TIME, ANACOSTIA

Yan Huáng was still enjoying the glow from the medal ceremony during which she was awarded a Bronze Star with a bronze V that denoted that it was earned in combat. Technically, she wasn't "in combat," but her role in the extraction of Doctor Lín was, in the director's mind, close enough. She was also awarded a Legion of Merit for her intelligence analysis on the PLA Navy.

With the debriefing of Jun over, Yan was back at her desk studying reports on the tests of the PLA Navy's anti-ship missiles when Captain Rainbow appeared at her cubicle. Yan stood at the appearance of a senior officer, who said, "I think you'll be interested in this. Technically, your clearance doesn't give you access, but since you were intimately involved, you should know this."

Captain Rainbow held a folder with yellow crosshatching around the words in large capital letters that said, Top Secret Specially Compartmented Information.

"Sir, what does it say?"

"The Spanish tracked Hop and Yanlin Yuhang to Madrid International Airport. There, under different names, they boarded an Air China flight to Beijing. Also, the Mexicans have traced the movements of Guozhi and Xue Tsao from Cancun to Mexico City where they boarded an Air China flight to Beijing under different names. There's no doubt in my department's and in the CIA's mind that this was a deliberate attack. Some might call it a test in which many people paid a terrible price."

"So what is going to happen now?"

"Short answer is I don't know. It will be, I am told, a discussion item between the president and his counterpart in Beijing right after the first of the year."

Yan glanced through the message and thanked Captain Rainbow for sharing. When he left, she wondered what could the President of the U.S. really do?

SATURDAY, JANUARY 3ᴿᴰ, 2004, 9:17 P.M. LOCAL TIME, SAN DIEGO

Both the CIA and DIA used their influence to encourage a medical research firm in San Diego to hire Jun. Thanks to her PhD in virology from the San Diego State University, they were delighted to have her.

Tao's business, San Diego Real Estate Development Corporation, helped Jun buy a two-bedroom, two-bath house in Rancho Santa Fe by guaranteeing the mortgage. This would help Jun, as a new U.S. citizen, establish credit. They did the same for an Indigo blue Volkswagen GTI with a six-speed transmission. The salesman suggested that she buy a red one, but Jun said the red paint would remind her of the PRC. She wasn't sure if the salesman understood, but she drove off the lot with the blue car.

One reason Jun loved the house she bought was that it had a small backyard with a hot tub. She was luxuriating in the tub and laughing as her mother, who was on the phone, was describing learning how to drive a car. Now that she was in the U.S., it was something she had to learn to do and she was the only adult, much less a senior citizen, in a class of 15-year-olds.

Tao created a position in his firm's accounting department for Liang who enrolled in graduate-level accounting courses and in an English course. Her goal was to pass the CPA exam. Liang preferred living in a two-bedroom apartment in a building that Tao's firm owned.

Now that both Jun and Liang had sworn allegiance to the U.S. and renounced their citizenship in the PRC, the one condition left was they must pass a U.S. citizenship course before a U.S. passport was issued. They enrolled in an evening class that was filled with future citizens from all over the world. When they were in the classroom, the instructor insisted that the only language that was permitted was English. It was, she said, good practice for when they became citizens.

Her mother changed the subject from her comments about the teenagers in driver's ed. She became more serious as she spoke. "Jun, I need your help."

"Why?"

"I need to create a profile and your English is much better than mine."

"For what?"

"A dating site that has many lovely older women like me."

"Mother, how about I come over tomorrow sometime? It will make it easier for me to help you."

"Fine, how about I make lunch as payment?"

"Wonderful, mother."

Before Jun could hang up, her mother said, "I think you need to find a man, and the sooner the better."

Jun said, "Good-bye, mother" and hung up the phone." She tossed the phone on a towel and leaned head back, luxuriating in the hot water. Already, men at work were flirting with her.

TUESDAY, JANUARY 6ᵀᴴ, 2004, 10:00 A.M. LOCAL TIME, WASHINGTON, D.C.

The People's Republic of China's ambassador to the United States was ushered into a conference room in the State Department just a few steps from the Secretary of State's office. The room was selected because the secretary wanted to show the PRC's ambassador that he was brought to the "inner sanctum" to emphasize the importance of the meeting.

Only two people were in the room – the PRC's ambassador and the U.S. Secretary of State. The PRC's embassy was told that their ambassador would be given the opportunity to quietly resolve a crisis that could, if unresolved and became public, ruin the relationship between the two countries.

The Secretary of State was waiting in the conference room when the ambassador was ushered in. Next to where the secretary sat, there were several thick folders containing several inches of paper.

After thanking him for coming, the Secretary of State said, "Mr. Ambassador, we have irrefutable proof that the People's Republic conducted a biological warfare attack on the United States, Mexico, Spain, and the Netherlands. It did so even though it is a signatory to the Biological and Toxin Weapons Convention. In this attack, agents of the People's Republic released a new mutation of the polio virus called Oilop-03 on the *M.S. Amsterdam*, a ship flying under the flag of The Netherlands while in port in Cartagena, Spain and at the Krystal Cancun Palace resort in Cancun, Mexico."

The PRC's ambassador shifted in his chair and then raised his hand. The Secretary of State stopped speaking. "That is preposterous. It is a fabrication of the CIA. We would never do such a thing."

Smiling, the Secretary of State opened one of the folders and slid the top sheet across the table. It was an analysis by the FBI lab noting that the propellant in all the recovered bottles was made only in the PRC. He then took another sheet. "This was taken from a Top-Secret PLA report in which Special Lab #62 located southeast of Nanning that named the new strain of polio as Oilop-03. Until it was released on *M.S. Rotterdam* and in Cancun, the strain was confined to the provinces of Guangxi and Guangdong and unknown to the rest of the world."

The ambassador shook his head, "All fabrications and forgeries."

Nodding his head, the Secretary of State continued. "Mr. Ambassador, protest all you want. The president of the U.S. has authorized me to offer this deal and it is not negotiable. One, the People's Republic shares all, and I mean all, its data on Oilop-03 with the World Health Organization and the United States within ten days of this meeting. Two, it deposits one billion U.S. dollars that the United States will put in a fund to compensate the victims of this attack. Another two billion must be deposited in an account to fund the development of an Oilop-03 vaccine to prevent more of your citizens and those around the world from being infected. If the PRC does not agree to these terms within forty-eight hours, the United States will release to the worldwide press all the documentation it has on Special Hospital #326, Special Lab #62, and the Oilop-03 epidemic your government has been covering up for years."

Standing up, the PRC's ambassador, said, "I do not have to listen to this garbage. It is an insult. You sir, and the United States will pay a heavy price if you release such false information."

The Secretary of State stood up, "Sir, before you leave, you may sift through some of our documents. The contents may change your mind."

Curiosity got the better of the ambassador and he looked at several documents, particularly those which were in Mandarin. They had all the right markings and formats. He pushed them to the side. "As I said, this is garbage. They are not even good forgeries."

Smiling the Secretary of State said, "Mr. Ambassador, remember, forty-eight hours from the time you walk out of this office we release what you see here plus much more. By the way, that will be Friday morning, Beijing time. Thank you for coming. A member of my staff will escort you out. Good day sir.

Thirty-six hours after the meeting at the U.S. State Department, a message was delivered to the Secretary of State accepting the settlement and asking where the money should be deposited. The PRC also asked if the money could be transferred on Monday, January 12th, 2004.

WEDNESDAY, JANUARY 14*TH*, 2005, 11:08 A.M. LOCAL TIME, SAN DIEGO

After running along the beach for the run part of her workout, Adrian walked to a bench near where her car was parked. She sat and faced the sky, enjoying the warmth of the sun that had burned off what the meteorologists called the marine layer.

The urge to write sent her back to her car and she took out her laptop and began to write in her diary about the emotions she was experiencing. When she started writing a journal, she found it an excellent way to explore her feelings and deal with the separation caused by Derek's first cruise. Now, she made daily entries that described in intimate detail her life, emotions, and sexual fantasies. Often, when alone, she'd reread some of the passages describing her dreams and they turned her on.

Adrian saved a couple entries to a separate file, changed the names, dates, made them look like passages in a manuscript and drove home. After a shower and a quick lunch, she headed to the Mercury Adult Book store. Rosa was, as she hoped, there, restocking a shelf.

Seeing Adrian, Rosa said, "Well, look what the cat dragged in. Haven't seen you in a while. What brings you here?"

"Rosa, I need a favor?"

"And that is?"

Adrian put a dozen sheets of paper on the counter. "Please read these and tell me if they, if woven into a plot, are good enough for a book."

Seeing it was 12 pages, double-spaced, Rosa said, "Look around while I read."

Adrian was at the far end of the store when she heard "Whoooeeee, girl!!!" Rosa de la Cruz was grinning. "This is very good. What's the book about?" Adrian described what she had outlined in her mind.

"You write it and then I'll help you find a publisher. Remember, it must have a plot, not just one gratuitous sex scene after another."

Driving home, Adrian was consumed by the thought of writing the novel. Thursday morning Derek and she were leaving for the house they rented for the winter in Mammoth. The owner of the one they rented last year decided not to sell so she found a smaller, three-bedroom, three-bath condo around the corner and a short walk to the Canyon Creek Lift. Over the winter, they could have friends come up for long weekends, or they could go by themselves.

Entering her house, Adrian had a plan. She could write on the days Derek was in Groom Lake. She had no idea how Derek would react, even though he was very open-minded. He might, she thought, encourage her. How her writing would affect their marriage she did not know, but she was afraid it might.

THURSDAY, JANUARY 15TH, 2005, 6:46 A.M. LOCAL TIME, BEIJING

Senior Colonel Fang Sun hurried along the sidewalk from where his apartment was in Beijing to the People's Liberation Army headquarters. It was dark and brisk outside, which to Sun made the two-kilometer walk even more enjoyable.

His mind was on his day's agenda as he strode at a brisk military pace about two meters from the curb amongst others headed to their jobs. Sun didn't notice the car in the street slow and the window roll down. Nor did he notice the end of the barrel of the dart gun used by wildlife game managers to subdue animals resting on the windowsill. He did not hear the soft pffft when the dart gun fired.

Sun felt the pinprick as the dart embedded itself in his thigh and emptied the small syringe filled with a colorless liquid. He fought panic and thinking he had been poisoned, Sun yanked the dart out wanting to give it to the doctors to figure out what had been injected into his body. As he did, Sun tripped on the uneven concrete and the dart flew out of his hand and into a street drain.

Sun expected to feel drugged and was surprised when he didn't. He showed the doctors where the dart hit him and he was sure that someone tried to poison him. At the dispensary in the General Staff office, a medic drew blood and he was transferred to a local military hospital for observation.

The lab tested for all types of poisons, even the special ones used by the PRC and their Russian counterparts for assassinations. None were in Senior Colonel Sun's bloodwork. As a precaution, the doctors kept him in the hospital overnight. At noon on January 9th, Sun was released and was back at his desk by one.

Around two in the morning on January 17th, Fang Sun felt nauseous and had a booming headache. He had his wife call his office at seven to let them know he was sick and was staying home. At noon, his wife took his temperature was almost 39^0 Celsius (102^0 Fahrenheit) and called an ambulance.

In the hospital, Fang Sun complained that his muscles were weak, his joints were stiff and at times he couldn't move his arms and legs. X-rays showed his lungs were clear. At times, he struggled to breathe and was connected to a positive ventilation system.

Five days later, on January 24th, his temperature was closer to normal at 38.4^0 C (~101^0 Fahrenheit). When Fang Sun awoke, he couldn't move his legs at all. On January 25th, the fever broke and Sun's paralysis was more extensive. Now he couldn't move his arms, hands, or fingers along with his legs. Breathing was also difficult.

The doctors told Senior Colonel Sun on January 26th, that there was a good chance most of his paralysis would be permanent. How extensive, they did not know and would not know for another six months.

Before an ambulance took Senior Colonel Sun to the airport for a MEDVAC flight to Suixi on January 29th, he was informed that he was being transferred to Special Hospital #326. The doctor patiently explained that this facility was the best in the PRC for treating the aftereffects of polio. Their specialty was helping those severely affected by polio to learn how to live with their paralysis.

Sun didn't mention that he knew all about Special Hospital #326. Another ambulance ride brought him to the admitting room at Special Hospital #326 just before lunch on January 29th.

When Fang Sun, now PLA Senior Colonel Retired was pushed down the sidewalk in a wheelchair to the admissions lobby of Special Hospital #326, he had recovered some arm movement and could flex his wrists but could not use his hands or fingers. He was essentially paralyzed from the neck down.

A smiling Dr. Ting Zheng waited as Fang Sun was pushed into the room where new patients were admitted. She held her withered left arm above the wrist so Sun could see what his hands and arms would look like in a few years. At least he had some arm movement, which her left arm did not have.

"Senior Colonel Sun, it is so nice to see you again. Welcome to Special Hospital #326 where we will take excellent care of you. You must be patient and follow our instructions. As you will learn, rehabilitation for polio victims is hard and slow. We do not know how much movement and strength you will recover, if any. If you are like most of my patients, the improvements, if any, will be small. You will never be as you were before you became sick. You are, just like me, now a polio survivor."

Fang Sun tried to smile. He still couldn't believe this was happening to him. It was like a bad dream that had become very real. Two weeks ago, he was a normal, healthy army officer with a bright future working at a job where he had power and influence. Now, he was medically retired from the Army and a helpless cripple who could not dress himself or tend to his basic physical needs.

Dr. Zheng continued. "I see from your medical records you still have trouble breathing so at night, we will put you in an iron lung until we are sure you can breathe throughout the night on your own. I think you'll like the iron lung. Most of our patients do. It gives them a sense of security, knowing that they will not suffocate."

Retired Senior Fan Sun pursed his lips. Before *Insidious Dragon*, polio was something other people got. It was, or could have been, a weapon. Once he left Special Hospital #326, he would find out who fired the infected dart and how he or she got the virus. He wanted to start making a list but couldn't use his hands to write or even tap on the keys of a computer. Mentally, he kept adding names and repeating them so he would remember. *Maybe that was the first step in rehabilitation?* "How long will I be here?"

"Good question. Most stay for between six months to a year. Some never leave since we are one of the facilities prepared to take care of all their physical and mental needs. That is something, Colonel Sun, you should consider."

Sun looked around and then at the wheelchair in which he sat. No matter how much he willed his arms to move, he couldn't get them to the wheels, much less push them. "What about a battery-powered wheelchair?"

Dr. Zheng smiled, enjoying the power she now had over Sun. What the senior colonel did not know was that the likelihood of Fang Sun ever leaving Special Hospital #326 was somewhere between slim and none. He needed full time care – people to feed him, people to help him dress, people to help him get in and out of bed, people to help him on and off the toilet, and then clean him.

The list of Fang Sun's rehabilitation needs was long, and since she was in charge of Special Hospital #326, Dr. Zheng would ensure he would never leave. Soon, Fang Sun would learn that those over whom he held power or could provide information to or do favors for would know that he was no longer an asset. They, along with his wife who was planning to divorce him, would disappear like a dissipating fog.

Dr. Zheng knew it would take time for Sun to realize that the best place for him was as a resident of Special Hospital #326. It was now his world. How long, Dr. Ting Zheng did not know, but she was sure that Sun would eventually come to that realization that he could be in her facility's care for the rest of his life. When he did, it would make his stay more bearable.

"After the hospital better understands what you can and cannot do, we will design and build a chair for you, but not until then. The last step in our formal admission process is a visit with me, so I will see you later. Enjoy your orientation and, if you need anyone to help you onto a toilet or eat or drink, just ask. We are here to help you."

Senior Colonel Sun glowered at the former wife of his good friend thinking that Ting Zheng was enjoying his situation far too much. He would add her to the list or potential co-conspirators.

From her conversations with Jun Lín, Dr. Zheng knew all about Special Lab #62 and its work. She couldn't wait to travel to Zhanjiang to her friend's place and call the number Jun gave her to say that the special package had arrived and was now in her care.

MEET THE AUTHOR

Marc retired as a Captain after twenty-six years in the Navy and is a combat veteran of Vietnam, the Tanker Wars of the 1980s, and Desert Shield/Storm. He is a Naval Aviator with just under 6,000 hours of flight time in helicopters and fixed wing aircraft. Captain Liebman has worked with the armed forces of Australia, Canada, Japan, Thailand, Republic of Korea, the Philippines, and the U.K.

He has been a partner in two different consulting firms advising clients on business and operational strategy, business process re-engineering, sales, and marketing; the CEO of an aerospace and defense manufacturing company; an associate editor of a national magazine, and a copywriter for an advertising agency.

The Liebmans live near Aubrey, Texas. Marc is married to Betty, his lovely wife of 53+ years. They spend a lot of time visiting their seven grandchildren.